TOUCHING DISTANCE

Rebecca Abrams

TOUCHING
DISTANCE

MACMILLAN

First published 2008 by Macmillan
an imprint of Pan Macmillan Ltd
Pan Macmillan, 20 New Wharf Road, London N1 9RR
Basingstoke and Oxford
Associated companies throughout the world
www.panmacmillan.com

ISBN 978-0-230-01555-5

1 3 5 7 9 8 6 4 2

A CIP catalogue record for this book is available from
the British Library.

Typeset by Set Systems Ltd, Saffron Walden, Essex
Printed in the UK by CPI Mackays, Chatham, ME5 8TD

For my mother,

Sonia

This is all as true as it is strange:
Nay, it is ten times true, for truth is truth
To th' end of reckoning.

William Shakespeare, *Measure for Measure*

And however our eyes may be dazzled with show, or our ears deceived by sound; however prejudice may warp our wills, or interest darken our understanding, the simple voice of nature and of reason will say, it is right.

Thomas Paine, *Common Sense*

Aberdeen, 1790

Part One

Ignorance

It proceeds generally from violent affections of the mind, as grief, despondency and the like; from the drinking of strong liquors, or caudle too highly spiced; from obstructed perspiration and evacuations.

Thomas Cooper, *A Compendium of Midwifery*, 1766

The predisposing cause of this disease is a vitiated state of the humours: for it is generally observed to be most prevalent in an unhealthy season, and among women of a weakly and a scorbutic constitution.

Henry Manning, *A Treatise on Female Diseases*, 1771

1

January

The hobnails on Alexander Gordon's boots strike sparks the length of the Spittal as he makes his way down the hill towards the New Town. The bold bright tattoo of his feet on the stone cobbles matches step for step, beat for beat, the bold, bright hue of his satisfaction. It could be gauzy high summer, so airborne are Alec Gordon's spirits, but in reality the winter's night shrouding the way is black as pitch, the air spiked with needle-sharp shards of ice. The cobbles beneath his feet are barely visible, nor his boots, nor the Gallowgate gibbet swinging slackly in the wind, nor the hulking mass of the Gallow Hills themselves. There's no moon tonight, nothing but the different densities of darkness and the road itself, shouldering forwards like a nervous heifer. From out beyond the Links, where the blackness is so solid it is more a physical presence than a mere absence of light, comes the drone of the waves crashing on to the beach. Alec's pace never falters.

A good birth. Nothing compares with it.

Past the ruins of the lepers' house. Past old Mallie's tomb (long since robbed of its contents, the boulders which once secured it all awry now, like a mouthful of crooked teeth). Past the waymarker. Stonehaven. Dundee. Edinburgh. Sensing rather than seeing the familiar landmarks. Following the spine of the hill towards home. Making notes in his head as he goes.

Six hours from first contraction to delivery. An excellent duration. Not so slow as to tire the mother, nor so fast as to hinder the natural dilatatory processes. Two touchings — the first to ascertain the positioning of the head, the second to determine that of the os uteri. Both entirely necessary. No unwarranted bleeding. No damage to the perinæum. The wombcake delivered unaided and intact. Mother and infant both alive and well at the end of it.

Ample reason, then, for satisfaction. Six ample reasons, to be precise (and Alec Gordon is a man for precision, wherever possible). Seven, if one regards the survival of the mother and that of the bairn as separate cause for celebration. Eight, if one views 'alive' and 'well' as distinct states of health, which common sense alone insists one should. Does not his livelihood depend to a very considerable degree on the gulf between the two? Why! If 'alive' and 'well' were coupled as effortlessly in life as in common parlance, there'd be no further need of physicians in this world. A utopia indeed – and his livelihood extinguished at a stroke!

Is it immoral to be grateful, if only in the strictest privacy of one's own reflections, that life gives rise to sickness? Alec shrugs off the question. Immoral or not, it is a fact.

Eight reasons, then, and leave morality for the kirk.

Recalling the scrap of new life he'd held in his hands just a short while before, Alec smiles to himself. He has done his work well tonight. That is what matters. That is the thought that lightens the darkness as he pushes on towards the lamps of the New Town. No matter how many labours he attends, the miracle of a good birth never palls. Never yet has he found himself insensible to the wonder of it: the deliverance of new life, immaculate in every detail, from each tiny coral fingernail to all the hidden marvels of heart and lungs and bones. Midwifery: the short cut to poverty, the quick route to an early grave. That's what the London physicians warned them, Osborn, Clarke and Denman. But all the same: the miracle of birth, the way it makes him feel, when it all goes well.

How cross, though, this particular miracle had been, and how comical, with its wizened, old man's face and gaping little-bird mouth. Not fully human yet. Something amphibian – reptilian even – about the scaly skin, the egg-shell skull. There'd been a bad moment when the head emerged: it had hung there, limp and still, between the mother's thighs. But with the next throe, the shoulders appeared, and then the rest of the body was slithering straight into Alec's outspread hands. The infant opened first one eye, then the other, took a brief squinny at the world and, mightily displeased by the sight, commenced a high, furious bawling that set everyone in the room laughing and sighing with relief, knowing the worst was over.

A crabbit wee babbity and no mistake. Jenny Duncan'll have her hands full with that one.

Some bairns were born trouble and there was no answering for it. At least his presence at the birth meant there'd been no unnecessary mischief, no washing down with spirits, no stuffing with gruel. Above all, no swaddling. He has taken the midwives to task for it times beyond counting: when every brute in nature is born with its limbs free so it may find its dam and suckle, why bind a newborn infant so tight it cannot even turn its head, must be lifted to the breast like a senseless block of wood? But Alec is no fool. He knows full well his orders are flouted when his back is turned.

The road ahead forks and Alec branches left into the Gallowgate. The bells have struck eleven and there's no one about. The shops are all sealed up, the bairns long since hauled indoors and into their beds. Only the occasional student passes, scurrying back to his lodgings, gown flapping, a clutch of books pressed to his ribcage.

Past the gates of Marischal College and into Broad Street. Alec sets his shoulders against the biting wind that bowls up to greet him, hunching the collar of his greatcoat as far about his ears as it will go and sinking his face into his woollen muffler, its fibrous warmth moist with his breath. A dog jack-knifes out of the darkness, barking madly, belly low to the ground, chasing a rat or something. Alec falters, curses, regains his footing. Along Netherkirkgate and past St Nicholas's, skirting the kirkyard, and on into Schoolhill.

There are no lights in the squat rows of houses that line the street; the buildings sit silent and dark as tombs, hunched against the wind and sleet, not that the darkness troubles Alec. He knows these roads too well, cobbled or mud-mired; has walked them countless times, at every hour; has grown up walking far darker paths than these, in fair weather and in foul: four miles of pitchy gloom from Miltown to Peterculter and four miles back again. Singing all the way. Marching songs, love songs, ballads, airs. *A beg-gar man cam owre the lea.* Anything will do so long as it keeps the wee ones moving. *An mony a fine tale he tal me.* Anything to stop them seeing faces in every shadow, cringing to a standstill each time a twig snaps or an owl shrieks. Willing to terrify them still further with threats of ghasties and goblins if that's what it takes. *Dinna dachle or the kelpie'll get ye!* Just keep them moving. One foot in front of the other. That's the way. The five of them traipsing through the darkness. Sandy Gordon's peelie-wally brood: Alec and his twin brother Jem taking turns to haul the others on to their backs whenever the mud gets too deep or the path too icy; Chae, two years younger, puny and piss-scared, but doing his best to hide it; Rabbie, all snot and snivel, the breath crackling out of him like his lungs are on fire; and Jeannie, the youngest, the doe-eyed darling of them all, gold-headed as an angel. Singing like a bunch of maddies to keep their minds off the frost seeping into their boots, their bones. No trace of daylight for weeks on end in winter and the dominie's tawse in store for those who are late – and their father's when they reach home again, if he gets to hear of it.

But that's all in the past. Miltown and Peterculter and his father's wrath. Sandy Gordon is long since in his grave, and Rabbie and Jeannie too, God rest their souls. There's just the three of them left now: Jem, raising cattle and turnips up the coast in Buchan. Chae, fattening like a goose on lawyer's fees. And himself: the physician. Not bad for the peelie-wally brood of a tenant farmer.

No, all things considered, he's not one to fear a bit of dark; he's used to it, likes the way it sharpens his mind, likes the feel of the freezing air stinging his eyeballs. Besides which, Alec is mightily relieved the weather has turned at last. Advent was over before the first snows finally came, bringing an end to the long, waterlogged autumn that had draped itself like a wet rag on every weak chest and stiff joint for miles around. And even then the colder weather had not fully settled. Sudden blizzards blew in from the sea, blinding the town, swathing flagstones, railings, rooftops in a fine veil of white, only to stop as abruptly as they'd begun, the clouds sweeping inland towards Ballater and Braemar. The skies cleared in an instant. Sunlight glittered on the house fronts. Granite turned to silver. Within moments the snow had melted away, corrugating the streets with ridges of icy slush that caught under the horses' hooves and sent them slithering and sliding over the new-paved streets. For a physician, a mild winter is as much to be feared as a harsh one, brings as many evils as it wards off; these past few months the press of patients has felt more a plague than a privilege, and there have been times when Alec has caught himself scanning the air in front of him in a futile attempt to see the invisible vapours that wreak such havoc.

Two days into January now and the mild weather gone with the old year, or so it would seem: the deserted streets whipped by a bitter north-easterly. Capricious weather, indeed. Only a week before, on Christmas morning, they'd emerged from chapel into pale gold sunshine, climbed Castle Hill with it bright on their faces, catching on the sails crowded in the harbour, flashing off the white underbellies of the gulls wheeling high overhead. Alec and Chae had gone ahead with Mary between them, flinging her up into the air. *One . . . two . . . three* . . . Mary squealing with delight and fear, her feet flapping in the blue air. The women had followed more slowly, Isabella leaning heavily on her sister's arm and laughing at her own breathlessness, her rolling gait beneath the heavy folds of her winter cloak the only visible sign of the child that would soon be born.

When Chae announced his engagement to Isabella twelve months before, Alec and Elizabeth had thought it a fine thing: two brothers married to two sisters, strengthening the bond of each to the other, drawing them closer still with these new ties of legal kinship. If Chae and Bella's happiness has been the source of less harmonious sentiments on some occasions since, Christmas Day, thankfully, was not one of them. Jem and his wife Megan joined them soon after and, with the dusk, a veritable clan of Harvies had descended on Belmont Street, swelling their number still further: Aunt Barbara, widowed now and lonely in the empty farmhouse she refused to leave, fussing and fretting about the journey back to Midmar from the moment she arrived; Rabbie, of course; Aunt Janet and her boys, Alistair and William, with their goodwives and bairns; Aunt Grace, stouter and shorter with every year, though not a whit less talkative, with her man Thomas, silent as a stone, and their two lassies, Maggie and Jean, dark-eyed like all the Harvies, with their mother's tongue on them and their father's weak chin. Only Aunt Rae had declined to join them – a blessing in Alec's opinion.

Not for the first time Alec found himself thinking that old Grandpa Harvie must have had sturdy stuff in his skinny Midmar loins: all eight of his bairns had survived into adulthood, had in their turn spawned twenty-nine Harvies of their own. Like a great net. This is how Alec imagines his wife's family. Stretching across the entire county and far beyond, with their influence, their wealth, their connections. Fingers in more pies than you could eat in a month of Sundays. Marry a Harvie and you were caught forever in the mesh: there was no falling, but there was no escaping either.

The evening had passed in a whirl of jigs and reels. Mary, unlooked for in the throng, ran through the maze of flying skirts and spinning legs in a delirium of excitement. Even Bella insisted on a little dancing, although Megan and Elizabeth pleaded with her not to, being so near her time; Alec, too, advised against it, to no avail. The music infected them all, adults and children alike, released something in them, which for that day at least no one had a mind to resist. When, at the evening's end, Jem struck up with the tune of old Skinner's reel, tired as they were, they'd all found breath enough to belt out the closing words:

> 'May dool and sorrow be his chance,
> Wi' a' the ills that come from France,
> Wha e'er he be that winna dance,
> The Reel o' Tullochgorum.'

Ills indeed, with the king of France and his Austrian queen prisoners in their own palace and the mob wild for their blood. Such times they were living through; turmoil whichever way you looked. War raging between the Russians and the Turks. Sweden as set as ever on victory. Scotland's own peace still fragile as eggshell in old folks' memories. Well, then, they'd been in need of a wee spring right enough, and who gave a fig what the low-churchers thought of the Gordons and the Harvies for raising such a merry din.

They had been happy. For one whole day. It was as simple as that. A day-long moment of grace. Even Elizabeth seemed light of heart that night, her cheeks flushed, her eyes shining as she danced. Alec watched Chae leading her up the set, leaning in to say something to her, making her laugh: the startling red of her lips against the pale oval of her face; the curling strands of black hair fallen loose from their pins; the blue shadows pooling above the ridges of her collar bones. Watching his wife dancing with his younger brother, a confusion of regret and longing had come over Alec; he saw her as a stranger might, as someone with no connection to himself. A fine-looking woman and no question.

Later, much later, in the curtained darkness of their bed, he had reached for her, sunk his face into the softness of her, the warmth of her, bracing himself for the usual resistance but encountering none, sliding into the folds and ridges of her, the first time in a long time, as clumsy and urgent as a boy, mutely grateful for her acquiescence.

Thinking of his wife, Alec feels a pang of guilt. He's close to home now, but it's not Belmont Street he's making for, but the Dispensary in Hope Row. One last stop at the Dispensary, he tells himself, then straight home.

Stamping in out of the cold a few minutes later, however, he finds not only his apprentice waiting for him, but another older man, whom he does not recognize. Rabbie Donald leaps to his feet, plainly relieved at the sight of him.

'Mr Harding's been here since nine, Doctor. It's his daughter – James Garrow's wife.'

The old man has leapt up too, his face a sickly yellow in the lamplight, his eyes wild.

'Please! She's dyin'!' Harding clutches at the lapels of Alec's coat, his foul breath gusting into Alec's face. 'I beg ye!'

'All right!' Alec pushes the old man away. 'Calm yourself!'

Garrow. Elspet Garrow. He reels in the name, filleting it for information. Elspet Garrow from Woolmanhill. Brought safely to bed of her second child a week ago. Married to the wheelwright, the big fellow with the mashed arm. Out of work since his accident last year. So he's Harding's son-in-law, is he? And hadn't Harding's other daughter died recently? Delivered of a still-born the week before Christmas. Yes, it's coming back to him now. The mother might have lived had Mistress Blake called for him at once, but it was the usual argument: childbed was women's business, a lying-in was no place for a man, that's what the old howdies believed. Four pints of blood lost by the time he got there and nothing to be done to save the woman. But with the sister there'd been no such difficulties. No complications of any kind, in fact. Alec had been in the following morning to check all was well and found the usual crowd, knitting and gossiping at the bedside, and Elspet Garrow herself, pink-cheeked and smiling, the bairn at her breast and her tow-headed three-year-old at her feet. The laddie was dangling a length of string just out of reach of a small tortoiseshell cat, which was pouncing and prancing across the counterpane, performing all manner of acrobatics in its efforts to catch the maddening thing. Alec had watched and laughed with them for a while before continuing on his way. That was five days ago, no more. And now gravely ill. From what possible cause?

'Let's away then,' Alec says, turning back towards the door. 'Girnin here won't help Mistress Garrow.'

2

Gripping the wrist bone between his thumb and middle finger, Alec lifts one of the arms and lets the weight of it hang from his grasp. Rigor mortis has not yet set in. The skin is cold even so, slightly damp to the touch. He releases the wrist and the arm concertinas back on to the mattress. The sheet is water-marked with sweat and other, darker stains, which someone has tried to wash away. No amount of water, however, can mask the stench coming off the corpse, rich and gamey as turned meat. From the beached flatness of the torso, Elspet Garrow's belly rises full and round as the hull of an upturned boat. One might almost have thought the baby *in utero* still, the deceased mother full-term and ripe for birth.

Alec glances behind him. James Garrow is hunched in a chair at the foot of the bed, his head bowed. The womenfolk are clustered in the corners of the room, as far from the bed as possible, some sitting, some standing, sprigs of dried rosemary pressed to their noses. Alec regards them with distaste, wonders briefly what manner of remedies they have been busily dispensing to the woman now lying dead before him. The little room is stiflingly hot. He considers ordering them to open the shutters, then thinks better of it. It goes against custom. The windows must remain closed until the corpse is safe in its grave or the spirit will go a-wandering and stir up who knows what mischief. To insist would only cause offence and what's the point? Mistress Garrow has no further need of fresh air, that's for sure. In the hearth lie the remnants of a recently doused fire, faint wisps of steam still rising from the damp peat. To the right of the fireplace is a small cradle, untended and motionless. No sound comes from beneath the wooden hood.

There's a sudden commotion from the forestairs and Mistress Blake bursts into the room, puce in the face and wheezing like a pair of bellows. Before she's even through the door, she's blurting out explanations, her eyes darting anxiously this way and that, her shawls twitching and trembling about her bulky shoulders like seaweed caught in low-tide shallows.

'She wis havin a bad spell. Then the fever set in. Worst I ivver seen. Sweatin an shiverin the whole time, she wis. Screamin wi the pain.'

The midwife's words are addressed to Alec, but her eyes are glancing past him at Mr Harding, as if she can't decide which of the two is to be the more feared.

'Twas the weid, Dr Gordon. But in all my life I nivver seen it like this afore. Nivver sae bad as to kill a body.'

Harding takes a step forward. 'Twas you killed her. An ye know it!'

'Quiet!' Alec snaps. 'Both of you!'

Placing himself squarely in front of Harding, he addresses the midwife. 'The pain was acute, you say. Where precisely?'

'The afterpains.' The old woman nods. 'In her back an her belly an all doon her legs.'

'What of the pulse? You did take the pulse?'

A glint of indignation enters Mistress Blake's expression. Aye, she says, she'd taken all the usual steps. Stoked the fire. Bound the belly. Dispensed warm caudle by the hour. But there was no helping the poor quine. Nothing made a jot of difference. The fever went from bad to worse. One minute she was burning up with heat, the next shivering with the cold. And the pain she was in! Worse than the travails of labour itself and awful to witness.

Alec interrupts her. 'When did the fever commence?'

The midwife hesitates a moment. 'Four days ago.'

'*Four days!* In God's name, woman! Why was I not called sooner?'

Mistress Blake purses her lips and pulls the ends of her shawls tighter about her. 'I didna think it necessary.'

'I see.' Alec fixes his gaze on the rafter above his head in an effort to master his anger. 'Perhaps you'd like to tell me what you did think necessary?'

The midwife flushes and scowls at her feet. The other women shift uneasily. No one speaks. The smell in the room is frightful.

'Permit me to observe—' Alec's tone is thick with sarcasm – 'that by the time you thought it *necessary* to call for me, Mistress Garrow was beyond the help of a physician and rather in need of an undertaker.'

It is too much for Harding. 'You killed her!' he bellows. 'You damn meddlin carlin!'

Leaping past Alec, he hurls himself at the midwife, hands reaching for her neck. The other women scatter, upturning chairs and colliding with one another in their panic, as Mistress Blake staggers backwards out of the old man's way. Alec and Rabbie dart forward and catch hold of Harding's arms. It's all they can do to restrain him.

'That's enough! All of you!'

Until this moment James Garrow has remained motionless beside the bed, seemingly oblivious to everything but his dead wife. Now he stands, a bear of a man, huge in the overcrowded room, wide as a sideboard, head grazing the ceiling. At the sound of his voice, everyone falls still. The rage drains out of Harding's body. Alec feels it: the biceps softening, the sudden limpness beneath his grasp.

Garrow's gaze settles on Alec. His face is heavily stubbled, grey from lack of sleep. His right shoulder hangs lower than the left, the crushed arm drooping uselessly below it.

'Will that be all now, Dr Gordon?'

Alec hesitates. He knows he should just say yes, leave the women to lay out the body, leave the family to mourn its loss. Aaccept there is nothing more he can do. But acceptance is not Alec's way. His mind has fastened onto the problem before him, piecing together the symptoms the midwife has described, measuring them against the symptoms he can see for himself, trying to fit what he knows into a picture he can recognize, shape it into something he can put a name to. Elspet Garrow was all but dead by the time her father set out for his help. That much is clear. But dead from what? Alec looks again at the dead woman. Under the paper-thin skin of her cheeks, a tracery of blue veins is visible. Her hair, still damp with sweat, lies in dark matted clumps around her head. The lips are pale, cracked, slightly parted, as if on the point of death she had been about to speak. Alec takes in once more the flatness of the chest beneath the cotton shift, the grossly swollen belly, the two thin reddish-purple feet protruding from the shift.

'There is one thing.' Alec slides a circumspect glance at the wheelwright. The man seems in control of himself, but Alec knows he must form the request with care if he is to stand any chance of success. 'As Physician to the Dispensary, I am required to record the precise cause of death.' He clears his throat. This is never an easy moment. 'I would be greatly assisted in this task if you would permit me to examine the corpse.'

Perhaps 'corpse' had not been the best choice of word, Alec has time to reflect in the fraction of a second in which it seems Garrow may not have understood, in the brief lapse of time before it becomes clear that Garrow has understood only too well.

'Over my deid body! I willnae hear o it!'

Physically imposing before, Garrow is suddenly immense, towering over Alec by a full foot, every muscle of his bulky frame taut with repugnance.

'But what harm can it do? Be reasonable, Garrow. It is common practice, you know, in other countries. Will you not consider it at least? For the sake of—'

'Other countries be damned!'

Garrow's face and neck have flushed a dark crimson. His

head is thrust forward. His one good hand is clenched into a fist, primed to strike at any further provocation.

'Not a single hair on her heid! D'ye hear me, Dr Gordon? To hell wi ye and yer filthy examinashuns!'

Garrow turns from Alec to face the room.

His Elspet gone. His wife. His lovely, laughing girl.

'Get out!'

He unleashes his grief. Blasts them with it. 'To hell wi the whole damned lot o ye!'

3

Elizabeth is trying not to listen to the silence, the way it gathers and unfurls like a flock of birds in her head. The clock hands mock her glances. The evening's work is done: the fires laid for the morning, the lamps lit or extinguished as necessary, the glass polished, the silver cleaned and locked away, the shutters all secured. Two hours have passed since she ran out of tasks. Seeing Annie in the doorway, twisting her skirt between her fingers, fully aware that her mistress had no need of her other than to keep time from standing still, Elizabeth had had no choice but to send her up to bed. Now there's nothing to do but wait. Outside the wind punches at the shutters. A tile skitters loose.

On summer evenings there are fine views and sunsets to help pass the time, the sky shading from crimson to violet to purple and every shade between. So unlike the brusque shift from day to night that she can still remember from her childhood, where every evening fell like the sudden drawing of a blind. All year round, the same. The abrupt dismissal of daylight, the sudden exile into darkness. So long ago now. So different from here. In summer this far north the sky is never fully dark, even at eleven, twelve o'clock; even when the sun has finally dropped below the horizon, the sky is translucent, milky, light enough to read by. Now, though, in the depths of winter, there are no views in the evening, only the tar-black night. Belmont Street marks the westernmost edge of the town. There's nothing beyond, nothing out there in the darkness but the crashing waters of the Denburn, swollen with rain and snow-melt, and beyond that a straggle of crofts and the bulky mass of the hills.

Elizabeth sighs to herself and shifts in her chair, easing out the cramp that is starting in her left leg. It could be hours yet before her husband returns, or he might walk in that very moment; there was no way of knowing. *Don't wait up for me if I'm late back*, Alec had said as he'd set out, pushing a kiss on to her cheek as an afterthought. *Get some sleep.* She would like to sleep. She's so tired tonight, tired at the very centre of her bones. But how can she, knowing he is out there, in the foul black night, breathing in who knows what poisons in the homes of the sick and dying, facing who knows what manner of dangers to life and soul? And how can she contemplate the prospect of him returning to a cold hearth and empty chair with herself slumbering peacefully upstairs? What sort of wife would that make her?

Under the rough linen of her shift, her nipples itch. The fine linen has gone to Widow Thom's for washing and won't be back till the end of the week. She rubs herself through her dress with the edge of her wrist and listens to the groan of the gale gathering strength in the night outside. The sound of it takes her mind back, despite herself, to Christmas night: the weight of Alec's body on hers, the sounds he'd made. Ashamed, she pushes the thought away. Somewhere above her head a floorboard creaks. Mary, perhaps, turning in her cot, disturbed by a dream or the storm. She should go up and see. Instead, she waits, tensed for further sounds of movement from upstairs, relieved when none comes. She leans forward and pulls her sampler from the sewing basket at her feet. She checks that the fabric is taut across the frame, then holds a needle up to the light and threads it with a strand of pale green twist. Tonight, she will finish the leaves, tomorrow start on the lettering.

The rhythmic motion of the needle is soothing: the low hiss of the thread as it pulls through the fabric. It reminds her: of soft waves sipping at white sands. Hot air on bare skin. Beads of sweat sliding between her shoulder blades. She was only seven when they left, but the memory is deep inside her still, imprinted there, like the impressions of seashells on small stones. She'd find them sometimes, little fossils, tangled in the gulfweed in the coves below the plantation. She liked to trace the strange whorls and ridges with her fingers, wondering who put them there, or press the tip of her tongue into the tiny cavities, lap out the saltiness, pretending to be a cat with a bowl of milk, while the great fat sun beat down and the sea breeze caressed her hair like a soft hand, stroking away the hurt.

A sudden riot of barking from somewhere outside the house returns her to the present. She looks at the embroidery between her hands, allows herself to imagine how it will be when Alec finally returns: how she will look up at him as he comes through the door, rise from her chair, hold out her arms and take his coat and hat, the wet dog smell of the wool in her nostrils; how she'll lead him to his seat by the fire, ease his feet from his boots, let the heat from the logs bring the feeling back to his toes; how she'll bring him broth and bread and porter, then settle at his knee, while he relates the events of his day and the tiredness ebbs from his face. *Stop it!* She jabs the needle into the circle of cloth, furious with herself. *It will not be like that.* The point misses its mark, embeds itself in the pad of her index finger. Tears sting the backs of her eyes. Why does she persist in thinking these things? Alec will not thank her for waiting up or fetching him broth. He has no use for her at the end of these long nights, prefers to be alone, silent, shut tight as a clam. The bead of blood is sweet on her tongue. *Why does it not get any easier?* Self-pity assails her, then curdles into shame. She must not give in to such thoughts or where will it end? Such an easy time the devil has of it on these long evenings, whether she occupies her hands or not.

Will you be late tonight?

The moment the words left her mouth she knew she should

not have asked, hated the sound of her own wheedling, the note of complaint in her voice that always brings that terrible blankness to his face.

Aye, most likely.

She hates herself for it, but hates still more that he has no idea how she is suffering, every moment, while he is away tending the suffering of others, gone for days at a time when he's called to the country. Every second he is out of the house she is in dread of some disaster befalling him; sometimes fears she may cause disaster with thinking about it.

I am a physician. This is what I do.

And I am your wife. Does that count for nothing?

The air between them will be rotten with unspoken grievance for days, as it always is after these outbursts. She is a disappointment to him, she knows, although he would never say it outright. He had hoped for a companion to share the burden and the triumphs of his work. Instead, with her fretting and clinging, she adds to his burden. And she, what had she hoped for?

In her mind's eye, Elizabeth pictures Alec as a young man once more. Wide fingers on thin knees, awkward as a heron on the edge of Aunt Rae's damask sofa, rough-edged and out of place amidst the fine furniture. They'd met for the first time at the annual New Inn ball. She was nineteen years old. They nearly had not gone, on account of her aunt's head cold, but at the last moment Aunt Rae revived and the phaeton was called. She and Bella were living with Aunt Rae by then. Their father's death, five years before, had left them not only orphaned but penniless. Aunt Rae seldom referred directly to her generosity in rescuing them from their disgraced state, but she let it be known in countless other ways. The sudden head cold on the day of the New Inn ball was not unusual, nor its sudden disappearance just as all hope of going had finally been abandoned. By the time the phaeton drew up outside the house, Elizabeth was in low spirits, any pleasurable feelings of anticipation eroded by her aunt's repeated raising and crushing of expectation. She hadn't wanted to go, could foresee no joy in another occasion governed by her aunt's despotic and unpredictable rule. It was Bella, coaxing her into dressing, arranging her hair, holding the glass up to her reflection, who had restored in the end sufficient courage for the evening ahead. She'd worn her mother's amethysts round her neck, a lilac sash about her waist. She wore her fragility, too, in the grey depths of her eyes, although she did not know it.

The moment she entered the room she noticed him: standing near the musicians, grinning at something his companion – his younger brother, Chae, she later learnt – was saying to him. She'd liked the grin, the broad open face, the unkempt hair. Joe Simpson made the introductions. They danced five reels and she liked him still more with each one. Then: nothing. Not a word nor glimpse of him. The weeks passed. The ice thawed on the loch. Lapwings blew in on the spring storms. Not a word. Alec Gordon seemed to have vanished into thin air.

It was April before they met again. A fine blustering day and her disappointment almost conquered. A multitude of folk had turned out to celebrate the inauguration of the new road and the cheerful cacophony of the crowd was competing loudly with the drums and pipes of the military band. Painted flags and banners, strung from the hawthorn trees, lined the route of the future Belmont Street. The air was filled with the smell of hot-bakes and small beer from the refreshment stalls. Ribbon sellers and jugglers, fishwives and pamphleteers busily plied their trade. Guildsmen and burgh dignitaries, resplendent in shining braids and medallions, strutted back and forth with all the self-importance they believed their position warranted. Drifts of creamy blossom gusted over the heads of the crowd from the branches of the hawthorns, settling like confetti on the women's bonnets. And suddenly there he was, with his brother, leaning on one elbow on the counter of a pie stall. He was taller than she remembered, his expression more serious. If he'd been laughing, perhaps she would have turned away, but his face brightened the instant he saw her, and, surprising herself with her boldness, she'd asked Aunt Rae if the brothers might join them. More surprising still, Aunt Rae, who was not inclined to regard farmers' sons as suitable company for gentlemen's daughters, had agreed.

'Your father – one of Lord Irvine's tenants, is he not?'

Elizabeth winced at her aunt's imperious tone, although, Lord knows, she should have been used to it by now.

'Was, ma'am. We lost the tenancy when my father died. My brother James manages Colonel Tower's estate now in Buchan.'

A tiny curl of pastry caught in the gingery stubble on his upper lip.

'And you? When you're not dancing reels and eating pies. What do you do with yourself?'

'Training for a surgeon, ma'am.' The pastry curl fluttering with his words, pearly white against the red of his mouth. 'I have recently returned from Leiden and go next month to London to secure my certificate at Surgeon's Hall.'

'Surgeons!' Aunt Rae gave a loud sniff. 'Quacks and mountebanks, the lot of them.'

Further exchange was ruled out by the approaching procession of dignitaries and musicians, accompanied by great cheers from the crowd. Stepping back to let the procession pass, Elizabeth found herself at Alec's side. 'This would be a fine street to live in one day, Miss Harvie, don't you agree?' He did not look at her as he spoke and his words were all but drowned out by the drummers, but she heard what he said and understood and blushed, and then blushed some more for showing she had understood.

He was like that from the first. So sure always of what he wanted. So unlike the other young men she met. Ablaze with ambition. He was not yet twenty-five, a student still, but when he spoke of his plans for the future, there was nothing wistful about it. It was never mere dreams with Alexander Gordon. It was always certainties waiting to happen. In his physical appearance he was not so remarkable: buff-haired, ruddy cheeked, with sharp blue eyes and strong hands and a wide smile, indistinguishable from a hundred other Aberdeenshire lads who, when they weren't learning their letters in the schoolhouse, were out in the fields with their fathers and brothers, battling with a soil and climate more suited to gorse and heather than barley and oats. It was when he spoke that you felt how different he was. Everything he said revealed an informed and independent mind. There was an unmistakable sense of purpose, a resolute energy about young Mr Gordon that Elizabeth was irresistibly drawn to. He had conviction. (Her father, she thought, would have liked that about him too.) He spoke of progress as if it were a marvellous journey. He spoke of knowledge as if it were an exquisite jewel. With so much certainty in him, she had thought, there must be some to spare for her. With such a man at her side, she would be able to face the world. She adorned herself in his talk, swathed herself in his passionate assertions about the power of knowledge to transform society. In the light of his convictions she had felt herself transfigured into a bolder, surer version of herself. All the vague dissatisfactions and apprehensions of her life found firm contours when she placed them in the impressions left by his solid tread. She could imagine for the first time a life beyond the confines of Aunt Rae's rule. She was happier than she'd ever been, felt clearly defined in a way she had never done before.

They courted for three years. He was too proud to ask her for her hand without financial means of his own. She understood. She waited. The very day his commission came through, he rode up north to put a ring on her finger, but it was a further twelve months before they were finally wed. Belmont Street had grown by then into two proud rows of granite houses, the colour of dove's wings on a fine day, built in the new style with elegant fanlights over the front doors and three stone steps leading up to them. The fourth house from the end, on the eastern side of the street, its back to the town, was their home.

It was only in the weeks leading up to their marriage that she began to suffer again. The plaguing headaches and fits of trembling. The old shadows creeping along the edges of her vision. Marie, Old Amos, McKenzie. She ignored them, refused to acknowledge their return, said nothing to Alec.

They were married in St Paul's on a dismally wet morning in late February. Joe Simpson and Chae were their witnesses. After two days' honeymoon at Peterhead, Alec was obliged to leave once more. It was all farewells in those years. Farewells and waiting. Six more months to serve in the navy. Six months after that in the London hospitals to complete his training. She'd wanted to be with him in London: it seemed wrong to be living still with her aunt and sister now that she was married. But Alec firmly rejected the idea, emphatically so once they discovered she was with child. The English capital was worse than a madhouse, he told her, with ranting lunatics roaming the streets day and night, and poor plackless devils, drunk out of their skulls on gin. To step into the street was to risk your life from the carts and coaches that thundered without cease along the narrowest of thoroughfares. Chief of Alec's objections, however, was the state of the air: from dawn to dusk so thick and dark you hardly knew what time of day it was or what season of the year, the poisonous miasmas spreading contagion to rich and poor alike. Far better, Alec insisted, that she remain in Aberdeen, where the streets were admirably free from filth and the air as sweet as any in the British Isles.

We must endure the separation as best we can, a few short months apart, then a lifetime together.

She'd cut out his words, placed the folded scrap of paper between the portraits of her parents in the silver locket that had been her mother's. Kept his injunction, his promise, round her neck and in her mind all that year, kept the darkness at bay with them.

They'd been apart for so much of those ten years, and although she tried not to dwell on the thought, it began to dawn on her that her husband might transpire to be a man who journeyed alone, that progress far from bringing her closer to him might simply take him beyond her reach, that his passion for knowledge might blind him to the existence of other treasures of equal value. Five years of marriage have proved her fears correct. She can scarcely see anything else. His certainty has not abated with the years, but she has not profited by it. The shadows plague her more than ever. Alec notices nothing. Only Mary sees. Her daughter's baleful gaze is almost more than Elizabeth can bear at times. Makes her feel there is nowhere left to hide.

She must not be ungrateful. Ingratitude is a sin and Alec is a good man, in so many ways. A husband to be proud of. There's no physician to match him this side of the Tweed. Isn't that what George Bannerman says? Isn't that what they all say these days? Even Mistress Glegg, the minister's thin-lipped wife, has been heard to admit that the young doctor appears to know what he's about: that the living do seem more likely to stay that way since he took over at the Dispensary. He has the town's confidence now. The patient list grows ever longer, the doors of the Dispensary daily more pressed with people seeking his help, like the Lord's creatures flocking into the ark. Elizabeth smiles a little at this thought, amused by the idea of her husband as a modern-day Noah. But Alec deserves their confidence, to be sure; has earned it many times over since his appointment to the Aberdeen Dispensary. Four years of hard work and tireless commitment. No obstacle is too great if it stands between Dr Gordon and the public good, no hour too late if it might save a man or woman's life, no disease too far advanced if it threatens the life of a child. Word of

Alec's dedication runs after him, around him, ahead of him, like a pack of faithful dogs, through the wide streets of the New Town and the narrow lanes of the Old, and out into the surrounding villages. His standing has never been higher, with the public or his colleagues. Dr Skene and Dr Bannerman are forever calling upon him for his opinion of their cases. Students from the college are always at the door with some question or other they have to put to him that very instant. Even the Infirmary physicians, the loathsome George French and his clutch of sycophants, require Alec's help on the wards most weeks – as if his hands weren't full enough already with his own practice, and the Dispensary, and the lectures, and the committees. Oh, the committees! Who would have guessed a town of this size could support such a quantity of committees? Yet it seems it can and it seems her husband must sit on each and every one of them.

Elizabeth leans back in her chair. The embroidery lies in a tired heap in the shallow pool of her skirts as if it too were exhausted by the thought of all Alec's industry. If only she were as busy as he. If only her hands were as full. Mary turned five two months ago. She is grateful for that, of course she is. You can relax a little when they get to five. It isn't that she's not grateful. But every week it seems another woman's child is born, brought into the world as often as not with her husband's help, while her own womb remains as still and empty as the room she's sitting in. It is her own fault, she knows, but what can she do? There is no one to ask. No one to tell her how to turn the hourglass so the flow of time is reversed, so the sand falls upwards. No one to explain how to forget.

4

It's the back of midnight and the gale is blowing hard as Alec makes his way through the town for the second time that night, grimly grateful for the wind's pummelling and buffeting, for the impersonal ferocity of its attacks. He'd sent Rabbie on ahead, preferring to be alone for a while. His earlier good humour has been replaced by a hard smouldering knot of indignation. Garrow's rebuttal is a darkening bruise on his pride, swelling and spreading with every step. The ignorance of these people! The block-headed ignorance of them! How is any progress to be made when they cling to their absurd beliefs? Nothing now will bring Elspet Garrow back to life, but an inspection would at least have shed some light on her death. Couldn't Garrow see that? In Leiden, there would be no such nonsense to endure. In Leiden the public understand the value of anatomy. Openings are commonplace and men of science are able to pursue their investigations in a civilized manner. No unseemly struggles in Leiden over still-warm corpses. No passing of purses and greasing of palms. No need for side doors, back doors, trap doors and a million other demeaning little ruses and subterfuges that are all part of his lot here in Aberdeen. And why? Because people persist in clinging to custom; prefer to stumble in the dark ages of fear and superstition, than to walk new pathways they are unfamiliar with. *What if her soul's no ready to depart? How d'ye know for sure she's deid?* Why, you damn fool, he wants to say, because she's stiffer than a length of wainscot and stinking to high heaven. That is why!

But how do you convince folk whose thoughts are brimful of ghoulies and ghasties that what remains concealed from the physician's gaze remains beyond the reach of the physician's art? How do you persuade them that the mind can only describe what the eye can see? That external appearances show only a small part of the true story. That diagnosis without dissection is like a book without its final chapters. So: the weid killed Elspet Garrow. That's what they want to believe, is it? An implausible ending to a tale if ever he heard one, convincing as a fox in a hencoop. Why should an illness only ever seen in a mild form and never known to be fatal suddenly snatch a woman in the prime of life, in good health and of sound mind, after a confinement distinguished only by a complete absence of complications? It made no sense whatsoever, but they would believe it anyway.

A rock and a hard place and himself between the two: that is how Alec sees himself at times. If it's not the townsfolk standing in the way of progress with their damn fool notions, as like as not it's the physicians. Alec frowns at the disagreeable memory of *that* quarrel; it was nigh on four years ago, but the recollection still rankles. The managers' case rested solely on their assertion that the public bath, having been neglected by the townsfolk, for whom it had not long since been built, could no longer be kept up without considerable loss to the funds of the Infirmary. Alec reckoned this a most extraordinary argument, the rate of bathing for a whole year not exceeding half-a-guinea a head. Cold bathing was of obvious public benefit, not only beneficial to the general constitution, but the most efficacious method known for washing effluvia from the surface of the body, *ergo*, an invaluable means of preventing infection. Alec could see no counter-argument of any merit, yet support for the closure had been stubbornly maintained. He began to suspect that the true arguments were not of a kind guaranteed to win public support, a suspicion confirmed by a perusal of the town plans one afternoon. Several of the senior physicians, it transpired, owned sizeable portions of the land being feued out for the bath and stood to make substantial gains by its sale. What angered Alec, beyond the dishonesty and hypocrisy of his colleagues, was their assumption that he would bow to their wishes, support their flimsy case for the closure against all the scientific evidence opposing it, against the public interest, against common sense. What did they take him for?

Alec let his discovery be known in a letter to the Board, mentioning no one by name of course, but when it became clear that even this had failed to swing opinion against the closure, he was left with no choice: he set out the argument in a pamphlet, had Chalmers print up two hundred copies, and called a public meeting. Elizabeth questioned the wisdom of opposing the Infirmary's wishes so soon after his arrival in the town, but he had no qualms: closing the baths would cost the Infirmary in the long run five times what it would save (or make) in the short term. In any case, he would not pander to liars and hypocrites, whoever their fathers and grandfathers. Self-interest was a sickness to be purged like any other. The pamphlet won the day: there was a public outcry and plans for the closure were quietly shelved. An unpleasant business, all in all, but it had made Alec's name. Overnight he became the poor folk's champion, the public's hero. Amongst the physicians, however, sentiments were more mixed. He'd earned their respect, but at a price. He had drawn attention to himself too soon; set himself above them in authority; exposed unscrupulous conduct in persons of public repute. In short, he had made enemies. A rock and a hard place indeed.

Elizabeth has fallen asleep in the chair by the hearth, her head tilted up and back at an awkward angle, small gutterings of breath escaping from her open mouth, the stretch of her throat white above the dark knot of her shawl. The tail end of a fire shifts quietly in the grate, its meagre light falling over her neck and shoulders, casting the rest of her body in shadow. The sight of her, lost to sleep, so slight against the high frame of the chair, brings Alec to a standstill. Tenderness washes through him, followed by remorse. For a moment he forgets Garrow and everything Garrow stands for, abruptly and fully conscious suddenly of the lateness of the hour; the distress he knows it will have caused her; the distress he knows *he* causes her.

Elizabeth startles awake with a little cry of alarm, disturbed by his presence in the room.

'It's only me.'

'Alec?' She pulls herself into alertness. 'Are you all right? Where have you been?'

That querulous note in her voice. Alec's heart sinks.

He crosses the room and, with his back turned to her, pours some wine from one of the decanters on the sideboard.

'You shouldn't have waited up. It only tires you.'

He sets the decanter back down on the sideboard with a hard little thud. How genteel they are, he thinks bitterly. Not one decanter, but two. And crystal no less. Her family, of course, not his. There were no crystal decanters in any house he grew up in. He raises the glass to his lips, opens his throat to let the wine slide into his gullet, feels the claret slip into his bloodstream. Even with his back turned, he can see the reproach in Elizabeth's expression, feel the nudge of it between his shoulder blades. He watches the wine settle back into the bowl of the glass; it nestles in the palm of his hand, a warm dark red. How many times has he told her not to wait up? Why must she persist in doing so when he has expressly asked her not to? The irregularity of his hours upsets her, he knows that, but what choice does he have? He is not some shopkeeper or clerk to order his time by the clock. How can she expect it of him, with all the patients she knows he must attend? There were four hundred names on the book when he took over from George French; now there are fourteen hundred. It is a triumph. It is *his* triumph. Yet his own wife seems not to rejoice in his success, but rather to resent it. What would she have him do? He cannot simply abandon his patients to their fate for the sake of her nerves. The greatest physician on earth cannot dictate precisely when an illness will strike, nor how long it will take to run its course. Why can she not understand this?

'Could you not have sent Rabbie?' says Elizabeth. 'With some word of your whereabouts?'

His *whereabouts*? In the nether regions of Alec's mind the word strikes a hard seam of obstinacy. With the wheelwright's hatred on him like a brand? With the stench of Elspet Garrow's corpse filling his nostrils? He has walked eight miles or more tonight in freezing sleet. In the space of an hour he has held life and death in his bare hands. And the woman desires to know his *whereabouts*?

'Robert Donald is my apprentice,' he says, turning back to the decanter and tipping another slug of wine into his glass. 'Not some message boy to be running round Aberdeen with little notes for you.'

'Little notes?' Her voice has risen sharply.

She cannot explain: about the silence and the fears that crowd it.

'You know what I mean.'

He'd only taken on Rabbie as a favour to her. He could have had his pick of any of the students, but had agreed to her cousin at her particular request. He'll not have her telling him now what he may or may not do with the lad.

'No,' she says. 'I do not know what you mean.'

'In God's name, woman!' Alec's fist comes down on the sideboard with more force than he'd quite intended. 'There was a birthing at one end of the town, then a patient with a fever at the other. That is all there is to know. Now let it rest, will you?'

He drains his glass and fills it a third time. Why does he not just tell her the truth, tell her the patient's name, tell her the wretched woman is dead? With everyone else in the world he is direct and honest to a fault, but with Elizabeth, the exact opposite: this terrible impulse to prevaricate and dissemble. But why? To protect her? To protect himself? The death of a lying-in woman is bound to ignite her concern with Isabella so near her time, but how does it help to try and keep the facts from her? She will find out soon enough in any case. All business is the business of all in Aberdeen. There is no place like it for wagging tongues and burning ears. One would think birth and death exotic occurrences, not everyday events, from the excitement they occasion: the faintest rumour of a lying-in, the vaguest mention of a low fever or a touch of the rheumatics, and the local women flock to the bedside like rats to a granary to see for themselves. Mistress Troop would have told her, or Isabella. Why trouble to conceal it?

Weariness envelops him suddenly. His ineptitude with Elizabeth is a mystery to him. He does not understand it. He, who is so competent in the world, so assured and skilled in every other area of his life! Yet his own wife is more baffling to him than a thousand illnesses together. These constant disagreements between them are the symptoms of a malady beyond his comprehension, like an invisible poison seeping through the circulatory system of their marriage. As long as he keeps moving, on to the next place, the next patient, the next crisis, he's all right, feels sure of what he's doing. It's when he stops at the end of the day, when Elizabeth starts her questioning, that he begins to doubt. Things catch up with him: what he's seen and done, what it means or fails to mean, how little sense he can make of it sometimes, this endless battling with nature, this thankless quest to keep death at bay, to cast light on the wastelands of ignorance. The expression on Garrow's face this evening, the look of horror and disgust in the wheelwright's eyes, sums up everything he is fighting against, everything he hopes to conquer, sometimes fears he cannot.

But this sitting up does no good, that is for sure. Far better if she'd just go to bed when he's called away at night. He has offered her sleeping draughts, but she refuses to take anything, clings to her anxieties instead, hoards them like a miser.

Alec risks a quick glance at Elizabeth. She has pulled the sewing basket on to her lap and is bent over it, making a show of sorting the contents. He knows there is no need, it is all in perfect order already. The sensation of heaviness assails him again. Of airlessness. From the upstairs landing comes the ticking of the long clock. The silence between them is impenetrable. He knows he must say something, but no words come to him. After a while she stands. Her shadow extends towards him across the floorboards. The sewing basket is clasped to her chest, like a barricade.

'I'm going to bed.'

He responds with a slight movement of his head. She puts the basket back in its place and takes the candle from its bracket by the fire. She crosses the room, pausing for a moment in the doorway. Still Alec does not move. Five feet of floorboard between them and a chasm of misunderstandings. As her footsteps recede down the passageway and up the stairs, he continues to stare moodily into his glass, swilling the wine around and around, watching the pink film on the inner surface of the glass form and dissolve. Had he looked up he would have seen Elizabeth's shadow thin and taper behind her, then buckle and vanish altogether. The silence settles around him. A rock and a hard place and betwixt the two a great ocean of ignorance and prejudice and worse.

5

It has been raining since dawn, an unrelenting downpour that is not quite snow but wants to be, the insistent pounding on the roof of St Paul's Chapel competing with the equally dour barrage of the sermon. The minister had slept badly, the hide-hard beef he'd eaten at supper lodged all the night like a boulder in his gut, causing much discomfort to himself and much complaint from his wife, who'd shortly banished him to the landing for disturbing her rest. Pressing just as disagreeably on the minister's thoughts this morning are the words 'imminent' and 'bankrupt', words mentioned with some frequency and heat the week before Christmas at the last Quarterly General Court of the Infirmary Board, words which are his particular burden this Sunday, it being the first Sunday in January, in other words, Hospital Sunday.

From the peeling interior of St Paul's, the tiny Quaker meeting room in Rottenholes, to the newly decorated nave of St Nicholas, the congregants of each and every denomination must be exhorted to dig deeply into purse and pocket; reminded that in the midst of life they are in death, and that the exact amounts raised today by each one of the town's twenty-four places of worship will be set down in flowing copperplate in the large leather volume that contains all of the Infirmary's annual business and proceedings. It must be spelt out, moreover, for any particularly dull-witted sheep in the assembled flocks, that the Directors and Managers of the Infirmary Board will be able to see at a glance precisely which of those twenty-four places of worship has given generously, and which has not.

No need just yet, it was unanimously agreed at the December meeting, to share this other fact lately laid bare by the

36

Clerk's twirling goose-feather: that the sums raised have for some time been declining, with the result that there is now a considerable disparity between the figure inked in under 'fixed and certain funds' and that linked in under 'expenditure'. A disparity to the tune of six hundred and eight pounds, nine shillings and threepence. Hence the 'imminent' and the 'bankrupt'. Hence the raised voices at the Quarterly General Court. Hence the unmistakably dangerous look in Provost Cruden's eye.

Pressing his still tender gut into the hard edge of the lectern, Glegg scowls down at the heads of his congregants and rallies himself for this year's assault on purse and conscience.

'These days and weeks of Epiphany are of the utmost significance in the holy calendar, the time when we recall that the Truth is made manifest *strictly* in accordance with the will of God.' He leans a little further over the lectern, eyeing them sternly. 'And in just what manner was the Truth first made manifest?'

Alec, seated three rows from the front, slides a glance at Mary, who is tracing a path with her forefinger through the pattern of her shawl. Elizabeth, beyond her, is staring into her lap where her gloved hands are tightly clasped. She has not spoken to Alec since their argument two nights before.

'Through miracles!' Glegg's voice booms over their heads. 'Through the great miracles of healing!'

With the hunched bulk of his shoulders, the pronounced brow and heavily hooded eyes, the minister bears a strong resemblance to a bad-tempered bird of prey and it is with a distinctly hawkish expression that he is glowering down at them now. Reverend Glegg may worship as an Episcopalian, Alec thinks, not for the first time, but the man's a Calvinist, through and through. They all are. Regardless what prayerbook they use. It's in the blood and bones of them, as the granite hills are.

Beside him, Mary has given up tracking the pathways in her

shawl and is now twisting the tassels of the fringe into tight little knots. Alec reaches over, enclosing her hands in his own. Her fingers fall still. He is surprised by how cold her hands are beneath the warmth of his own. She looks up at him, wondering if she's done something wrong; he smiles back at her, gives her hand a reassuring squeeze.

Glegg's voice thunders on. 'He went amongst the people and healed the sick. He cleansed the leper of his disease. Lifted the sickness from the servant of the centurion. Drew the fever from the mother-in-law of his disciple Peter. Rich and poor, old and young. He made no distinction. He cured those possessed with demons. He gave sight to the blind and hearing to the deaf. He made the lame to walk. He restored breath to the dying.'

The chapel smells of dank wool and tallow smoke. A continual sniffing and coughing punctuates the minister's words.

'It is as the prophet Isaiah foretold. *He has borne our infirmities and carried our diseases.* Chapter fifty-three, verse three. *Upon him was the punishment that made us whole and by his bruises we are healed.* Let no one here today forget this.'

Signalling for the collection plate to start its rounds, Glegg pulls himself to his full height.

'From first to last, Christ's ministry on earth was a healing ministry, showing us that healing lies at the heart of the Christian faith. Are we not blessed, then, that here in Aberdeen the healing vocation thrives? Are we not blessed to have in our midst dedicated physicians of the first rank, who, in their own humble way, work healing miracles each and every day? Are we not blessed—' lingering on the word, injecting it with the necessary note of recrimination – 'to have in this town a fine and well-appointed hospital, in which the sick may receive the very best care in their hour of need?'

In his mind's eye, Alec sees Elspet Garrow, entirely beyond care, her bloated corpse beyond healing of any kind. He had woken in the night, the remnants of a dream edging from his memory. He lay on his back, listening to Elizabeth's steady breathing in the darkness beside him. She was turned on her side, away from him. He moved his leg to touch hers, but she was fast asleep and did not respond. The curve of her buttocks against his hip made him stir and stiffen. For a moment or two he'd considered the likelihood of his advances being tolerated again so soon. Soon? Ha! Resentment flared in him, wilting his erection; he would not force himself on her; would not be reduced to that. He trained his mind instead on the sounds beyond the room. Rain was falling, a one-note patter on the pantiles. A night bird called through the darkness, a warning cry. He tried to remember the dream that had woken him, but it was gone. From the direction of the woods a fox barked. He was wide awake now, distilled to alertness by the blackness all around him, his senses straining for purchase on the darkness, his thoughts closing in once more on the puzzle of Elspet Garrow. There was nothing uncommon in a fever after birth. A lochial disorder, most probably, incorrectly treated, the trapped secretions running to putrefaction when not quickly enough purged: this seemed the most likely explanation for her death, and yet it did not entirely satisfy him. There was something else, just beyond reach, like his vanished dream; something on the peripheries of his memory that he could not quite recall.

'Infirmity and disease await each and every one of us.' The minister's voice intrudes once more on Alec's thoughts. 'In this brief span of earthly life, therefore, let none of us neglect to do Our Lord's business. We cannot all be healers, as we cannot all be assured of salvation, but let none of us forget the words of St Luke: *Whoever has two coats must share with anyone who has none, and whoever has food must do likewise.* Recall, also, the words of St Matthew: *If thine enemy hunger, feed him; if he thirst, give him drink.*'

Glegg's voice lifts above the rain, the hacking coughs, the

ceaseless evacuation of nasal passageways. 'Today of all days, let no one in *this* congregation fail in his Christian duty.'

The organ at last takes over from the minister and the opening chords of the hymn fill the chapel. Glancing over his shoulder, Alec inadvertently catches James Garrow's eye. The wheelwright is watching him with a look of outright hostility. Alec feels a rush of indignation. It is hardly his fault the man's wife died! But he knows that is not the point: folk need someone to blame for a death, and who better than the physician?

6

'A rousing sermon,' George French says, lifting his glass in the minister's direction, 'and, if I may so, a most excellent leg of mutton, Mistress Glegg.'

The minister's wife lowers her eyes modestly as if to imply the mutton is the Good Lord's doing rather more than her own. Her upper lip, nonetheless, puckers at the compliment.

'Pearls before swine.' Provost Cruden spears a slab of meat and inserts it into his large, fleshy mouth. 'Short arms and deep pockets,' he adds, chewing with vigour. 'That's the trouble with this town.'

Reverend Glegg eyes him gloomily. The best part of a fine claret has already vanished down the Provost's throat. The man might display a little restraint, he cannot help thinking, not to mention a few manners.

'Let's wait for the collections,' George French says in a pleasant tone. 'No reason to despair just yet.'

'Don't hope for too much.' Cruden holds out his empty glass. '*By their fruits shall ye know them.* Isn't that so, Minister?'

Glegg grunts his assent, filling the proffered glass with some resentment.

'Of course,' Cruden continues, 'we wouldn't be in this mess if the baths had sold. Curse the man! No thought for anything but his own fool arguments.'

'Any more, Provost?' says Mistress Glegg, signing to her husband to pass the meat platter. 'Would you be referring to Dr Gordon?'

'I would, madam.' Cruden turns and waves the point of his knife at the minister. 'Your man, Glegg. Cost me a pretty penny, I can tell you.'

Glegg blinks and reddens. 'My man?'

'Twas your coat tail he was clinging to when he secured the post, was it not?'

'*My* coat tail?'

'Your pig tail then. I don't mind which.' Cruden smiles benevolently. 'But let's have the facts straight. *You* were his sponsor, were you not?'

'I am acquainted with his wife's uncle, if that's what you mean.' A nerve is ticking on the side of Glegg's neck. Resentment is burgeoning into something less governable. 'I wrote to Mr Harvie at your request, Provost, as I recall. And he gave most generously.'

'Aye,' Cruden nods, 'and could afford to. Which is not, sir, to deny my point.'

'Being?'

'Perhaps, Provost, this is not—' George French intervenes.

'Being?' the minister says again.

'Gentlemen!' Alice Glegg's hands flutter like moth's wings in the candlelight. She has not served choice mutton for it to be ignored in this fashion. 'No quarrelling on the Sabbath! If you please!'

7

Three streets away another disagreement is coming to the boil.

'There must be some risk,' Chae is saying, 'of contagious air spreading from one ward to another.'

'And from one house to another,' Alec retorts. 'It makes no difference in the epidemic season.'

'Aye, but in general,' Chae persists, 'surely a woman is safer in her own home?'

'At the mercy of ignorant howdies? With no knowledge of anatomy, no training in chirurgy, no understanding of physiology? Why, they would not recognize a contagion if it sat down to spin with them!'

They have been arguing the point for the past quarter of an hour.

Elizabeth, who has been following the exchange with mounting disquiet, can contain her feelings no longer: 'How thoughtless you men are! Please! No more talk of epidemics and contagions!' She places her hand on her sister's arm. 'Flemming is the best nurse in Aberdeen. She attended all Lady Cologhun's lying-ins. You have nothing to fear.'

Isabella hears the loving intention behind Elizabeth's words and answers her with a smile. But they both know it's not true: every lying-in is attended by danger. It is ordained by God. *In pain shalt thou bring forth children.* There is always cause for fear.

The afternoon wears on. The table is cleared. The fire burns down and is replenished. Rabbie reads to Mary from the Bible. Elizabeth and Isabella sew. Alec and Chae bicker about the news from France, the unrest it is giving rise to at home, the recent survey of the town's water supply, the draining of the loch. Outside, the wind picks up, flings itself in spiteful fits against the walls of the house. Daylight, what there is of it, subsides into dusk and dusk into stormy darkness. Tea and ginch-breid are proposed and rung for. No one is minded to quit the warmth of the fireside. Shortly after five o'clock the calm is broken by a violent hammering at the front door. All sewing, reading, bickering stops abruptly. A man's voice is heard to shout from the street: 'Dr Gordon! Is Dr Gordon there? I need to see the doctor!'

Alec is on his feet at once, signalling to Annie to go and see who it is, then going after her to see for himself. A thin, dishevelled man half-steps, half-falls into the hallway. Rain-water streams from his hair and coat. Fear rises off him like steam from a dung heap.

'What is it? What's happened?'

'It's Jenny.' Andrew Duncan is close to tears. 'She's burnin wi fever. Screamin wi pain since yesternight.'

Not again, Alec thinks, but there is no question in his mind, not a moment's hesitation. He is reaching for his cloak, fumbling in his haste to get his arm into the sleeves, casting around for his medicine chest and his hat. Rabbie is hard at his heels. Elizabeth has followed them into the hall.

'Don't go, Alec. Please!'

'I'll be back later.'

She puts out her hand, catches hold of Alec's cloak.

'It's only a fever,' she pleads. 'The milk coming in. It'll pass.'

He stops, one hand already on the latch, stares at her. 'Are you mad, woman? Elspet Garrow died this week of just such a fever.'

But Elizabeth knows nothing of Elspet Garrow.

'Send one of the others. Please, Alec! Bannerman or Skene can go. You're forever helping them. Can they not do something for you for once?'

But he has gone, Rabbie Donald and Andrew Duncan after him, her words trailing uselessly in their wake.

8

The men walk in single file, heads bent down against the driving rain. The wind is blowing hard off the sea, sighing and moaning in dour harmony with the distant thrash of the waves down on the beach. The streets are deserted, the town bolted and shuttered against the storm.

'Over here!'

A child's voice cuts through the darkness. A boy, no more than eight or nine years old and pitifully thin, is standing a short way in front of them, sheltering from the rain as best he can beneath a strip of canvas, holding a lantern as high as the length of his arm will permit. The lantern rocks violently in his hand, tugged this way and that by the wind. The slur of light does little more than fall on to the boy's head, casting deep shadows under his eyes and cheekbones, lending him a ghoulish appearance. They have come to a halt in front of a low timber dwelling. Duncan takes the lantern from his son and raises it to illuminate the short flight of wooden stairs leading to the upper storey of the house, where the family has its living quarters. Alec goes first. He braces himself as he pushes open the door, but even so is unprepared for the stench. It hits him the moment he steps foot inside the room and for a second he is confused: he knows this smell, this vile sweetness.

The room is stiflingly hot. In the hearth a fire is piled with logs and burning fiercely. The casement is lined with a roll of blanket; even the keyhole has been plugged with a twist of paper. The throng of women gathered around the bed obscures the patient from Alec's view. At the sight of their massed backs pressing in on the bedside, a cold dark rage rises through him.

'The doctor! The doctor is here!'

In one smooth cringing wave the women shrink back to the edges of the room. *The way paper curls from the heat of a flame*, Alec thinks, the small evidence of his influence affording him an instant of bitter pleasure, the feeling dispelled at once by the sight of the patient before him.

Jenny Duncan is lying on her back in an odd stiff attitude. Her face is pallid and waxy, except for the skin around the nose, which is faintly blue. Her hair is drenched from a recent sweat. As Alec approaches the bed, she turns her head very slightly to look at him. Her eyes are huge: two dark points of distilled terror. Alec looks away, fighting an urge to bock. A pewter basin on the floor by the bed contains a pool of greenish-black vomit. The piss-pot beside it is full, the urine streaked with black. Beneath the sheet, which is pulled up to the patient's chin, the abdomen is hugely swollen. Alec sets down his medicine chest. At the same moment Jenny Duncan is seized with a violent rigor. Her body shakes so violently that her bones seem to liquefy. The wooden bedstead on which she is lying is thrown repeatedly against the wall behind. Andrew Duncan leaps forward, wrapping his arms around his wife's juddering frame, as if trying to overcome the rigor's strength with his own. His face is bleached with fear, almost as pale as that of his wife. After two or three minutes, the rigor subsides. Almost immediately, it is replaced by a low fit of shivering.

'Mistress Duncan?' Alec leans in close to the patient. He can smell death on her skin. 'Can you hear me?'

The miserable woman nods her head a fraction.

'Are you in pain?'

She nods again, and moves her head very slightly to indicate her right side, her face clenching with distress as she does so. Alec takes one of her hands in his own and finds the pulse, faint and frantic against the pressure of his fingertips. The skin is hot and dry, as drained of colour as her face, except for the knuckles, curled towards him, which are flushed a deep red.

He counts, measuring the pulse against the second hand of his fob watch. A hundred and forty strokes to the minute.

'Is the lochia stopped?'

The question is addressed to the room in general.

'Aye. Since yesterday.'

Without turning, Alec recognizes the voice as that of Mistress Elgin.

'When did the fever commence?'

'Just after six.'

Lifting the sheet with his left hand, Alec slides his right on to the hard mound of the woman's belly. The pressure of his palm is light, but it is enough to produce an instant scream of pain.

Alec straightens up. 'She must be bled without delay.'

The women in the room stare at each other and at him, openly appalled.

It is Jennifer Elgin who dares to voice what they are all thinking. 'But Dr Gordon – ye cannae bleed a lying-in mother!'

At once the others add their voices to hers.

'She'll ne'er survive it.'

''Tis no cure for the weid.'

'The very worst cure for the weid!'

Alec has no time for this.

'Mistress Duncan does not have the weid. '

His voice is too loud in the airless room.

He turns to Andrew Duncan. 'Your wife must be bled at once or I cannot answer for the consequences.'

Duncan looks down at his hands and, without looking up again, nods his assent. Alec turns to Rabbie.

'I will need your assistance, Mr Donald. There is no time to call the operator. We will apply a fomentation to the abdomen, then proceed at once to venesection.'

He shuts out the quivering dismay of the other women. Shuts out the tight-lipped disapproval on Jennifer Elgin's face.

Shuts out Andrew Duncan. The stifling heat. The stench. Closes his mind to everything but the patient and the necessity of action. He folds back the lid of the medicine chest and takes out the instruments he will need. Places them in a neat row along the edge of the bed. Tourniquet, lancet, bleeding bowl. Rolls up his shirtsleeves.

'We will take eight ounces in the first instance. The oppression in the blood must be drawn off as quickly as possible.'

To the other women he says: 'I need water and fresh sheeting.'

No one moves.

He spins round to face the assembly of mistrustful women. Bawls at them: 'Water and sheeting! Now! And in God's name, open these windows!'

This time, reluctantly, they do as he commands.

9

With a little sigh Mary turns on to her back, away from the candlelight, flinging her arm out over the top of the quilt. She does not wake. Elizabeth stares at the small white hand resting on the cover. Unsettling, the way it lies there. The pale little hand with its maggoty fingers. Just lying there. The crows will mistake it for something they can eat, so small and white like that. Old Amos said it was a bad, bad omen, a crow flying into the bedroom at that very moment, but Marie said not to listen, it only came to show the way. Papa shot it anyway. Strung it up from the veranda later, where it swayed in the breeze and drew the flies. When she asked who would guide Meg's soul now, no one would say. The nights were filled with the sound of muffled weeping. A cockerel's claw, boiled and dyed red with beetle juice, swung outside the women's hut. To ward off evil spirits, Marie said.

Elizabeth's shadow is huge over the slumbering child. It spreads over the counterpane like a stain, crawls along the wall like something intent on evil. She holds the candle up, away from herself, so that the light falls directly on to her daughter's face: the dark crescent of lashes, the bow of parted lips, the smudge of nose. Elizabeth's heart constricts, looking at her. Earlier that evening she'd caught Mary looking inside the long clock, fiddling with the pendulum. She'd wrenched her away, lifted her right off her feet, startled by how light the child felt, and limp, like a rag doll dangling from her grasp. She had gone at her, even so, slapping at her legs, swatting at her in furious little jabs, beside herself with rage and something else she did not fully understand. Mary had not cried. She'd recoiled from the blows, but had not cried, just looked at her mother with an expression that made Elizabeth afraid. For herself. For both of them.

Somewhere overhead a loose casement rattles in the storm. Alec and Rabbie won't be back for hours yet. From the far end of the landing, she hears the long clock's low reproach. *Want – Not. Want – Not. Want – Not.* She retreats from its accusations. The soles of her shoes make a harsh, pecking noise on the wooden boards; her skirts slip down the stairs behind her, hissing like grass-snakes.

Alec's study seems to know what she's come for. *Thou shalt not steal. Thou shalt not tell a lie.* A pile of books occupies one corner of the desk, a stack of papers the other. She glances at the top sheet. Case notes. The Board requires that Alec keep details of every patient he attends, their name, age, place of residence, illness, treatment, cure. He is scrupulous about this, as he is about every aspect of his work, transcribes the notes himself in his clear, firm handwriting, won't trust anyone else to write up the cases, not even Rabbie. What is it he says? *One can only be as accurate as one has been observant.* She hears his voice so clearly it is as if he were in the room with her, had spoken out loud. It is one of his refrains. She has heard it so often it is lodged in her head. *Authority without facts is nothing but opinion.* There is another. *And opinion without authority is worth less than a barleycorn.*

Five quills in the leather quill-stand, nibs sharpened and ready for use. Inkwells full beneath their silver lids. Sealing wax. Blotter. Hour-glass. The miniature in its tortoiseshell frame. Her wedding gift to him. Everything ranged along the desk in a perfect line. Nothing out of place. Except herself. Elizabeth picks up the portrait, peers at the face of the young woman she sees there. Her features, but somehow not her face. The nose too small, the eyes too round. A younger, prettier, softer version of herself. That Elizabeth would know how to do what's expected of her, how to love her daughter, how to wait patiently for Alec's return. That Elizabeth would not pace the house at night like this, like some mangy cat scavenging for scraps. What has happened to that Elizabeth, the one in the picture, if she ever existed? Sometimes Elizabeth thinks that she lost a part of herself when Mary was born, but there are other times when she thinks she has always been lost, as far back as she can remember, as far back as the white sand and the hot sun stroking her skin and the black bird swinging on the veranda.

She replaces the picture on the desk, careful to put it back where it belongs. On the wall in front of the desk hangs the framed engraving they'd quarrelled over. He'd wanted it hung in the dining room. *A dead bairn, Alec? In the dining room?* She holds the candle up to the picture. An 'anatomical drawing', that's what he preferred to call it. Elizabeth leans closer, studying it properly for the first time. The baby is tightly furled in its confining chamber, head down, knees drawn up, arms wedged in close to the little chest; the head is huge, as big as the whole of its body; a few faint wisps of dark hair, delicate wet curls, show above the tiny ear. Only the baby's face is hidden from view, covered by its left hand, as if already turning away from the world it would never know. What was it Alec had said? 'A peerless addition to the sum of medical knowledge: a nine-month-old human foetus, depicted *in utero* on the very point of birth by one of the finest artists in the business.' *And the mother, Alec? What of the mother?*

Along the shelves of the far wall are rows of jars, each one labelled with the physic it contains. On the long table in front of the shelves are the tools of her husband's trade: a pair of weighing scales; a pestle and mortar; a wooden pill board; the oak pharmacy chest; two leather cases containing his knives and saws; a pewter glyster; a wooden speculum. Dangling from hooks above the table, like a string of fly-blown carcasses, are three pairs of forceps. Elizabeth looks away. To her right is the door to the storeroom, locked against intruders and prying eyes. No one goes in there but Alec himself. She has seen inside the storeroom only once, a fleeting glimpse one morning when she'd surprised him there. He'd hurried out, locking the door behind him, but not before she'd seen the banks of shelves within, rising from floor to ceiling, stacked with glass jars of every size and shape, inside of which hung strange, shadowy forms, drifting in a state of eternal suspense.

On an impulse Elizabeth goes to the door and tries the handle, but the storeroom is locked. She turns back to Alec's desk and carefully sets the candle down on the leather top. Flanking the desk are a pair of large leather globes, one celestial, one terrestrial, each mounted on a gleaming mahogany stand. With the tips of her fingers, she gives the top of the celestial globe a little shove. It glides away from her touch; slows once more to a standstill. Orion straddles the curve, sword in hand, Sirius snapping at his heels. *Orion is not the only hunter here tonight.* The thought drops into her mind like a stone: she is forgetting herself, she must get on.

A sudden draught sucks at the candle on the desk and the shadows flare in the bucking flame. A thin jet of smoke quivers towards the ceiling. She waits for the light to steady, listening for sounds of movement outside the room. She can hear her heart crashing against her ribcage, but the house is still. She turns to the bookcase that lines the back wall of the study. Her fingertips trail over the spines of the books. The gilded letters are cool and smooth between the softness of the leather binding. She will come to it soon enough. Can feel it waiting for her. *Doucement, ma petite, doucement.* Marie's voice speaking to her still, after all this time.

Astruc, *Traite des maladies des femmes* ... Burton, *A Complete New System of Midwifery* ... Cooper, *A Compendium of Midwifery* ... Denman, *The Art and Practise of Midwifery* Hoffmanni, *Medicina rationalis systematica...*

She can feel it, closer all the time, approaching her, low-backed and stealthy. Is she hunting it, or it her, she suddenly wonders. She starts to move faster along the shelves. Johnson ... Millar ... Manning. *A Treatise on Female Diseases* ... *Traite des maladies des femmes grosses* ... Mauriceau ... de la Motte. So many books! All these men, these learned physicians from so many countries, all these volumes of books, these pages and pages of words on women and their bodies. Such a quantity of knowledge about things she knows nothing of, although they concern her so directly. These books know her better than she knows herself. They seem to peer at her as she passes, the names and titles squinting at her in the dim light. Hundreds of inquisitive eyes. Skene ... Smellie ... Sydenham ... Strother ... Tissot.

She must have missed it. She retraces her steps, looking more closely, reading the words gilded on the spines more carefully this time. And then, there it is. No author given, only the title. *Ladies Friend*. Five small sunflowers embossed in gold on dun-coloured leather. Her index finger is on the lip of the spine and she's tipping the book out of its groove, the weight of it subsiding into the palm of her hand. She's slipping the volume into the pocket of her skirt, snatching up the candlestick from the desk, drops of wax spilling from the melting pool at the base of the wick, forming a thin white trail on the wood where it cools. She's out of the study, pulling the door behind her with a bang, scurrying down the passage that leads to the kitchen − the last place he'll look for her when he comes in − her feet almost breaking into a run, shielding the candle with her hand so it won't blow out, the flame singeing her palm, but she doesn't stop.

She stands with her back pressed against the door, catching her breath, arguing with herself. How else is she to find out? How else is she to know? Alec says not to worry, it will happen in time. But time is passing: days, weeks, months, years, great gulps of it, and no sign of anything. Another physician is out of the question. It would reflect badly on Alec, and besides, she could not bear the shame of it, could not find the words. Once or twice she's been on the verge of confiding in Bella, but each time something has held her back. Bella cannot remember; she was not there. She was born in Aberdeen, two years after they left Antigua. She knows nothing of that time.

The heat, the crows, the mocking eyes. Marie is just a name. McKenzie less than a name. For an instant, Elizabeth sees her father's face as they stood for the last time on the quayside, looking out at St John's harbour, his hand enclosing hers. *It is over now*, he had said. *Everything will be all right now.* Seven years later both Mama and he were dead.

She seats herself at the kitchen table and draws the book from her pocket. She places it on the table.

THE LADIES FRIEND,
or
COMPLETE PHYSICAL LIBRARY

Her hands are shaking. Slowly, almost reluctantly, she opens the book. Beneath the title, in smaller print, it reads:

> For the BENEFIT and particular Use of the Ladies of Great Britain and Ireland; TREATING of the Nature, Causes, and various Symptoms of all their Diseases, Infirmities, and Disorders, natural or contracted, both before and after Marriage: WITH AN APPENDIX, Containing a Number of the most Valuable and Modern Prescriptions for Family Use.

Below this is the author's name: S. Freeman, Esq, Physician, e Collegio Regio Aberdonensi, Author of *The New Good Samaritan* and other Medical Writings. On the facing page, in an untidy hand, is an inscription in Latin, followed by the words: *With my everlasting gratitude and sincerest admiration, Stephen Freeman.* Elizabeth casts through her memory for a Stephen Freeman. No one of that name comes to mind. An apothecary's son, perhaps, his degree obtained by other means than studying for it? It does not matter. When she tries to turn the page, however, she discovers that the book is still uncut. Whatever ties once connected her husband to the author of the *Ladies Friend*, it would seem that Stephen Freeman's admiration is not returned. The book has not been read.

She fetches a knife from the dresser drawer and carefully slits open the first few pages.

> Wishing never to withhold so valuable a jewel from the lovely sex as the following mode of restoring to themselves health without other assistance, or without divulging their delicate sentiments to any person living, or even mentioning the nature or cause of their disease . . .

Admired by her husband or not, Mr Freeman seems to have intuited her own predicament precisely.

> . . . I have nevertheless left out of this edition a few pages, which upon a further revisal appeared to be too immodest for the chaste ear; instead of which, I have added some useful observations upon the nerves, and disorders in general arising from the womb, which affect the head sand stomach.

Elizabeth rifles forwards to the next chapter:

> OF WEAKNESSES CONTRACTED BEFORE MARRIAGE, WITH PROPER ADVICE IN EVERY RESPECT WHATEVER.

She leans back in her chair, light-headed with relief. Closes her eyes. Now, perhaps, she will find the answers.

10

Jack Morrison's place is on the northern edge of the town, not convenient for anything or anywhere. It is late afternoon when Alec reaches the workshop. Morrison is nowhere to be seen, but signs of his industry are all around: lengths of wood of assorted sizes in various stages of preparation cover the floor; saws, clamps, hammers and axes hang from hooks in the walls; from the rafters dangle other bits of wood, parts of objects that Alec cannot readily identify; contraptions in mid-creation. One entire side of the workshop is taken up with the official products of Morrison's trade. Three large coffins are ready and waiting by the window, two smaller ones have still to be nailed together. At the foot of stairs, there are five little ones, no bigger than lobster pots.

The back door swings open and the carpenter staggers in from the wood-yard, bow-legged with the weight of the timber he is carrying. On seeing Alec, Morrison's weathered face creases into a broad smile. Morrison likes the Dispensary physician, has a deal of respect for him, too. His youngest son would have lost an eye last Lammastide had it not been for the doctor's swift and skilful intervention. Alec returns his smile.

'Come for your wee whigmaleerie, I suppose?'

'Is it ready?'

'Aye, and a right fykie task it was!'

The carpenter is a small wiry man in his fifties with greying hair and shrewd blue eyes. Despite his slight build and his age, his voice is surprisingly deep and melodic, a beautiful voice, as unexpected as the delicate tapered fingers, which seem more suited to a tailor than a carpenter, until you look more closely and see they are cross-hatched with scars and calluses.

Morrison leans forwards and lets the armful of timber

thudder to the ground. Straightening up, he wipes his forehead with the back of one forearm.

Alec gives the coffin nearest to him a light tap with the toe of his boot. 'Trade's good, I see.'

It is an old joke between them, the see-saw link between their livelihoods: when business is swift for one, it is swift for the other, but with the opposite effect on each man's pocket: while the carpenter's purse grows heavier as the body count rises, the doctor's grows lighter. And vice versa. *Dinnae do yer job too well, Doctor, or I'll be beggin at the Castlegate with Wee Bobbie Blaney*, the carpenter likes to tease him, to which Alec's response is always the same: *Dinnae fash yerself, Morrison. Till there's a cure for mortality, you are safer than stane hooses.*

The trouble is, Alec's own livelihood is a great deal less secure than houses. Too few patients and the Board begins to ask questions; too many, especially those with lingering or incurable conditions, or those too poor to pay, and the Dispensary's meagre funds are rapidly depleted. Already this winter, with the outbreaks of influenza, the incessant sore throats and fevers, the reserves are worryingly low. Treating the poor gratis is good for his standing in the town, but how the devil he's to pay his own bills he cannot say.

In the corner of the workshop a stepladder leads steeply up to a suspended platform that creates a second room under the rafters. Morrison clambers up the ladder now and vanishes from sight. A succession of thumps and thuds ensues. Eventually the carpenter's face reappears at the top of the ladder. He points to a brown blanket on the floor by the hearth. Alec throws it to him and Morrison vanishes again. More scufflings and shufflings filter through the floorboards. When Morrison next emerges, he is holding a bulky object concealed inside the folds of the blanket. He lowers it carefully over the platform edge towards Alec's outstretched hands.

For a long moment Alec can only gaze at Morrison's handiwork in silent astonishment. It sits on the workbench in its cocoon of wool, glossy as a new-hatched conker. Alec passes his palm along the silken surface, up and around and over the smooth arc of the wood, letting his fingertips absorb the texture of it, the warmth and softness of the polished grain.

'Does it work?' he says, at last.

Morrison laughs. 'D'ye take me for a fool, Dr Gordon? Of course it works!'

Only then does Alec pick it up, cautiously manipulating the two outer blades, apart and back together again, noticing how cleverly the wooden pin that holds the two parts in place has been concealed behind the central shaft; how precisely and skilfully the central shaft itself has been fashioned to resemble the lower section of the spine, the sacrum and coccyx. The more he explores the contraption, the greater his admiration for the carpenter's achievement. To make each part of the model easily identifiable from a distance, Morrison has used different types of wood: elm for the big curved paddles of the hips; chestnut for the ischium; oak for the spine; walnut for the pubis and – with surely a touch of humour in his choice here? – a gleaming nub of cherry wood for the joint connecting the pubic bones.

Morrison has far exceeded Alec's expectations. Not only do the iliac bones tilt back and forward exactly as in life, but a discreetly positioned screw behind the sacrum allows the width of the pelvic opening to be increased or decreased as required. The consequences for the mother of a too narrow pelvis, or a too large infant, or an abnormal presentation are as clear as day. The spine has been fashioned from a series of small blocks, hinged together in such a way as to mimic the natural movement of the bone. Over the main skeletal structure, Morrison has applied paper-fine sheets of pale ashwood to represent the ligaments. Most ingeniously of all, suspended within the outer framework of the pelvis, by means of a mesh of barely visible threads, Morrison has suspended an inner shell, worked in birch, to show the soft tissue of the gravid uterus, the dilated cervix, the birth canal and the perinæum. The more closely he inspects Morrison's work, the more evidence Alec finds of the care and intelligence the carpenter has brought to his realization of the commission.

'Astonishing,' he says at last. 'Perfect.'

Morrison nods, pleased. 'Aye, well, high time that wee swellhead shared a bit of the applause.'

At which Alec, too, cannot help but grin.

Folk made the journey from Glasgow and Edinburgh to hear the Wee Swellhead speak, not just once, but twice, three times, or more. In the crammed lecture hall, Alec had found himself standing shoulder to shoulder with men of every rank and station. Merchants and lawyers, watchmakers and mill-wrights, joiners and smiths. All gathered to hear the mathematician. Within moments of Patrick Copland's appearance on the rostrum, Alec understood why. He'd been as mesmerized as the rest. Copland spoke without notes and he spoke in the language of the common man. No learned terms. No theory. Not a word of Greek or Latin. Every principle illustrated by experiments so that the dullest wit amongst them could follow with ease. And then there were the models. Exquisite working miniatures in wood and metal. Cranes. Corn mills. Inkle looms. An exact replica of Vauloue's pile engine. Another of Arkwright's Spinning Jenny. And the applause! Wave after wave of it thundering up to the raftered ceiling.

A great itch had started up that night in Alec's brain, a fine idea he'd been scratching away at ever since.

Bannerman had dismissed the plan out of hand. 'Save your breath, Gordon. Mechanics are one thing, midwives quite another.'

'They've got knowledge of a kind. Intelligence too, many of them. I see no reason why they cannot learn, if they are given the chance.'

'How? How will they learn? Half of them cannot spell their own names.'

'Then I won't ask them to,' Alec replied, more stubborn by the moment.

Bannerman folded his arms across his chest and sucked on his pipe, unconvinced. Mothers should be attended by trained accoucheurs who knew what they were about, not ignorant women. That was Bannerman's view, and he was sticking to it. For a man of Bannerman's ilk, this was radical enough. There were plenty of physicians who held that men had no place at all at the bedsides of labouring women, and plenty of midwives who agreed with them. Birth was women's work. Childbed a natural business and death a natural part of it. That was just how it was. It was not a question of education. Bannerman admired Alec, respected his skill as a physician and often sought his counsel, but he was a man who preferred things done as they'd always been done, unless the benefits were immediate and unlikely to provoke controversy. It was younger men for the most part, like Alec himself, who were challenging these assumptions; men from humble backgrounds, apprenticed in the old way as surgeons or apothecaries, but trained out in the world, in the new disciplines of anatomy and midwifery, ready to do anything that came their way, and able to, ready to discard tradition where it stood in the way of progress.

As Alec tried and failed to bring Bannerman round to his view, he understood for the first time the distance between them. George Bannerman was from another world. His forebears were provosts and professors as far back as the Alliance, men who'd always known there'd be meat on their plates when they sat down to eat. Wasn't there a bridge named after his grandsher, for heaven's sake! Bannerman didn't know what it was to wonder where the ten pounds would come from for the entrance fee to Marischal College, or the money for gowns or books or lodging once he got there. Dr Skene was the same: did not his uncle live in one of the finest houses in Aberdeen? Educating midwives? Whatever for? It was all new-fangled nonsense, as far as Bannerman was concerned. Alec could do as he wished; they would soon see which of them was right.

Opposition had merely strengthened Alec's resolve. He would have not just lectures, he decided, walking away from the tavern that night, but models too, and the devil with caution!

It had been scarcely less trouble, however, to persuade the carpenter. He hadn't the time, he said, was fully occupied for six months to come on Copland's commissions.

'Forget Copland! You're the only man for the job, Morrison. No one in Aberdeen can carve a whistle compared to you. No one in all of Scotland.'

It was no exaggeration: Morrison was an artist when it came to wood. He knew timber the way some men knew women. He understood its different moods, could draw out the particular beauty and capability of each different wood. Knew how to cut along or down or across the grain to suit his purpose. Could plane a length of birch so finely that it would bend without snapping. Could turn a chair leg so surely that the stoutest man in Aberdeenshire could land his weight on it without the slightest fear of it breaking. He knew exactly where to find the palest ash, the supplest rowan, the strongest elm. His skill was exceptional. But more than that, he had the ability to turn ideas into reality, was able to release all the latent possibility of a design, transform the ingenuity of the abstract conception into an object that could be touched and held and moved. Alec told him all this. Cajoled and pleaded and flattered. When all else failed, he resorted to lower stratagems. 'No matter, then, if you're not up to it. I'll send to London.'

That had done the trick.

Now he has it in his arms. Cumbersome as a newborn colt. Beautiful. A work of art indeed. The only one of its kind in the whole of the British Isles. Now he'll show Bannerman what progress looks like, what modern nonsense can achieve.

Now he'll show them all what stuff he's made of, how far from Miltown of Drum he's travelled.

He is already at the entrance to the workshop, his head full of triumph, when Morrison interrupts his reverie, one foot firmly barring the way, one hand firmly extended in Alec's direction.

'My fee, Dr Gordon. If ye dinna mind.'

11

Mary comes clattering down the stairs in her wooden clogs. *Daddie! Daddie!* Charging at him in a flurry of pinafore, wrapping her arms around his knees, butting him with her forehead, demanding to know where he's been, why he wasn't there when she woke that morning, why Rabbie came back without him, what's in the blanket he's holding. Alec laughs, lifting his precious cargo out of her reach.

'Steady, my wee pettie! Steady!'

He bends to kiss her hair, breathing in the caramel scent of her hair, but Elizabeth steps between them, pulling Mary away from him, fingers pinching into the child's arm.

'Let your father take off his coat before you're all over him.'

Mary looks from one to the other, trying to marry the warmth in her father's smile with this swooping fury in her mother. But Papa's not smiling any longer. He's looking at Mama in a way that says he's angry at her and sorry for her at the same time.

'Let her be.'

Alec stretches out his hand and lets it rest for a moment on the crown of Mary's head. Mary knows that he shouldn't be doing this, that Mama will not like it. But Mama simply shrugs her shoulders, purses her lips into a single thin line, then nods her head in the direction of the front parlour.

'They're all here. There's not a chair left in the house.'

Elizabeth is not exaggerating. The parlour is crammed to bursting. There is barely room to open the door. He'd expected ten, maybe fifteen, but they have come in numbers far exceeding his expectations. Mistress Blake is there, sitting on what looks very like a footstool, and young Mistress Anderson, too, perched on the creepie from the nursery. Beside her, Agnes Chalmers and Meredith Philp, more comfortably settled on two of the dining-room chairs. Alec wants to shout out loud at the sight of them all, but contents himself with a quick grin at Rabbie, who's squeezed up against the piano at the back of the room. There must be thirty bodies in the room at least. Some he doesn't even recognize. Alec is cock-a-hoop. Here is a result there's no arguing with! Here is his front parlour stowed out with local women, every one of them got up in their Sunday best, though it's only teatime on Tuesday. And every one of them hungry for knowledge, eager to furnish themselves with the rudiments of an education that Bannerman and his kind take utterly for granted. It is just as Alec predicted. He is jubilant. So jubilant he is almost angry with it. No one will make him doubt himself again on this score. He will shake this town to the soles of its grey stockinged feet. Purge ignorance wherever he encounters it, whatever Bannerman has to say, or any of them. He will teach them all what good practice really is, educate them to value real understanding, to recognize the importance of evidence you can see with your own two eyes. This is a revolution he is leading, nothing less.

As he waits for the buzz of the women's chatter to quieten, his gaze falls for a moment on the painting of the harbour hanging on the far wall. It was one of the first possessions that he and Elizabeth purchased together after they were married. They commissioned it, laughing at themselves, from a visiting artist, whose advertisement in the *Aberdeen Journal* had caught Alec's attention at breakfast one morning, and since the fellow had temporary lodgings with Mr Samson the shoemaker and since Elizabeth had decided a man in Alec's position could not go about in the same old boots he'd worn as a student – *You may tramp the streets if you wish, Dr Gordon, but there's no reason to do so looking like a tramp!* – it was decided to kill the two birds with the one stone and visit both men at once. The painting was ready three weeks later, delighting them both. The harbour was where they'd first walked and talked, free of the constraints of Aunt Rae's watchful eyes and ears, the buffeting wind obliging them to draw close and closer to make their words heard. Alec never looks upon the painting without it kindling within him that same sensation of hopefulness he'd felt then. He feels it now, weaving through the flotilla of chairs to the front of the room.

The women fall quiet. Alec carefully sets the model down on the table. He wipes his hands on the side panels of his frockcoat and clears his throat.

'Welcome!'

He attempts a smile of greeting, but his facial muscles have grown unaccommodating and he feels his expression take on a lopsided grimace, which he quickly abandons; clears his throat a second time instead. There will be twenty-four lectures, he informs them, every Tuesday at six, providing full and comprehensive instruction in the art of midwifery in a manner easily comprehended by all. The mechanisms of labour will be demonstrated: the workings of the pelvis, womb and uterus; the purpose of the various fluids that accompany this state of nature; also the function of the contractions, or pains of labour, as they are commonly known. The principal object of attention this evening will be the perinæum, a part frequently neglected by accoucheurs and midwives alike.

A profound hush settles over the room. Is this the right note to strike? He's not quite sure. He wants to inspire them, not patronize them, knows them too well for that. The perinæum is hardly the obvious place to begin, but these are midwives he's addressing, not medical students. These women will be delivering bairns not in six months' time, but tomorrow and the next day and the day after that.

Alec turns to the table behind him. 'To facilitate your understanding, I have commissioned this model—' he folds back the blanket, gratified by the audible gasp from his audience – 'a working replica of the female pelvis as it appears in labour.'

The women are craning forward to see; those at the back of the room have risen to their feet to get a better look.

'You will see, ladies, how the bones of the pelvis are represented by these two long curved blades. Here, we have the tail of the backbone, correctly termed the coccyx. Here, the pubic bone. And here, in the lighter wood, you can see the soft tissue of the uterus. The bairn I have left to your imagination.'

There's a ripple of laughter, but it quickly fades: they are as amazed as he'd hoped they would be. If only he'd thought to invite Bannerman this afternoon. That would have settled their argument.

The perinæum, he says, pointing to the narrow band of birch suspended on the underside of the model: a part often subject to laceration in the course of labour, and the cause of great misery to women in childbed, and thereafter. He is aware of his heart quickening against his ribcage. Balling his hand into a fist, he traces a path through the birth canal, ending with a succession of quick little punches to convey the pressure of the baby's head on the hammock of muscle.

'Laceration varies greatly, in both direction and extent, from one birth to another,' he says, his fist deep in the wooden pelvis. 'I know of one case in which the entire part ruptured, leaving no natural barrier between the vagina and the rectum. The physician in this instance supplied the want by the palm of one hand, like so–' he places his free hand underneath the band of birch – 'thus guiding the child's head through the proper passage.'

The midwives shift uneasily in their seats. *Vagina* and *rectum* are not words you'd expect to hear uttered in gentle company. This is probably the first time that anyone in the room besides himself has heard the correct terminology for these parts of the female anatomy spoken aloud. He presses on. Everything he tells them must have immediate practical application. If in one evening he can convey the importance of this business alone, he will have made great progress.

'In my experience,' he says, looking out at the sea of faces and unintentionally catching the rheumy eye of Mistress Blake, 'much evil is done by the erroneous belief that a good labour is a speedy one. Whereas nothing could be further from the truth.' He pauses, trying to gauge the midwives' reaction. 'When the head of the child is insinuated within the external parts, if these do not easily yield, it is customary to dilate them manually, to allow of the more speedy passage of the head. This method of proceeding, far from preparing the parts, contributes significantly to the risk of laceration. Likewise, the pernicious custom of anointing with unctuous applications. To put the matter plainly: unless the forceps are required, all artificial dilation of the parts is to be forborne and avoided. On this point I cannot emphasize myself sufficiently. The perinæum is not torn because the head of the child is large, or passes in any particular direction, but because it passes *too speedily*, or presses *too violently* upon the parts before they have acquired their dilatability. The proof is beyond dispute. Consider for yourselves how rarely the perinæum is lacerated in very slow or difficult labours.'

The silence has a viscous quality. Dense, laden, heavy. Hardly daring to look at his audience now, knowing there is no turning back, Alec pushes on to his next assault on common custom. He holds up the wooden pelvis.

'There is another way in which accoucheurs and midwives obstruct where they might assist.' He rotates the pelvis so that the pubic bone faces forwards, with the spine behind. 'It is usual for the mother to be placed in bed upon her left side, with her knees drawn up towards the abdomen.'

He takes the pelvis through a quarter turn to illustrate the position he is describing.

'Though convenient to the birth attendant, this position occasions a projection of the child wholly unfavourable to the perinæum. A more natural position, and one that is widely chosen by the mother and her attendants in some other countries, is to place the mother upon her hands and knees, like so—' He twists the model through another quarter-turn, so that the pubic bone is face down, towards the table, the spine now on top. 'In this position, as you can see for yourselves, the head or other presenting part would, by its gravitation, lessen both the pressure upon the perinæum and the risk of its laceration.'

For the past few minutes the atmosphere in the room has been growing more and more charged, but this is too much.

From the back of the room an outraged voice bursts out: 'Gweed preserve's! He'd make farmyard brutes of good Christian women!'

'And greit fools o us!' cries another.

Agreement is rising from the midwives like a spring tide. A third woman, whom he recognizes as Mistress Carnegie, leaps to her feet, face flushed with indignation.

'No woman I know gies a hoot for a rent periwinkle, be it red, blue or dancin a jig. Not after three days in mortal agony an herself as near deid as the stanes in Rudshill Quarry.'

She plumps back down in her seat amidst a growing clamour of assent.

'Please!' Alec holds up his hands, but it is too late and he knows it. He has lost them. He should not have tried for so much so soon.

12

Now that Elizabeth has the book to guide her it's no trouble to send Annie to the market or to the apothecary's shop for the things she needs, or even to go herself. She has a little money, tucked away in the loose panelling behind the bed; not much, but enough to pay for an ounce of gum Arabic or a few grains of columbo root, enough to make up the necessary draughts and decoctions that Freeman recommends. It's too early in the year to gather the plants in the fields behind the house, but there are dried herbs in the pantry, and many of the other ingredients she can come by easily enough in the home apothecary. Far harder to come by is time when she can be sure not to be disturbed. Last Friday, when she thought she had the house to herself, Baxter and Annie had returned a full hour earlier than she was expecting. Normally on market days, they were gone until noon at least, but on this occasion a long-simmering tension between the cook and the butcher over the quality of his cuts had finally flared into a full-blown altercation. Baxter was still quivering with rage when she and Annie arrived back at Belmont Street, the cook's voice, raised in indignant anger, alerting Elizabeth at the last moment to their return. She managed to shove Freeman's book and the medicine jar into one of the dresser drawers before they came in, but there was no time to conceal the pan bubbling over the hearth.

'Tha's no the way to make an infusion!' Baxter exclaimed, shaking her head in dismay at such incompetence. What a day it had been for folk not knowing the first thing about anything!

'The water's boilin too hard. You'll steam the goodness from it.' The cook sniffed suspiciously at the acrid vapour rising off the liquid. 'It doesnae smell right neither. Those stems shouldnae be in. 'Twill be too bitter to drink.'

Baxter bustled the pan off the fire and begun straining the liquid into a smaller pot. Elizabeth stood by and watched helplessly. All her careful preparations – ruined. She'd wanted to weep.

Since then she's been more careful, choosing only recipes with ingredients she can get hold of in small quantities and at short notice, the ones she can prepare quickly and easily, without using the kitchen at all. The powders are the most convenient. She can lock herself in the bedroom, away from prying eyes, combine the ingredients at her dressing table, or sitting on the floor if needs be. It has helped that Alec has been so busy in the past week that he has taken to leaving his medicine chest unlocked. Since discovering this, she's been able to help herself to what she needs with no difficulty at all, the ingredients already pulverized and ready for use. All that remains to do is mix the powder with some wine or a little brandy and add the solution to the barley water that sits by her bed as a matter of course. No one need know the bottle contains anything else. Her efforts are paying off: already the faintness and dizzy spells are occurring less frequently. The nausea has abated a little too. Yet the improvements do not seem to last; after only a day or two the symptoms return. Dr Freeman insists upon the importance of continuing with the treatment until all the symptoms have disappeared, but how long will that take?

Lately, she has stumbled upon a cure of her own: a grain of opium added to Dr Freeman's recipe transforms her usual fitful slumber into a languorous, dream-dense repose. It is not sleep exactly, but something between awake and sleeping, a place filled with gently floating shadows, soft as goose down, in which colours and sounds are vivid but at the same time distant and muted, as if viewed through the wrong end of one of Alec's telescopes. In this curious half-slumber, she too floats, as if she's lying in a cradle in a darkened room, rocked gently back and forth, towards and away from the surrounding darkness.

She has known it before, this rocking and this darkness, so airless it's like a bolster pressed to your face, so you think you will suffocate on it, although it's only air. You lie on your side, eyes wide, trying not to sleep at all, although the misery of awake, with the rolling ship and the answering pitch of your belly, is hardly preferable. Night after night of it. Day after day. Until at last the storm passes and the waves flatten into blameless little folds and you're allowed back on deck, where the daylight hurts your eyes and you feel flayed, skinless.

Going home, her mother said, the word 'home' infused with an unmistakable note of finality. *At last!* Mama's tone seemed to imply. Such hatred, such dark-red loathing in her voice. It had made no sense to Elizabeth. Antigua was home, the only home she'd ever known. Coconut palms and orange trees. Scarlet hibiscus and sun-baked earth. The hillsides dotted with windmills, white sails splicing the lilac sky. She could not imagine anything else. Had no notion of what this other 'home' might be, this town on the far side of the ocean where they said she'd been christened, but of which she has not the smallest recollection. And why were they not all making the journey? Why just herself and Mama and Papa? Where were Marie and the other servants? Mo would be so lonely without her to visit him, would go hungry without her to take him the kitchen scraps. And what about the boys? Willie and Tommy and Charlie? Why were they not here with them on the boat? Who would look after them with Mama and Papa not there? Who would make sure they were safe at night?

There had been a fire; she remembers that: a foul-smelling bonfire in the front courtyard. There were nights broken by low voices and sudden bursts of shouting, the darkness quivering with torchlight. Men's voices, the sound of their boots, the clattering of hooves on the driveway. For three days she'd been locked in her room. Marie brought her food, pulled her away from the window, scolded her for opening the blinds, refused to answer her questions. And then, without explanation, they were leaving. The china and linen packed into tea-chests, the pictures turned to the wall, the furniture shrouded in dust sheets. *Going home.* But why, if going home was such a good thing, did Mama turn her face to the cabin wall each night and weep and weep as if her heart were breaking?

13

At first the treatment seems to help. After opening the vein a second time and taking a further ten ounces of blood, leeches are applied to the abdomen. Mistress Elgin is instructed to prepare a hot poultice, large enough to cover the whole belly, to keep up the heat and moisture. On his next visit to the Duncans, Alec is pleased to find the pulse a little slowed, from 140 strokes to 136. The laxative given in the morning has the desired effect. The other symptoms, however, continue unabated. The blood exhibits a thick inflammatory crust, the lochia are suppressed, the urine scanty and voided with pain. Alec prescribes a blister to the abdomen and small doses of tartar emetic in the saline mixture, in the hope of purging the illness. But on returning that evening, he finds the sweat has disappeared and the swelling of the abdomen seems, if possible, to have increased. By the following day, the disease has made rapid progress in spite of the remedies he's employed, the pain and tension extending now over the whole of the abdomen and up into the ribs. An uncontrollable diarrhoea has set in. *The case is hopeless*, he tells himself sternly. *She is dying*. And in the acutest agony. He administers opium, externally and internally, to mitigate the pain. It is all he has left to offer. When Andrew Duncan stops him in the doorway to ask in a low voice: *How much longer?* Alec loses his temper. *I'm a physician, not a soothsayer! I'm doing what I can*.

He hates to fail.

He wakes Rabbie early the next morning and they are out of the house before daybreak. The temperature has dropped sharply in the night and the frozen darkness is oppressive, a solid counterweight to be penetrated with each step. Around them the town is waking slowly, stretching, creaking into motion. The few people who are about keep their heads down, go about their business in silence: opening shutters, sluicing down doorsteps, emptying close-stools, fetching peat to load the grates, breaking the ice on the water-troughs. Acknowledgement of others runs to a curt nod, if that. The talking will come later, with the daylight, but they are in the depths of the year still, the earth's back turned to the sun for all but a few hours. Daylight is a long way off. The servants, the porters, the coopers and fleshers, all burrow their way along the narrow lanes, tight-lipped against the cold. Only the horses, restive in their bridles, challenge the sombre mood, stamping their hooves on the flagstones, chafing at their bits, snorting plumes of warm breath into the black air. Gradually, as the darkness lifts, the bustle and commotion gather strength, spreading through the town from the quayside, where already the gulls are shrieking, roused to a frenzy by the unloading of the night's haul. The fishwives will be dragging the nets clear of the water, heaping their baskets with herring, salmon and cod. It takes two men to heave the loaded creels up on to each woman's back. Later, when the catch is sorted, the women will toil up the hill to the market place, where they'll sit and squawk on the Planestaines by the Cross, like a rowdy flock of starlings in their drab greys and browns, until the fish is all sold and the baskets empty.

Alec and Rabbie turn off North Street into the narrow pend that leads to the Duncans'. A few scrawny chickens squawk and scatter as they approach. A pig lifts its snout from the midden heap it is excavating, eyeing them with mild interest. Above the roofline, banks of pewter-grey cloud are massing slowly upwards, like a roomful of old women heaving to their feet. There's a laden stillness to the air that presages snowfall, and in the queasy half-light the courtyard and buildings look more bedraggled than ever, the timber struts clearly rotten in places, crumbling patches of wattle and daub plainly visible between.

Alec lifts his cane and raps on one of the shuttered windows. At once the door at the top of the forestairs flies open. To the amazement of both men, the flushed face looking down at them is luminous with joy.

'A miracle, Dr Gordon!' the locksmith cries. 'A miracle!'

Beaming at the doctor and his apprentice, arms flapping up and down with excitement like an ungainly bird attempting to take flight, Andrew Duncan is near ranting with happiness.

'She's cured, I tell ye! Come an see for yourself!'

The little room, which only two days before had been shrouded in an atmosphere of bleak despair, is transformed beyond recognition, filled now with an air of jubilation. The aroma of spiced wine has partially replaced the smell of rotting flesh and on the table by the fire are cheese and bread and ham, festive fare indeed for this time of year. The room is as crowded as before, but the women are now bustling about, folding bedding and setting out the best crockery, chatting and joking between themselves. At the foot of the bed sit a fair-headed girl of about four and the boy who had met them with the lantern, pink-cheeked with relief at their mother's recovery. There are smiles on every face. Jenny Duncan herself is sitting up in bed, deathly pale still, but she too is smiling. Her belly is no less swollen than when Alec last saw her, but when he touches and then presses the mound of flesh, far from screaming out, she remains entirely composed.

'There is no pain?'

'None, Doctor.'

'You see!' cries Andrew Duncan, beside himself with delight. 'Didna tell ye?'

The pulse is rapid still, but very faint now, the blood no longer twitching and throbbing beneath Alec's enquiring finger-tips. There is just the merest flutter.

Jenny Duncan looks up at him with timorous hopefulness.

'May I see my bairn, Dr Gordon?' she says in a whisper. 'I do so long to hold her. Surely there canna be any danger in it?'

Her hand, resting lightly in his own, is icy, so thin and insubstantial he could crush it with ease, and for a brief instant he is filled with an insane desire to do so. He forces himself to return her gaze.

'Of course,' he says at last. 'Of course you may. In a day or two. As soon as you are quite better.'

'And can she take a knap to eat, Dr Gordon? She's had nothing for days. A wee drop o broth surely wouldnae do her any harm.'

'Aye,' Alec nods, his eyes resting on Mistress Duncan still. 'Whatever she wants.'

He writes a prescription for an opiate draught, in case the pain should return, and a short while later he and Rabbie are ready to leave. Andrew Duncan accompanies them back down to the close. As he turns to go, Alec puts out his hand and catches his forearm.

'It's too soon to be absolutely sure. I have seen—'

But Duncan interrupts him. 'Nae fash yerself, Dr Gordon, she's all right now. A wee bit gowsty, but the worst is over.'

He flings another jubilant grin at Alec, then bounds back up the stairs to rejoin his family.

14

Snow comes in the early afternoon, not the short-lived flurries of previous weeks but a curtain of heavy, silent flakes that shroud the town in premature twilight, bank rapidly on the walls and rooftops, settle in arching drifts against the window-panes. Towards six in the evening Duncan's boy comes with the news. Alec has been expecting it, but it still winds him. He sees Andrew Duncan's foolish grin all over again, and the trust in the poor woman's eyes as she'd asked to hold her bairn, not knowing it was already dead. He can see the lamplight shining off the wee girl's hair, the pink of her fingers entwined with the ghastly white of her mother's. And another memory rising to take its place: the same smell of rotting flesh and soured sheets; a woman screaming, her head thrown back, one gold tooth glinting in the ruin of her mouth. The lying-in ward at the Westminster: as near to hell as he's ever been. In his mind's eye, the two images cavort: the daughter's hair, the gold filling. He pushes them away.

When Alec returned to Aberdeen, after the years away in Leiden and Edinburgh and finally London, it was as if a long period of preparation had reached its conclusion and his real life, the real work of his life, could now begin. It was as if everything had been leading him to this point in time and the true purpose of his existence would now become clear. As he'd come down the gangplank and stepped on to the quayside, excited at the prospect of seeing Elizabeth again and meeting for the first time his newborn daughter, he'd paused for a moment and glanced up at the sky. Months had passed since he'd really seen sky. In London, there were chimney stacks and smoke and glimpses of grey or blue or black between the rooftops, but never real swathes of sky. Now overhead, stretching over the entire town, was a great bank of livid cloud, its edges fringed with fiery gold from the sun behind, wide streamers of light fanning out over the top. Even to Alec, a man not given to portents and auguries, it had seemed a sign of some kind, a divine greeting, a promise of great things to come. And since then, despite the setbacks and disappointments he's met with, his sense of purpose has not abated. He had his plans then and has them still. Such plans! There's scarcely enough time in the day: for his patients, his students, the midwives, the books he intends to write. There is so much to do. So much he *wants* to do. He wakes full of it each morning, thanks God for it, the sense of purpose that drives him forwards, the sensation of tilting at the day, head on. From the first moment when he wakes his mind is teeming with ideas. They propel him into the day, and on through it. He is an ambitious man, he would be the first to admit, but it is not ambition for himself alone that drives him. He is part of something far greater than his own small existence: like the waters of the Dee and Don flowing out to meet the sea, he feels himself part of a vast unstoppable tide of energy, ideas and genius, all pouring forth from his homeland, from the universities and churches, the taverns and coffee houses, flooding the world, changing the course of human understanding everywhere, from the leading cities of England to the farthest shores of America. He is part of this great movement towards the future, this flood of progress. He knows it. In whatever field you cared to choose, there was another of his countrymen staking a claim to posterity, pushing forward the boundaries of knowledge: the Hunter brothers in London, the Gregorys in Edinburgh, William Cullen, William Smellie, James Hutton – there seems no end to the success of Caledonia's offspring. And he, Alexander Gordon, is part of this tide of greatness, carries within himself through each day the unshakable conviction that he is contributing to it, moment by moment, with his skill, his energy, his dedication. He hears it in the sound his boots make as they strike the Gallowgate cobbles, sees it in the trusting faces of his patients, feels it in each newborn child that tumbles, slippery and steaming, into his hands. Even Elspet Garrow's death and now Jenny Duncan's, and the foreboding they strike in him, cannot dislodge this certainty in his soul.

It is a matter of determination, as it has always been, from the earliest days when he dragged his younger brothers through the woods to school each morning, worked doggedly at his lessons each night; when he walked the wards of the Westminster, wore fatigue like a second skin and only the thrill of knowledge kept him standing though his whole body yearned for rest. He knows how to endure hardship, prides himself on it. *Look to the rock from which you were hewn, and to the quarry from which you were dug.* Isaiah, 51. He has only to look around him, at the granite walls of the houses, at the surrounding hills, at the unflinching ground, to know who he is and why. One learnt a certain stubbornness, growing up on this soil, in this climate; learnt to endure, to set one's face to obstacles and keep going. It was a case of knowing one's own mind, deciding for oneself what was right and wrong, keeping faith with one's own convictions. No good will come of dwelling on things past mending. *He has borne our infirmities and carried our diseases.* He must not succumb to doubts, regrets. *Out of his anguish he shall see light; he shall find satisfaction through his knowledge.* There is only one direction to move in and that is forwards: towards knowledge, towards the light.

15

February

'Are you seriously proposing that the Good Lord was – ' Aunt Rae can hardly bring herself to say the words – '*a negro?*'

'I am proposing nothing. I am merely relaying the opinions of Mr Hunter, who has made a special study of the matter. These are his conclusions.'

'That Adam was – *an African?*'

Across the table, Elizabeth is glaring at him. Aunt Rae has only recently forgiven them for the previous summer's upset over the inheritance. This was supposed to be an agreeable occasion, a small dinner after the charity concert, an opportunity to appease her aunt, not to infuriate her anew. Elizabeth had spoken to Alec as they were leaving the concert hall. Emphatically. No talk of religion. No talk of science. No talk of politics. Now here he is, blundering headlong into a disastrous conjunction of all three, and Aunt Rae's eyes bulging with indignation.

Alec puts down his wine glass. He'll be damned if the old woman will intimidate him. Taking care not to gratify her by slipping into Scots, he says, 'That is the implication of Hunter's argument, yes. Since God created man in his own image – therefore – yes.'

Rabbie is dabbing at his mouth with his napkin, stifling the urge to laugh. Neither the gesture nor its purpose are lost on his aunt.

'I trust *you* have some objections to this preposterous suggestion, Robert,' she snaps. 'And you, Provost Duncan? What do you have to say?'

Provost Duncan looks up in confusion, caught unawares.

He has no idea what the preposterous suggestion is that he is being called upon to reject, having been pleasantly engrossed in conversation at the other end of the table with the younger Mistress Gordon. They had been discussing the merits of Monsieur Scherer, whose delightful new sonatas for harpsichord and violin they've heard that evening. The Provost had been in the midst of comparing the Swiss composer's compositions with those of Haydn and Corelli, a subject on which he happens to be particularly knowledgeable and Mistress Gordon, apparently, particularly interested. Duncan opens his mouth to reply, then shuts it again, finding it impossible to contribute to an argument he has paid no attention to without risking further offence to his interrogator. Chae, seated on his aunt's left, saves him the trouble by replying for him.

'It *is* a somewhat extraordinary theory, Alec, even you must admit. What is Hunter's evidence?'

'Skulls, mostly.'

'Skulls?'

Alec nods. 'Hunter has conducted a close study of many different species of mammal, human and animal, and found intriguing evidence that the angle of the frontal lobe reveals a gradual and continual chain of development from the lowest to the highest. Proof, Hunter believes—'

'Tush! Proof!' interrupts Aunt Rae. 'It's all you young men think about. I am sick of the very word! You will be saying Bishop Ussher is mistaken, too, I suppose?'

'I am prepared to believe that he was somewhat in error in his calculations,' Alec replies, cautiously. 'The discovery of marine fossils on the upper slopes of Ben Nevis lends strong support to James Hutton's theory that—'

'Really, Dr Gordon! I am amazed you are so suggestible. It is perfectly obvious to anyone possessed of the least *common sense* —' she stresses the words pointedly — 'that all these absurd theories prove but one thing: their authors' desire to shock the world into noticing them.'

'I assure you,' Alec retorts, 'no man could be less interested in what the world thinks than Mr Hunter. He is a scientist of the first rank, indefatigable in his quest for truth and wholly beyond any man's persuasion or influence. Mr Hunter's opinions are based on no authority but the facts before his eyes.'

'Is it true,' Isabella asks, attempting to divert the conversation into calmer waters, 'that he keeps a menagerie of wild animals in his garden?'

'It is.'

'And a stuffed giraffe in his London home?'

'I have seen it myself,' Alec says.

'But in this instance,' Chae says, 'with regard to the Africans, he must be mistaken, since it is well known that the Africans are greatly inferior in intelligence to the Europeans—'

But Aunt Rae has risen to her feet. 'It is bad enough that the Africans are nowadays writing books without having to endure such repellent notions as those put about by Mr Hunter. He is obviously a most unpleasant individual and I have heard quite enough of him for one evening. Elizabeth, it is time the ladies retired. Isabella, you are fatigued. My shawl, Charles, if you please.'

The discussion thus brought to a definitive halt, Chae gets up to help Aunt Rae with her shawl, arranging it several times before it meets with her satisfaction. Alec turns to his sister-in-law, relieved when she meets his eye with a small smile of sympathy. Isabella, at least, has not been offended. Over her head, however, Alec catches sight of Elizabeth's face. Her cheeks are flushed and her mouth is drawn into a thin, tight line. The look she shoots him is one of outright hatred.

'Permit me to assist you, Mistress Gordon.' Provost Duncan has moved forward to take Isabella's arm. Short of fighting the older man for his sister-in-law's arm, Alec has no choice but to step aside.

Left alone in the dining room, waiting for the other men to return, he gives in to a sense of gloomy bafflement at his own stupidity. How could he have let the conversation take such a turn? Only a moment before they had been harmlessly discussing Mr Burns's *Poems in the Scottish Dialect* (a volume highly praised by Dr Skinner in the *Journal*, but of dubious merit in Aunt Rae's opinion). It was in fact Chae, not Alec, who'd introduced the subject of the negroes, by referring to the astonishing success of another recent publication: Olaudah Equiano's account of his life as a slave. The *Interesting Narrative* had sold well over a thousand copies, Chae informed them, and while he could not vouch for it, having not yet read the work himself, he'd heard from several who had that it was exceedingly well written and in excellent English. When Aunt Rae expressed scepticism on this score, it had seemed only natural to introduce Hunter's theories into the conversation. At least, Alec consoles himself now, he'd had the sense not to mention Hunter's theory on hermaphrodites. He has little doubt what Aunt Rae would have made of that.

In the grate by Alec's feet a log shifts, releasing a spray of red-hot embers; they flare brightly for a second then fade and fall. The blank circles of the soiled dinner plates regard him balefully. They would have known to keep quiet. *Damn! Damn! Damn!* He wants tact, as Elizabeth repeatedly reminds him, and will certainly lose no time in telling him again the moment their guests have departed. Worse, the disputed portion will go now to one of the cousins; even Elizabeth has no idea how much they have need of it themselves.

He had sat down so full of good intentions, resolved to offend no one for once. In the moment, however, in the heat of the exchange, he forgets everything but what it is he wants to say; forgets that what so excites his imagination is, in equal measure, obnoxious to the minds of others; can see only how wrong they are to think as they do.

'Well, Alec man, that was well done!'

Chae sits down at the dining table beside his brother, half-turning his chair to face the fire. Seeing Alec has not yet done so, Chae picks up the bell and rings for the plates to be cleared. Annie, looking flustered, pokes her head into the room.

'*Before* the coffee, sir?'

'No, no, see to the women first. And bring more wood, will you?'

Provost Duncan and Rabbie rejoin them a moment later and Alec, after a dig in the ribs from Chae, recollects his duties and fetches the brandy.

'So, this Hunter fellow—' Duncan says.

Alec scowls and says nothing.

'Bad news for the West Indies, if his theory gets about. Let the negroes hear of it and there'll be no holding them. Tobago's in uproar already. Two planters burnt to death by their own slaves in the recent riots, so I'm told.'

'You think the negroes are wrong to want their freedom?' Rabbie ventures.

'It's not a question of freedom, young man. It's a question of trade. The planters are facing ruin with all this talk of liberty and equality. Plantations abandoned. Cane fields razed. The hills full of maroons. Where will it end? That's the question. Look at France! The country's bankrupt yet all people talk of is freedom. One bad harvest and, free or otherwise, France will starve. You think the slaves will work if they're not made to? Well, then, you're a fool! They'll sit on their fat black arses and let the cane rot under their fat black noses.'

Duncan concludes this speech by taking out his snuffbox and inserting a generous pinch into one of his own large nostrils. He snorts smartly, then gives a loud sneeze.

'I take it you are not in favour of abolition,' Alec says drily, watching the flecks of orange mucus tremble on Duncan's chin.

'A little freedom is a dangerous thing,' Duncan misquotes with insouciance. 'Especially for those unused to it.'

'And all men are not born equal?' Alec persists. 'In your view?'

'Equal? Certainly not, sir! Tis all claptrap and nonsense. My father knew the West Indies as well as any man and he'd be turning in his grave to hear such talk. Forty years on Coddrington's estate. He knew a thing or two, I can tell you. Had tales to shatter all these fool notions of equality. A wise and prudent man, my father, may he rest in peace. I thank heaven for his good sense and judgement in leaving when he did.'

'But you have interests still—'

Duncan bridles instantly at the implication. 'As, I understand, do you, sir!' He looks around at the other men: 'As do you all.'

It is true enough. Elizabeth's father sold everything when he left Antigua, but her uncles' estates are in the family still. It is sugar that paid for their house in Belmont Street. Sugar, too, had assisted considerably in securing Alec's appointment to the Dispensary. Along with a bill of payment from John Harvie to the Infirmary, there'd been a timely letter of recommendation for a certain young naval surgeon newly arrived in town and in want of employment. There was no need to spell out for the Infirmary managers that the eager young surgeon was also recently married to Mr Harvie's eldest niece, for everyone knew it.

'What interests me,' says Chae, 'is whether freedom can ever be achieved without bloodshed. We pride ourselves on being rational beings, but when vast obstacles stand in the way of convictions passionately held and objectives passionately wished for, violent action seems always to be the result. Whether France or Tobago, it matters little. Reason begins the process, but violence seems inevitably to end it. Is it not as Mr Hume said? "Reason is slave to the passions."'

'Hume was wrong,' says Alec, with quiet vehemence. 'Reason is what sets man free. Without reason, we are nothing.'

16

The hills beyond the town are snow-clad. The sea beyond the Links is iron-black. Three more women die. All in good health. All delivered of living bairns after relatively easy births.

Jean Anthony, twenty-five years of age.

Alison Mennie, twenty-seven years of age.

Agnes Smith, thirty-one.

All carried off within a week of their confinement.

Jean Anthony was delivered by Alec himself, assisted by Rabbie; the others by Mistress Elgin, who had not called for help until the disease was too far advanced for any intervention on Alec's part to be of use. When he'd upbraided her for not calling him sooner, she'd stiffened with indignation, spat back at him: Why should she? A touch of fever is not so unusual after a lying-in, nor a bit of pain and discomfort. No need to go greetin to the doctor at the slightest little thing. She's an experienced midwife, after all, one of the best in Aberdeen; was delivering women in childbed when he was still parsing Latin verbs in the schoolhouse. What does he think they all did before they had a Dispensary, or a physician to it? She's lost bairns in her time – they all have – but never once a mother. She knows milk fever and after-pains when she sees them, knows what to do without having to ask any physician's opinion of the matter, however many degrees he has, however many grand letters after his name. If he wants *her* opinion, what killed those poor women was his insistence on bleeding them when it was clear to the rest of the world that they'd not the strength to survive it.

Alec, for once, had held his tongue, but he knows better. Once you've seen this illness for yourself, you don't mistake it for anything else, however much you may want to. The suspicion of it, nudging at his memory since Elspet Garrow's death, had become certainty the moment he set eyes on Jenny Duncan. The time and manner of attack, the symptoms, the smell. The smell! That alone was unmistakable. How many cases had he seen that year at the Westminster? Twenty? Thirty? Near to fifty women were seized in the space of three months; more than half died. Not quietly or peacefully, but in greater agony than any he'd witnessed before or since. Worse torture than the pains of labour, they said, those who were able to say anything at all. And now it is here, in Aberdeen. The witch at the christening, come to spoil all Alec's plans, to curse his new beginnings, blight his progress in its lovely infancy. The midwives have never encountered the disease before, have never even heard of it. He will have to speak out eventually, give the condition its proper name, but now is not the moment. It is still too soon. Even the other physicians have failed as yet to recognize the disease. How could they be expected to, in all reasonableness, having neither interest nor experience in this particular field and having never before come across the condition in their own practices? In the flesh, as it were. Alec thinks of young Jean Anthony at the end, delirious with the pain, her empty belly grotesquely huge beneath the bedclothes, an unstoppable flood of black diarrhoea pouring from her bowels though she's eaten nothing for days. Truly, this is a disease in and of the flesh. The riotous emanations of shit and piss and puke; vile-coloured, vile-odoured fluids frothing and foaming from every orifice, as if some monstrous guest were lodged inside the patient and there grew fat and foul from feasting on her innards, relieving its gluttony by regurgitating the masticated remains. Childbed fever. A gentle sounding name for so violent a disease. Puerperal fever, to give the illness its proper designation. Not words to utter lightly under any circumstance. Not words to utter in your worst nightmare.

17

Robert Donald is the first to be told.

'Childbed fever?'

They are on their way to the Infirmary in response to an urgent summons from Dr French. It is early afternoon. Tiny flecks of snow skitter in playful whorls in the muted light, blowing up under the brims of their hats, fluttering against their faces, lodging in sticky clumps in their eyelashes.

'But I thought – ' Rabbie is not sure how to put it – 'I've only ever heard of it—'

Rabbie is a conscientious young man, keen to advance in his chosen profession. What free time he has, he spends absorbing the contents of the volumes on Alec's shelves. He is familiar with the name, has read some accounts of it.

'On lying-in wards?' Alec helps him out. 'Aye, you're right. Dublin, Edinburgh and London. Twelve recorded epidemics in the last forty years. All of them in hospitals. Until now.'

'You think the disease is in its epidemic state?'

'Too soon to be sure, but five deaths in six weeks—' Alec considers. 'That's five more than in the past two years.'

They trudge on in silence, the snow creaking under their boots, the boughs of the trees bordering the road heavy with it. Every branch, each twig bearing its own white replica. The air filled with that muted silence that comes with snow. They cross the footbridge over the Denburn and continue up the hill in the direction of the hospital. Despite the cold, the first snowdrops are starting to appear, the green of their stems bright against the snow, impossibly delicate beneath the tiny ice-white bell of petals. In the fields, rooks flap and squabble, black and raucous above the smooth white land. Alec sees death-tolls not snowfall. Nineteen seized at the Westminster, fourteen of whom died; twenty-eight at the British Hospital, of whom twenty-four died; thirty-four on the lying-in ward in Edinburgh, not one of whom survived.

Rabbie sidles a glance at Alec. 'I suppose it is an opportunity—'

Alec looks at him sharply, not understanding.

'To study the condition at close quarters, I mean.'

Alec stops in his tracks then, laughs out loud. His apprentice is throwing his own teaching back at him. What can he do but laugh? He should have thought of it himself.

'Yes indeed, Mr Donald, you are absolutely right! Observable facts. Firm evidence. An epidemic in Aberdeen is just the thing!'

Up on Woolmanhill the hospital is overflowing. Extra beds have been set up on the military ward and one of the bedlam cells has been turned over. Still there isn't space. Any patient well enough to stand is made to get up and help, their bunks stripped almost before they're out of them. One or two flout regulations and die before there's time to prise them from their beds and send them home. Mistress Farquhar is sluicing the floors four times a day to try and clear the air of the noxious effluvia. Plumes of steam rise off the icy boards, giving the ward the appearance of a washhouse.

For the next few days Alec hasn't a moment to reflect on puerperal fever, epidemic or otherwise, too busy with this sudden outbreak of erysipelas. *Erythros*, red; *pelle*, skin. They call it also St Anthony's Fire, on account of the pain that scorches the epidermis like the furnaces of hell. Even trivial scratches redden and blister and blacken. Minor wounds pucker into gangrenous sores that weep and seep and ooze unstoppably. The amputation rate is shocking. Men who the month before were fit and strong are rendered cripples, faces grim-set to the future, wondering how they'll feed their wives and bairns now they've no means to ply their trade. Alec has never seen such eruptions of decay, such kaleidoscopes of colour: purple, scarlet, moss-green, slate-grey. His lips are cracked from breathing through his mouth, the only way to control the urge to retch. French doesn't bother. He does his rounds with a scented handkerchief clamped to his nose, or finds an excuse not to do them at all. Only the students are cock-a-hoop, wielding their saws and scalpels with unconcealed glee. Real bodies at last! See how the flesh yields to the blade. How the blood vessels near the wound are bloodless, white as the underlying bone. They are queuing up at the Infirmary doors in the morning, eager to be first in line, to get first stab, literally, at the previous night's casualties.

Alec tears between Woolmanhill and Hope Row, his own patients disgruntled by his absence when they need him. How endlessly available a doctor is expected to be. How infinitely divisible. Alec has yet to meet a patient who accepts with good grace that a doctor may have more pressing cases to attend to than his own. Illness is a tyrant and makes tyrants of its prey.

Elizabeth cannot understand why he wastes his time on Infirmary patients.

'One word from Dr French and you jump like a performing dog. On top of everything else you have to do. And he doesn't pay you a penny!'

'French needs me. That's worth a good deal.'

'Oh, aye, a fine deal and no mistake! And George French the sole beneficiary, in case it had escaped your notice. I have to manage with one maid and you work for nothing.'

But Alec holds his ground.

'It's only by treating the sick that my stock will rise. It's time I had a hospital appointment, you know that, and how else is French to calculate my value to him? He is a physician. A man of science. This is his currency.'

'George French is a man of the world,' Elizabeth replies.

'The only currency that interests him is one that will purchase his own advancement.'

Alec tries to appease her with a kiss, but she twists away from him and his lips graze the side of her head.

During the day there is scarcely time to think, but at night, in the seconds before sleep engulfs him, Alec's mind reels with what he has seen: the peacock brilliance of a sore, the creep of pus, the scarlet hole of a mouth. There's been too much of such things in recent weeks; ever since Angus Robertson got caught beneath his upturned cart, a month back now, it's been one thing then another. The lying-in mothers, the putrefying wounds at the hospital, the miller and his leg. The horse had skidded on a patch of ice just after crossing between the narrow parapets of the Brig o' Don, almost dragging the cart over the edge and into the ravine below. That would have been the end of both horse and driver, but somehow the unfortunate miller had managed to hold the horse's head long enough to keep the cart running along the road on just one wheel; when it finally toppled over, he had been caught beneath it.

By the time Alec arrived, the man was losing blood so fast that Alec knew he'd die if something wasn't done at once. At first they'd tried to lift the cart, Alec and Rabbie and the miller's lad, but then they realized that the wheel trapping the miller had shattered and that he was not only lying under its weight, but pinioned by its broken spokes. The force of the cart's descent had driven one of the spokes clean through the man's lower leg and into the ground. Alec had performed the operation then and there, one swift circling cut through the skin, then down through the fat and muscle to the bone, pausing only long enough to tie the major blood vessels and change the knife for a saw, before hacking into the bone itself, amputating the leg well above the knee, while Rabbie gripped the man's shoulders and the miller's son, white-faced, had tipped whisky from the doctor's hip flask down his father's throat.

'A limb for a life, lad,' Alec had said, through gritted teeth, his head full of the sound of the amputation saw grating its way through the miller's thigh bone. 'Better peg-legged than dead.'

It was a desperate piece of work, though. He'd caught his finger on the blade at one point, drops of his own blood mingling with the miller's in the mud. In the end it was all for nothing: gangrene set in and within a week the scene was closed.

It is the miller, Alec finds himself thinking as he reaches his front door one evening, bone-weary, blood-and-gore-weary. *It began with the miller.* But he knows the idea is absurd. What connection can there be between a chance accident on an icy road and the outbreak of skin disease now raging through the wards of the Infirmary? It is just the amputations that have linked the events in his mind. After all, there was nothing diseased about Robertson's leg. It was clean, healthy flesh through and through, only ran to gangrene after. Not like the stuff he's been cutting away these past few days. However long he stands at the sink in the outhouse, scrubbing and soaping, he cannot get rid of the smell. It pursues him. He catches it on his fingers when he lifts a glass to his lips, when he loosens his cravat. Yesterday Mary had pulled away from him when he tried to kiss her cheek. 'You stink!' she'd complained, wrinkling her nose in distaste.

Alec tips more water into the stone basin, then picks up the block of soap, works it hard against the palm of first one hand then the other hand, like a scrub-board and a piece of soiled linen, pushing the soap along the tops of his fingers, so the shavings wedge in behind the nail. Every now and then he pauses, lifts his fingers to his nose, sniffs and shoves them back into the water. The fifth time he does so, however, he is arrested by a sudden thought and stands stock still, left hand midway between chin and nose. Icy water trails down the inside of his wrist and congeals inside his sleeve, but he hardly notices.

There *is* a connection. It's in Hamilton. Somewhere in his account of the Edinburgh epidemic. Alec is sure of it. Something about the state of the air. How at certain times it was capable of producing symptoms of erysipelas on the surgical wards. And how when such a state of air was present on the surgical wards, the same contagious atmosphere could produce outbreaks of puerperal fever on the lying-in wards. At the same time, but at no other. Yes, there is a connection! The skin disease blooming on the surgical wards; the puerperal fever picking off victims in the town.

But even as Alec thinks this, he questions it. How can it be so? All previous epidemics of childbed fever have occurred on lying-in wards, as his apprentice had pointed out. While Hamilton's claim made some sense within the confines of a single hospital – given the concentration of vapours arising from the patients crowded there, it was not implausible that vitiated air might pass somehow from one ward to another – how could that be the explanation for the two diseases occurring at the same time here in Aberdeen? How could the same contagious air both give rise to erysipelas on the surgical wards up at the Infirmary and simultaneously kill people in their own houses down in the town? Houses, furthermore, where hitherto there had been no illness, no vapours, no putrid effluvia of any kind? And why one house, one woman, but not another?

Questions without answers. Always questions without answers. Soapsuds drip off Alec's hands on to the flagstones at his feet. It makes no sense. And yet the coincidence is too interesting to dismiss. He feels it in his bones, a hard pure instinct. This is not merely coincidence; there is a connection, and somehow or other he must track it down, whatever it is; however hard it tries to elude him, to shake him off its trail with riddles and puzzles, he must follow its scent until he has sniffed it to ground. Something has taken shape in his mind, dimly still, its contours hazy, like a creature briefly glimpsed through mist, but he has it in his sights, a marked quarry: he knows now what he is after.

Alone in the scullery with the suds darkening at his feet, excitement floods through his body, like pure water, sweeping away the physical fatigue in his limbs, the silt of questions in his head. A glittering, hard-edged euphoria drenches his mind. In place of the turmoil of a moment before, there is stillness, clarity, certainty. This is what he is meant to do.

Briskly, he dries off his hands and rolls down his sleeves, seeing with brief annoyance the puddle he's been standing in. The scent of new-baked oatcakes drifts through from the kitchen, and from the other side of the hallway, the high burble of Mary's voice. *I'll write to Denman*, he thinks, going through to join the rest of the household. *Put the matter to him.* He pictures his old friend and mentor, standing on the podium in the lecture hall of the Westminster Hospital, shabby coat patched at the elbows, grey hair flowing over his shoulders, surveying the sea of faces before him with an expression as ferocious as any kirk minister, eyes blazing, leaning forwards to emphasize his point, one hand gripping the lectern's edge, the other held aloft, index finger pointing heavenwards, a medical pantocrator. *The dead may further our scientific understanding, but we are in the business of life. Never forget this. Our task is to keep the living alive, not profit by their deaths.* Afterwards, pushing and shoving their way into the amber warmth of the alehouse, the apprentices would quote Denman's words, hilarity mounting with inebriation. Wedged together like salt herring on the wooden benches, they'd propose toast after toast to the business of life, until they were sufficiently drunk to forget how many patients they'd seen sacrificed to that very business in the past few days.

Yes, Denman's the man to ask.

'Music!' Alec cries, stepping into the front parlour.

Elizabeth looks up from the wool that she and Mary are winding. Rabbie lowers his book and stares at his uncle.

'Stop gawping at me wi that smoutie phiz o yours, Mr Donald. Tis not Lent yet. Fetch your pipes and gies a wee spring!'

18

Three days after her husband's birthday, as she is bending over to stoke the fire, Isabella's waters break. The labour is quick and without incident. The baby has a shock of feather-fine black hair and a tiny ruched mouth like an unfurled poppy. Chae is as proud as if she were the first bairn ever to grace the town and he the first father. 'Did you ivver see sich a bonnie wee lassie?' he asks everyone in turn, forgetting his vowels in his excitement, not waiting for the answer, which he knows already.

Alec would have been there, but at the last minute was called away to an urgent case twelve miles out of town, where a young woman at the paper mill had caught her hair in one of the presses and been scalped clean before anyone realized what was happening.

'Alec, man! At last!' Chae cries, when he finally appears on the doorstep in Broad Street. 'Where've ye been? Come and see your new niece! The bonniest wee lassie in all of Scotland!'

The baptism takes place on a fair morning with high scudding clouds and sudden bursts of sharp-edged sunshine. Lozenges of silvery light from the three small windows set high in the south wall jitter across the flagstones. Alec arrives late, squeezing along the row to take his place beside his wife and daughter just as the congregation is rising for the first hymn. They are renowned for their singing, the pixies of Aberdeen. Wesley himself had commented on it when he visited the town, and so, a few years later, had the celebrated Dr Johnson, passing through on his tour of the Highlands. All around Alec now the voices swell in unison. The English tunes still jar on his

ear, strike him as floridly irreligious. There were no English
hymns at the Peterculter kirk. No pews either. Not for the
sons of tenant farmers at any rate. You stood at the back on
your own two feet and hoped the sodden straw you'd packed
your shoes with wouldn't freeze before the sermon was over.
It is Elizabeth's faith they follow, not his.

Beside him, Alec feels his wife sway slightly, the weight of
her upper body leaning into him for a moment.

> 'His power increasing still shall spread;
> His reign no end shall know...'

The music swells in volume and density, building towards
the concluding bars, reverberating off the walls, slowing and
expanding until the air is saturated with sound.

> 'Justice shall guard his throne above,
> And peace abound below.'

The moment the hymn comes to an end the congregation
subsides on to the benches. Elizabeth stops pretending to sing
and sits too. She feels light-headed. She hasn't eaten since the
night before. The sight of the grey sludge of porridge on the
breakfast table had made her stomach turn. In an effort to
steady herself, she stares hard at the stone pillar in front of
her. Flecks of light, the colour of churned milk, quiver over its
surface. It makes her dizzy to look at them. She raises her
eyes, fixes them instead on the whitewashed wall behind the
vicar. That helps at first, but then the whiteness too begins
to tremble and shift. The longer she looks, the less certain she
becomes that the wall is white at all; a strange blackness seems
to be seeping through from the stone itself, spreading into a
dark grey stain just above the vicar's head. It reminds her of
something, a painting she'd once seen, years ago, propped up
against a mound of packing cases on the quayside, on its way
to the colonies. She went often to the harbour with her father
when there were shipments to oversee. Sometimes it was cargo

he was expecting, other times merchandise he was sending on. Whatever it was that day, there'd been an argument with the captain of the vessel, something to do with the fee that had been agreed being insufficient for the quantity of goods to be stowed. She'd wandered off, well used to amusing herself while these business matters were sorted out. The painting had been perched on top of a long low crate, about level with her head. It was a copy, she later learnt, of a work by the Dutch master Rembrandt van Rijn. The blanket covering it must have slipped or been lifted off by the wind because for some reason most of the canvas was exposed to view. Without knowing the name of the artist or the painting, she recognized the scene at once.

In the centre of the picture stood Belshazzar, surrounded by his courtiers, clothed in a magnificent fur-trimmed cloak embroidered with gold and studded with pearls. A golden platter lay on the table before the king; in one hand, he held a golden drinking goblet. The guests, too, held goblets of gold; their robes were laced with precious stones; strings of tiny pearls gleamed in the women's hair. The scene was one of opulent festivity, but the faces of the guests were etched not with merriment but fear. Belshazzar himself was on his feet, staring at the wall behind him, plainly terrified by what he saw there. A hand had appeared from nowhere – just the hand, nothing else – and, before the gaze of the cringing king and his guests, had inscribed three lines of writing on the wall, the letters blazing like firebrands against the blackness of the wall. Elizabeth had no more idea how to read this strange God-sent message than Belshazzar himself; the symbols meant nothing to her. But she knew the story from her Bible, knew by heart what the Hebrew letters meant. Standing amidst the noise and bustle of the quayside, gazing at the painting, she had under-stood well enough, as had Belshazzar and his guests, that the writing on the wall spoke a terrible inescapable truth. This was judgement. This was the word of God. Spelling out the king's fate for all to see. *You have been weighed in the scales and found wanting.* She had stared and stared at the painting, unable to tear herself away, oblivious to the clamour of the docks all about her. Even when she heard her father calling for her from along the quay, she had not moved. She had felt pity for the king in his silly little crown, with his wet mouth drooping open, his eyes stupid with fear. But she had also felt his terror at the sight of that spectral hand, its soft white fingers emerging from the blackness. Those three rows of strange blazing letters had seemed to her not divine, but diabolic.

Alec's hand on her elbow, guiding her out of the pew, jolts Elizabeth back into awareness of her surroundings. He steers her towards the font, only releasing her arm when they are standing right in front of it, alongside her sister and brother-in-law. Alec is saying something to her under his breath, but Elizabeth isn't listening. She's distracted by another sound: a high desolate keening. At first she thinks it's a bird of some kind, stuck in the rafters most probably, then she realizes it's not a bird she can hear, but a baby.

As Reverend Glegg recites the christening vows, she hears it again. She's not imagining it. There is a baby crying, without a doubt, not the baby the minister is holding over the font, not Isabella's baby, but another one, somewhere up above their heads. The crying baby must be hidden somewhere up in the rafters over the nave. She mustn't look up, though. Somehow she knows that this is very important: she must not draw attention to the crying baby. She must pretend she cannot hear its crying either. Now Glegg is tilting the bundle in his arms towards the glassy water in the font. High overhead the thin wailing continues.

'I name thee Elizabeth Charlotte Gordon.'

Afterwards she cannot explain, even to herself, exactly what happened. How, at the moment Reverend Glegg pronounced those words, the names began ringing in her ears, her niece's names, her mother's names; how the quiet crying of the baby concealed in the rafters had expanded into a deafening roar, filling her head not just with noise, but with a heavy blackness, which had borne down on her, like a vast hand, pushing her into the ground. Ashes to ashes, dust to dust. She'd been unable to withstand the blackness or the heaviness; they had fused into a single irresistible force, pressing her into the ground, as if a massive weight were pushing her downwards, lowering her in seven slow beats, *e liza beth char lotte gor don*, into the cold stone floor. There was nothing she could do but sink beneath its pressure, succumb to the simple logic of the darkness, until all that remained was that original mournful wailing, a single thread of dark-grey woven into the fabric of nothing, like the humid airless nights that went on for ever and ever, like the suffocating shaded days. Until eventually even the crying stopped. And then there was nothing at all, an even greater nothing than before, an emptiness so intense that, even then, Elizabeth had known for sure it could never be filled.

19

Alec keeps her in bed for the next week, dosed with four hourly draughts of camphire julep to quiet the nightmares and still the storms of weeping that follow. He questions Annie with a ferocity that succeeds only in scaring the girl into tongue-tied silence. Had she noticed nothing amiss? Had her mistress given no signs at all of illness? The interrogation takes place in the kitchen, where Annie is soaking the sugar papers to extract the dye. Her fingers are blue with it.

'Nae, sir, nothing, I swear.'

'Nothing, ye glaikit feel?' Alec storms. 'Have ye no eyes? No ears? No brain?'

It is himself he is furious with.

He can learn little more from Elizabeth. Something about a bird trapped in the chapel roof that makes no sense. Her complexion and pulse are as normal. She complains of neither flatulence nor costiveness, the usual indications of hysterical disorders. He prescribes a course of steel filings to cleanse the belly, which she assents to meekly enough. It occurs to him that she has not been right since Mary was born. He has seen this in other women often enough, a perplexing laxity of spirit that is the devil's own business to cure.

'Fresh air will do most good,' he tells her, 'and a plain, vegetable diet.'

'I think I'll sleep a little now,' she says in response.

For a while it seems that the deaths may have stopped. The disease claims only one more victim that month. Warily relieved, Alec gets back to the usual business of burns and boils and fractured bones. The cases of inflammatory sore throats are still excessive for the season; the erysipelas, too, continues to appear at the site of the slightest scratch. When Alec is not occupied with the Dispensary patients or up at the Infirmary, he has his private practice to attend to. Since January he's had hardly a moment for his private patients, but he cannot afford to neglect them: they pay more than all his other work together. Now, finally, he begins to catch up. He gets over to Queen Street to see Mistress Byron about her son. As he suspects, there is nothing to be done. The foolish woman should have followed Skene's advice when the boy was born. He recommends her to the bootmaker in North Street; if he cannot oblige, she will have to send to the capital. A letter comes from Denman at last.

February 20th, London

> *My apologies for not replying at once, but urgent business called me from town for several days. I regret to say that I find every reason to agree with your diagnosis; the symptoms you describe are too familiar to me to admit of any doubt. Pay no attention whatsoever to vulgar opinion. Confronted with a condition they know nothing of, local women will always cling to custom sooner than admit their ignorance. What never was can never be: that, my friend, is the deplorable philosophy you are up against! Take my advice and trust in your own infinitely superior knowledge of these matters. Your nose, in any case, will tell you more than any quantity of local opinion, for this is assuredly the foulest smelling malady known to mankind, both before death and after.*

> *Whether or not it is in an epidemic state I cannot say, but so many deaths in so short a space of time permits scant scope for complacency. It is perfectly true that all previous epidemics have occurred in hospitals; whether that means an epidemic could never occur out of one, I am unwilling to speculate.*

> *In treating the disease, happily, we are on surer ground. Hot applications to the extremities and warm diluents, in small quantities, often repeated, I have found frequently effective in*

shortening the rigors. Fomentations, vapour-bathing, or the warm bath, may sometimes be used with advantage; but I think that a folded flannel well sprinkled with brandy is one of the best applications to the abdomen. Frequent quantities of chicken-water, beef-tea or barley-water should be given, as plentiful dilution is necessary. Tea of almost any kind may be drunk at pleasure. The necessity of vomiting I have ascertained beyond doubt and everything possible should be done to produce this operation. The practice will expose you to much hostility from the midwives, but I have found that many desirable purposes are answered by it. Purging draughts are likewise essential. An emollient clyster should first be administered, followed by antimonial powder in small quantities to bring on the evacuations, or if the patient is of a delicate constitution or much weakened by the disease, two ounces of purging salts dissolved in a pint of thin gruel.

On the question of bleeding, I must advise caution. When the attack is violent, and the constitution feeble, it may be more expeditiously serviceable to draw blood by scarification or by the application of eight or ten leeches to that part which appears to be principally affected. In general, emollient or purgative clysters should be resorted to instead, remembering that opiates must afterwards be given to procure a respite.

To your final question. Alas! Short of forbidding fornication, a measure unlikely to meet with general approbrium, I know of no sure way of preventing this disease. Childbed fever accompanies childbed, as coughs and colds come with the winter months and swallows herald the start of summer. The evidence on this point is as conclusive as it is lamentable and I fear we must resign ourselves to it.

My warmest felicitations,
Thomas Denman

20

March

There is snow still on the hilltops and in the north-facing glens, but in the fields beyond Belmont Street early buds are thickening on their stems. Clumps of wild primrose have succeeded the snowdrops and in a few sheltered spots, feathery new leaves have begun to soften the stark outline of the branches. The sheep have been set free from their winter confinement and the first lambs teeter knock-kneed in their wake, mewing for milk and respite from the wind. As the horizon begins to relent and dip away to the south, the days are lengthening. The farmers ready themselves for the spring sowing, driving teams of oxen across the still-hard earth, breaking up the compacted soil, banking up the flints into low wide dykes that shine like mirrors in the cold, waterlogged daylight. Squalling winds wreak havoc in the fishing villages along the coast.

In Aberdeen, the rains thrash the streets and houses, leave the town as clean and fresh as new-washed linen. Water droplets cling to every gutter, drainpipe and railing; noisy torrents cascade along the gullies that flank the newly laid roads. The milder weather turns roads to mud, miring wheels and hooves and boots alike. The bairns don't mind, happy to splash in the puddles or douse themselves under the run-off gushing from the gutters and water-spouts, but their mothers shore them for it when they catch them. Ice is better than mud: it takes less washing off and drying out.

Alec is beginning to hope that he's been over-hasty in his fears of an epidemic, but in the second week of March, two more women take ill and die. One after a case of *placenta praevia*, in which he'd had to reach in, turn the baby and deliver it right through the placenta. The other was a breech and had required the forceps. Both mothers survived the birth, only to be carried off in the first few days of their lying-in.

As if strengthened by its brief repose, the disease now attacks the town with renewed vigour, striking without warning or pity and killing without mercy. Far from being spent, it seems it had merely been catching its breath. By St Patrick's Day, there have been four more cases, each meticulously logged in the pile of notes amassing on Alec's desk, none shedding any light on what has gone before or what will happen next.

'It is a disease like no other,' he tells the medical students, taking advantage of the official theme of the afternoon's lecture, the classification of diseases, to pursue the problem that, day and night, is beginning to obsess him. 'Young or old, rich or poor – it makes no difference. The disease is promiscuous as a whore, cares nothing for character or conduct; preys as readily on the saintly as the sinful, the robust as the sickly. It confines its attack to lying-in women, but none can say how or why it selects its victims. Whether inflammatory, putrid or contagious, remains a mystery; whether caused by something noxious in the air, as Dr White believes, or generated within the body as a result of the changes of pregnancy and the upheavals of childbirth, as Dr Leake and Dr Burton have proposed; whether brought on, as Dr Kirkland maintains, by the migration of rancid milk from the breasts, or by suppression of the lochia, as suspected by Dr Cooper. In short, gentlemen, we know next to nothing.'

It verges on the heretical for a teacher to admit to such ignorance, but Alec is as stubborn on this score as on most others. Feigned certainty will not save lives. He looks over the faces of the score of young men who, four months before, had subscribed to be his disciples, and wonders if he has succeeded in teaching them anything; if they have any idea what he is talking about, or why it matters. He lets his eye travel over the familiar countenances: McGrigor with his aquiline features and keen bright eyes, every bit as intelligent as he appears; snub-nosed Holmes, quick-witted as a lump of clay; weasel-faced McRae, clever but lazy; Rabbie Donald, serious, diligent, too soft-hearted for his own good. What kind of surgeons and physicians will they make? Since October they have listened, notebooks in hand, to his twice-weekly lectures; they have trotted at his heels round the streets of Aberdeen, visiting the sick, the dying and the all-too-evidently malingering; they have walked the wards at his side, watched him cut stones, cauterize wounds, amputate limbs, remove growths of every size and description. They have taken turns to pin down the writhing victims as he's performed the necessary operations. He has shared everything with them, held nothing back: from his experience as a surgeon and his knowledge of midwifery, to the precious gems of his anatomical collection. He has gone beyond the scope of his duties and taught them how to prepare and preserve specimens for collections of their own. He has helped them to procure subjects whenever occasion has allowed. Everything he knows he has endeavoured to pass on. He has done all he can to inject his knowledge into their veins, not merely facts, but a whole philosophy, founded on the need to look and see with their own eyes. *Learn from nature, not from books.* He has said this to them more times than he can recall. *Look, touch, smell, taste. Amniotic fluid has a flavour like brine. The diabetic's urine has the odour of violets. Take nothing for granted.*

Now his lease on their minds is almost over. The university term is drawing to a close and they will be gone soon – all except Rabbie, who is apprenticed to him for another twelve months. Will they put to good use what he has given them? Holmes, for sure, will bury everything he's learned and never dig it up again. McRae is unpredictable, could apply or squander his skills. McGrigor will go far. All of them are restless today, though. Alec can sense their thoughts moving beyond the walls of the lecture room to the apprenticeships they have secured. Edinburgh, Dublin, London and Leiden are beckoning. For most it will be the first time they have set foot beyond Aberdeen.

'Before one may treat a condition correctly,' he continues, 'one must first classify it correctly. Mr McGrigor — if you please — the necessary steps are—?'

McGrigor reels off the answer as smoothly as Alec knew he would: 'First, distinguish *the immediate cause*, that which is sufficient of itself to produce the disease; secondly, identify *the predisposing cause*, that which precedes and leads on to the immediate cause; and thirdly, determine *the occasional cause*, that which succeeds and promotes the predisposing cause, and which combined together form the immediate cause.'

Out of the corner of his eye, Alec can see Holmes scribbling furiously in his notebook. McRae appears to be sketching the back of McGrigor's head.

'Very good, McGrigor. And how would you apply this procedure to the puerperal fever?'

McGrigor looks down uncertainly at his notes and does not reply.

'Any of you?'

There is silence for a while as the students consider the problem, then McRae pipes up: 'Is it not just a case of examining the facts, Dr Gordon?'

McRae has an innocent expression on his face that doesn't deceive Alec for a moment.

'Aye, McRae, but which facts? Have I not just explained that some of our most eminent physicians argue, *from facts*, that the immediate cause is putrefaction, while others, equally eminent, insist putrefaction is the predisposing cause? Perhaps, Mr McRae, seeing as you're so confident of your opinion, you'd grace the rest of us with your superior intelligence on this matter: the immediate cause, if you please?'

Playing to his audience, McRae gets to his feet, puts his head on one side, index finger to his lips and makes a clownish show of pondering the subject. The others wait with gleeful anticipation.

'I would say tis a putrid disorder,' he announces at last, 'for by all accounts it has an awfy bad smell!'

He pinches the end of his nose and pulls a face before sitting down amidst laughter from the others. Alec waits for the noise to subside, then turns to the thin earnest boy bent low over his notebook near the back of the class.

'Ogilvie, come out of hiding, lad! Make us a case for this being a putrid disease.'

Stricken at finding himself the centre of attention, Ogilvie stares down at his lap, his heart-shaped, pox-scarred face scarlet with embarrassment.

'Come, come, lad. You must be able to think of something. Some small indication of *prima facie* putridity – besides smell.'

Rory Greig raises his hand. 'Evidence of internal putrefaction in the deceased?'

'Not bad, Mr Greig. But here too we have a wee problem. Does putrefaction prove the disease is putrid by nature, or merely that it becomes putrid with time? How, moreover, do you propose to distinguish between the putrefaction that occurs in all corpses and that caused by the disease in question prior to death?'

A fly, newly hatched and roused by sunlight on the glass, is buzzing crossly against the fanlight above the door. Alec follows its dazed attempts at flight, while the students sit with the puzzle he has set them. Rabbie, gratifyingly, is the first to work it out.

'Perhaps it is not a putrid disease at all,' he says in his slow thoughtful way. 'There is evidence to support the contrary argument – to indicate an inflammatory condition.'

'Pray, explain further, Mr Donald – for the benefit of this flock of featherbrains.'

'At the onset of the puerperal fever, many patients complain greatly of acute pain in the hypogastric region. This suggests that the internal organs in that area are in a state of inflammation.'

'Excellent, Mr Donald.' Alec turns to the rest of the class. 'And those of you who have been minded to read Dr Hulme's invaluable treatise on the disease will know that dissections of its victims frequently reveal evidence of extensive inflammation of the internal parts.'

'You mean it's not a putrid disease?' Holmes is crossing out the notes he wrote earlier, a bewildered look on his face.

'I mean, Holmes, that controversy reigns. That there are persuasive arguments on both sides.' Alec is talking not just to Holmes but to the whole class now. 'Physic is not a matter of rote learning. You must weigh the existing evidence, then gather new evidence. Only when you have sufficient facts in front of you, can you make a proper assessment. Above all, you must never forget—'

The students recognize what is coming and join their voices with his, reciting the doctor's favourite maxim with loud enthusiasm: 'Authority without facts is nothing but opinion, and opinion without authority is worth less than a barleycorn.'

21

Alec pauses at the head of the brae to catch his breath. There's a fine view of the town from here, as far as the Seton Hills to the north, across to Gilcomston and Forresterhill to the west. Despite all the building work – the widening of some streets, the straightening of others, the new houses springing up on every side – the centre of the town is still as neat and compact as a wheel, with St Catherine's Hill at its hub, encircled by Ship Row, Netherkirkgate and Putachieside, and radiating out from there the crooked spokes of Castle Street, Broadgate and Schoolhill. To the south lies the harbour, and beyond that, the mouth of the Dee with its maze of sandbanks. After graduating from the schoolroom at Peterculter to the Grammar School in town, Alec spent most afternoons down on the quayside, sometimes alone, sometimes with the other boys, Charlie Gibbs and Sandy Flemming and the rest. He liked to watch the coasters and coracles meandering up the estuary, negotiating the sandbanks and shingle that littered the wide, slow-moving waters of the Dee. Only the shallower vessels could safely navigate the river as far as the town harbour; the merchant ships were obliged to dock further out at Torry, then transfer their goods to smaller craft. This arrangement, necessitated by nature and so far resistant to the efforts and ingenuity of the town's engineers, greatly increased the traffic of small and middling-sized vessels plying the route to and from the pier, ensuring a constant state of bustling activity in the harbour itself. Trade had slowed in recent months with the troubles in France, but when Alec was a boy the quayside had been a continual carnival of noise and motion, with cargo of all shapes and sizes arriving from every major port in Europe. Flax, hemp, linen yarn and timber from the Baltic. Oak from Norway. Onions, bacon and tomatoes from Holland. The bounty from the Netherlands seemed infinite: sacks of clover seed, wood-ash and linseed, candlesticks and clocks, spinning wheels and copper pots, ribbons and corsets, flutes and harpsichords, pens and paints and paintings. Everything the civilized man or woman could possibly need to adorn their lives was there, hauled out of the boats in an inexhaustible array of crates and sacks and boxes and baskets, heaped up in orderly confusion the entire length of the quayside beneath the frantic gulls and the steely gaze of the harbour master. The merchants took their cut and handling fees and shipped most of it on to Zeeland, Virginia and the West Indies, bulking out their holds with local goods: soap, candles, books and prints, woollen cloth and velveret, pewter plates and worsted stockings. There'd been a trade in children too, way back, but it was a time no one spoke of now.

To Alec, as a boy and then as a young man, it seemed that Aberdeen must be the centre of the world, sitting as it did at the heart of all this prosperous clamour. In only a matter of days barley grown in the lochland fields would be on sale in Rotterdam; salmon caught on Monday in the River Dee would by Friday be filling bellies in London and Ostend; bricks quarried and baked not half a mile away in the Seaton kilns built houses for gentlefolk in far-off Riga. Aberdeen might be a town at the most northerly end of the kingdom, eight hundred miles from the English capital, but the view from the harbour was the world itself.

It has never left him, the stir of excitement at the sight of the quayside, and the estuary dotted with sails. He loves this town, with its restless shifting light, its thousand shades of grey; loves the way it nestles in the embrace of the Dee and the Don, yet boldly tips its face towards the world. He loves the wide sweep of the new streets, the sweet-sharp air blowing in from the surrounding hills; especially he loves this sensation of being in the centre and on the edge of everything, at one and the same time.

Alec turns to face north once more, letting his eye travel over the familiar landmarks: the blunt tower of Marischal College, the domed crown of King's and, in the distance, the roofs of the Old Town and the metallic glint of the Don. Things come in twos here: two rivers, two towns, two universities. But to the east, the ace to trump them all: the uncompromising singularity of the sea. Whichever way you're heading, it is always there, behind you, ahead of you, to one side or another: the great pewter platter of the ocean stretching into the distance as far as the eye can see.

Back in his study, Alec turns to a clean page in his notebook and at the top, in his neat, clear hand, writes the words:

Inflammatory or Putrid?

It is all very well to lecture on theories of classification, but patients do not exist in the realm of theory. While theories take gradual shape, patients live and suffer and die. Twelve women carried off while he gropes his way blindly towards understanding. The physician must act. Must respond to present and pressing necessity. Controversy may reign in the kingdom of theory, but here on earth action is required.

Putrid or inflammatory? That is the question. One of the questions. He cannot treat the disease with confidence until this matter is decided to his satisfaction. If putrid, the disease must be treated with hot compresses, warming cordials. If inflammatory, with purges and bleeding. It cannot be both. It must be one or the other. Alec has combed his study shelves in the past weeks, read every word on the subject he can find there, but there is nothing in any of his books to assuage concern. It has a name, yes, but what use is a name when so little else is known? No two authorities are agreed on any aspect of the disease, besides its name and its symptoms, and not always that. For every physician who argues it is inflammatory, another insists it is putrid; for every one who proclaims the disease is contagious, three more assert it never is; for every one who argues for a single cause, half a dozen others say it comes from many different causes. It is not just controversy that reigns, but downright confusion. Ignorance and opinion parading as conclusive evidence. Scant facts manipulated by first one author then another to suit their own particular theory. Uncertain description transformed into certain proof. How is one to proceed in any direction with such wildly contradictory signposts to guide the way? How, moreover, is one to break the news that a disease as deadly as the plague is even now seeking out its next victim, when almost nothing else is known for sure? Neither cause, nor means of prevention, nor cure.

Alec goes over the facts again, listing them under the heading he has made.

A disease that only ever arises in lying-in women.

Fact.

A disease that is connected in some way to pregnancy and labour.

Fact.

He thinks of the swollen hands and thickened ankles of his pregnant patients, the bloating they complain of as their wombs swell and their blood thickens; he thinks of the heavy veined breasts, the distended labia; of the uterus gradually rising out of the pelvis to fill the cavity of the abdomen; of the foetus slowly expanding in its dark lake of amniotic fluid.

Both natural physical states, accompanied by a large number of natural physical changes, all of which are essentially inflammatory in nature.

Fact.

Alec leans back in his chair and sighs. How and why should a disease that arises from a physical state that is essentially inflammatory, and that manifests with inflammatory symptoms in its earliest stages, suddenly become putrid? There is no way to account for such a great reversal. Which is the predisposing cause and which the immediate: the inflammation or the putrefaction? Dr Hulme, whose opinion Alec respects on most matters, is certain the chief predisposing cause is the pressure of the gravid uterus against the intestines and omentum, the immediate cause being inflammation of these parts. Yet both Sydenham and Boerhaave, the greatest authorities of all, have asserted the disease is putrid in nature, pointing to the symptoms of suppression, the 'awfy bad smell' as McRae so succinctly put it, the ample proof of putrefaction on opening victims of the disease. And yet, and yet.

The evidence points in both directions.

Fact.

Alec puts down his pen and presses both palms against his face. He lets his hands hold the weight of his head for a moment; kneads his forehead with his fingertips. *Forget authority*, he tells himself. *Go back a step. Don't rush at it.* He has always rushed at everything, all his life.

He turns to a fresh page of the notebook and writes a new heading.

External Symptoms

He underlines the heading with two thin lines, then starts to list all the symptoms he can think of. The last entry reads:

Face flushed – a deep red colour on cheeks

He hesitates for a second before adding the words:

also on joints – elbows, knuckles &c.

Two rivers, two towns, two universities. And now two diseases. Erysipelas and puerperal fever. Nothing to link them but this odd discoloration of the skin and the timing of the outbreaks, both of which could be nothing more than coincidence. But if there *were* a connection? Erysipelas is known to be an inflammatory disease. Is it just stubbornness that pushes the two conditions together in his mind, as irresistibly attracted as magnet ends? It goes against reason. There is no evidence to support the idea, and how many times has he exhorted his students to be wary of ideas without evidence?

With a groan of exasperation, Alec pushes the notebook away. In the fireplace the last log settles down into its bed of greying ash. The room has grown cold as he's been working and he is sitting now in near darkness. Earlier that afternoon, as he'd looked out at the sea from the head of the brae, an unsettling sensation of exposure had suddenly gripped him. There'd been something unnerving about that vast expanse of ocean. Holland is out there, he'd told himself, and Norway and Denmark, and further still, Iceland and Greenland. But the feeling of precariousness remained. It hadn't helped, knowing that the earth curved away in a never-ending surface of land and water, water and land, that there was no edge. He still could not shake the feeling that the wheeling gulls, the granite hills, the heavy seas might catch him up in their vertiginous motion and pitch him into the emptiness; that there was nothing out there, just the grey sheet of the waves and, beyond the waves, the emptiness of space.

Proof. He needs proof.

Outside rain is falling. The weathervane creaks and moans in the wind.

All right then. It must be done, and soon, before the weather turns. The Annual General Count is approaching and he will need to account for himself. Diagnosis based only on outward appearances is like trying to read a book by its cover. To learn one must open the boards. Read the message written inside, inscribed on the organs, muscles, arteries, bones: the revealed truth. He must see for himself. With or without the families' consent.

22

Advertised for sale in the *Aberdeen Journal*, Tuesday, 23 March 1790

China silk STOCKINGS (white) for ladies and gentlemen; also, glazed, silk and lawn Umbrellas, Bathing Caps, and Hat-Covers, Jewellery, gold Wares, and Silver Plate – Pistols, Powder Flasks, Shot Bags – Telescopes, Microscopes, and other optical instruments. Also, Mitts and Purses in great Variety.

RED and WHITE CLOVER SEEDS, of the best quality

PAINTINGS, in Landscape and History, copied from the works of West, Kauffman, Cipriani &c. Also, Silver Buckles and other articles of Plate, Watches, Jewellery &c.

Field of SEVEN ACRES, including Clay-pits, barn, stable, kiln, mill and utensils of every kind, and style, used for brick manufactory.

Lavoisier's ELEMENTS of CHEMISTRY, with 13 plates, 8vo, 7s boards. *Also* Smellie's PHILOSOPHY of NATURAL HISTORY, 4to, 2s boards, Rotherham's Letter to Smellie on the Sexe of Plants, 1s.

Broad and narrow CLOTHS, Hunters, Duffles, Shalloons, Fustians, Linens, Durrants, Temmies, Flannels, Callimancoes, Camblets, Cambletees, Corduroys, Velvets and Velverets, Printed Cottons, Muslins and Muslinets, Sattin, Sewing Silk, Hair, Thread, Metal and Hair Buttons, &c.

FRUIT TREES, an excellent assortment, viz Apples, Pears, Cherries, Plumbs, Nectarens, Peaches, and Apricots, all from Brompton Park, in England.

MAREDENT's DROPS, the first Antiscorbutic extant, for the relief of the Scorbutic, Scrofulous and Leprous.

23

Mistress Glegg settles herself on the chaise longue by the window and casts an appraising glance about the room. The clock on the mantelpiece has not been wound and the upholstery of the sofa is threadbare in a place or two, but otherwise everything appears to be in order. But then appearances, as Alice Glegg knows, can be deceptive. She has made sure to call regularly, ever since witnessing the strange turn the doctor's wife took at her niece's christening. Twice a week at eleven o'clock, Wednesdays and Fridays. It is quite an inconvenience when she has so many other poor souls to visit, but Mistress Gordon has such a distracted air about her these days that Mistress Glegg regards it as the least she can do. All the same, it's a little much to be kept waiting like this, when she's come across town in such drabbly weather. A little refreshment would not have gone amiss. But the maid has shown her into the parlour and disappeared without even offering to take her cloak and bonnet. Another small sign that all is not quite as it should be in the doctor's household.

Hearing a low rustling outside the parlour door, Mistress Glegg adjusts her expression of disapproval to one of greeting. The child who enters stops the moment she sees her and stands motionless in the doorway, staring at Mistress Glegg with huge dark eyes, not saying a word. Then the maid is swooping down on her, pulling her away from the door.

'Mary! Get awa oot o there! Ye musnae go troubling—'

Catching sight of Mistress Glegg watching them through the half-open doorway, Annie stops tugging at Mary, remembering suddenly that she has not taken the minister's wife's wet cloak, and wondering whether or not she should do so now, but at that moment Elizabeth arrives. Her cheeks are

flushed and one hand is raised to her hair, thrusting her cap
pins into place. Annie and Mary fall back, out of her path.
Elizabeth passes them without a word or even a glance, as if
she hasn't seen them. She pulls the parlour door shut behind
her.

'Mistress Glegg – I'm so sorry – so kind of you to – have
you been offered anything?'

The minister's wife, gratified by so much evidence of
disarray in so short a space of time, smiles graciously.

'Please don't be worrying about me, Mistress Gordon. It is
you we are all concerned for.'

Elizabeth feels herself dwindling under Mistress Glegg's
unctuous gaze.

'Really, there is nothing the matter. I am quite better
now—'

She takes a seat and tries to compose herself, but Mistress
Glegg is not to be deflected.

'Better? Nonsense, my dear! But I'm afraid I am spoiling
your sofa with my wet clothes—'

'Oh! Forgive me!' Elizabeth cries, leaping up again and
giving the bell a sharp ring. 'That stupid girl! What was she
thinking of!'

Annie, waiting on the other side of the door, appears at
once, red-faced and as flustered as her mistress.

As soon as Annie has retreated with the dripping garments
Mistress Glegg resumes. 'You are too much alone for your
own good, my dear. When my sister-in-law moved to Derby-
shire, you know, her spirits became quite depressed for want
of company.'

'I have my sister, and Mary—' Elizabeth counters faintly.

'Och, a wee girl's no company. And with your man as busy
as he is.' The minister's wife lowers her voice and adds: 'Such
a terrible business! How many is it now? I heard six.'

'Twelve.'

The second the word has left her lips, Elizabeth regrets it.

The 'terrible business' is Mistress Glegg's favourite topic of conversation. Now she's on her rock, she will cling to it.

'Twelve! Indeed! That many? My sister-in-law met a physician from Manchester who'd lost sixteen on the lying-in ward there in the space of three months.'

Elizabeth closes her eyes, trying to stifle a sudden curling surge of nausea. She reaches again for the bell.

'Will you take tea, Mistress Glegg? You've come all this way and had nothing.'

But Mistress Glegg waves the offer aside.

'I don't know what Dr Gordon thinks – ' Mistress Glegg's voice has dropped to a low conspiratorial note – 'but Reverend Glegg considers it a sign.'

'A sign?'

'Aye, a sign, Mistress Gordon. A warning to folk to mend their ways. There's too many bairns born out of wedlock, Mr Glegg says. Too much wickedness and wantonness and folk turning a blind eye on all sides.'

An avid gleam has crept into Mistress Glegg's pale blue eyes.

'You're not suggesting – ' Elizabeth can hardly bring herself to say it – 'that Mistress Duncan – Mistress Anthony—'

Mistress Glegg nods serenely. 'Who knows what lies hidden in folk's hearts? Only the Good Lord knows for sure. Nothing is hidden from Him, of course. Now, I'm not saying anything against poor Jenny Duncan, but let's not be forgetting that her own mother sat six weeks on the punishment pew for her wickedness. I was only a wee girl at the time, but I remember it well. It may be their own sins or the sins of the parents, Mr Glegg says, but it is always, to be sure, just punishment for some thing or other.'

With a great effort, Elizabeth moves her hand to the bell and shakes it. She passes the hour that follows in a dream. Annie brings the tea. It is poured and sugared and sipped. The theft of William Mitchell's white mare is talked of, and the forthcoming sale of hosiery at the Schoolhill manufactury. A kirkhouse is to be built at Beaulie, the minister's wife informs her; the Musical Society is to perform a new composition by Mr Peacock...

When Mistress Glegg finally departs, Elizabeth has no strength left to face the day and retires to her room, telling Annie not to disturb her. She lies on the bed with the curtains drawn against the unsteady spring light, drifting in and out of sleep, half-listening to the muffled noises of the street outside, the modulating keys of the household as it shifts from afternoon to early evening. She hears the bell ring for the post, and Annie's feet racketing back and forth from the scullery to the front door, hears her singing to Mary, and the high reedy answer of the child's voice joining in. There are sudden showers of rain, followed by flares of feeble sunshine, then another downpour. From the shrouded bed she follows the shape of the day with her mind, but Alice Glegg's words are an imprisoning web from which there is no escape. Can it be true? Is there such wickedness in the town? Have those poor women forfeited their lives for it? Worse than the rack, Alec said after Alison Mennie died: a torture worse than labour itself. For what crimes exactly? It is too horrible to contemplate.

The slaves were punished for stealing or disobedience or laziness. Just punishment, her father used to say, a necessary evil. Any leniency and they'd have their own lives to answer for it, as other planters had. John Tanner was dragged from his bed and burnt to death in his own yard. Ten years' investment reduced to blackened stubble in a single night. Tanner's wife and children escaped with their lives, but nothing more. The negroes were savages at heart, indolent by nature: the only law they understood was the whip. Her three brothers nodded their agreement whenever Papa reminded them of this, but Elizabeth sometimes found it hard to see what the punishments were for. Merely for standing still, or so it appeared from the glimpse of the cane fields she could see if she looked sideways out of the upstairs windows. Even when there was nothing to be seen out there but the long wavering lines bent low over their hoeing and digging and staking, you could still, throughout the day, hear the whine of the lash, followed by the high crack it made as it split the air. It gave her the same feeling as when Willie and Tommy pulled the wings off butterflies, or cut the tails and ears off the squirming bodies of the mice they'd snared. They mocked her for crying, but it made no difference to the way she felt inside, the same way she felt when Papa took off his belt and beat one of them for some act of disobedience. That, too, just punishment.

She was kept indoors on public whipping days, even the veranda was out of bounds, but the noise of it carried up the hill on the breeze. Old Amos wore his long face all day and would not look at her, and Marie made so much banging with the pots and pans in the washroom that Mama would sigh and grimace and sooner or later go and have words. At night in the throbbing heat that turned the bed-sheets into damp ropes around her legs and arms, her brothers would tell her what they'd seen. How the negro was laid out on his belly, face to the ground, his neck weighted with irons, his hands and feet fastened to four stakes driven into the earth so he could not move. How he struggled and squealed at first, but after a while fell silent and soon lay perfectly still, not moving at all. How the sun beat down and made them sweat. How one or two of the female negroes wept and were thrashed for it. How, after sixty lashes, there was nothing to be seen of skin any more, it was just gore from waist to calf. How McKenzie ordered the overseer to pickle the wounds. How he laughed while it was done. Tommy chuckled too in the darkness, remembering. Later still, after the boys had finally tired of their tale and fallen asleep, Elizabeth would lie awake listening to the hectic clicking of the cicadas and the low singing that drifted up from the huts, a sound so sweet and slow and melancholy it made her chest hurt. Sometimes, drawn by the music, she would creep over to the window, pressing herself against the screen to let the night air cool her sticky skin. Below the Great House the darkness lay in thick folds except for flickering pockets of light from the fires. Shadowy figures shifted about in the orange glow.

For a day or two after it was as if the ground were covered in shards of invisible glass. The house-slaves kept their eyes to the ground, placed their feet with care. Everyone moved more slowly than usual, not only the servants. Mama hardly moved at all, just sat on the veranda in the rocker with her veil pulled down over her face so you could not see her eyes, just the thin straight line of her mouth. McKenzie alone seemed in high spirits, riding up to the house to ask if the boys would like to go fishing, doffing his hat to Mama with a festival air, his blind eye rolling in its socket. 'Thank you, McKenzie, but not today,' Mama would say in the cold voice she used when she disapproved of something. It was the voice she always used when she spoke to McKenzie, and Elizabeth was glad of it. Even first thing in the morning he smelled of drink and cruelty. She was relieved when he turned and rode away again, his whip coiled on the saddle, his long rifle bumping against his shoulder-blades. But her brothers complained bitterly at being denied these expeditions, Tommy especially. He was nearly eleven, old enough to take care of himself. McKenzie knew all the best places and Papa never had time; couldn't they please go, just this once? Mama always said no, always had some reason why today was not the day for fishing or swimming or tracking. Elizabeth could tell that Mama did not like McKenzie's blind eye either, or his twisted smile, or the way his gun nudged at his back as he rode off down the drive.

24

The capped toe of Bannerman's cane connects with the floor-boards in hollow little beats. Toc-toc-toc. The impatient rhythm is the only sound in the icy garret.

'Seems your lads have let us down, Gordon.'

The other men grunt their assent to Bannerman's opinion. They've been waiting over an hour now, wrapped in their cloaks and mufflers to keep as warm as is possible until the very last moment. A full moon shines through the skylight, casting a clean white lozenge of light on to the empty table. Beside it, the bucket of sawdust is full and ready.

'They'll come,' Alec says.

'Aye,' Bannerman grumbles, 'and we'll freeze to death waiting for them.'

Bannerman pulls out his flask, takes a swig and offers it to Skene. Alec stamps his feet on the boards to try and bring the circulation back to his toes. The conditions are perfect. Where the devil have the lads got to? Trouble with the watch is all they need. McRae swore it was all arranged. The faces of the assembled men are shadowed and impossible to read, but the atmosphere is tense. As the minutes have passed, they've grown more and more uneasy. None of them wants to be found here and the delay is making them nervous. In any case they must be out by dawn and the bells have already struck two.

There's a dull thud at last from downstairs as the door on to the street opens and then swings shut. The sound is followed by a low whistle.

'About time,' Skene says, getting to his feet.

Several pairs of feet are mounting the stairs, accompanied by a good deal of muttering and cursing. Alec signals to Rabbie to unlock the garret door and a moment later McRae,

McGrigor and Ogilvie appear, staggering under the weight of the sack they are half-carrying, half-dragging between them.

'Where d'ye want it?' McRae's voice is nonchalant.

'What kept you?' Alec barks. 'There!' He nods towards the table, shrugging off his coat and jacket, rolling up his sleeves.

'A close run we had o it tonight!' McRae's eyes are shining under the wide brim of his hat. This is his kind of study: night-lit and risk-filled, not sitting on his backside taking notes in classrooms. 'We'd to wrap it in Ogilvie's cloak an prop it upright atween us on the cart. Told the watch twas a fellow colleeginer, a wee drop the worse for wear. Said we was jist seein him to his bed afore he came to ony mair harm.'

'Never mind that,' Alec snaps. 'Get it up here and be quick about it.'

There's a good deal more pushing and heaving as McRae and the others jostle the sack on to the table. That done, McRae pulls out his knife. With a harsh ripping sound the hessian splits apart and the released contents spill out.

'Catch it!'

Rabbie leaps forward, just managing to break the body's fall before it hits the ground. McRae and Ogilvie start to snigger. Alec, too, feels an urge to laugh at the sight of the corpse lolling in his apprentice's arms, its head resting affectionately on his shoulder, one hand draped lovingly around his neck.

'Stop laughing and help me! She stinks!'

It's only when the corpse has been manoeuvred out of Rabbie's arms and back on to the table that Alec's glance travels from the tell-tale mound of the swollen belly to the face. The laughter dies in his throat. The features, illuminated in part by the lamplight, in part by the moon, are altered by age and by death, but are nevertheless as familiar to him as his own. A face he'd once searched for in chapel on Sunday mornings. A face he'd held between his own two hands more often than he can remember, lovely then as a flower. Cheeks he'd covered with kisses. Lips he'd drunk from. That whole long summer he'd wanted nothing but to lie in her arms, breathe her in, taste her skin, the spice scent of her on his fingers. It was the summer after his mother died, but all he could think of was Mary McDonald's honeyed limbs and cornflower eyes.

'Where did you get—?'

'Gilcomston kirkyard,' McRae sounds pleased with himself.

Behind him, Skene clears his throat. 'One of mine,' he says. 'Day before yesterday.'

'Oh! I—'

But what does it matter now whose she is or was. The present is the clue to the past. James Hutton has said as much of rocks and the same is true of bodies. That is all that matters now.

Alec makes the first incision, from just below the breastplate down to the pelvic bone, scything through the layers of skin and fat and muscle. As the blade pierces the wall of the abdomen, a great belch of gangrenous air fills the room. The other men recoil in disgust. Even Alec has to pause for a moment, knocked back by the smell. A flood of stinking liquid gushes through the opening he has made. Rabbie grabs a basin to catch the fluid as it seeps over the sides of the corpse to the floor. The others cover their noses and press closer to get a better look as Alec peels back the flaps of outer flesh. The abdominal muscles are sound, but the scene beneath the muscle wall makes him pause again. From the pelvis to the intestines, the entire abdominal cavity is swimming in a thick yellow liquor. Floating about on its surface are lumps of pus, like globules of grease in a bowl of broth.

'*Christ!*' Skene exclaims. 'What a mess!'

The intestines themselves are greatly distended, as if someone had taken a pair of bellows and pumped them full of air. They are blackened in places and glued together with small parcels of a white fatty substance. Alec pushes them to one side to find the liver. This, too, is grossly swollen and pressed up hard against the diaphragm. Alec scoops it out and hands it to Skene, who examines it briefly, then passes it round for the others to inspect.

Gritting his teeth against the smell, Alec turns back to the corpse. It's hard to know where to begin with the mangled remains before him. What should have been the protective curtain of the omentum is in an entirely mortified state. Pushed out of place by the distension of the other organs, it is now lying rumpled up against the arch of the colon, which, from its caput along the whole course of the ascending arch, is inflamed and running into gangrene. It takes Alec a moment even to recognize the stomach: bloated to more than twice its normal size, almost nothing is left of the ruggae; its ridged surface is as smooth and slippery as a freshly peeled egg. Alec prods the membrane with one finger. Taut as a drum skin. Sliding his hand under the stomach, taking care not to dislodge the connecting tubes, he lifts it out of the abdominal cavity. Signalling to Rabbie to hold the bowl in place beneath it, he punctures the membrane with the point of his knife. With a hiss of stinking air, followed by a dark gush of liquid, the stomach deflates.

'One quart,' Rabbie says, when the flow finally stops. Alec drops the emptied organ on to the sawdust at his feet, conscious suddenly of his own loud breathing, the cold trickle of sweat on his temples. The left ovarium is sound, but the right is totally wasted. The perinæum is badly ripped from the birth, but not diseased. Only the uterus, tucked neatly under the pelvic bone, small and contracted, is as it should be.

From out in the street, the teller rings the night bell. Four in the morning. They must be out, the body removed at once. Alec straightens up, rubbing his hands. 'Well, gentlemen, I think we've seen enough for tonight.'

He leaves the students to stuff the organs back into the

corpse and close it up. They will have to hide it somewhere until a safe moment comes to bury it, out in the hills or on the moor. But that's no concern of his. Better the physicians don't know certain things. Safer for them all. A bucket of cold water stands by the door. Alec gives his hands a quick rinse, splashing the water up to his elbows to detach the little shreds of skin and tissue that have caught in the hairs on his arms, then rolls down his shirtsleeves and pulls on his jacket. He, for one, has seen enough.

'So what are you saying?' Skene asks, as they walk away from Bannerman's house a short while later.

Dawn is breaking over their heads, the darkness thinning into milky light. It will be a fine day.

'That it's not a putrid disease.'

'In Christ's name, man!' Skene stops in his tracks and stares at Alec with unmasked incredulity. Rabbie too looks surprised. 'There was nothing there but putrefaction!'

'A consequence of the disease, not its cause.'

'Your evidence?'

Alec does not reply at once. They are standing at the top of Marischal Street, the wide expanse of the Plainstanes in front of them. The square, always so crowded and noisy by day, is silent and perfectly still. The imposing façades of the court and town house have a brooding look to them. In the dawn light the dressed granite is a pearly grey.

'How long was she ill?'

'Ten days in all.'

'And you treated her with?'

'Heating cordials. The usual remedies.'

'Precisely! You treated it like a putrid disease, when in fact it was inflammatory. Or started out as such. The extensive putrefaction was the consequence of letting the inflammation go untreated.'

'Are you suggesting I am to blame for the woman's death?'

'I couldn't give a fig who's to blame. Don't you see? Those parts not yet putrified were all in a state of inflammation. The uterus, where you'd expect greatest damage, was sound.'

'In this case, perhaps.'

'In every account of every case I've ever read! I tell you, Skene, we have all this time been confounding consequence and cause. I am convinced of it.'

It's only afterwards, alone in his study, too wide awake for sleep, that he thinks about her as a woman. Thinks of the implications of those devastated organs. Of her suffering. Worse than the torments of labour. Rotting away from the inside, putrefying and dissolving as she lived. Ten days in mortal agony. It was a wonder she'd endured as long as she had. Not only her, all of them. The external symptoms were the mere shadow of the beast, the faintest trace of its full fury. No wonder they screamed out when he touched the swollen abdomen. No wonder they could scarcely breathe. The slightest additional pressure on the internal parts must have caused them the most exquisite pain.

He pulls his notebook towards him. Affixes a new nib to the quill. Dips it in the inkpot.

Interval Between Onset of Fever and Death

He draws a single vertical line down the centre of the page and makes two sub-headings, one for each column; writes *Time from first attack* at the top of the first, and *Number of cases* at the top of the second. Sifting back through the case notes, he extracts the relevant figures and starts to insert them in the table he has just drawn. He is sure now of one thing: the site of greatest decomposition varies from one patient to the next, depending on where the disease first concentrates its attack and for how long it remains untreated, but once the initial inflammation has become putrid, the disease is beyond remedy.

Alec adjusts the lamp wick, and studies the completed table in the renewed pool of light.

Time from first attack	Number of cases
24 hours	0
36 hours	0
three days	1
five days	8
seven days	3
ten days	1

It's staring him in the face. The sample is small, admittedly: twelve cases of his own, plus Skene's, but of those, the majority have died on the fifth day. The fifth, then, must be reckoned the critical day, the day when the crisis proves salutary or otherwise. If the disease is not arrested by the fifth day there can be little chance of recovery. The implications expand rapidly in Alec's mind. If the disease must be arrested by the fifth day, then the disease must be borne out of the body considerably *before* the fifth day. And if this is correct, if a cure must indeed be affected within just five days, why then, he must greatly increase the force of his assault on the disease. Like must cure like. The treatment must be equal in vehemence to the illness itself, the methods employed must be as violent. Yes, *this* makes sense. It is an inflammatory disease, and must be treated as such. Whatever the midwives say, whatever the tracts and treatises by other physicians say, the proper treatment for the disease must be venesection, and not only in the late stages but at the very beginning. Denman is wrong. Clarke and White are wrong. Cooper is wrong. They are all wrong. Alec can see his own mistake, too: until now he has been bleeding not too freely, but not freely enough. He has been taking not too much blood, but too little. Thirteen cases. All of them bled too little, too late, or not at all. It is too soon for him to be absolutely sure, but it is something: it is a start.

25

April

When John Webster's wife gives birth a week later, Alec is ready. He instructs the midwife to keep constant watch and to call him at the slightest sign of fever or pain.

'It may look to you like after-pains or milk fever, but however it appears, Mistress Philp, you must send for me without delay, do you understand?'

And for once the midwife does as she is told. When the first rigor strikes, five hours after the birth, she calls for Alec and he in turn wastes not a moment.

'We will bleed right away, Mr Donald. Eighteen ounces, if you please.'

Rabbie looks at him, unsure if he has heard correctly.

'Eighteen, Dr Gordon?'

'That is what I said.'

Without another word, Rabbie applies the tourniquet to the upper arm, positions the bowl under the elbow and with a swift sweep of the lancet incises the vein. Like a misconceived rainbow, the blood bursts from the cut in a bright arc of scarlet, before slowing to a steady pulsing stream. He watches the fluid creep up the calibrations on the bowl. Eight. Ten. Twelve. Eliza Webster's eyes have glazed over and are rolling back under the lids.

'She's fainting!'

'Keep going.'

Fifteen. Sixteen.

Rabbie looks past the bowl at his feet. The tips of his shoes are spattered with tiny droplets of blood. On the bed beside him, the woman has lost consciousness.

'Surely that's enough, Dr Gordon,' Mistress Philp intervenes, no longer able to conceal her agitation, but Alec ignores her.

'Quiet!'

Seventeen.

'You will kill her!' The midwife's voice is shrill with alarm.

'And if I stop now,' he replies coldly, meeting Mistress Philp's terrified gaze full-on, 'the disease will do the same.'

Eighteen.

'That's will do!'

Rabbie at once staunches the flow. He feels sick and faint himself. He has never taken so much blood before. In the bowl on his knees, the crimson pool lies thick and velvety, the sizy puckering already at the edges. For the first time since being apprenticed to Alec, he finds himself doubting his judgement. Can it be right to draw so much?

'Keep her quiet,' Alec is saying to the midwife. 'You may give an opiate draft if the fever returns and a clyster every four hours. Keep the room well aired and on no account give heating cordials, do you understand? She must be kept cool and quiet. Call me at once if her condition worsens.'

But he is hopeful as he and Rabbie step out into Castle Street. More than hopeful. He feels in command once more, does not notice the younger man's stricken expression. 'Is it really safe?' Rabbie asks. 'To take blood in such quantities? If she dies . . .'

But Alec cuts him off.

'I have seen pregnant women lose upwards of two to four pounds of blood in the case of flooding and afterwards make good recoveries. In the case of pneumonic inflammation, a man of tolerable strength may lose four to five pounds of blood in the course of two or three days and be none the worse. It is custom not science that dictates otherwise for women in childbed.'

His apprentice says nothing.

'Trust me,' Alec says, more gently. 'The cure is severe, but it is short. It will cure the patient in a few days, or not at all.'

And for two days it seems the treatment may have worked. The fever abates. The pain subsides. On the third day, however, the symptoms all return. By the evening of the fifth day, the scene is closed.

'Eighteen ounces was not sufficient,' is Alec's verdict. 'With twenty-two we would have had success.'

26

The midwives do not share Alec's view.

'Echteen?'

'Aye, and sworn to take passin aat the next time.'

'The man's ta'en leave o his wits.'

The women have gathered at the Plainstanes, not by any official arrangement but by some unspoken consensus, as the starlings in autumn know, without any audible command, to rise from the boughs of the trees at the precise same moment, conjoin in midair and twist, in artlessly synchronized motion, to left or to right.

'He muthert Eliza Webster,' says Meredith Philp, her voice tremulous with the memory. 'I watcht him do it wi my ain een.'

'An no just Eliza,' says Jennifer Elgin, darkly. 'All the ither afore her.'

In the high walls of the Tolbooth the mica crystals flash. Overhead the gulls wheel and shriek.

'But if he's set on bleedin,' says Alice Blake, 'fit are we to do? A howdie's word has no weight agin tha physeeshun's.'

'True enough, an tis we'll be getting the blame for the deiths if this wags on.'

The other women nod.

'We mus let it be known,' Jennifer Elgin says at last. 'Aboot the bleedin.' Her long, bony face has a resolute cast to it. 'Or, mind my words, tis wirsels will pay the price.'

27

Elizabeth was taught to speak in the English manner, first in Antigua, where all the children learnt a mangled tongue of English, Scots and Creole, and later in Aberdeen under instruction from her governess. It is another obstacle between herself and the townfolk, the women in particular. As if being the physician's wife weren't obstacle enough. They suspect her of being privy to their secrets, when in truth she knows nothing. Seeing the group of midwives gathered on the steps of the Plainstanes, she ducks her head and skirts around the far side of the Castlegate, tugging Mary after her, reluctant even to bid the women good morning lest in so doing she should give them any further cause for enmity. She and Mary are on their way home, having been to see Isabella and the baby, who is beginning to smile: a wide gummy piece of enchantment that makes Elizabeth think of Meg, although she tries to shake off the memory as quickly as it takes hold of her. It is not only her niece who reminds her, everything these days conspires to drive her thoughts in unwanted directions: the new lambs tottering in the fields behind the house; the goslings skittering over the surface of the Denburn; the young women coming from market with their bairns strapped to their breasts. Other things too remind her: rain falling on the birch leaves, a silver-backed hairbrush, a sheet billowing on a washing-line. Her mind has become a close-meshed net, snaring every minnow that swims its way. Sometimes the past seems so near at hand it is hard to remember that she is a married woman with a child of her own, that the past is the past and there is only today and tomorrow and the next day to be got through, that nothing of the time before will ever change, no matter how many tomorrows she is granted or spared. Hearing Annie calling for Mary that morning, it was Marie's voice she'd heard. *Venez vite! Depêchez-vous!* And at once she was back at Harvie's End, with the carriage standing in the drive and about to leave without her if she did not come at once.

Every Sunday without fail, except in the hurricane season, they took the carriage into St Johns. There was only the one road: down the hill, past the boil-house and the cane fields, through the forest to the coast. Papa rarely came with them. Even when he was home there was business on the estate to attend to: machinery to be inspected, correspondence to catch up on, accounts to be settled. The carriage was stifling, with or without Papa: the curtains drawn, the six of them pressed up against one another, Charlie wriggling in his Sunday britches, Willie and Tommy pinching him when Mama was not looking, making him squeal and squirm all the more until he earned himself a sharp slap from Mama, the imprint of her fingers blooming on his bare leg in four thin scarlet welts. Elizabeth, wedged between Marie and Mama, held herself as far apart as she could from the heat of their bodies, tilting her face to the carriage window to try and catch a dusting of air on her cheeks.

Long before they saw the town, they could smell it: salt-cod and rotting vegetables and the sharp tang of human sweat. A quarter of a mile to leeward it filled the air, but there was no other way into town, no avoiding it. Along the roadside trailed a steady line of negroes, swaying towers of baskets perched on their heads, dust clouds billowing round their ankles. Elizabeth sometimes tried to catch a glimpse of the women's faces as they passed, but the curtains and the jolting of the carriage made it hard to see. If Marie saw anyone she knew, she never gave any sign of it. Soon they could hear the clamour of the market ahead of them: voices shouting and calling to one another; poultry squawking; pigs squealing; dogs barking. Then they were passing through the thick of it, the throng of negroes and mulattos on every side forcing the carriage to slow to a walking pace.

The slaves had been gathering since daybreak, come from all over the island to sell anything and everything they could. Yams, edda, cassava and shaddock. The carriage crawling forwards now. Okra, plantain and soursop. So very many of them. Mango, guava, pomegranate, star apple. Haggling and bartering, lounging and laughing, jabbering and arguing, sweating and pissing. Not a white face to be seen. On the plantation they never seemed so many, though Papa never tired of reminding them of the facts. *Fifty of them to every one of us and don't ever forget it.* But here at the market, the negroes seemed to have multiplied in number. ('Like rats,' said Tommy inside the sweltering carriage to no one in particular, 'like cockroaches.') Hardly moving forwards at all by this time, the immense press of slaves all about them, and Elizabeth able to see all she wants. Necklaces of cowrie shells and beaten tin; ladies' fans inlaid with mother-of-pearl or brilliant with plumes; wooden dolphins, arrested in mid-leap; dancing figures carved from turtle shell and cedar wood, and everywhere, everywhere, the slaves: the men so bold in their nakedness, wearing nothing but tattered breeches, a scrap of shirt; the women like exotic birds in checkered headdresses, striped petticoats, patterned shawls. The whirl of colours making Elizabeth's head swim. The confusion of smells – sweet, sour, fresh, foul – making it hard to breathe. Only when they were out the other side did Mama bang on the roof of the carriage with her cane: the signal to Amos to stop and set Marie down. They'd collect her again on the journey home. By then the market would be over and the singing and dancing would have begun. The men would be playing their toombahs and banjars and shak-shaks, the women twisting and bending to the music, clapping their hands so fast their fingers a blur, shaking their shell-strings with sudden high whoops and piercing wails, jiggling and wriggling their shoulders and hips, leaping and spinning, stamping the earth with their bare feet, flinging their arms up into the air and down again, to one side then the other. The strangest thing, to Elizabeth's mind, was how happy they looked as they danced, with their shining eyes and their faces upturned to the sky. She had never seen that expression on the face of any white she knew. That thought made her head spin too.

After the terrifying crush of the market, the cool interior of the church was always a relief; within its solid walls, Elizabeth felt safe again. Mama knelt straight away to pray, head bent low over her hands, lips moving silently. Mama never looked more beautiful than when she was in church, praying like this or sitting – perfectly still, straight-backed – intent on the minister's words. She was like a painting: pure, untouchable. At these moments, Elizabeth felt a sensation of mingled love and yearning that almost overwhelmed her, felt acutely her own insignificance, yet at the same time was filled with a boundless aching devotion: she would willingly have died for Mama if she had commanded it.

Directly after the service, they walked round the side of the church to the graveyard. The gravestones were so small they could not be seen from the path. Two little slabs side by side on the sun-singed grass. Elizabeth hung back as Mama placed fresh flowers on the graves, not liking to think of her sisters trapped there in the dark earth. ('They're dead, you stupid!' Tommy said, his upper lip curling. 'They don't care.') It was not Mary she minded for, but Meg. She was just a baby herself when Mary was born, had no memory of her, alive or dead. But Meg had dimples in her cheeks when she smiled and her eyes shone with pleasure when she saw Elizabeth's face. When Elizabeth bent over the crib to kiss her, Meg stretched out a plump little fist and grabbed hold of her hair, clutching it with all her might, as if she would never let her go. Tommy and Willie and Charlie had each other; Meg was hers. She was allowed to carry her around the bedroom and out on to the veranda, a bulky bundle that filled her arms. She helped Marie to bathe her and dress her, and when that was done, she watched her suckling, the little pink mouth tugging greedily at the long black dug. She liked to sing to her, or tickle her belly to make her laugh, rock her crib to help her sleep. Once Meg learnt to crawl, they would scuttle back and forth along the upstairs landing, or lie on their backs in the grass and watch the leaves shifting above their heads. 'Dat baby got sunshine in her soul,' Marie said. Even Mama smiled sometimes when she saw them together, would lift her hand and graze Elizabeth's cheek with her gloved knuckles, say what a kind sister she was, what a good little mother she made. But then, one morning, Meg lay in her crib, blue and limp, and no amount of tickling or singing would wake her. It was Marie who found Elizabeth there; Marie who wrenched her away and seized up the baby, shaking her, rocking her, crying *No! No! No!* over and over; Marie who ran from the room with Meg in her arms, screaming for the mistress, the sound of her shrieking filling the house.

Things changed after that. Uncle John rode over from Falmouth, spent long hours shut up in the study with Papa. Aunt Rae came from Grenada to look after Mama, who stayed all day in her room with the blinds down. Elizabeth and the boys were left to themselves. Eventually Aunt Rae went home and Mama got up, but she seldom spoke, except to give Marie or Amos their orders. After Uncle John left, Papa took to shouting, perhaps to compensate for Mama's silence. When Willie upset the gravy boat at dinner one evening, sending brown streaks over the white table cloth, Papa sprang forward out of his chair and struck him round the head with such force it knocked him to the ground, and when Tommy smirked at his brother's misfortune, Papa hauled him straight from the room and birched him, there and then, in the hallway. When he returned and tucked his napkin back into place, no one dared move or even raise their eyes from their plates, for fear of what else Papa might do. His face was red and there were trickles of sweat at his temples, but he picked up his knife and fork and began eating his pork and potatoes as if nothing had happened. Mama watched him from the far end of the table. 'And McKenzie?' she said at last. Papa did not answer.

Only Marie was as before. Brushing out Elizabeth's hair at night with firm steady strokes, the scent of coconut oil lifting from her fingers, the warm, comforting bulk of her. 'She wid da angels now, missie,' Marie whispered to her through the shadows. 'No devils get her now.'

With no one to play with, Elizabeth trailed round after Marie as she did her chores, following her down to the reservoir to fetch water, or to the wood stack for kindling, wandering after her into the yard to feed the chickens, sitting in the scalding steam of the wash-house as Marie scrubbed the sheets, watching from doorways as she scoured the bedroom floors. When Marie sat down to her mending, Elizabeth crept up beside her and settled at her feet, hiding her face in the folds of Marie's skirts. Eventually Marie lost patience. 'Don't need no white phantoms hauntin me,' she scolded. 'Plenty phantoms enough out your long face hauntin me day an night.' It made no difference. The only time she let Marie out of her sight was when the governess came, but the moment lessons were over she'd go in search of her again.

One morning, however, she failed to find her. She tore through the house, from one room to the next, a red film spreading behind her eyes, panic swelling in her ribcage, but Marie was nowhere. Amos was chopping wood in the yard, but he just shook his head when she asked him, went on chopping like she wasn't there, swinging up the big axe, sinking it into the wood, the long white scars across his back rippling like waves along the surface of his skin. Across from the yard was the wash-house. Hearing something move inside she pushed on the door and opened it, not wide, just far enough to peep inside. McKenzie's back was to the door, his gun a dark diagonal against his shirt. Marie was between McKenzie and the wash-house wall. Her skirts were rucked up and her bare legs stuck out on either side of McKenzie's body. In the shaft of light from the open door, Elizabeth could see Marie's head over the top of McKenzie's shoulder, jerking up and down like a marionette. Her face was all screwed up, as if she were in pain, but she wasn't making a sound. The only noise in the wash-house was Marie's head banging against the wash-house wall and McKenzie's grunting.

Mo came not long after. Papa brought him up from the fields one afternoon, dropped him at her feet.

'He must live in the kitchen,' Papa said. 'If I hear he's been upstairs, he goes straight back to the huts.'

Elizabeth didn't love Mo as she had Meg, but she liked to play with him or feed him scraps of food she'd saved. They were about the same age, but Mo was much smaller. He had stiff black hair that stuck straight up from his scalp and creamy brown skin. One of his legs was shorter than the other and when he danced he rolled from side to side like a broken cart. In the rainy season they made mud pies in the yard and held tea parties under the veranda with billycans and palm leaves for cups and plates: she was always Mama, and Mo her Amos. When her brothers were about, she took care to hide Mo in the pantry. If Tommy saw him, he'd kick him or pull his hair. But mostly her brothers ignored him, as Papa did.

Mama could not bear the sight of him. 'Get that brat away from me,' she'd say, flicking at him with her fan. Only Marie was fond of Mo. Elizabeth sometimes saw her cradling him on her lap in the kitchen. At those times she hated him, pulled his stupid tufts of hair and pushed him away when he came sidling up wanting to play. Elizabeth's last sight of Mo was on the day they left, standing in Marie's shadow on the steps of the Great House as they drove away. Marie was holding him firmly by the hand. Elizabeth thought it was in case he tried to run after the carriage, wanting to go with her.

28

William Mitchell's mare is washed up on a sandbank on Maundy Thursday, its white throat cut and an old feud settled. In the streets of Aberdeen the schoolboys jostle and taunt each other.

> 'Bloodthirsty Dee
> Each year needs three,
> But bonnie Don
> She needs none.'

Alec hears the familiar chant and ponders.
   Two rivers, two towns, two diseases . . .

29

'Ah! Dr Gordon!'

George French does not need to say, 'At last'; his tone articulates the words loud and clear. Alec takes his seat beside Bannerman at the end of the table. He is late, no denying it, but to hell with the man. How many patients has French treated that morning? How many miles has French walked in boots so old the leather has finally split from age and wear? Is French obliged to wade through acres of cowshit to reach bothies and steadings hardly fit for human habitation? One glance is enough to assure Alec that the Infirmary physician had risen at a civilized hour to find his shirt pressed, his wig combed and his boots polished; had broken his fast at a leisurely pace and quitted his house to mount a horse that was almost as buffed as his boots. Alec cannot, in actual fact, see French's boots as they are concealed by the expanse of the oak meeting table, but he is willing to bet they are miraculously free of the mud and worse that stain his own. He had risen at dawn to find his own horse holding her forelock off the stable floor, as useless as a bucket full of holes. His own fault, of course. Spilt milk. He'd ridden her too hard on the way back from Belhelvie, had ignored her wincing tread the following day, the telltale falter in her stride. Not so much ignored it, Alec mentally corrects himself, as not had the opportunity to attend to it. Now, if *he* had a valet, a groom and a stable boy.

'Apologies, gentlemen.' Alec nods to the Board with as much docility as he can muster. 'I was unavoidably detained.'

Baillie Cruikshank gives a derisory sniff. 'We all have calls on our time, Doctor.'

Alec opens his mouth to object, then catches Bannerman's eye and shuts it again. Cruikshank is a ponced-up nobody, a drunkard. No point demeaning himself in argument with Cruikshank. He looks along the table. The full complement of managers appears to have shown up for the occasion of the Annual General Court, thirty-five of the town's most influential and respected men, private habits notwithstanding. Alec's gaze falls on Thomas Livingston. He notes the patches of yellow on the old man's cheeks, the tumour bulging visibly on the side of his neck, the size of a goose egg. *He'll not last out the year*, Alec thinks, and for some reason the thought restores his equanimity. This is what he does, this seeing and knowing. This is what he's good at. And what better moment, it now occurs to him, to prove it to the Board. As soon as the opportunity arises he will announce the epidemic and his means of curing it. It is the ideal occasion, with them all assembled in one place.

Provost Cruden calls the meeting to order and the roll is taken.

'To the day's main business then,' says Cruden, peering over the rim of his spectacles in the direction of the Treasurer. 'Mr Birnie?'

William Birnie gets to his feet, opens the ledger book with an officiousness that irritates Alec all over again and begins to read out the figures. Account of soap to Mr Robert Thinne, 5 shillings and 6 pence. Account of spirits to Mr James Henderson, 2 pounds, 15 shillings and 6 pence. The sum of 100 guineas, given to the House by Mr Callender on November 15th last, to be placed and applied to the Account of Stock ... Birnie's voice drones on. He's a short, stocky man with a barrel chest and no neck to speak of, the huge cravat he wears to hide the defect serving only to draw attention to it. Today, in his bottle-green coat, he bears a marked resemblance to a large, squat toad, a similarity that merely increases Alec's disliking for the man.

Across the table, several heads are nodding. With the heat from the fire, Alec is beginning to feel drowsy himself. To stay awake, he concentrates his attention on Provost Duncan's lower lip, on which a bead of spittle is quivering in time to the rise and fall of his chest. With each exhalation, the silvery mucus sags a little, lengthening inexorably into a drool and threatening at any moment to break away and land on the gold badge of office, gently rising and falling on the slumbering man's bosom. If the Board is in agreement, the Treasurer is saying, might it be proposed that all sums of money hereafter given to the House, whether legacies or donations or under whatever other denomination, excepting annual contributions to the amount of £20 or upwards, be added to the Stock Account and not applied to the annual expenditure? A short discussion ensues, following which the proposal is agreed and duly minuted by the Clerk. Birnie glances across to Provost Cruden and by a brief flick of the Provost's fingertips receives permission to continue.

'The annual collection for the Infirmary,' he announces in a portentous tone sufficiently loud to waken the dozing members of the Board.

Alec, too, sits up. Now they're coming to it.

'Made as usual at all churches in the counties of the northeast on the first Sunday of January last. The sum collected amounting to – ' Birnie allows a little pause to be sure he has everyone's full attention – 'five hundred and thirty-nine pounds.'

'Putting the deficit at—?' Baillie Paul prompts.

Mr Birnie frowns. 'I am just coming to that. Putting the deficit at – ' he looks down at the ledger book, as if to be quite sure – 'at two hundred and twenty-two pounds, four shillings and three pence.'

A sombre silence falls over the meeting room.

'Well, gentlemen,' Provost Cruden looks around the table. 'I think you will all agree, we have a crisis on our hands.'

Dr French rises smoothly to his feet. 'If I may be permitted to respond?'

Cruden nods and all eyes turn in French's direction. It seems to Alec that the man is dressed with even more care than normal. Dressed for the occasion, one might even say, his cravat perfectly tied, his wig powdered to a snowy white, his well-cut jerkin and waistcoat immaculate down to the last velvet button.

'Demand for the services of the House,' French begins, 'have been unusually great in the past twelve months. The outbreaks of dysentery and scarlet fever last summer, combined with the stationing in town of the garrison, have placed an exceptional burden–'

'Yes, yes, Dr French,' Baillie Paul interrupts. 'Spare us the excuses. What solutions do you propose?'

'– on the Infirmary purse,' French continues, as if the other man had not spoken. 'In light of the disappointing result of the kirk collections, I'm sure everyone will agree that it is now imperative on the House to reduce its costs. One possibility before us is to cut the laundry bill by sending out bedding fortnightly rather than weekly, as is the current practice. Further savings could be made by restricting the claret consumption, which has more than doubled in the past twelve months, I believe.'

French looks over at the Treasurer, who confirms with a small bow that this is indeed the case.

'I cannot see how either of these measures will help,' objects Mr Gibbon of the Society of Shipmasters. 'Surely, Dr French, they will save only trifling amounts?'

'Certainly unequal to the grumbling they'll cause,' Bannerman mutters, raising a few guffaws from the men close enough to hear.

'Thank you, Mr Gibbon, and a fair point,' French replies. 'If I might continue, gentlemen, a more significant saving could be achieved by stringent enforcement of the entry requirements.'

Alec is not the only one taken aback by this proposal.

Provost Cruden looks as surprised as anyone. 'The Infirmary exists to support the sick, Dr French, not to turn them away at the door.'

'So it does, Provost, but there will be no Infirmary if things continue as they are.'

'President, gentlemen.' Livingston is rising painfully from his seat to speak for the first time. 'If I might add to my colleague's comments, many of those applying for our care of late are either incurable, in which case they are ineligible for treatment according to the statutes of the House, or of an age that would render them better suited to treatment in their own homes.'

Alec is astonished. Livingston seems to be implying that the Dispensary is failing in its duty. He is on his legs at once.

'It may interest the Board to know that in the past month alone the Dispensary has treated two hundred and twenty patients in their own homes – a three-fold increase since last year's accounts were heard.'

A tiny smile crosses French's lips. Almost the moment Alec sees it, it is gone.

'Yes, Dr Gordon, that is true – and a large part of the problem.' French turns away from Alec to address the rest of the assembly. 'The Dispensary currently represents a very considerable burden on the Infirmary accounts—'

'On the contrary, sir!' Alec is aware of his temper rising. 'The Dispensary relieves the Infirmary of a great number of patients it would otherwise be burdened with!'

'No one is questioning the importance of your contribution,' Provost Cruden says. 'Dr French is merely observing, perfectly correctly, that the Dispensary's costs are met in large part by the Infirmary. You use the apothecary shop, do you not?'

There's something in the Provost's tone that would instil caution in a more diplomatic man. Alec hears only the grinding of old axes.

There was a time when he took his place at these meetings with unalloyed pride. Whilst never feeling himself less than equal to the distinguished assembly, he had also been sensible of the privilege of holding a position within it. That had all changed with the argument over the public bath, which had diminished not only his respect for his colleagues but his pride in being one of their number. The row had, in addition, raised considerably more ill-will towards him than he'd realized at the time. A whole year later, Livingston had referred to the business not once but three times as the reason the Infirmary was in straitened circumstances, when the real reason was obvious to anyone who troubled to consider how much of the physician's time was spent on the wards and how much of it in the gaming house.

'As I understand it,' says Baillie Paul (another one, it belatedly occurs to Alec, whose opposition to the closure had so exasperated him five years previously), 'the funding arrangement was intended to help establish the Dispensary, not to support it in perpetuity.'

Provost Cruden turns to Mr Birnie. 'And if the Dispensary were to meet its own costs? What saving would that represent?'

'Twenty-five pounds, nineteen shillings and eight pence at current rates of demand.' Birnie appears to have the figure at his fingertips.

'This is an outrage!' It's only Bannerman's boot connecting smartly with Alec's shinbone that keeps him from shouting. 'Demand for the Dispensary has never been higher. I am treating more patients than ever before. Patients who would otherwise be taking up space in Infirmary beds. The Dispensary cannot survive without the Infirmary's support.'

'And the Infirmary,' French replies steadily, 'cannot survive with it.'

Only then does Alec understand. George French has prepared for this moment, planned and plotted for it. Mr Birnie is a close friend, more than a friend, related by his youngest sister's marriage to French's cousin. French must have known the situation for some weeks now. Cruden and Livingston, both, must have been primed beforehand.

'The savings would put the finances back on an even footing,' French's silken voice runs on, 'and, in addition, enable the Infirmary to appoint a third physician, which it urgently needs to do to meet the great and growing demand for its services. Even allowing for the cost of a third physician, the Infirmary would be considerably better off financially than it is currently with the expense of supporting the Dispensary.'

Nods and murmurs of agreement ripple round the table.

Alec looks about him at the well-fed faces of the Board members. He has been cornered as surely as a dog in a blind alley. There is no way he can announce the epidemic now. He needs the third physician post as much as the Dispensary needs the Infirmary's financial support. Whatever he says, they will cut off the Dispensary; if he continues to object, he will cut himself out of the running for the appointment. But how will the Dispensary survive on subscriptions alone? The two institutions will be fighting over the same scant pot of gold. More to the point, how will he himself survive? He has already drawn on his own salary of three months in succession to meet the physic bills for his poorest patients. Has assisted Skene and Bannerman more times than he can remember, without ever once quibbling over payment for his services. Assisted French, too, when he could have been attending to his private patients. Elizabeth, it seems, was right.

A vote is taken and the hands are counted.

'Motion unanimously carried,' the Clerk declares.

30

Elizabeth suspects there are things he's not telling her. About the deaths. About the Dispensary. About other things she has not even thought of. She suspects he is avoiding her. He rarely comes to bed before the small hours and is gone before she wakes. She feels him going, the mattress lifting as he slides out from under the covers, the chill air creeping along her back. Through the fog of sleep, she hears him pissing, then the whisper of dressing, the murmur of cloth, hooks, buttons. Then the distinct silence of absence. She cannot move. Her mind registers his leaving, but her body hears nothing, as though the two were entirely separate. Her legs are dead-weights beneath the blankets. Her arms are blades of grass between the pages of a book. With her mind she wants to reach out, call to him, but her body is in another place, too far to be reached. His departure fills her head with a sense of loss, but she lies immobile, stranded. It strikes her with a cold rinse of grief, his slipping from the room, but it is a relief too: the relief of not having to hold herself apart, of not having to keep him at bay. She must wait until the treatment is complete. Even in sleep she must not yield to the comfort of his warmth. Alone, she can relax at last, sink into real sleep, fall into its embrace, let it envelop her completely for a while. When she finally wakes, hours later, the morning is sharp with noise from the masons' hammers, the vendors' cries, the dogs barking at the wheels of every passing cart, the clatter of hooves on the cobbles, the shrieking gulls. Every morning now this sensation of being out of step with the day, of the hours leaving her behind, the world turning faster than it should. She waits for the noises to settle, sift down into recognizable shapes, then she rolls on to her side and reaches under the bed, fingers groping back and forth until they close on the cool barrel of the clyster. This is her first task each morning. Pouring the required amount of the decoction into the canister, securing the cap so none of it spills, holding herself open with one hand, manoeuvring the steel nozzle into position with the other, the shock of the cold metal, her muscles clamping down in the involuntary spasm she is both ashamed of and welcomes, her insides liquefying even before she begins to press down on the wooden handle.

How can it be wrong when it will heal her?

After a while, the decoction reverses itself, seeping back out of her like a turning tide, its cool lick slipping along her thighs, running down into the cleft of her buttocks, pooling under her. Sugar of lead. Roch allum. White vitriol. She must lie quite still now, let it do its work, wash out the wickedness. It is forgivable, surely, the inadvertent consequence of the operation? Not something she is doing to herself, not something she wants. Just something that happens. Perhaps Dr Freeman had not thought of this. He is most emphatic on the crime of self-abuse and since he has prescribed this very treatment as a cure, how can it be wrong? It worries her all the same. She wonders if it will counteract the intended purpose of the remedy.

She cannot remember how it began. It had simply happened. Her hand pressed between her legs, her fingers idly stroking the softness of her skin, not for any reason, not with any intent, certainly not with any idea of wickedness or any knowledge of the misery it would bring. Simply the comfort of it, no different from the hot sun on her head, or Marie's warm palm running over the sheet of her hair as she brushed it out each night before bed, quiet and soothing. And when one night her fingers had moved, of their own accord it seemed, to the source of the soothing, had found their way to other places, and the small, quiet waves had become something more than soothing, she had not known it was wrong, had no knowledge of all the evil consequences it would lead to. All she'd known was the simple logic of her own touch, everything else falling away in the melting whiteness. The creaking of the rockers on the veranda boards. Mama's weeping. The bonfire in the courtyard. McKenzie's laugh. No one had told her or she would not have done as she had. She could cry out at times with the weight of her shame. It is like a physical pain. No one until Freeman had explained. She'd been horrified as she read, yet it all made sense: the shooting pains in her head, the nightmares, the nausea, and above all, her own coldness, her indifference to her own husband's embrace. What were Freeman's words?

> When a woman can charge herself with such a course of self-abuse as hath sensibly weakened and damaged her organs of regeneration, hath she not all the room in the world to be for ever uneasy, in the remembrance of her folly and wickedness, and to believe, with justice that another woman, in her case, would not be infertile?

Forever uneasy. Was there to be no end to it then? It had taken two weeks to make up the remedy. Procuring the ingredients, measuring, mixing, setting, filtering, pouring off the scum till it ran perfectly clear, as Freeman directed. She couldn't find a way to heat it, which he also recommended, but it was not, he said, essential. *Designed for those who have debilitated themselves greatly.* Is she so wicked that even the treatment should lead to more occasion for sinning?

The trickle of liquid has stopped and the stinging has begun. It will be with her all day, a reminder of her guilt. Well, so be it. It is no less than she deserves. She must not weaken now. The cessation of her courses, Freeman says, is still further proof of how deep-rooted the corruption is, but he seems sure that the decoction can restore the decayed parts.

> If continued a sufficient time, it will seldom fail of answering the end desired, especially if the Enliven-

ing Balsam be also constantly applied in conjunction
with it.

She must find a way to make up the balsam. If only this
dragging fatigue would lift for a moment. The nutmeg, mace
and cloves present no difficulty, but she has still to obtain the
musk and civet, the essences of cantharides and ambergrise.

Mix well together upon a tile, without fire. Anoint
the parts, both internally and externally, morning and
evening.

Even when she is not carrying out his instructions, she is
thinking about them. The next dose, the next application, the
next injection.

31

The letters are written and sealed. It was Chae's idea.

'Stake your claim, before someone else does. They can scarcely refuse you now.'

Alec intended initially to give the letters to Rabbie to take over, but a sudden scruple made him change his mind, a last-minute instinct that they were safer delivered by his own hand. He'd had to drum up some other pretext for having called Rabbie to his study at such an early hour, so had set the lad to replacing the preserving liquid in the specimen jars. Rabbie clearly thought at first that it was some joke on Alec's part, had stared at him in open astonishment. The storeroom had always been strictly out of bounds, and now here was the doctor holding out the key as if it were quite the everyday occurrence. Rabbie could not guess at the pang of anxiety Alec felt as he handed over the key. But perhaps after all there was nothing to worry about, Alec consoles himself now: it would take Rabbie some time to reach the shelves at the far end of the storeroom. With luck he would be back by then. The first of the two letters is already delivered; there's just French's manservant to be circumvented now and he's done.

Pugh opens the door with his customary expression of scowling mistrust. All callers at French's door, of whatever rank and standing, whether they come on foot or by carriage, are greeted with Pugh's habitual mien of deep-rooted disgust for human-kind. The man has never been known to show the slightest fondness for anybody, his affections reserved solely for his dog, a flea-bitten mutt with a countenance as twisted as its master's.

'Give this to Dr French,' Alec says, ignoring the hostile glare with which Pugh is welcoming him. 'Be sure to see he receives it this morning. It concerns a matter of the utmost urgency.'

Gravedigger at St Peter's for twenty-eight years, Pugh had been apprehended two winters back burying a coffin full of nothing but stones. The shroud was recovered soon after, hidden behind a spade in the kirkyard. The body was never found. Evidence was insufficient to condemn the fellow out-right, but there was no question of him remaining in the kirk's employ. French had taken him on soon after, for reasons that were clearer to some in the town than others. The Bitch and the Brute: that's how French and Pugh were known, at least in the back booths at Wylkie's Coffee House.

Pugh is looking from the letter to Alec and back again with an unpleasant leer.

'Here!'

The coin is taken and stowed almost before Alec has extended his hand. He jabs the letter at Pugh's chest.

'See he gets it!'

Perhaps, Alec thinks as he walks away, it would have been better, after all, to have given the letter to Rabbie, who would have roused less curiosity in Pugh. The letter will be steamed open and read before it reaches French's hand, that is certain. Perhaps it was unwise to have written to French at all. But Chae had insisted: a letter to Cruden and a letter to French. As President of the Board, Cruden would be obliged to reveal its contents to the rest; French would not then want to appear in ignorance of the matter. Well, it is done now.

Alec turns his attention to the day ahead of him. The morning is brightening about him, the air cold still, sharp and clean in his lungs. All along the wayside the grass stems are veiled in spider's webs, beads of dew glistening like tiny pearls on the gossamer threads. The sky is busy with birdsong. Gradually Alec's anxiety is displaced by a simple sensation of pleasure. How can one not feel hopeful on such a morning? Each breath renews his spirits. French will receive the letter; the post will be his; Elizabeth will be content.

He is level now with the southern end of the physic garden.

The high stone walls bounding the garden are directly in front of him. He pauses for a moment, thinking of his unlocked storeroom, then pushes open the iron gates and steps into the scented silence.

A broad path leads from the gates through an avenue of yew trees to the herb and flowerbeds. Beyond the beds is the well, a grand affair of sculpted stone, topped with a statue of a prancing bronze Pan, and beyond that, at the northernmost end of the garden, is the hothouse, an elegant structure of iron and glass, in imitation of the one at Kew. The part of the garden in which Alec is now standing has been set aside for trees, mostly indigenous, but interplanted here and there with imported varieties of hydrangea and rhododendron. Upkeep of the garden has been neglected since old Farquhar died (the Board is still squabbling about his replacement), but the somewhat unkempt appearance is not unpleasing, lending a natural look to this end of the garden. The apothecaries' apprentices have been and gone, gathering their bundles of herbs and flowers and scuttling back to their benches before the sun spoils the precious juices and their masters' wrath spoils their day. Later there will be patients from the infirmary pottering along the pathways and lounging on the benches by the south wall, soaking up the first warmth of the spring. For now, though, the garden is empty, and so peaceful it's impossible not to want to linger a while. Alec can hear small animals scratching about nearby in the undergrowth. From somewhere above overhead, a blackbird opens its throat to the morning and pours forth a burst of song. Almost at once, from a neighbouring branch, comes an answering stream of notes. And then a woman's voice:

'Good morning, Dr Gordon.'

Turning in the direction of the voice, Alec sees a figure standing a little way off in the dark shadow of the yews.

'Listening to the birds?'

The woman steps forward on to the sunlit path.

'Mistress Anderson,' Alec says, trying to hide his surprise. 'Why, good morning to you.'

The young midwife is smiling as she walks towards him.

'I wouldn't have thought you'd have time for such frivolities,' she says, a teasing note in her voice.

She has come to a standstill directly in front of him. Her auburn hair is loosely pinned under the white dab of her widow's cap. Her eyes, which are nearly level with his own, are a startling shade of green, pale as jade, with darker flecks around the outer rim of the iris.

Her eyelashes are the colour of burnished copper.

'They sound happy this morning,' she says, turning away from him to look up at the branches over their heads.

As if to oblige, there's a further flourish of song from the courting male. Janet Anderson laughs.

'It's the sap rising,' Alec says. 'They feel it too.'

Immediately, he is seized with embarrassment, cannot think what possessed him to speak in this way. But the midwife seems untroubled. All she says is, 'Aye'. No smile this time, just a simple nod of agreement. She is looking up at the trees still, scanning the branches for signs of the blackbird. All about them the morning is fidgeting and rustling with hidden life. When she starts to walk in the direction of the flowerbeds, it seems the most natural thing in the world to fall into step beside her, the most natural thing in the world for them to be walking along together, as if they did so every day of their lives.

'It is beautiful, is it not? God's design for the world.' She is referring to the first of the beds, which they've now come to. 'These miraculous pairings in all forms of life.'

He can only agree, for it was he who'd argued for the garden to be replanted according to the Linnaean system, in these logical couples of male and female plants; it was his voice that helped to silence objections to the expense of adopting the new scheme.

'And yet,' Janet Anderson is saying, 'almost more miraculous to my mind is the great diversity of life. So much variety stemming from a single source. *That* is truly to be marvelled at, do you not think?'

Alec is not sure they share the same understanding of the phrase 'a single source', but it is too early in the day for theological arguments and he is not, in any case, inclined to argue with Mistress Anderson at this moment.

'There is certainly much to learn from plants,' he says carefully. 'From all life forms.'

Janet Anderson has paused beside one of the beds.

'But how unjust,' she continues, 'that flowers should reproduce themselves without any of the suffering that invariably accompanies the reproduction of human life.' She turns her head to look at him. 'How would you explain it, Dr Gordon? Is it simply that flowers are innocent and we humans very wicked?'

Alec cannot help but laugh. She is such a beguiling mixture of innocence and knowingness.

'*You* do not seem to think so,' he says.

'I do not know what to think. But when I see the plants laid out like this, the husbands and wives so sweetly paired and so harmoniously arranged, I do wonder that we humans should come into the world with such a struggle and find it so very hard to live peaceably thereafter.'

'Why, Mistress Anderson, you are a philosopher!'

'Alas, no!' She shakes her head. 'Merely inclined to idle speculation. I own it has become something of a habit since my husband's death.'

Her voice remains light, but for a moment her face is touched with sadness. Alec sees it and feels an answering flush of emotion within himself. It is unlike him to be moved in this way, but it's as if the fresh rawness of the spring morning has stripped him of a layer of skin. The glimpse of vulnerability in the young midwife stirs something in him that he is unfamiliar with and unequal to, some hidden current of longing and loneliness within himself that he would not normally be aware of. He is still wondering how to respond when, recovering her former composure, Janet Anderson starts to speak again.

'I read recently that plants have been discovered on the islands of the Pacific that cannot be identified with any known species.'

'Aye, that is so. You take a keen interest in botany?'

'My brother Wullie taught me a little of his profession before he went to London.'

'Wullie?'

She points to a low spreading plant a short way ahead of them.

Alec looks from the midwife to the wild ginger and back again.

'Wullie Forsyth is your brother?'

Wullie and he had been close friends as boys, had shared the same bench at the grammar school, thrown stones at the same dogs, played shinty on the loch when it froze over. Ardent, headstrong, skinny-shanks Forsyth! Tall as a beanstalk, handsome as an angel, obstinate as the devil! When Alec had left for Leiden, his friend had quitted the town too, his path taking him south to the capital, where he'd done very well for himself, securing a position at the Physic Garden in Chelsea. A few years later, when Alec was in London himself, he'd been over to Paradise Row to see his former schoolmate. Wullie was the Gardener at Chelsea by then. Alec had purchased some seeds to send back to Elizabeth for their own little garden in Belmont Street and Wullie had been pleased to show Alec the grounds, pointing out with great pride the imports he'd procured from his connections in the Indies and America. His particular interest at that time was the diseases, defects and injuries of fruit and fruit trees: he intended a great work on the subject. As the tour of the garden continued,

Wullie had begun to unburden himself of other sentiments than pride. He had complained bitterly about the restrictions placed upon him by the Garden committee and the general ingratitude that his labours met with. It was with the utmost indignation that he told Alec how he was obliged to raise his three bairns above the greenhouse, despite the danger from the stoves and flues; yet when he'd pointed out that the rooms were not fit for young children, or anyone else, he'd been told it would cost too much to replace the flues and if he was not satisfied, he could secure alternative lodging elsewhere at his own expense. 'Not satisfied – I'll say not!' Wullie exclaimed. 'Twenty-five pounds a year it costs me to live in that smoke-house! And my wages not exceeding forty!'

Not long after, Alec read in the *Journal* that Wullie had resigned from the Physic Garden for an appointment to his Majesty at the Royal Garden of Kensington. (No details were given of the accommodation accompanying the position, so Alec could only hope that they were an improvement on those at Chelsea.) It was largely thanks to Wullie Forsyth that the physic garden in Aberdeen was so well stocked. The wild ginger in front of them now, with its dark, kidney-shaped leaves and ugly little flowers, was just one of his many gifts, and an invaluable one, its root a potent emmenagogue, sudorific and abortifacient. More than one woman in Aberdeen owed her life to WullieForsyth's gift.

So, Janet Anderson is Wullie's sister!

It seems hard to believe, looking at the young woman in front of him, that he had not noticed her when they were younger. He can see the resemblance now: she has all of her brother's good looks in a softer, more graceful version. She is looking at him with her steady green eyes, amused by his surprise, her lips slightly parted. Her skin has a luminous quality, as if the light were shining through from the inside. Her hair is a red-gold flame in the sunshine. Alec looks away, and they walk in silence for a while. Reaching the herb-beds, she pauses once more, kneeling down to pick a few feathery leaves from a low bush.

'Sweet cicely.'

She holds the bunch out for him to smell. Obediently, he lowers his face and sniffs the delicate aniseed scent of the leaves.

'Strange, is it not, how two plants can look produce such different effects? Sweet cicely so harmless and hemlock so deadly. Yet almost impossible to tell apart this early in the year.' She pauses. 'Like the symptoms of diseases, I sometimes think.'

He looks up sharply and meets her gaze. She knows! She understands!

He has seized her hand without quite realizing how. 'But that is just what the others refuse to see!'

Again there is that quiet, small nod of the head. 'They will come to understand,' she says, softly. 'Give them time. They will listen in the end.'

They are standing very close to each other, so close that Alec can see the texture of her skin, the tiny cross-hatching of lines at the corners of her eyes. Below the left eye, on the ridge of the cheekbone, there is a tiny scar. The brilliant morning is all around them in a blur of light and colour and sound – the birdsong and sunlight, the loamy smell of warming soil, the new shoots greening the branches. Without allowing himself to think, Alec dips his face towards hers. Falls into the simple logic of her sympathy. For a moment there is nothing but the softness of her lips, the loveliness of her, the dissolving warmth of her body against his. Only when she pulls away does he abruptly recall himself.

'Forgive me,' he says, horrified. 'Please – forgive me.'

She leans forward, kisses him once, lightly, on the cheek. 'There is nothing to forgive,' she says, before turning and walking quickly away.

Part Two

Knowledge

Plentiful, but proper bleeding with a cooling regimen is, in general, absolutely necessary.

John Burton, *An Essay Towards a Complete
New System of Midwifery*, 1751

Unless the pains are very great, we should not bleed, at least for the first eighteen or twenty hours ... Nervous and hysterical women cannot bear the loss of much blood, wherefore, when it is necessary to bleed such patients, the quantity at first taken away should be small.

Thomas Cooper, *A Compendium of Midwifery*, 1766

Venesection ... I have never seen of any use, excepting in a few cases, where there seemed to be a combination of peripneumonic symptoms along with peritonitis; and even in such cases it only had the effect of alleviating the severity of the symptoms.

Joseph Clarke, *Observations on the Puerperal Fever*, 1790

32

May

If you angled the stone right, held it lightly in the palm of your hand, with just enough pressure to tip it slightly as you set it loose, it would fly out over the water, scudding across the surface, like a dragonfly dipping for midges, six, seven arcs of flight before the weight of the water finally pulled it down for good. Hours they'd spend, whole, long afternoons, in search of the perfect stone, the perfect angle, with the curlews looping and gliding high above them, and not a thought in their heads but this single goal, this momentary defiance of gravity. Jem was the best, taking his time to find the smooth flat pieces of shingle that would cut through the air, weightless as shadows. He piled them up at his feet, a heap of ammunition that he refused to share, working his way through them with silent determination long after the others had exhausted their supply. It was the same methodical tirelessness that he brought now to the raising of stock and the tending of crops. Then it had seemed a kind of genius: the way Jem's stones bounded across the water, as if his hand imbued them with life and they were no longer simply bits of rock, but living things, unravelling towards some destination of their own choosing. Even as Alec watched his brother perform this alchemy, animating the inanimate, he'd known it was not magic, merely skill, but no matter how closely he scrutinized Jem's technique, he could never match it; his own pebbles never flew so far nor so low.

When the breeze was too strong and the surface of the water too rough for skimming stones, they'd wander further afield, tracking the burns up into the hills to the shallow places where they could wade across, the water so cold it felt as if your legs were turning to stone beneath you, the pain burning up through your shin bone and into your thigh though you were only ankle-deep. They'd try to block the water's flow with dams of rocks and mud and bits of brushwood, plugging the gaps with rushes and clumps of heather, the tough stems ripping the palms of their hands and the cuts stinging like mad at first, until the icy water numbed all sensation, their fingers turning red then white then red again as they worked furiously at their impossible task. For a minute or two the dam would hold. They'd retreat to the bank, shouting with glee, hopping from one frozen foot to the other while the water pooled on the upstream side, pondering its next move. Then a trickle would work its way through, a thin black seepage, always where you least expected it, and they'd crash back in, yelling orders at each other, as the mud walls started to shift and slide under the pressure of the water massing against it. *It's dinging doon! The foons are ganging!* Frantically, they'd pack on more mud, more stones, as yet another segment seeped away, their hands slapping frantically at the crumbling barricade. But once the dam was breached there was no stopping it. Weaker sections would break away first, softly yielding to the force of the water, then the remaining structure would collapse into the gap and be swept away downstream, their labour dissolving to nothing before their eyes. Those few jubilant seconds were enough, though, when their dam held back the burn; that was all that mattered, that and the inextinguishable belief that the next one they built would be bigger and stronger, would withstand the water for longer.

In high summer there were fish to catch. They'd bait lengths of string with worms that they'd dug from the loose mud, then tether the lines to stout sticks driven into the river bed, in imitation of the stells erected by the fishermen. But it was hard to wedge the stakes in deep enough and it was no great trouble for the salmon to catch the bait and swim off with it, the stake bobbing along behind like a bit of kindling.

Other times they'd hold the lines themselves, the silvery trails wavering beneath the surface, while they perched on the bank, waiting for the telltale shadow, the sudden jerk of the bite. If they succeeded in hauling the weight of it out of the water, the fish as often as not would simply twist away mid-air in an outrage of flashing motion, flop back into the water and vanish again. When they made it as far as Gordon's Mills, they could tickle for them, and then they'd have more success. Jem was the best at this too, able to tighten his grip on the writhing mass long enough to flip it out of its course and on to the bank, the scales every colour of the rainbow as the fish thrashed and flailed at their feet. Dolphins died this way too, the skin shimmering through pink, red, blue and gold as the last air left their lungs. His father had heard it from the whalers, who caught dolphin whenever they could on the long run home from Greenland, feasting on the rich flesh, succulent as cured pork, a welcome change from weeks of salt cod and dried biscuits. Alec had never tasted dolphin, but he'd seen them often enough, from the Seton hills north of the King's Links, alone or in pairs, curving in and out of the waves in great liquid hoops. Occasionally there'd be the sighting of a whale, and once he'd seen a humpback, no more than half a mile out to sea, thirty feet long and black as coal, the vast bulk of it rising up through the waves, splitting apart the grey skin of the water's surface, pulling the ocean into itself and at the same time forcing a massive causeway through the waves. He's sometimes wanted to share with someone his memory of that splitting, breaking sea: the nearest thing in nature he's ever seen to the way a woman's body opens at the moment of birth: the elemental force of it.

Alec and his brothers were not permitted to join the crowd that thronged to Pocra jetty when the *Hercules* or *Latona* returned from the Arctic, but they went anyway, threading their way through the press of bodies, as eager as everyone else to see the gargantuan hunks of flesh being dragged ashore, reassembling them in their imagination to see the fallen leviathans entire again. Down at the bleach greens, the jawbone of a whale rose from the sand, the relic of some earlier voyage, as high as the gates of St Machar's cathedral, so wide a wagonload of hay could pass through with ease. It was said that the open mouth of a Greenland Right could swallow a boat full of men, and looking at that archway of white bone you could well believe it. As for the whalers themselves, they seemed scarcely human, swaggering up the jetty with their frost-blackened faces and sunken eyes, making straight for the saloons along the quayside to drown their recollections in grog. Everyone cheered them as they passed, mindful of what hardships they'd endured, and grateful: the whalers' cargo fattened the town, brought oil for lamps and soap and candles, for currying the leather and dressing the wool. Whale grease kept the mill wheels turning. Whalebone stiffened the womenfolk's skirts. So they welcomed the tattered crew like conquering heroes, but at the same time took care not to get too close, for everyone knew that whalers were unpredictable, more than a little mad. Cross Old Creedie's path and he'd pull a handful of bones from his pocket and shake them in your face: they were the toes of Creedie's own left foot, lost to frostbite. He kept them strung together on a length of hemp like a bunch of keys to ward off bad luck and to frighten the loons.

When the whaling was good, the stench from the boil-yard hung over the quayside in great poisonous clouds for days on end, the stink of dissolving blubber the whale's last revenge as it yielded up eight, sometimes ten tons of its precious oil. Before Alec and his brothers reached home they'd take off their shirts and run with them held high over their heads like kites to try to lose the smell, but their mother was never fooled. She'd catch it on their skin and in their hair and start up fretting and scolding them for risking their health breathing in the fumes from the blubber. They weren't afeard though. What did they care? Death was nowhere and everywhere, could take or spare a soul as it pleased, in sickness or in health. The chance to see a whale or walrus, or even a glimpse of a sea-unicorn, was worth the risk.

Strange, to be remembering those things now, Alec thinks as he trudges along the wooded track that leads to the Brig o' Don, his feet slithering a little in the mud. Strange how these images come to him at times, sharpened with the passage of time, as if they'd been stored somewhere in the depths of his mind, the shapes and colours and smells perfectly preserved. A world away that time seems, yet in some ways what had changed? When you stripped away the lineaments of manhood was Jem not still the determined boy, intent on his own ends; was Chae not still the one for a good meal and a quiet life; and as for himself, was he not the same as he'd always been: the one after the answers, the one for taking the risks? He might have settled for a modest private practice as a surgeon, fallen in line with the Infirmary physicians, followed the dictates of accepted wisdom. How different his life could have been. But there was always that voice in his head asking, *Why? How? What if?* Never willing to take anyone else's word for it. Never prepared to accept limitations, in himself or others. Always wanting to improve things. Always driving himself on. Forever seeking out problems and searching for solutions (or, as Elizabeth would say, making difficulties where there were none).

When he and Jem lay side by side on their backs in the field behind the farm, looking up at the night sky, Jem had seen constellations. Pegasus, Orion, Cassiopeia. But Alec had seen questions. What he'd felt was the overwhelming desire for answers.

How much had changed since then, and how little.

33

Whoever bound the stump has used the wrong bandages, making slow work of Rabbie's efforts to change the dressing. Filaments of cotton have shredded into the wound and accreted to the congealed blood. He teases the threads of the ruined bandage away from the flesh, moistening the fibres with water from the bucket at his feet. His fingers are slender and nimble, well-suited to the task. Rabbie works on steadily, sighing from time to time at the poor workmanship that has gone before him; the oozing wound and the smell of decomposition do not bode well. The previous night's storm is still blowing itself out, shoving irritably at the outer walls and girning in the chimney flues, but the ward itself is quiet, most of the patients asleep. The man winces and groans under his hands. Through the skylights unsteady sunshine flares and fades, tipping the room from watery gold to grey to gold again.

It is peaceful in its own way, this painstaking picking over the bandage amidst the silent play of light and shadows and the slumbering patients, or perhaps it is just the contrast with what he's come from that makes it seem so. Lancing boils and splinting bones are second nature now to Rabbie, but chirurgy he still finds an ordeal. The cataract was on the left lens, awkwardly placed, and as the knife slid into the soft tissue of the eyeball, Rabbie felt his stomach liquefy, his own nerve endings recoil in horror. Despite the liberal quantities of whisky the patient had consumed in preparation, his body bucked hard against Rabbie's arms and he let out a shriek of pain that flayed them all. Alec's hands were perfectly steady as he continued the operation, which was taking place on the gamekeeper's kitchen table, but his face was chalk white. The man needed his sight: with six bairns to feed, it was more than vision that would be restored – if he survived the operation at all. Rabbie feels unbounded admiration for his master on these occasions, for his ability to focus all of his attention on the practical task before him, to remain unflustered by the patient's suffering. It is an art to be cultivated, this apparent hardness of heart, but it takes its toll, even so. Alec looked drained as he put the knives away afterwards; beyond issuing a few curt orders for the patient's care, he did not say a word. They rode away from the cottage in silence, parting company at the crossroads, Alec having decided to complete the home visits alone.

Footsteps and raised voices disturb the calm.

'I have not forgot the matter – ' it is Dr French speaking, his tone taut with annoyance – 'and I would thank you for allowing me to handle it as I see fit.'

A second voice replies, but Rabbie cannot make out the words.

'There is no dispute, Dr Robertson. We are in perfect agreement. A third physician is an urgent necessity.'

There is more indistinct mumbling, then French's voice again, loud and hard-edged as before.

'I imply nothing, sir. I merely state the facts.'

The argument continues as the two men draw nearer, their footsteps finally coming to a halt outside the ward.

'I see no reason to continue this discussion further. I will consider your request in due course. Now good day, sir.'

A moment later French strides through the doorway. Seeing Rabbie, he stops, clearly displeased to find him there. Rabbie stands and lowers his head respectfully.

'What are you doing here, Donald?'

Dr French dislikes the medical students at the best of times and in this current frame of mind he's in no mood to conceal his hostility.

'Changing the dressings, sir.'

'On whose authority?'

'Dr Gordon's, sir.'

French comes closer and peers over Rabbie's shoulder.

'Well, it's a damn mess, man! What the devil's he been teaching you?'

Rabbie says nothing, knows French won't stay long if he's not provoked. Sure enough, after a cursory inspection of the other patients, a procedure carried out from the safe distance of the ends of their beds without so much as lifting a sheet, the Infirmary physician storms off. Alone again, Rabbie quickly finishes cleaning the wound and applies the new dressing. That done, he makes his way quietly down the corridor and out of the hospital, leaving by the side door and skirting the edge of the building, out of sight of the windows to avoid being seen. As soon as he is clear of the grounds, he breaks into a run.

34

'Dr Gordon! Dr Gordon!'

His voice echoes back at him, high and girlish. The house appears to be deserted. Standing in the silent hallway, Rabbie is suddenly embarrassed by his impetuousness. The meaning of the exchange between the two physicians no longer seems as clear as it had; the words he'd taken as a clear warning seem now less substantial, too ambiguous to be worth reporting. Perhaps he's misunderstood French's intention entirely. It is Friday in any case; Alec is unlikely to be back before dusk. The rush of alarm that had propelled him down the hill from the Infirmary has drained away, replaced by a sense of unease. Belmont Street has been his home for the past two years, but suddenly he feels like an intruder. The house seems to be watching him, waiting, holding its breath. Baxter and Annie must still be at market, but it's strange to find neither Elizabeth nor Mary at home.

As he makes his way through the empty rooms, Rabbie notices for the first time countless small signs of perturbance and disarray. Candles down to their stubs. Sheet music dropped on the floor. Discarded embroidery. In the kitchen, he finds outright mayhem. The dresser doors are gaping open and two of the chairs are upended on the floor. On the table, amidst a carnage of pots and pans, a sticky trail leads from the honey pot towards a hunk of bread it was intended for but never reached; abandoned beside it, a bowl of greying porridge.

A faint noise catches his attention, like the mewling of a kitten. He looks around, unable to source the sound at first, then realizes it's coming from under the table. He bends down, peering in the direction of the noise.

'Why, Mary, whatever are you doing down there?'

Mary, huddled in a ball, legs tight to her chest, head down between her arms, does not move.

'Come out of there, lassie. You cannae stay hiding there.'

When his coaxing does no good, Rabbie gets down on his hands and knees and crawls under the table himself.

'Hush now, Marykie, it's all right.'

Gently he puts his arms around the small rigid body and pulls the little girl towards him, rocking her until she slowly softens, lets her head fall on to his chest and her body lean into him. He waits until she's quite calm before loosening his hold a little.

'Where's your ma?'

Mary stiffens at once, looking up at him in alarm.

'Mammie's sick. She musnae be disturbed.'

'Where is she?'

But Mary does not answer. She has nuzzled back down beside him again, her thumb in her mouth. Against his forearm, Rabbie can feel the rise and fall of her ribcage, slowing as her distress fades. He can smell the warm animal scent of her skin. As moments pass and they continue to sit there in the shadowy cave of the table, an immense tenderness gradually comes over Rabbie, a feeling of deep protectiveness towards the child. She is as dear to him, he suddenly realizes, as if she were his own sister. A fierce indignation rises in him as he recalls how often in recent weeks he's found her alone in the house, waiting patiently for someone to remember to feed her or dress her or simply recall that she exists. Alec is fond enough when he's there and not distracted, which is ever less often, but his cousin seems intentionally to avoid the child, as if the very sight of her were distasteful. At his side, Mary shifts and sighs: a little sobbing inhalation followed by a long slow release of breath. Rabbie bends his head and lets his face rest in the musty nest of her hair. Only once she is quite calm does he attempt to move.

'Stay here,' he says. 'Promise me.'

He cups her cheek with his palm. She nods solemnly.

Outside the bedroom, he hesitates, listening for sounds of movement, but all is quiet. He presses down on the latch and pushes the door open a little way. Through the crack in the door he can see Elizabeth stretched out on the bed. She seems to be asleep and does not stir as he enters the room. Even when he's right beside the bed she does not wake. She is lying on her back, dressed only in her undershift, the laces undone to below the waist. Rabbie looks away, but not before he's seen the exposed curve of her breasts and, below, the soft swell of belly between the parted lips of cloth, and the dark line traversing the skin from the navel down into the folds of fabric.

'Lizzie,' he whispers. 'Coz.'

Elizabeth's face is paler even than usual, her unpinned hair jet-black against the white bolster. On the bed beside her, the chamber-pot contains a greenish pool of puke. He moves the pot to the floor.

'Lizzie!' He gives her shoulders a little shake. 'Wake up now!'

His voice is a shiver of leaves in the forest she is dreaming of. Not a Scots forest of pine and birch, but the forests of her childhood. Cedar and palm and tamarind. Broad dark leaves glossy with heat. She has been walking for hours, for so long now, her feet are sore, scratched and bitten and bleeding in places, but she must not stop, she has to get back, before it's too late. The parrots are screeching at her from the branches. It's hot. So hot. If only the wind would blow. And there! She hears it now, the quiver of it in the trees. Calling her. *Lizzie. Lizzie. Lizzie.* Calling her name, again and again, the wind stronger now, shaking the branches, tossing them this way and that. The storm is coming. The first fat drops of rain are on her forehead. *Can you hear me? Lizzie!* She's being shaken. Someone is shaking her. She opens her eyes.

Rabbie is looking down at her.

'Lizzie! Are you all right? I found Mary under the table.'

It takes her a moment to remember where she is, who he is. She seizes his hand.

'I'm not well!' Her eyes are huge and dark with fear as she stares up at him. 'Truly, Rabbie, I am not well.'

He thinks she must be dreaming still. She seems unaware of her state of undress. Sitting down on the bed beside her, careful to keep his eyes on her face, Rabbie places his free hand over hers.

'You must have fallen asleep,' he says.

The statement, or perhaps the kindly tone in which it is expressed, acts on her like a purge. It all pours out of her: all her fears and anxiety. The bad dreams and headaches. The dizziness and the horrible sickness. The enervation she cannot shake off. Her courses stopped for three months now. She is silting up with evil humours. Losing her mind.

Rabbie hardly knows what to say. Is it possible she would not recognize the symptoms? Surely after the first time? But then he has heard of women brought to bed in the belief they have nothing more than an ache in the belly. Another glance at his cousin's stricken face assures him she has no idea. Is it right that he should be the one to tell her? But given her distress, how can he keep it from her?

'You're not mad – ' He cannot stop himself from breaking into a smile. How shall he put it? 'You are with child.'

35

French is standing by the window with his back to Cruden, his attention apparently fixed on the street outside, where a drover is steering a herd of cattle towards the harbour, his dog darting in and out of the beasts' legs in response to the drover's low whistles and the noisy lowing. The letter lies open on the desk between them.

'I think you should read it,' Cruden says, for a second time.

French turns reluctantly from the window. With an expression of distaste, he picks up the letter and reads aloud.

> 'Gentlemen,
>
> 'As I understand it has been signified by Dr French that the duties of the Infirmary require additional assistance, I beg leave to inform the Board that I have formerly assisted for that Gentleman and I am ready on the present occasion to give gratis every Assistance the house may require. If you shall proceed to make any appointment, I hope that my long Public services and other considerations with which I presume all of you are well acquainted, will incline you to give me the preference. I trust that my pretensions will not be the less regarded because without using interest or soliciting individuals I have thought proper to rest my success on the Merits of my claim.
>
> 'I am with great respect . . .'

'Etcetera, etcetera.' French tosses the letter back down on the desk and folds his arms across his chest.

'Without using interest!' Cruden spits the words. 'The merits of his claim! Who does he think he is? The insufferable presumption of the man!'

'He needs the money, of course,' French replies in a level tone.

'That is scarcely our concern. To think we can be bought in this way! His ambition is intolerable!'

'And if the Dispensary goes under?'

Cruden gives a contemptuous snort. 'Presumably his "long public service" will insure against it.'

'I'm not so sure.'

Cruden looks sharply at French and a more thoughtful expression dawns on his fleshy features. He taps the letter with his forefinger.

'There are others, I suppose? Equipped to take on the responsibility? Should he choose to go.'

'It might even be advisable under the circumstances.'

A poised stillness has filled the room. The two men are watching each other across the desk, circling one another's intentions, like a pair of jackals round a carcass, cautiously negotiating their share of the kill.

'What circumstances did you have in mind?'

French turns back to the window. He doesn't need to watch the Provost to know what effect his words will have.

'His insistence on venesection. He is entirely adamant on the subject. When the families protest, he accuses them of killing his patients.' French permits himself a glance over his shoulder at his colleague. 'Such conduct scarcely rebounds well on the rest of our profession, on our standing in the town. The man is becoming something of a liability.'

Cruden meets his eye with steady comprehension.

'Well then, Dr French,' he says, standing and extending his hand towards the Infirmary physician. 'We find ourselves in perfect agreement.'

36

Mary is running, arms out wide like the wings of a bird. She is flying. Rising on the air currents, skimming the clouds. She is all air and light. Her mind a blur of blue and white and gold.

'Mary! Mary!'

Her ears full of the crashing surf. The sound of her name so faint she hardly hears it. She circles to the left, dipping one wing in a wide arc, turning, heading for the dunes. The grass whips her ankles and calves as she flies on, following the narrow pathways through the dunes. She knows he's behind her, but she does not stop. The sky turns dark. His shadow falls over her, over the marsh grass, over the sand paths. On she flies. Then his arms are around her, pinioning her wings to her sides, lifting her off her feet.

'Got you!'

She wriggles and kicks with all her strength.

'Let go o me! Let me go!'

But Alec holds her tight, her small, sturdy body against his chest, strands of her hair in his mouth as they fall, tumbling, laughing, on to the soft sand, the silky grains subsiding under them to form a cocoon, a burrow, in which they lie still for a moment, out of the wind, nestling in each other's warmth, catching their breaths.

'Look!' She points at the sky.

'What?'

'Look!' she cries impatiently.

Above their heads, a giant white fish, a leaping salmon, fin-tail raised. But even as they watch, it seeps away, elongating in the breeze, thinning into bland little wisps. He pulls her to her feet.

'Come on! Ye musnae catch cold.'

At once she's running again, off like a whippet down the dunes, her bare heels lifting a spray of fine sand in her wake. He catches up with her at the water's edge, where the ridges of surf explode at their feet. They jump, clear of the white froth, Mary landing up to her knees in the icy water, shrieking with the shock of it, her father's hand tight around her own, anchoring her from the tug of the receding wave.

They ready themselves for the next; leap, hang for a moment in the shining air, then fall, their feet shattering the water into a thousand blinding fragments. Mary turns her head to look up at him. The sun, low in the sky now, is full on her face, glitters on the salt-spray caught in her eyelashes, gleams on her flushed cheeks. She is laughing up at him. Offering him her happiness. Surfeited with it, though her teeth are chattering with cold. She would play this game all afternoon, let the sun set before she tired of it. But Alec is pulling her away, back up the beach. 'We must get you warm,' he says, when she protests. Kneeling in front of her, he wrings the sea-water from her dress, unbalancing her a little in the process so that she has to rest her hands on his shoulders to steady herself. He dries each of her feet in turn with his shirt, brushes off the wet sand lodged between the toes and around the nailbeds, dusts away the fine grains clinging to the upperside of her foot, suddenly conscious of the intricate maze of tiny bones beneath the fragile sheath of skin.

They make their way up the beach, following the long fingers of shadow that stretch and bend over the sand, Mary pausing every few steps to poke at sand-coils and gather shells that catch her eye. What are shells made of? she wants to know. Where are the creatures that live in the shells? Does God make the shells, like he made Adam and Eve? They must be very old, then. Older even than Aunt Rae. When she is finally too tired to walk, too tired to ask questions, Alec picks her up and carries her.

As the sun sinks behind the hills, the light and warmth

drain from the air and the land. Fishermen, returning for the evening, have pulled their boats up on to the shore and are lighting small fires on which to bake a herring or two. Ribbons of woodsmoke, sweet and resiny, drift on the breeze.

'Good catch?'

The fisherman looks up at the sound of Alec's voice.

'No bad.'

He takes a herring from the pile at his feet, and with one deft movement slits it open from gill to tail, letting the guts slither out on to the sand. Holding the gutted herring up by the tail, he slices a strip of flesh away from the backbone and flicks it into the pan, then repeats the action on the other side. Alec and Mary watch. The scent of roasting fish fills their nostrils, draws the juices into their mouths. Spearing a piece of cooked fish on his knife tip, the fisherman holds it out to Mary.

'Want some, lassie?'

Mary nods. Alec leans forward to take the fish for her, twisting her off his back as he does so, but at the same moment Mary reaches out her own hand and her weight unbalances him. He stumbles, veers to one side, his outstretched fingers grazing the edge of the knife. He feels the cool of the blade as it slides into his skin. Cursing softly, he sets Mary down on the sand, then lifts his hand to the firelight to inspect the wound. A thin line of blood is seeping from the cut. It swells and oozes over his palm, along the creases there, pooling for a moment on the rim of his hand, before the first drops break away and fall. Five scarlet beads falling onto the sand at his feet.

37

Elizabeth hadn't known what it was to begin with, hours of it, or so it seemed at first, a great swell of twittering and chirruping, thinning the darkness. She woke to it, day after day, startled and frightened by the strange riotous clamour outside the window, as alien as the grey air that clung to everything in this new place, crept into her as she slept, so that she woke every morning chilled to the bone, could never stay warm no matter how many blankets were heaped on her at bedtime. The dawn chorus, Papa called it, and slowly over the years she had grown to love it. This wondrous spillage of joy in the half-light.

There was no birdsong where she'd come from. Birds but no song. The nights had bristled with other sounds: a multitude of scuttling, scratching, scurrying things busying themselves inside the house and out, from sunset to sunrise; a hectic, furtive feasting on floorboards and food-crumbs and human flesh. Cockroaches and chiggers, scorpions and centipedes. The hiss and shriek of lizards and snakes, the racketing of cicadas, the whining mosquitos. Rats, too, hundreds of them, squealing their way through the cane fields. It didn't scare her, this nocturnal cacophony. Marie greased her legs with cassava oil to keep off the bête-rouges, and even when the cockroaches slithered across the bed nets, their pincers snagging in the mesh, she felt quite safe, with her brothers fidgeting in their sleep close by and the sound of Marie's slow, steady breathing from her mat in the corner. But in this new world they'd come to, she slept alone, with no milky tent to protect her from the unfamiliar noises that broke into her dreams, no soothing breathing from the corner of the room. The shrieks of the barn owls terrified her. The north wind soughing in the blackness outside froze her blood. She believed herself transported to a land of demons and impenetrable darkness.

Elizabeth closes her eyes, now, listening to the birdsong filling the air. She is sitting in the garden in a sheltered spot close to the house, the afternoon sun warm on her face. She lets her ear disentangle the different sounds: the short plaintive song of a robin; the scolding click of a wren; from the direction of the blackcurrant bushes, the thin, wavering song of a dunnock; from high in the branches of the birch tree, the liquid, descending scale of a willow warbler. Calling to each other. Singing for no one's sake but their own. Rejoicing in the lovely afternoon. The trees and bushes full of their eager rustling. The sunlight glows red-black through her eyelids. She can smell honeysuckle on the air. She is tired, but agreeably so. Isabella had been to see her that morning and the company seems to have done her good, for a pleasant languor has come over her since. Bella had been so evidently happy at her news, and happier still to show off the baby, kissing its plump cheeks every few moments and laughing delightedly at its gurgling smiles. When Mary had brought her face close up to the baby's own, the wee thing had reached out and grabbed hold of her nose so hard that Mary squealed and started to cry.

'Naughty baby!' Bella scolded, covering the fat little fists in kisses. 'What a naughty baby!'

'She'll be crawling soon, Bella,' Elizabeth warned, 'and then you'll get nothing done for weeks.'

Isabella had smiled. 'Then you must come often, Lizzie,' she'd said, 'and do nothing with me.'

Elizabeth's hands move now to her stomach, her palms spreading over the slow swelling of her belly. Perhaps it will be easier this time. Perhaps with this child she will experience some of that happiness she reads so plainly on her sister's face. But then happiness comes easily to Bella and always has. Elizabeth was relieved today to find herself struggling less with the feeling of resentment that so often comes over her in her sister's company, an undertow of bitterness that, to her own dismay, has only grown stronger as the years have passed. She'd been friend, sister and mother to Bella when they were young. They had clung together as their mother sank into madness, and grown closer still after she died. Two years later, Papa, too, was dead, as if with no more purpose for living once she was gone. Isabella had needed her then, and Elizabeth had willingly occupied herself with her care, cleaving to the task that saved her the trouble of her own distress. As time passed, however, Isabella had gently but determinedly unshackled herself from her older sister's clasp, revealing a quiet assuredness and independence of spirit that Elizabeth resisted and resented in equal measure. It had unwillingly become apparent to Elizabeth that Bella no longer needed or wanted her anxious hovering concern. Marriage to the Gordon brothers had concreted their attachment only in law. In more important ways, Bella's betrothal to Chae had created an invisible wall between them that Elizabeth could never break through. Cast out from her sister's confidence, she found herself painfully alone. Perhaps she would not have minded so very much had her own marriage enjoyed more of the ease and comfort of Bella and Chae's, but as it is, the unwanted exile is a constant wound: a goading image of all that her own life lacks. She has built walls of her own, of course, but they never prove quite as solid as she hopes. The sound of laughter still drifts through the bricks. The sun still seems to cast its light on Bella's side of the wall, the shadows on her own. She can feel them on her, within her: a darkness in her veins; a slow seepage at the periphery of her vision, sullying her thoughts and actions, spoiling all her efforts to banish the past. Some days it seems the shadows are everywhere, dragging at the foundations of the life she has tried to build for herself, whining in her ear as the mosquitos once had.

She opens her eyes. Not far from her chair, a young robin is rooting about in the soil beneath the bushes, digging for insects with its beak. She can see its little brown head and pale red breast through the veil of low branches. She closes her eyes again, remembering suddenly the humming birds in the garden at Harvie's End, a rowdy little family of them in the calabash tree, their bright green feathers tinged with reddish gold, the brilliance of their plumage compensating for the monotonous drone of their song. She'd thought of them as tiny flying jewels. One morning, sitting with Mo in the shade of the tree and sucking on slices of pineapple that Marie had brought out to them, a much larger bird had flown into the nest and made off with one of the fledglings. The furious mother had set up pursuit, hovering over the kidnapper's head until she was close enough to land on its back. Though the other bird was ten times the hummingbird's size, it could not shake off its attacker. After a short, frenzied struggle, the former dropped out of the sky like a stone and the mother returned victorious to its nest. When Elizabeth crept over to where the dead bird lay, she saw a mess of grey and red oozing from the hole that the hummingbird had drilled in its skull. She hadn't liked the flying jewels so much after that.

A shadow falls over her, cutting out the sunlight. She opens her eyes again, this time to find Alec standing in front of her. Something is wrong. She can see at once from his face.

'What? What's happened?'

He holds out a copy of the *Aberdeen Journal*. 'It seems you were right.'

Elizabeth looks from her husband to the newspaper and back again, not understanding.

'Here!' With his forefinger he jabs to a point midway down the front page.

She takes the newspaper from him and, after a moment, finds the item he's indicated.

> Letters from Dr French and Dr Gordon with the
> Representations of Motion of Provost Cruden,
> confirmed and supported by Dr George Skene,
> having all been deliberately considered, the meet-
> ing are unanimously of the opinion that it is
> expedient and necessary that a 3rd physician
> should be appointed to the Infirmary. Being all
> perfectly satisfied of the ability and qualifications
> of Dr William Robertson for filling that place,
> they have unanimously appointed the said gentle-
> man to be 3rd physician along with Dr Livingston
> and Dr French.

She looks up at him, appalled. 'How can they do this? How *can* they?'

All around them the birdsong, the lavender and honey-suckle, the whispering leaves.

'After everything you have done! All your assistance!'

Alec does not look at her.

'Baxter will have to go,' he says, his eyes fixed on the ground at his feet.

'What! But how will I manage? With the baby coming? I cannot make do with Annie alone. I cannot!'

Alec shakes his head. 'You must. There is no choice.'

38

June

Out in the world, revolutions are occurring. Wars are fought, tyrants are opposed, time-worn wisdoms are overturned. Undaunted by recent defeat at Reval, the Swedish fleet prepares for a second major offensive against the Russians. In the Austrian lowlands, the Belgians rise up against the oppressive yoke of their new emperor, Leopold II. From the prison of the Tuileries palace, Leopold's sister nervously follows his efforts to quell the rebellion: in her darker moments, she suspects her own future may depend on it. Beyond the palace walls, labourers, monks and soldiers toil shoulder to shoulder in the midday heat to excavate a giant amphitheatre for the great pageant that will mark the first anniversary of the Bastille's fall; on the Altar of the Fatherland will be inscribed the words: *All mortals are equal; it is not by birth but only virtue that they are distinguished.* In London, Mr Edmund Burke puts the finishing touches to his new work, predicting that the revolution will end in disaster.

Throughout the civilized world, new ideas are taking shape. New forms of government are carved from the worn rock of old regimes. New words form on the lips of scientific men. Nitrate. Sulphuric acid. Hydrogen. Discs of gas are discovered floating among the stars. The shoelace is invented. The first dental drill is put to use. A young jeweller launches a company to manufacture a new drink he has created: an artificially carbonated mineral beverage that Herr Schweppe is calling 'soda water'. In Suffolk, Mr John Frere discovers flint tools in the crumbling yellow soil; he believes they are evidence of prehistoric humans. The theory is greeted with widespread derision, although privately some wonder if Mr Frere may not, in time, be proved correct.

In Aberdeen, too, old certainties are collapsing, falling away like shelves of soft sand beneath the onslaught of waves and salt and wind. There is emptiness where there was once firm ground. There is blank space where there was order. Inchoate darkness where there was light. The world is not flat. The sun does not revolve around the earth. And now, it seems, contagion is not in the air but somewhere else, as yet unseen, unimagined.

Thankfully, perhaps, Alec's attention is directed towards other, more immediate concerns for the inoculation season is now come.

He begins on the first of the month at Baillie Duguid's home, where three-year-old Master Duguid and his little sister are to undergo the operation. The matter has been kept in a closed phial for some time and when Rabbie pulls the cork, the stench that issues forth causes Mistress Duguid some uneasiness as to the wisdom of the operation. But her husband, who is also present, overrides her concerns and insists the procedure be carried out as planned. Rabbie holds the lad still while Alec makes the scratch on his left arm and inserts the threads. They then repeat the procedure with the little girl. By twelve o'clock they are on their way to Mr Irving's in Broad Street. All five Irving children are to be done at once. Alec has prescribed four doses of physic to be taken in advance and a purifying regimen of light, easy nourishment with a strict abstinence from animal food of all kinds to take off the inflammatory diathysis. The children appear healthy; the eldest is nine years of age, the youngest two. The six-year-old is more afraid than all the others put together: she stands trembling in front of Alec as he makes the cuts, with huge tears streaming like watery pearls down her pretty cheeks.

Three days later, the dressings and threads are ready to be removed, all except for those of the younger Master Irving, in whose case the threads are still stuck. The wounds in the two older children are a good deal inflamed and a little matter has formed. By Thursday, the youngest Miss Irving is feverish, but all the others are well. Master Duguid has been taken with sickness and puked twice. Three spots have appeared on his cheeks and the sores are beginning to run. Alec orders Gascoigne's Powder. Two days later the boy is still indisposed and very fractious. The Irving children are all sick now, the two girls in general being the easiest.

Besides the Irvings and the Duguids, Alec receives instruction from five other families, which is not as many as he'd hoped, but better than none. Inoculation is not a procedure he enjoys and the pouring rain that has fallen with sullen insistence all week makes it none the pleasanter. The bairns themselves hate it, of course, and their mothers too, although they try to conceal their anxiety by scolding the children for fretting and fussing. One wee laddie bolted under the bed at first sight of the physician and no amount of threatening would lure him out again. It is the children's distress that makes it so wearying a business, that and the risk that one of them may prove unequal to the ensuing infection. But Alec prefers not to dwell on that, prefers to think of the evils he may succeed in averting rather than those he knows he cannot.

39

The rain eases. Stitchwort and campion bedeck the hedgerows and the woods are carpeted with dog violet and yellow pimpernel; the cliff-paths are pink with flowering thrift, the air laced with the scent of gorse. In the fields, the oats are in and the biggs sown; now the drilling of the turnips is under way, the farmers seeding and harrowing from dawn to dusk to make up for the time they've lost. For a few days at a stretch the disease lies quiet, then it strikes again. Alec notes everything he can about each case, stockpiling information like ammunition against an enemy he cannot see, however long and hard he looks. He knows it's out there, nevertheless, waiting for its next chance to attack. Three women have recovered so far, all three when he'd been called in time to bleed early and sufficiently, but far more continue to die. There are too many obstacles in his way: the midwives concealing the disease from him until it is too late, then opposing his treatment, although they have nothing else to offer but useless cordials and clysters; the husbands, too, withholding their consent until the narrow window of opportunity for saving their wives has been missed. Alec is at a loss to know how to combat their opposition. It is like fighting back the sea: this ignorance and fear he encounters again and again. The three successes, however, do give him some small room for hope, convince him he is correct in his choice of treatment, however unpopular it is with the rest of Aberdeen. *Let nature do her work*, he urges, pleads, bawls. *Nature must be assisted. It is the only way.* When the families still refuse permission to bleed, Alec prescribes emetics, diaphoretics, purgatives without their knowledge, lets them believe he is writing prescriptions for physic to ease the pain.

*

Late one evening as Alec is writing up his notes, Dr Bannerman knocks at the door in a state of considerable agitation. An urgent case in the Hardgate. One of his private patients. The woman has been in labour for two days already and is dangerously fatigued. The baby appears to have given up the struggle and abandoned its efforts to be born. Should they give it more time, or try to save the mother at least? The midwives won't touch her. Skene is at a loss.

There is something evasive in Bannerman's account of the situation, some piece of information that he is withholding and which prevents him from meeting Alec's eye; some mis-adventure, Alec suspects, which he prefers not to admit to. But there can be no mistaking the gravity of the woman's predicament.

'You've examined her?'

'Every few hours,' Bannerman nods. 'No progress at all since yesterday. You opinion, Gordon, would be invaluable.'

As he follows Bannerman out of the house, it occurs to Alec that he has not yet discovered the name of the patient he is to visit. Both this and the reason for Bannerman's evasiveness become clear the moment Bannerman halts in front of William Cormack's door. Always in the past the Cormacks have come to Alec for treatment; they were among the first to seek his services after he took up the Dispensary position; it was he who'd confirmed Mistress Cormack's pregnancy four months back. When had they become Bannerman's patients? Banner-man himself had certainly omitted to mention it. Still more to the point, what reason had the Cormacks for their sudden change of allegiance? It was he, not Bannerman, who was acknowledged the best accoucheur in Aberdeen. Bannerman was not a bad physician, but he had little skill or reputation in this area of practice: what the devil had induced them to entrust their health to Bannerman rather than to him? He could have told them before today it was a decision they'd regret.

They are admitted by a servant who leads them upstairs to

the lying-in room on the first floor of the house, overlooking the garden. The blinds are lowered, but one of the casements is a little raised and the room is cool and clean. Among the women gathered about the bed is Widow Chalmers, the midwife in attendance. Mistress Cormack, herself, is barely conscious. Her eyes are closed and the hair at her temples is drenched with perspiration. Alec orders the room to be cleared, with the exception of the midwife and two others. As soon as the women have gone, he lifts the sheet and slides his free hand up on to the mother's belly, pressing rapidly on one side then the other to ascertain the baby's position, relieved to find it is neither transverse nor breech. Parting the woman's legs, he inserts his index and forefinger into the vaginal passage, pausing for a moment before carefully introducing the rest of his hand up to the hilt of the thumb joint. With the tips of his fingers he can feel the hard rim of the cervix stretched tight as a barrel hoop around the top of the baby's head; through the thin membrane of the fontanelle he can feel the throb of the baby's pulse. Very gently he traces the edges of the skull plates, deciding after a moment that what he's touching must be the diamond shape of the superior fontanelle. The baby's head is well down, but flexed too far forward. He withdraws his fingers a little way, feeling for the spines, and after a moment he finds them a little way below the head and not over much protruded. Reaching in again, he starts to ease the cervix back over the baby's head: it's slow work and there's not much time, but if he goes too fast there's the risk of rupture. The mother still has not moved.

'Give her something to drink,' Alec instructs the midwife, his fingers nudging all the while at the rigid lip of the cervix. 'Something cold. She must be brought round.'

After another five minutes, he's succeeded in freeing the head from the cervix. Straightening up for a moment to ease out the muscles in his back, he inspects his fingers: there's a little blood and mucus, but nothing untoward.

'It'll take forceps to get this one out,' he says to Bannerman in a low voice. 'You and you – ' he orders the two women, 'we need to move her down the bed. Get behind her and lift her up. And you – ' to Mistress Chalmers, 'when I say, you're to press down on the belly, hard as you can.'

As Bannerman and he shuffle the inert mother down the bed, she at last begins to moan and revive a little.

'Give her a slap,' Alec orders. 'Keep her awake.'

He opens his bag, feels his heart rate quicken as he takes out the forceps and unscrews the blades. How often he has done this, but never yet without this cold rush of apprehension. The mother is propped up now between the two women, with her legs hanging over the end of the bed. Alec folds the sheet back over her belly, out of his way, ignoring the muttered objections to this impropriety. Holding the entrance of the vagina apart with one hand, he inserts the first blade, sliding it carefully forwards until it is high up around the side of the baby's head. The second blade is harder to position with the first in place: there's no space in the passage and the right spine is in the way of the second blade, directly below the skullbone. He has no choice but to angle it hard into the wall of the birth channel before he can get it up alongside and then past the head, an operation that elicits a cry of pain from the patient. When both blades are finally in position around the skull, he attaches the connecting plate and tightens the screw to lock them securely into place.

'All right,' he tells the midwife. 'Now start pushing on the belly, like this –' he demonstrates a sharp downward motion with his free arm. 'Go on! Aye, like that. But harder. And again. Hard as you can!'

The mother is fully conscious now and groaning loudly, as the throes once more take her in their grip.

'Good. That's good. Keep going. Don't stop till I say.'

Alec is half-standing, half-crouching at the foot of the bed, legs well apart to keep his balance. With both hands on the wooden handle of the forceps, he braces himself, then starts to pull slowly down on the baby's head. The mother's groans turn to screams. Keeping a constant pressure on the head, Alec continues to pull down on the forceps. It takes all his strength and concentration to keep the motion steady and gradual; he can feel the slow reluctant stretch of the channel as the head edges its way through the vagina, can feel the muscles in his back and arms strained tight and starting to burn with the effort of drawing the baby down. He sets one foot against the wooden frame of the bedstead to give himself more purchase against the body's resistance. By minute degrees, he drags the baby on through the birth channel, the mother's tortured shrieks filling his ears. Glancing up, he catches sight of Bannerman's face, grey as ash in the dim light. The baby's head inching downwards. It is like cleaving a rock-face.

'Nearly there,' Alec says, more to himself than anyone else. 'Nearly there.'

He suddenly sees, level with his eyes, the perinæum: paper-thin, bluish-pink.

'Bannerman!' he shouts. 'Get your hand here!'

But Bannerman has barely time to roll up his sleeves before the head begins to crown. The perinæum rips apart. There's nothing Alec can do: he needs both hands for pulling, down and now, at last, up, lifting the baby's head free from the birth channel and, with a final anguished scream from the mother, out. And alive. The marks of the forceps blades imprinted on either side of the infant's elongated skull. But definitely alive.

Alec passes the child to the midwife and turns his attention back to Mistress Cormack, who has once more reverted to a state of semi-consciousness. He gives the cord a gentle tug. Waits. Tugs again. Softly. And to his infinite relief feels the slow convulsion run through the mother's body in response. Seconds later the wombcake is expelled intact. No haemorrhaging then. Thank God.

His work done for the moment, Alec steps back from the bed and lets the women come forward to tend to Mistress Cormack. He is exhausted suddenly, can feel his leg muscles shaking slightly, the cold sweat filming on his back and sides. Picking up a discarded bed sheet, he rubs off his hands and arms. Bannerman comes and stands beside him, arms dangling like a big ungainly schoolboy. His sleeves are rolled up still. Below the elbow on the inner side of his left arm, Alec notices, there is a large, purple sore.

'What?' he says, with a touch of impatience.

'Thank you,' Bannerman says, reddening a little. 'You saved her life.'

Alec accepts the veiled apology without comment, but he shakes his head. 'She's not out of danger yet. She must be bled. While there's still time.'

'Are you out of your mind, man?' Bannerman's voice has dropped to a whisper, but the look on his face is loud with astonishment.

'You heard me,' Alec says. 'It's the only sure way to avert the risk of contagion.'

'There's no contagion here.'

'You think not? Do you know how many healthy women I have delivered in the past six months who have subsequently died of this disease?'

'She's half-dead as it is. Bleeding will kill her for certain.'

Alec regards his colleague in silence for a moment, then shrugs and turns to pack away his things.

'Very well,' he says. 'You are her physician. Have it your own way.'

Three days later, Bannerman sends a note to the Dispensary. The bairn is dead and Mistress Cormack gravely sick, with a racing pulse and raging fever. She is complaining greatly of pains in her belly.

Alec crushes the note in his fist and lets it fall to the floor. Scrawls a brief line back. *Too late to save her.*

He thinks of the sore he'd seen on Bannerman's arm and remembers: one exactly like it on Mistress Blake's arm at Elspet Garrow's lying-in; a lesion on Mistress Philp's leg way back, before Easter. How had it escaped his notice before now? Two rivers. Two towns. Two diseases.

40

A week after the threads are first inserted, the pock is come out well in all the bairns and more continuing every day. Master Duguid has many pimples up and down the body, and all are a good deal inflamed and pretty large. By the eighth day, the fever in the Irving children has gone off. The eldest Irving boy has about four or five pimples, the two younger boys about a dozen each. The youngest Irving girl has over a hundred, much inflamed and very tender. Alec instructs Rabbie to poultice the sores. By the tenth day the sloughs are coming out and the sores are almost all clean. Master Duguid is still weak and a little loose, but has no other bad symptoms. Twelve days after Alec's first visit, the pustules are almost gone and healing well. He declares the operation a success and prescribes jalap, to be taken three times a day at proper intervals. Baillie Duguid sends a brace of hare to Belmont Street by way of thanks.

What worries Alec more than the bairns he's treated are the ones he has not. He has offered to inoculate the poor gratis, but that has not been inducement enough for the families of Footdee and Torry, the ones most vulnerable to the disease and the least able to withstand it. He can understand well enough why they fear the procedure. To introduce disease intentionally into a healthy system runs counter to every shred of parental instinct. He can still recall his own misgivings when he inoculated Mary, and the terrible days and nights that followed, when it seemed she would not survive the operation, when it seemed that he might be responsible for his own child's death. She had survived, thank God, and two severe outbreaks of the disease since then have proved her resistance to its evil.

But how is he to convince others of what he knows to be the case: that instinct is not the best guide to action? That reason is a better master, though a harder one?

One afternoon, on a sudden inspiration, he recalls that a new plan of the town has recently been published. That same afternoon on his way back from the Dispensary he takes a detour to the Homer's Head, and after some negotiations, it is agreed that Mr Brown will sell a copy of the plan on credit on condition that the account is settled by the end of the month. Back in his study, Alec takes down the van Rymsdyk engraving and nails the plan up in its place. Mr Milne has made a fine job of it: every building, street and wynd and all the backlands are clearly drawn. Alec takes up a handful of pins and inserts one into each of the households that he has inoculated this year and last. That done, he sits down at the desk and surveys his work. His campaign map. Come next winter he'll show them beyond doubt. Make them see that the operation provides the bairns' best hope of protection, whatever instinct may tell them to the contrary.

Lowering his eyes from the map of Aberdeen, Alec's attention turns to the case notes on the desk. Progress has been made here, too, but progress of a most baffling kind. To his and Bannerman's astonishment Mistress Cormack is still alive. A week before, in desperation, Bannerman had ordered a large dose of opium to mitigate the excruciating pain she was in, and most unexpectedly the treatment not only allowed her some rest, but produced a copious sweat, which continued several days and seemed to take off the worst of the fever (although without any other sign of improvement in her condition). Surprised and intrigued, Alec had overcome his anger and turned back to the case. 'Keep up the opiates,' was his advice to Bannerman, 'and keep the bowels open with regular doses of senna.'

There was no doubt of internal suppuration, for the belly was large and hard and exceedingly painful to the touch. The fever, though somewhat reduced, never entirely left her. Neither man entertained much hope of a recovery and yet, precarious as her state was, Mistress Cormack stubbornly refused to die.

Reason tells Alec the woman should already be lying in her grave. Instinct whispers in his ear that somehow, against all odds, she will survive. He looks from the case notes to the pin-studded map and back again. He thinks of the sore on Bannerman's arm. Thinks of the bairns he's inoculated, and the ones he has not. In his head reason is silent. It is the clamouring of instinct he can hear.

41

Mistress Glegg will countenance no objection: the roup of silverware at the Gallowgate will provide excellent and harmless diversion; the rain has stopped for a while, and Mistress Gordon will assuredly benefit from a wee airing. What objection can possibly outweigh the advantages of the proposal? Elizabeth can think of a thousand objections, but cannot summon the power to voice them in the face of the other woman's insistence, so suffers her cloak and bonnet to be fetched, her arm to be taken and herself to be transported to the Gallowgate showroom, where a great throng of folk has gathered and a brisk trade is already under way. The showroom is filled with stands, on which are arranged innumerable items of silverware, large and small and middling size, every one of them buffed and polished to brilliance. People are walking up and down between the stands, pointing and admiring; the air hums with the noise of bartering and arguing. Mistress Glegg, her arm still tucked firmly through Elizabeth's, goes from one stand to the next, exclaiming at the beauty or otherwise of the items before them, and assiduously asking the price of each. 'Eight shillings!' she cries, in response to her enquiry of a little set of ladies' brushes, the silver backs engraved with leaves and flowers. 'For that sorry bit of nothing! Do you take me for a fool, sir! You may have four shillings, and think yourself lucky.' But the stallholder is as forceful in defence of his wares. 'Eight shillings, ma'am. Not a penny less.'

Elizabeth takes advantage of the argument to disengage her arm and move on alone to the next stand. Her gaze travels over the assortment of objects on display before her. In a glass case at the front of the table is a collection of brooches. One is engraved with a bouquet of roses, another with a winding trellis of tiny leaves, the veins of each delineated with the utmost care. A third bears a butterfly, wrought from silver filigree and set into an oval of onyx. Laid out on either side of the glass case in great profusion are yet more silver trinkets: tiny boxes for pills and salts and snuff; pepper bowls and sugar cutters; thimbles and card cases. Despite herself, Elizabeth finds her spirits lifting at the sight of so much loveliness. She has a secret fondness for pretty objects of any kind, for little extravagances pleasing to the eye or touch or both. Alec has never been one for such things, however, nor has their situation allowed her to indulge this predilection. Instead the early years of their marriage, Alec would present her with his more outlandish cases as another man might present his loved one with a pretty piece of jewellery or a new volume of verse. These were his tokens of love, and he offered them for her amusement and astonishment. 'Today,' he would begin, 'something extraordinary . . .' It reminded Elizabeth of her father, pulling surprises from his big leather bag, on his return from business in London or Antwerp or Paris, a china doll for her, a skipping rope for Bella. Whenever Alec spoke those words – *Today, something extraordinary* – she felt like a gleeful child again. Even then, in the early years when she considered herself fortunate in her marriage, even then her days contained little that was astonishing, rarely consisted of anything more diverting than paying visits and receiving them, and she relished hearing Alec's tales as much as he delighted in telling them. 'A worm, Lizzie, of prodigious size! Eighteen yards in length. Can you conceive of such a thing? And when I opened the corpse, there were twelve yards more wound round the man's intestines!' Or the tradesman's wife, a few months later, delivered of a baby boy, a monster: sixteen pounds and seven ounces, and two feet in length. Who would have thought mother or child could survive? But they did, and thrived. The boy, now a giant three-year-old, could be seen any day of the week, kicking his heels on the harbour wall.

Behind the glass cases, in tiers, are larger items: serving plat-
ters, candlesticks, biscuit jars, tea caddies. An elegant little tea
urn, mounted proudly on a plinth of its own, arrests Elizabeth's
eye. There is something especially pleasing in the urn's propor-
tions, neither too bulbous nor too elongated, and the detail is
exquisite: the handle of the lid has been fashioned into the
shape of a pheasant, and so cleverly done that the feathers of
the breast are readily distinguishable from those on its back and
wings. The artist has rendered the bird on the point of flight
with such exactness that it really seems as if it might lift off
from the urn at any moment, rise up into the air and away.

'Russian,' says the man behind the stall, noticing the direction of her attention. 'One o the Tsar's own, I shouldna
wonder,' he adds, 'judging by the skill o it.'

Elizabeth looks again at the little bird, at once poised for
freedom and eternally fettered. Reaching out her hand, she
strokes the pheasant's outspread wings with the tips of her
fingers. The tiny ridges of the feathers are cool to the touch.

'How much?' she asks.

For the rest of the day she cannot shake from her mind the
image of the silver urn and of her hand on the bird's wing.
They mingle with other images that rise unbidden and
unwanted in her memory. Her father's hands caressing the
bolts of silk in his storehouse. Her mother's hands folded
across her breast, white and still. Alec's hands held between
her own in bed at night when they were first married. His
hands had held a special fascination for her then. She thought
of them as instruments of deliverance, able to defeat death,
defy fate. He laughed at her for saying such things, but she
thought them anyway. Late at night, in the guttering candlelight, warmed with love-making, she would take his hands
between her own, turn them palm up and lightly trace the
whorled grooves of his fingerprints, the pathways of lines
crisscrossing the surface of his palms, as if she were a fortune-
teller reading the map of his life. 'What do ye see there, my

wee wumman?' he'd ask teasingly. 'Why, fame and fortune, of course!' she'd reply, and lace her fingers through his and raise them to her lips to kiss. What she really saw was knowledge.

It is strange to think how she'd loved his hands in those days, when now she cannot bear to have them near her, can think only of them prodding and prying, in corpses and other women's hidden parts. He seldom touches her now in any case, but at times even the sight of his hands is enough to make her recoil in disgust, thinking of where they've been. That morning he'd come to find her in the parlour, where she was sitting with her sewing, attempting to appear as if she were still the daughter of a gentleman, doing the things she had been brought up to do. He'd come up behind her and placed his hand on her shoulder. Instantly she caught the smell on his fingers, the odours engrained in his skin. She'd jerked away from him and he let his arm fall to his side and stood there in silence for some time.

'It'll be over soon,' he said at last. 'I promise.'

She hadn't known what he meant and hadn't asked, but she can still feel now, hours later, the precise place where his hand had briefly rested on her shoulder. In the depths of her belly, the baby stirs, a faint rolling motion, like the glimpse of a distant wave. Perhaps this was what he'd been referring to. If so it tells her only how little he knows of her, how far apart they have travelled in these years they've been married. Perhaps she should have told him: it is not the prospect of the birth, but confinement of a different sort that torments her.

42

'The first milk of all animals is naturally purgative and the best medicine that children can get.'

Alec's tone is not calculated to win over the midwives so much as bludgeon them into submission. The rain has returned and he is cold and ill-tempered in his wet clothing. It's been nothing but rain and mud and miserable bairns for days and he is in no mood for stockit howdies.

'Stuffing newborns with water gruel destroys their stomachs, gripes them severely and takes of their appetite for suckling. Filling them with syrups to purge off the meconium is, likewise, entirely contrary to nature and does far more harm than good. Some wise people have taken into their heads that it would be better for children to be brought up by the spoon entirely, but I assure you, nothing can be more monstrous, nor a greater perversion of nature's laws. All other animals wean their young gradually and in this, too, we should follow the example of the brutes. A child ought to live many months before it tastes anything but the mother's milk.'

'If it has a mither,' one of the midwives mutters.

Alec turns to her. 'You refer, I suppose, to the deaths?'

'I do.'

He has heard them gossiping and whispering. Seen their eyes sliding away from his when he greets them in the street, heard their grumbling, felt their shudders of disapproval when he calls for the operator. They are not avoiding his gaze now, but looking directly at him, openly challenging him to defend himself. First the physicians, now the midwives, Alec thinks, with sudden weariness. Where will it end? What price must a man pay for attempting to enlighten in this so-called age of enlightenment?

'Very well.' Alec puts down his lecture notes. 'Since you have raised the matter, let us turn to it.'

It astonishes him, frankly, that they should cling to their prejudices, but he has been aware for some while now of their mounting hostility, aware that neither his authority nor the proof of his methods are succeeding in reducing their enmity.

'The disease that has now claimed the lives of thirty-five women—'

Yes! He thought that would make them sit up!

'— is the puerperal fever. Some of you may have heard of it by another name: childbed fever. Call it what you will, it is responsible for all of the mothers' deaths in Aberdeen this year.'

How very much longer than six months it seems since that first lecture, when they'd flocked to his house with such eagerness, with such respect for his knowledge and his experience. Twenty-five weeks ago. Today there are just twelve women in the room, and not one of them has dressed for the occasion. He wishes they hadn't come at all. He is sick to death of the midwives and their opposition.

'You will grant, I trust, that a physician's training allows him to distinguish between symptoms that to the uneducated observer may appear indistinguishable?' He lets his gaze travel over their faces, his expression and his tone defying them to contradict him. 'So it is with this disease. To take an example familiar to you all, let us consider two plants you know well. Hemlock and sweet cicely.'

Janet Anderson is sitting at the back of the room, a little apart from the rest. Since their meeting in the physic garden, Alec has taken pains to avoid further encounters, but now his eyes meet hers. He looks away at once, tries to ignore the sudden jolt of longing at the sight of her.

'Two months ago these plants appeared identical, yet, as you all know, one of these will harm as readily as the other will heal. Only now that they have grown to maturity are they readily distinguishable. So it is with the childbed fever. To the untrained eye, the symptoms of this fever may resemble those of several others. To the trained eye, I assure you, the symptoms are utterly distinct.'

They want a fight: they shall have one. They want to know what is killing the women: he will tell them. He has kept his thoughts to himself long enough. Now it is time to speak his mind and he will leave them in no doubt as to who is right. As the death-toll has climbed, the indignation of all the midwives has mounted, but it is those whose patients have died who have protested most loudly. He finds himself picking them out now from the small crowd. Mistress Blake. Mistress Elgin. Widow Chalmers. Mistress Philp. But he will not allow individuals to cloud his judgement. It is not a matter of individuals, their particular innocence or guilt. The midwives must be made to see what he sees, all of them must be made to understand what he himself knows. They must be made to understand just how wrong they are.

'Many of you have informed me that I am mistaking the after-pains of birth for the symptoms of childbed fever. Let me tell you, in no uncertain terms, it is not I who am mistaken. With the after-pains, the discomfort is periodical, the pulse is unaffected and the abdomen is not in the least sore to the touch. In the childbed fever, the pains are continual, the pulse is always very rapid and the abdomen cannot be pressed without occasioning the severest pain.'

Milk fever, some of them think? Well, they are entirely wrong. Although attended by great heat and sweating, the chief characteristic of milk fever is fullness and pain in the breasts, while in the childbed fever, the breasts are unaffected. The stoppage of the milk is the *cause* of milk fever, but it is the *result* of childbed fever. Flatulent colic also can be discounted, for in this condition the pains move from one side of the belly to the other, while in cases of the childbed fever the pain remains in one place or spreads over a large area. Rheumatic pains, although they shoot through the legs and hips as do the pains of childbed fever, are never accompanied by shaking, fever and a rapid pulse, as they always are in this disease.

Alec's voice has risen to a shout, but he cannot help himself: with each instance of their stupidity that he cites, with each obstacle to his opinion that he tears down, the cold, dark rage is mounting inside him.

Typhus fever leads to pain in the head, but without pain in the abdomen. It sets in before delivery, seldom after. Childbed fever *always* sets in after, *never* before. Cholera: no constipation, severe vomiting. Childbed fever: severe constipation, mild vomiting.

'Cholera, moreover, is a seasonal condition, while this disease has spanned two seasons already and – ' he is roaring the words at them, all vestige of self-restraint abandoned – '*shows not the least sign of abating with the arrival of a third!*'

Afterwards he sits alone in the parlour, ashamed and shaken. So much for reason, progress, education. They lie in ruins at his feet. The midwives had shuffled out in silence, not looking at him, their mutinous expressions eloquent enough. Janet Anderson seemed on the verge of speaking at one point, half-turning in the doorway to face him, then thought better of it, dropped her gaze and left with the rest. What had come over him? What is happening to him? Increasingly he finds himself prey to this uncontrollable fury coursing through his veins, as if his reserves of reason were gradually being depleted to expose a wasteland of brutishness below. Impatient, intolerant, quick-tempered, yes, he can recognize these faults in himself. But this rage that comes over him now with such frequency, this is something else, a response from somewhere very deep and raw within himself to circumstances outside himself that seem beyond his control, beyond his understanding even. It feels at times as if he does not know himself, although whether

he is becoming someone he never knew, or discovering someone that was always there, he can hardly tell.

But it was necessary, unavoidable, was it not, to have spoken
as forcefully as he had? Surely they cannot continue to ignore
him after what they have been told? There are new cases
almost every week. There are outbreaks occurring now in the
villages. The disease is spreading, not abating. If he is not
called at once, there can be little hope of the patient's survival.
It is imperative that the midwives recognize the disease at the
earliest opportunity. Instead of which they dither and dawdle,
prescribe their own pointless remedies, then round on him
when the wretched patient dies. There is no other way: he
must have the midwives' co-operation. Their intransigence and
suspicion must be purged as aggressively as the disease itself.
They have left him no choice but to speak as he has.

43

Doubt, too, is like a disease. It creeps through some opening too small to discern with the naked eye and seeds itself in the mind, quietly setting down roots, delicate and inconspicuous as threads of lace, but growing steadily stronger with time, seeking out the nutrients it needs for survival, feeding on every passing shred of jealousy, fear, guilt and grief, putting forth its tender, venomed buds, until at length it blooms into full-blown vermilion rage.

44

It's after ten when he hears it: a slow, regular beat, like the indolent tapping of a bird's beak on a hollow tree trunk. Alec is at his desk, ordering, re-ordering his notes, arranging the facts this way, then that, convinced the answers are to be found there some way or other, that there is a key to this infernal puzzle, if only he looks long enough and hard enough. The sound intrudes only gradually on his consciousness, growing steadily louder, until he can no longer concentrate on his work. Alec lifts his head and listens. He can't make it out, thinks it must be a woodpecker working as late as he, somewhere out in the garden, except that, on paying closer attention, he realizes the sound is coming from the other side of the house, from outside the window on the street side. One of the town scavengers, perhaps, poking at pelt in the gutterways. But no, it's too regular for that, too loud and too near at hand. Rising from his desk, Alec crosses the room to the window and opens the shutter that he'd half-closed earlier to keep out the draught.

He sees them at once, cannot miss them in the milky, mid-summer twilight. Standing half on the pavement, half in the road, facing the house: a group of nine or ten men, their features shadowed by the brims of their hats. At the front of the group is a tall, broad-shouldered fellow. He is holding two stout staffs and banging the one against the other in a leisurely but deliberate fashion. The movement at the window catches the man's attention and he lifts his head. With a sickening lurch that starts in his belly and floods rapidly down into his bowels, Alec sees who it is. Striking the sticks together without missing a beat, James Garrow stares straight back at him. The other men have seen him now. 'There he is!' one of them shouts. 'That's him!' At these words the rest of the mob as one pull forth sticks and staffs from under their coats and begin hammering them in time with Garrow against the paving stones. Two of the men have stepped forward to stand shoulder to shoulder with the wheelwright, and Alec recognizes the faces of Andrew Duncan and John Webster. Behind them now he can make out other faces he knows: Donald Philp, Alistair Irvine, Robert Mennie. Strong working men all, not men to reason with, not with the din-raising mood on them and the fuskey flowing in their veins. The racket is growing louder by the moment, falling out of rhythm with itself into a deafening barrage that ricochets off the walls of the buildings behind and rebounds on itself in an ugly syncopated echo. Like beaters routing grouse from the heather. And all the while they stand there staring up at him, banging their sticks together in that unholy din, not one of them uttering a word.

It's not often that Alec feels fear. In late autumn sometimes out on the moors at night on his way to a patient, when the mist is thick about him and the bogs are treacherous as quicksand, ready to suck a man to his death and leave not a trace of him until the ground spits out his remains the following summer. Or sometimes in the woods after heavy snowfall, with his horse stumbling up to the shoulders in banks of drift, unable to struggle free again. Then he knows fear: a cold lurching in his gut. But it's different from the hot drench of anxiety he feels now with the men outside in the street, beating their sticks and staffs as swift and sure as if they were smashing them down upon his skull. Alec quickly steps away from the window, and with fumbling hands secures the shutters with the wooden bar. In the darkened room, his fingers gripping the bar still, he stands listening helplessly to the hard insistent beat of the men's fury. When the first stone strikes the window, he hears the dull crack of the glass splitting, the feathery sigh of the pane collapsing in pieces behind the shutter.

They will go eventually, he tells himself. They will vent their anger, then they will go. But his legs are shaking, his hand on the shutter bar is shaking, his whole body is shaking. *So, it has come to this*, he thinks, *and so soon*.

45

'But what did they want?'

Elizabeth is staring at him as if it were he who had smashed the windows.

'I don't know. I've told you.'

'But you must know *something*. Why our house? Who were they?'

'I don't know. Are you not listening, woman? I've said ten times already. I don't know! And for God's sake, come away from there before you cut yourself.'

Outside in the street, Annie is sweeping up the last fragments of glass scattered in front of the house. A crowd of youngsters has gathered on the pavement opposite, intrigued by the sight of the doctor's house bereft of its glass. As Alec moves towards the window to pull Elizabeth away, he sees Annie lift the besom and shake it at the crowd.

'Fit ye goupin at?' she yells across at them. 'Nivver seen a brak winnock afore?'

The mob had not finally dispersed until after midnight, by which time the entire household had been awoken by the noise. Rabbie had wanted to go for the bailiffs, but Alec would not hear of him leaving the house. They'd sat together in the back parlour, as far from the sound of shattering glass as they could get, though it was not far enough; Elizabeth and Mary huddled together in the wingback, Rabbie standing beside them, leaning over to murmur reassurances each time another missile struck the front of the house, almost as if he, not Alec, were man of the house. Annie sat bolt upright on a chair by the empty fireplace, quivering with a mixture of terror, excitement and indignation. Alec had paced back and forth, filling his glass and draining it, planning revenge and retribution, writing one long excoriating letter after another in his head, aware even as he did so that there was no one to whom such a letter might be sent, that somehow, without his noticing, he had become the cause of an outrage in others as great as that which he was now feeling within himself. *When I have dedicated myself* – he mentally deletes the phrase – *worked tirelessly for the public good* – deletes the phrase – *out of my own pocket, paid for their* – deletes the phrase – *to be subjected to the grossest display of ingratitude ever visited* – deletes the phrase. The words circle round and round on themselves as he paces the room, but they cannot find their mark: there is no audience for his recriminations, not even in the fevered space of his imagination.

Eventually, receiving no response and sating itself, as anger will when given no new object to provoke it, the attack ceased and the mob went home to their beds. With the morning had come the sorry spectacle of the damage they had inflicted: every pane shattered or cracked, jagged shards of glass dripping from the wooden beading. In the bright June sunshine the paving stones in front of the house glitter and dance with reflected light. Alec gloomily calculates what so much glass will cost him to replace.

Mistress Glegg is at the front door before the morning is out.

'Don't let her in,' Elizabeth hisses down the stairwell at Annie. 'Tell her I've gone to my sister's.'

But the door is already open and Mistress Glegg has already seen her standing on the half-landing.

'Mistress Gordon!' she cries, swooping into the hall like a carrion crow with her black cloak and black skirts billowing around her. 'I came the moment I heard. Such wickedness! Such sinful wickedness! What you must have suffered, my dear. And just look at the state of your house! The villains must be brought to justice, Mr Glegg says, before they think to come back again. Come and tell me everything.'

Elizabeth, however, has nothing to tell her and would not

tell her if she had. She had not seen the men, does not know who they were or what their motivation. Mistress Glegg nods knowingly, but her appetite for gossip is sadly disappointed and a half-hour later she swoops out again. Elizabeth stands in the empty hallway, twisting the little pheasant on the silver urn that now graces the hall table. Alec has left for the Dispensary. Rabbie has taken Mary to Mr Peacock's for her Friday morning dancing lesson. Upstairs, Annie is banging and scraping on the boards as she works her way through the front rooms, clearing up the debris. The house is broken, and with it the fragile peace Elizabeth has made with herself. She cannot stand to be in this shattered place another second, but she cannot think where else to go. Her bonnet is lying on the hall table beside the urn. On an impulse she picks it up, takes her shawl from the hook behind the door and steps out of the house.

The brightness of the day is shocking, like a rinse of cold water on her skin. It is days since she has left the house; weeks since she has walked out alone like this and she feels insubstantial in the sudden assault of light and space and sound, transparent, as if the air were washing right through her. Without quite knowing how she has got there, she finds herself at the end of the street. Ahead are the spires of the College; to her left the glinting waters of the burn and open land; to her right, the gentle rise of Schoolhill. She turns right. She has no particular destination in mind, only an urgent instinct to distance herself from the house and from the events of the previous night; to walk and keep walking. It is a surprise to find the streets so populated, so hectic and noisy with activity: masons chipping away at blocks of stone; brickmen rushing up and down, crying, *Make way! Make way!*, the hods towering over their heads; thackers perched atop ladders, mending the roofs; women down below, knitting on their doorsteps in the sunshine, the bairns playing at their feet; dogs tumbling round and about the bairns; chickens pecking and scratching in the earth; carts charging this way and that, piled high with barrels and baskets, the drivers shouting to one another as they career by, sparks flying from the wheels.

Elizabeth walks through the bright clatter and clamour in a kind of dream. Past Dr Beattie's house on Schoolhill and St Nicholas's kirkyard into Upper Kirkgate; along the narrow wynd that leads down to Netherkirkgate, where the corbelled turrets and coned roofs of Wallace Tower have the look of a French chateau; past the Quaker Meeting House and the back of Provost Skene's mansion, imposing even from behind with its crow-stepped gables and jutting casements; down Carnegie's Brae, the sun black and gold in her head as it flashes through the iron railings, and into the broad straight stretch of Putachieside; past the mercers and the pewterers and Mr Ross's chandler shop and the bookseller and Bruce's chinaware store. From an open window above the storefront, the sound of someone playing the piano. At the back of the houses, she can see the pleasure gardens rising up the lower slopes of St Catherine's Hill, like a great green skirt flaring about the waist of some giant dancing girl.

She turns off Putachieside, towards the Green, drawn by the hubbub of the Friday market, almost colliding as she does so with a gaggle of young women coming from the Green with skeels of water balanced on wool pads on their heads, laughing and chattering to one another. She steps out of their path at the last moment and the girls pass. One of them brushes against her arm and glances in her direction, then looks away again as if there'd been no one there.

Elizabeth ducks away from the crowds into a dark little wynd on her left. The buildings are so close on either side and so high that barely a shred of daylight penetrates the space between. The air is sharp with the smell of tannin and cat's piss, as dank and cold as if it were winter still. Elizabeth picks her way through the tangle of rubbish beneath her feet: food scraps, broken bottles, torn sacking, fragments of worn-out garments, rotten bits of rushing, ripped pamphlets and crumpled ballad sheets. The stinking debris is seasoned and smeared and daubed with the contents of countless bowels, animal and human. Living things squirm and rustle in the filth. Elizabeth can feel her heart beating hard against her ribcage. Every breath makes her throat constrict and her gorge lurch. The urge to run mounts with each step and finally she gives in to it, not stopping until she's reached the head of Fisher Row, where she stands, panting for air, the estuary breeze full on her face, the taste of brine in her mouth. Hadden's factory is to her right, a plume of smoke billowing upwards from its red-brick chimney. Below the factory is the barn where the lost bairns were held, now Mr Hadden's counting house. *No, not that way.* Elizabeth turns to look in the opposite direction, along the waterfront towards the quay. The harbour is filled with sailing vessels, the white sails dazzling in the sunshine. Out in the estuary scores of little boats twist their way through the maze of inches and sandbanks. Clear away across the glinting water is the Inch Dyke and the wide, winding band of the Dee. It is beautiful: the silver water; the shining sails; the limpid clarity of the sky, dotted here and there with tiny white clouds; the soft green of the Clayhills in the distance. And yet somehow the beauty of the scene gives her no pleasure, fills her instead with a sickening flood of emptiness. She walks on, quickening her pace to distance herself from the feeling. As long as she walks, she needn't think. Down Trinity Corner, past the great carved arch of the Trade Hall Gateway, with its thundering inscription: HE THAT PITIETH THE POOR LENDETH TO THE LORD AND THAT WHICH HE HATH GIVEN WILL HE REPAY. On into Ship Row, the shabby tenement buildings towering three storeys high on either side, lowering her head to shield her face from the curious looks of the old men, turned out of doors by their womenfolk and smoking their pipes on the forestairs, asking themselves what a trickit up quine like that is doing in this part of the town. The din from the docks growing louder with every step; the stink. Past the Shipmasters' Hall and the

Fish Market, down the steep descent of Shore Brae to the Quay Head, where at last she stops, arrested by the tumult that confronts her.

All is motion and commotion. The boatbuilders are occupied with their hammering and sawing, the boatmen with the tugging and winding and stowing of ropes, the fishermen with their nets and creels, the merchants with the overseeing of their cargo. Barrels and chests of every shape and size are being loaded and unloaded. A constant procession of porters and caddies trawls back and forth from the multitude of vessels tied up to the quayside or anchored close by to the great press of wagons and carts awaiting them in the street. There is shouting and roaring and cursing. There is crashing and thumping and banging and slamming. There are wheels grinding and hooves clattering. There are light things scraping heavy things, hard things striking harder things. There are men stripped to the waist, men in fine waistcoats, men in rough fustian. There are gulls, gulls everywhere, screeching and screaming in the high blue sky. There are memories, too, as pressing as the present scene: of her father in his brown frockcoat, standing on the quayside, surveying his stock, ticking off items on the chalkboard, scolding a man for clumsiness, commending another for his care, arguing with a captain who has cheated him of a bushel of something, a boll of something else; there are his dark eyes resting on hers for a moment, his smile, his hand enclosing her own. And there is Alec, young and handsome and full of ambition, his head bowed low to hers to make himself heard above the clamour, drawing their future with his fine, lilting voice: the braw bright future they will share together. And herself, there, beside him, leaning on the harbour wall, sheltering from the wind, her arm tucked through his, believing him, trusting him, as she'd trusted her father before him. High overhead, the gulls scream. All along the quayside the sails flash and the wheels turn. Doubt seeds itself. Sets forth its venomed buds. Blooms.

46

The public meeting is held on the last Wednesday in June in the hall of the Poor House. Rabbie Donald has arrived early and is watching the room as it rapidly fills, trying to gauge the expressions on the faces around him. Attendance is excellent, at any rate. Dr Bannerman and Dr Skene have taken their seats near the front, together with a number of the other town physicians. He knows Dr Selby and Dr Dyce by sight, but is not acquainted with them personally. Further along the row, he can see Provost Duncan and Baillie Cruikshank and near them the other Dispensary managers: Baillie Duguid, Mr Dingwall and the rest. The clergymen, too, are well represented; Reverend Glegg is here, of course, his wife at his side, and there is Mr Gibbon the shipmaster, with his wife and daughter. Mr Birnie has brought his entire extended family from the look of it. On the other side of the room but further back in a tight little cluster are a number of the Dispensary midwives. Behind and around them are many others whom Rabbie knows or recognizes: Mr Mitchell and Mr Aitken from the drug store; Mr Shirress, whose ware-room is directly across the street from the chapel; Willie Law, who is Alistair Milne's son-in-law and had done the drawings for the new plan of the town that now hangs in Alec's study. To his left, there's Robert Strachan, the tea merchant, and James Moir, with whom the doctor is currently in dispute over an unpaid grocery bill. Mr Chalmers, the printer, is sitting side by side with Mr Brown from the Homer's Head, somewhat unaccountably as the two men are known to be sworn enemies. At the back of the hall, where by now there is standing room only, are the poorer folk. James Garrow is clearly visible, towering head and shoulders above the crowd. The whole town, it seems, has an interest in today's proceedings.

A table has been set up at the top of the hall, and Alec is seated behind it, his attention apparently fixed on the wad of papers in front of him; Chae Gordon is on his right, in his official capacity of Clerk to the Dispensary; on his left is Alistair Ross, the Dispensary Treasurer, who is looking distinctly ill-at-ease and keeps leaning over to whisper in Dr Gordon's ear. Rabbie can never set eyes on Mr Ross, with his ludicrously pointed head and as ludicrously pointed nose, without an urge to laugh: it's as if each of his parents had grabbed him with the fire-irons the moment he came into the world and each pulled with all their might.

Shortly after twelve, Chae Gordon stands and opens the meeting. After a brief speech reminding the assembly of the great and extensive utility of the institution before their attention today, he hands over to Mr Ross, who reports the state of the funds and announces the short-fall. Chae Gordon gets to his feet again. As Clerk to the Dispensary, it is his task to declare the summary of records for the year.

'Patients treated: one thousand four hundred and eighty-five,' he announces. 'Cured: one thousand three hundred and forty-nine. Under cure: eighty-eight. Deceased: forty-eight.'

Chae is about to take his seat when a voice from the floor calls out: 'And of the dead, how many were women?'

Chae turns to his brother. Alec's lips form the answer.

'Thirty-seven,' Chae says.

'Aye, an whose fault is that?' a deep voice shouts out from the back of the room.

'Ask Dr Gordon!' someone else cries. 'He can tell you!'

Heads are turning in the direction of the hecklers. Rabbie turns too, but it is impossible to tell with any exactness where the voices are located in the crowd. Chae raises his hands to quieten the audience. Any member of the public wishing to see a full and accurate description of patients, conditions and treatments may do so, he says, in the books of the Dispensary, on application to himself at his house in Broad Street. But his announcement is ignored. The noise from the floor only increases as more voices join the demand for the Dispensary physician to explain himself. Rabbie looks from the faces in the audience, some puzzled, some intrigued, some plainly frightened by the ugly turn of the mood, to the expression of astonishment on Alec's face. Chae has turned to him again with a despairing look. Slowly, as if pushing upwards against an immense weight, Alec gets to his feet.

'Three times the number of patients have been treated this year than last,' he begins. 'Many of them at my own expense and with considerable success—'

'Tae the point, man,' someone shouts.

'Hear him oot,' returns another.

'The toll on lives has been greater than usual in past months on account of it being an exceptionally bad year for epidemical fevers. There have been severe outbreaks of the flux in Torrie and Footdee, two separate epidemics of scarlet fever, another, still current, of erysipelas – '

'Tell us aboot the mithers, Dr Gordon!'

'Let the man speak, will ye!'

Alec presses on: 'Commencing December last –' it is like watching a man drag his way across a desert, Rabbie thinks, while gradually losing all hope of finding water – 'there has been another disease in an epidemic state, one never seen before now in Aberdeen, a disease familiar, however, to every learned physician and rightly feared by every one, for it is more deadly than the plague – a disease known as childbed fever. It has been my chief business in the past six months to attend the victims of this dreadful disease, and I assure you, no man could have done more to lessen the miserable suffering it inflicts. But through constant vigilance and unceasing application, most fortunately I have discovered a cure, which I can announce to you now. A sure and certain cure—'

'Certain cure!' a voice bellows from the back of the hall. 'You call bleedin mithers to deith curin them?'

'Twenty-eight ounces!' a woman cries out. 'Twenty-eight ounces!'

'Aye!' roars a third voice, 'and happy to blame the howdies for it!'

'Order!' Mr Ross shouts, leaping to his feet. 'Order in the hall!'

But his voice is blown away like thistledown in a gale.

'The truth, Dr Gordon! We want the truth!'

The cry goes round the hall, accompanied now by a great stamping of boots on the scrubbed boards.

'The truth! The truth!'

Alec's face has flushed a deep crimson.

'Why?' he shouts out, raising his arms, stretching them out towards the crowd in a gesture of angry, hopeless appeal. 'Why would I kill my own patients? I am doing everything in my power to save these women's lives. It is in my power to save their lives. It's your own damn ignorance that's killing them. *That* is the truth!'

47

The spines of the books on the study shelves seem to taunt Alec with their sealed-up certainties. Orion, astride his eternal night, has a scornful air. The day-book on the desk before him is an open mockery. Ten shillings and threepence for a new tea urn, as if they didn't have enough of those already; thirty shillings on a new spinning wheel; seven pounds and four shillings for dining-room chairs to replace the old ones; sixteen shillings on gloves; one pound and fourteen shillings for winter cloaks and another one pound and two shillings for lining the hoods. Damned extravagances all! Why had he not kept a closer eye on things? Even with the three guineas saved on Baxter, Alec cannot see how the accounts are to be squared. The dismal sums go on and on:

> 10 *shillings a stone for candles*
> 5 *shillings for firewood*
> 11 *shillings for coal*
> 16 *shillings a boll for oatmeal*
> 10 *shillings a pound for tea*

Alec shuts the book. The prospect of discussing further economies with Elizabeth is not a pleasant one. She's taken Baxter's dismissal very ill, has hardly left her room since, refuses to speak to him. Annie is not much better: huffing and puffing about the place, and performing her new chores with such ill grace he's in half a mind to dismiss her too. The porridge was burnt and over-salted again this morning, for the third day in a row, and when she finally minded to bring the tea, she'd poured it so carelessly it had slopped over the cloth. Elizabeth, sunk in her own self-pitying reflections, had seemed not to notice. It is all vexing in the extreme.

'I realize it is hard for her,' Alec complains to Chae, 'but she does not help herself. She keeps to her room all day, when what she needs is company and exercise. She lays all the blame for our predicament at my feet, when it is in no small measure due to her own poor housekeeping.'

Chae does not share Alec's view of the situation. 'She needs a change of air. Take her out of town for a while. And Mary too. It would do you all good. Let this trouble die down.'

As Alec recalls his brother's words, he suddenly feels terribly tired, terribly alone. After all the battling of the previous months, with the disease, with the midwives, with the Infirmary, the debacle at the Poor House had been just one more humiliating defeat. He longs for rest and for peace. He longs for the clear view through the trees to Drum Castle and the Irvine standard fluttering atop the castle flagpole; for the sweet songs of his childhood, his mother's voice singing to them at night, the smell of oats hotting on the fire on cold mornings. He longs for the inevitable rhythms of the farm: the men coming from the fields to break their fast; the seedtime and the harvest; the feuing fairs and autumn trysts. With near physical pain, he longs for the simplicity of that earlier time, when he and his brothers bunked off to skim stones and build dams and fish for trout in Gormack burn; a time when everything seemed possible and his own mind fit to bursting with the sense of all that was ahead of him.

Whenever he hears now of a woman falling with child, there is a stirring of dread. God knows, he would ban fornica-tion if he could, if it would protect them from this invisible monster. And now Elizabeth, too. Their own child to be born in the autumn. At such a time. It is the very last thing he would have wished for. 'Are you not glad?' Elizabeth had asked, plainly hurt by his want of pleasure at the news when she had told him. Glad? With this contagion stalking the town? With childbirth tantamount to a death sentence? But he could not speak of that to her, could not bring himself to be so cruel. What would it achieve, anyway, but to terrify her? Her state is precarious enough as it is. Chae is right: he must make arrangements. She must be sent away, somewhere safe, where the disease would not find her, to one of her aunts perhaps, or to Logie, to Jem and Megan.

Alec forces himself to get up from his chair. What's done is done and there is work to do. He's to meet Bannerman at the Green by four. The post bell had rung a while back. Perhaps there will be a reply from Denman. It's over a week since his letter was sent, asking Denman for his opinion of Mistress Cormack's case. A remarkable thing had occurred about ten days before: an aperture had appeared in the woman's navel, and through it a very large quantity of purulent matter was discharged. The flow kept up for several days, whereupon the tumour subsided, the orifice closed and in only a little more time, Mistress Cormack was quite recovered. Alec is impatient to discover Denman's thoughts on the matter. Had Denman known anything of the kind in his own practice? Was this not proof that physic must assist nature by creating openings for the disease; that venesection, in other words, was the proper and urgent course of action? In Alec's own mind the matter is quite decided: here at last is the evidence to support his hypothesis. Far from seeking entry to the body, the disease rages through its victims in a desperate effort to find *egress*. Mistress Cormack's case confirms it.

There is another question, Alec reflects as he goes out to the hall (the post has brought a reply: he recognizes the hand at once) and returns once more to his desk, a question he had not put to Denman, for the simple reason that only in the past day or two has it formed itself clearly in his own mind: the action of the disease indicates a desire to exit the body, but how is it entering to begin with? There must always be some point of entry. In fevers in general, contagious miasmas settle on the skin, entering through the pores of the epidermis. In inoculations, the smallpox is introduced directly into the bloodstream by the application of pus on the threads. With erysipelas, it enters through an open wound; a mere scratch might be all that is needed, but great or small, there has to be an opening of some kind. And with childbirth? Now that the question has taken shape, Alec cannot get away from it, and yet at the same time, he cannot get beyond it. It squats in his mind like a great block of granite, stolid, obdurate, refusing circumvention, defying explanation. *What do you do if you cannot understand?* Look harder. Gather more evidence. Dissect the problem. Anatomize the dilemma. Cut away the skin until the muscle is exposed. Tease apart the blood vessels. Dilate the veins. There is no end to what man can discover if he only looks hard enough, close enough, long enough.

Alec opens Denman's letter and rapidly scans its contents, which are brief to say the least.

> *Bleeding may be necessary in very full, sanguine habits of body, but on no occasion would I sanction the quantities you propose.*

He pushes the letter aside. *On no occasion*. Well, then. To hell with Denman too. He turns to his case notes. He must place his trust here, and here alone. Forget opinion; forget authority. Stick with the terra firma of observed events, certain facts. Names, dates, death rates. The black of the ink on the cream of the page. He can rely on nothing and no one else.

Recently, he has begun reordering all the information he's gathered in the past six months, setting it out case by case in a single table, rather than on separate sheets of paper. No one has done this before to his knowledge, documented each case in an epidemic disease in tabular form. Laid out in this fashion, he can see at a glance the patient's name and age, her address, the date of lying in, who attended her, the state of the weather at time of first attack, the duration and outcome of the illness. The similarities and differences between each case are far easier to see now. He has been able to discount some factors to his certain satisfaction. The constitution of the atmosphere, for example, is an utter irrelevance: the women die in fine weather and foul, in rain or shine, whether the barometer stands at forty degrees or thirty-five, whether the wind blows from the west or from the north. Otherwise, dishearteningly, the tables reveal little that is new. Some midwives have had more cases than others. Beyond that, nothing.

Alec's mind constricts with weariness and perplexity. He's had his moments of failure and uncertainty, what physician has not? But always before there's been a reasonable explanation for it. In the early days it was simple inexperience. Then, as his knowledge and skill increased, it was more often bad luck or bad timing or other people's ignorance that were to blame. This is different. This is like blindness. Like gowping into a mist that never thins or lifts; so dense that however long or hard he stares, he sees nothing. Only the spectre of failure.

Lifting his head for a moment to ease the stiffness in his neck and shoulders, Alec's eyes fall on the map in front of the desk. Two towns, two rivers, two diseases. And beyond, the singular expanse of the ocean. It is fatigue playing tricks on his mind, he knows, nothing more, but as he stares at the map, the familiar shapes and ink marks shift and reform before his eyes. Suddenly the cartographic marks no longer depict Aberdeen and its adjacent countryside, but seem instead to delineate, quite clearly, the pelvis of a woman. The burns and roads and field boundaries are like rough sketches of veins and arteries; the fine lines that indicate the hills flanking the sea resemble scraggy patches of pubic hair; the densely inked area that previously designated the buildings of the New Town now show the blackened remains of a diseased right ovary. Above and below, the winding pathways of the Dee and the Don have metamorphosed into two spreading thighs; between them, the long stretch of the shoreline has become the gaping wound of a post-partum vulva.

Alec grips the arms of his chair and shuts his eyes, the image imprinted still on his mind. It is just fatigue, he tells himself again, his mind playing tricks on him. He must sit very still, steady his breathing, wait for the hallucination to pass. As he follows his own prescription – sits, breathes, waits – he gradually becomes aware of a noise coming from the hall outside the study: a high, light clattering sound. He listens for a moment. There it is again, followed by a series of little thuds. Glad of the distraction, he gets up and goes to the door.

At the far end of the passageway that runs from the study to the kitchen, he sees his daughter. Mary's back is turned to him, thin plaits bobbing against her shoulders as she hops and jumps over the flagstones, so intent on her game she doesn't hear him. She is playing beds, he realizes. The clattering sound that had caught his attention is coming from the pebble she is throwing. Pivoting on one foot, she turns now to pick up the pebble from one of the flagstones, then hop-skips her way back through the squares. Alec stays where he is, watching quietly from the doorway of his study. He can just make out the chalk marks on the beds, can't help but smile when he sees the 6 and the 9 have been written back to front.

There is something reassuring about the wordless certainty of his daughter's game, the pre-ordained, unquestioned sequence of moves; something reassuring, too, in the staunch set of her shoulders, the firm line of her back, her two small feet landing sturdily on the dark-grey flagstones. Alec leans his shoulder against the doorframe and watches her. This is what matters, is it not? This beloved child of his. Living, growing, playing. All the rest, the struggle to understand the disease, the ingratitude of his patients, the opposition and hostility mounting against him in the town, even his financial worries, what does it count for compared to the existence of this one little girl? It is all vainglory, vanity, worldly nothing.

Mary's arm swings forward once again and the pebble flies from her hand. It makes a low arc and lands in a square further along the grid. She begins hopping and jumping up the squares to retrieve it. From where Alec is standing, the flagstones have an elongated appearance, more rectangular than square, like actual beds. Up goes Mary's arm. Up goes the pebble. Arching through the air, up and over and down. Landing with a little click on the flagstones. Alec's head is heavy, clagged with lack of sleep and too much whisky. His whole body aches with exhaustion. Still he stands and watches, transfixed by the figure of his daughter, hopping and skipping through the grid of squares. She spins round, skirts flying, for the return journey. Hopping and skipping back to the first square. Her arm lifting again. The pebble flying once more ffrom her hand. Sailing across the emptiness. Arching up. Curving down. Falling towards its target. He can see the entire arc of the pebble's flight, from his daughter's hand to the ground, as clearly as if it trailed a ribbon in its wake; sees how the pebble goes where Mary's hand sends it, but nowhere else. And in that instant, as the pebble once more strikes the grey flagstone, Alec suddenly, finally, understands.

Part Three

Truth

[This disease] has occurred in many cases, in the most destructive form, where contagion could not possibly be supposed to have operated as the cause.

Robert Lee, *Researches on the Pathology and Treatment of Some of the Most Important Diseases of Women*, 1833

The conditions arise entirely within the patient's system ... Hard work and exercise are a preventive against the disease.

R. Barnes, *On the Causes, Internal and External of Puerperal Fever*, 1887

Antiseptics are worse than useless. Wash the hands at the patient's house before examining. Having observed these rules, do not bother about micro-organisms.

Dr Mears, *British Medical Journal*, 1906

48

July

They travel by post-chaise as far as Peterhead, the twelve shillings for their fares paid by Chae. The new road makes the journey less uncomfortable than it might have been, but the carriage is crowded and the incessant jolting and joggling against the other passengers takes its toll on Elizabeth, who seems to shrink further into her cloak with every mile. She is white-faced with fatigue by the time the post sets them down at the crossroads, where they have to wait nearly three hours more at the inn while Alec haggles for the hire of a horse and cart to take them the last ten miles to Logie. No room is to be had, and Elizabeth and Mary are obliged to sit on stools in the hallway, the innkeeper's wife relenting with very ill grace even to the stools, though the sight of Elizabeth's wan face and swollen belly eventually stirs her conscience sufficiently to procure for them a jug of small beer.

It is early evening before they reach the farm, the trees casting long thin shadows across the fields, the wavering grass silver in the low light of the sun. The farmhands are still at work and the sky is dotted with kites and kestrels, hovering in wait for mice and rabbits fleeing from the scythes. Mormond Hill sits at their back, its lower slopes purple with wild thyme and heather. Ahead of them glitters the sea.

'Alec, man.'

'Jem.'

The two brothers embrace for a moment, awkward and glad, each man's chest too full of love for the other to say any more just then. Jem holds the horse's head while Alec hands Elizabeth and Mary down. Megan is all smiles, scooping Mary up into her arms, exclaiming what a fine wee lassie she's growing into and the image of her mother, kissing her cheeks. Then she turns to Elizabeth and takes her hand.

'Come in and rest now,' she says, her voice full of kindness.

With the womenfolk gone, the brothers set about unhitching the horse, working at the buckles, one on either side of the creature's head, not looking at one another, not talking, knowing the time for talk will come later. Jem leads the horse to the stable and Alec follows, standing in the sweet scent of hay and dung, as his brother ties up the halter, fetches fodder and water, as sure and slow and steady in his movements as he had always been since a boy. It was Alec who'd gone quick and sharp at things, Alec who'd lose his temper when an axle snapped or the stots got out. *Our Jem got the cool head, our Alec the hot one*, their mother used to say. *Twas agreed betwixt the twae afor they were oot ma belly.* And now, in the quiet of the stable, with Jem moving about in his sure, calm way, Alec feels the old familiar sense of completeness he has always known in the company of his twin. A sense of safety. His strange other half, who'd so often enraged him with his difference, but whose presence at his side renders him whole in some ineffable way.

He sleeps soundly that night for the first time in months. Elizabeth and Mary share the big bed upstairs, he has the cot in the kitchen to himself, the darkness enfolding him, pierced by the lonesome cry of the peewits, as familiar to him as his own skin, soothing as a lullaby. He wakes in the morning to Megan moving quietly about the room, kindling the fire, hotting the porridge. He follows her movements with his mind, still half-asleep. Only when he hears her go out to the dairy does he open his eyes. The homely order of it all is like balm: the scrubbed table, the shining coppers, the dresser with its neat rows of pewter plates, the tender spirals of steam rising from the pot into the chill air. He hears the latch lift and then Mary is standing beside the cot, looking down at him with sleep-dark eyes, her hair matted in a black halo about her face. He lifts the edge of the blanket and she slides in beside him, her feet like ice on his warm legs. She nuzzles down into the crook of his arm, settles her head on his chest, her hair tickling his chin as he cradles her to him. He could lie like this forever, never move again, never give another thought to sickness and disease, to childbed fever, to Aberdeen. But then Megan is back with the milk and soon after her, Jem, come in from the fields for his breakfast and raising an eyebrow at Alec for still lounging in bed at this hour. Then the pottitch is on the table and Mary is up in a flash to have the first bowl, heels swinging under her chair, and there's no more holding the day at arm's length, for it has begun, whether he's ready for it or not.

For the next three days Alec goes with Jem to the fields, where all hands are engaged with sowing the summer's final crop of turnips and hoeing those sowed earlier in the month. They take their food with them or Mary runs down with it from the farmhouse. Megan keeps Elizabeth occupied too, drying herbs, pickling fruit and weeding the vegetable plot. The weather holds fine and dry and Alec is grateful for the hard physical labour, the lack of thought it requires. He is amazed at the new implements his brother is putting to use on the farm, the new methods he has employed for rotating the crops and liming the soil. Jem has laid down a system of four-shift cropping, and is growing drilled beans in place of the green crop. There is a fanner, for cleaning the hulled oats and other grain, and instead of sowing the turnip seed one drill at a time in the old way, Jem has an ingenious modern contraption, consisting of three rollers, two coulters and a pair of seed boxes, which permits him to sow two drills at one and the same time. 'Set them out at eight or ten inches like this and heel them down after second hoeing,' Jem explains, 'and they'll choke out all the weeks within a few weeks and sprout like lettuces.'

In the ten years since he took on the management of

Colonel Tower's farm, he has worked a miracle with the stiff tenacious Buchan soil, and Alec tells him so. They are taking a break for some cheese and ale, sitting beside the small burn that borders the end of the outfields. All around them is the evidence of Jem's successful industry.

'Aye well, I'm fortunate in Colonel Tower,' Jem says, deflecting the compliment. 'He's not afraid to take a few risks, or lay out the necessary expense to improve the land. And being away in London much of the year, he leaves me a free hand for the most part.'

Alec has pulled off his boots and is dangling his feet in the water. It breaks over his ankles in a cascade of shimmering droplets; below the surface his toes float bone-white in the limpid clarity of the stream.

'And the ruta baga? It looks to be doing well.'

Jem had told Alec about this new crop when he and Megan were staying with them last winter. After his triumph with the white turnip, he'd been looking for a new challenge and had found it in the ruta baga: a crop that could withstand the harshest frosts, its leaves and root equally nutritious for human consumption in the spring, and far better calculated for finishing off the cattle than the common turnip. No one had grown ruta baga in Aberdeenshire before, and Jem had a messianic gleam in his eye as he outlined its properties to Alec in December. He'd raised the seed himself, to be sure it was uncorrupted, and had been preparing the soil for the past twelvemonth. The first crop was sown in April.

'Too soon to be sure,' he says, in response to Alec's question. 'I won't know till next spring.'

Alec recalls his own use of those same words to Rabbie, months back, at the start of the epidemic. *Too soon to be sure.* Well, he's sure now. Fleetingly he wonders where he will be come the autumn.

49

Of all the places to be of a night, this is not the one Rabbie would choose, with the shadows huge on the walls, bending over you, leaning this way and that, with every little draught, the moaning and sighing of the patients making the shadows seem like living things. And of all the folk to be stuck with in such a place, on such a night, Joseph McRae is the last one in a thousand years you'd choose to be here with. But stuck here for the night he is and with McRae and not a thing to be done about it.

'Your deal.' McRae finishes shuffling the deck and pushes it across the table towards Rabbie.

The luck of the draw, who gets to watch the patients through the night, and it was their names that had come up. Six hours to go before Mistress Farquhar comes back on duty. Rabbie picks up the cards and shuffles again. McRae's won the last four rounds. He wouldn't trust McRae with a kebbuck of cheese. He splits the deck. Diamonds it is.

'Your man's in a wee spot of bother, I hear.' McRae is studying his hand, ordering the cards with quick, deft fingers.

Rabbie looks through his own hand. Nine of hearts. Three and six of spades. Two of clubs. Not a high card or trump in sight.

'Leastways that's what I've heard,' McRae says, laying down a jack. 'Folk daarna come to the Dispensary for fear o what he'll do to them.'

Rabbie plays his two of clubs. 'It's styte, McRae, and you know it.'

'The midwives dinnae think so. You should hear them on the subject.'

'And you should know not to go minding claik. He's a finer doctor than you'll ever be.'

McRae scoops up the cards, plays a second queen.

'Maybe, but what's the use of a doctor wi no patients?'

'Shut it, McRae!'

'If you ask me, he's finished in this town,' McRae goes on in the same careless tone, as if remarking on the weather. 'He's a deid man.'

'I said shut it!'

'All right, all right! Dinna get yer dinder up, Donald man. I'm no but expressing my opinion.'

'Aye, well, I dinna care for your opinions, McRae. Keep them to yerself.'

They play on, McRae whistling a little jig through the gap in his front teeth, Rabbie losing every hand. His mind is elsewhere. He's wondering how he can get rid of McRae for long enough to look at the record books. Alec asked him, before he left for Logie, to do this one thing for him: get hold of the figures, any admissions with erysipelas since January last. Just a wee whim that might shed light on things, he'd said. Rabbie thought at first of asking Dr French directly, saying he needed the books for his talk to the Medical Society, which was true enough, but it didn't take much more reflection to realize the ruse would not work. French hated the Medical Society. He'd done everything in his power to prevent it being instituted in the first place and, having failed in that endeavour, had brusquely rejected the offer of honorary membership, refused to attend any of the Society's meetings, denigrated its every achievement, and had never yet missed an opportunity to broadcast its least significant misdemeanours. Night duty had seemed the best chance – until he'd been saddled with McRae.

The sound of footsteps and muffled sniggers on the other side of the door brings the game to a halt.

'That'll be the others,' McRae says, getting to his feet.

'What others?'

'Just a few friends.' McRae grins at him.

He goes to the door and opens it a little way.

'Password?'

More snorts of laughter and a bottle is thrust through the gap.

'Good man!'

McRae takes the bottle, pulls open the door and ushers in his guests. There are three of them, patients from the military ward, judging by the red coats draped over their nightshirts, young men no older than themselves and not much wrong with any of them besides the King's Pox. The tallest of the three produces a second bottle from under his coat and sets it down on the table.

'Good, good man!' says McRae, clapping him on the shoulder.

'What in God's name do you think—' Rabbie begins, but McRae puts a finger to his lips.

'Hush now, Rabbie man. Jist a wee bit o crack. Nothing to worry aboot.'

'Who's this?' The tall man squints suspiciously at Rabbie.

'This, gentlemen, is my esteemed colleague, Robert Donald of Midmar.' McRae raises the bottle with a flourish in Rabbie's direction. 'May I propose a toast, gentlemen? To Mr Donald of Midmar. Physician Extraordinary to be!'

'Aye, aye! A toast!' The other men join in, grabbing for the bottle on the table and stumbling over each other to get their turn to drink. 'A toast to Mr Donald of Midmar!'

Rabbie stares at them in dismay. There's no way he'll get them out, not now they're settling down at the table, shoving and belching and cracking their knuckles.

'On your head be it, McRae,' he says, getting up. 'I'll be no party to your japes.'

He leaves the room to guffaws of derision from the company, hears one of the men mimicking his words in a woman's voice. He pulls the door to behind him. Out on the ward, all is shadowed stillness. A patient groans, shifts a little in his sleep, falls quiet again. Rabbie takes one of the lamps from its hook and makes his way along the ward and through the doorway at the far end out into the corridor. It's darker still here, without the lamps shedding their little ochre pools of light. His silhouette is the merest smudge of dark on the boards ahead of him. Why is he doing this? *You don't have to*, Alec had said, *but I'd be grateful*. If anyone were to discover him ... But McRae won't trouble him now and the house-keeper's fast asleep at the other end of the building. And how can he not do this one thing? After all the other things he has been told?

The office is locked, as he'd expected it would be, but the hospital keys are in his possession for the night. One of them should fit. His fingers are shaking as he tries the first few keys on the chain. At the fourth attempt, the lock turns and he's in. The record book is on the desk. From upstairs, the faint sound of drunken laughter, a snatch of song. He sets down the lamp and opens the book. Spreading across both pages, the sheets are marked out in columns. In the first, the date of admission. In the second, the patient's name. In the third, the complaint and progress of the condition. In the fourth, the outcome. In the fifth, the date of dismissal. Every single patient admitted to the Infirmary in the past six months duly noted in the varying scrawl of whoever happened to be in charge of entries for that day. Rabbie's mouth goes dry. This will take hours! He pulls out his notebook and pencil. Begin at the beginning. January. McRae's words whisper in his ear as he works his way through the lists. *A doctor without patients. A dead man.*

'Who will believe you?' he'd asked Alec the night before he left.

'They all will. They'll have to. It's the truth.'

One truth, Rabbie wanted to reply. Only one truth.

50

On the far side of the town, in the little house she's lived alone in since her husband's death, Janet Anderson is also awake. She'd woken from a dream, disturbed by revellers outside her window. She can still hear the staccato of their shouts gradually receding down the street, loud in the hush of the night. Unable to find her way back into the cocoon of sleep, she'd got up and gone downstairs, thinking to read for a while, but the sight of the drawings lying on the table had drawn her thoughts in other directions. Now she too is thinking about Alec Gordon.

It was late when the doctor came to the door, and though she was surprised to receive a call at such an hour, somehow she was not surprised when she realized who it was.

'I need to speak wi ye,' he said, all trace of English gone from his voice and slurring the words a little, so she could tell he'd had more than a drop to drink even before he was close enough to catch the smell of the whisky on his breath.

'Is that a good idea?'

'I'll nae bide long,' he said, and took a stumbling step forwards.

She moved aside to let him pass, taking a quick look up and down the street to be sure no one had seen him enter before closing the door. When she turned round, he was standing in the middle of the little room with his back to her, his upper body slowly listing to one side, like the mast of a sinking ship, until he corrected his weight and began slowly keeling to the other. She pulled up a chair and pushed him gently down on to it. He didn't seem inclined to talk, so she went back to the table where she'd been arranging and checking her drawings. Twenty-six botanical studies, complete at last and ready for the printers. A compendium of herbs for the treatment of women's disorders. One plant for each letter of the alphabet. By no means perfect, some of the studies much better than others, the colour still not quite right on the centaury flowers, the rendering of the shepherd's purse a little harsh, but on the whole she was pleased. It was hard to concentrate with him sitting there, blinking at the fire like a dazed rabbit. She glanced over at him; the sight of his exhausted face wrenched her heart. She wanted to put her arms around him, take his broad harrowed face in her two hands and kiss away whatever was troubling him. She turned back to her drawings.

'Fit are ye doin?' he asked eventually.

She held up the top sheet for him to see. He got up from the chair and came over to the table, overshooting a little and colliding with the table edge. He steadied himself and took the sheet, studying her drawing with an air of careful deliberation. 'Angelica,' he read aloud, leaning against her, his upper arm pressed against her own, although he seemed unaware of it himself. She could see his fingers crushing the edge of the sheet. Could tell he was no longer looking at the drawing.

'So?' she said, taking it from him and laying it back down on the table with the others. 'What is it you wanted to say?'

Her words seemed to surprise him. For a second he stared at her and his eyes darkened, as if he were struggling with himself, as if wanting to say something and at the same time wanting not to. Several times he seemed on the verge of speaking, but no words come forth. It was agony to see him like this. After a prolonged silence he lowered his gaze and began fumbling around in the pocket of his coat, eventually succeeding in pulling out a wad of papers.

She couldn't make it out at first. On one page there appeared to be a diagram of some kind, but it was little more than a mess of words linked by a tangle of lines and arrows. On the second page, the words occurred again, this time as a list. Blake. Elgin. Gordon. Philp. Flemming. Donald. Anderson. Skene. Each name was followed in brackets by a number. On the next sheet were the same names, now with a date, and after the date, a second name. Garrow, Duncan, Mennie, Webster.

'What is this?' she'd said, slowly, not sure if she wanted to know.

'Keep awa from them.'

'I don't—'

'Just keep awa from them. Right away. Promise me.'

'And the others?'

He shrugs. 'Too late for them.'

She looked at the names again.

'What will you do – with this?'

Alec shrugs again, but this time says nothing.

'Your name's here too,' she persists.

'And there's anither thing,' he says, ignoring her last words. 'I want you to attend on Mistress Gordon – when her time comes.'

After he left, she sat for a long time at the table, looking at the pages he'd thrust into her hand as he was going. Eventually she laid them to one side. From the pile of her botanical sketches, she pulled out two sheets and placed them side by side in front of her. The first depicted the fern-like leaves and tight-packed white flowers of the flowering sweet cicely, the second the sparser foliage and umbels of the ill-scented hemlock. Alone in the silent room, she began, softly, to weep.

51

When the wind blows from the east, it carries the sand inland for miles. Tiny grains dust the grass stems, settle along the grooves of leaf veins, insinuate themselves between collars and the napes of necks. Alec stands on the shore of the loch, watching the breeze riffling the surface of the water. The ocean is invisible from this point, separated from the loch by an expanse of marsh grass and wind-ridged dunes. He can hear it though, can taste the salt on his lips, can feel the sand chafing his skin. When he glances down at his coat sleeve, he sees the minuscule grains nestled in the weave of the cloth. The world, he thinks, is full of such things: infinitely small things – specks of sand, the veins of a leaf, dandelion spore – things that one can nevertheless see with the naked eye. And then there are other things that are smaller still, too small to see without the aid of a magnifying lens: the crystals in a piece of slate, the ragged surface of a strand of hair, the swarm of spermatozoa in a teaspoonful of semen. The air he's inhaling at this very moment is composed of elements that are known to exist, though they cannot be seen at all, even with the most powerful of microscopes. Not being able to see something is no longer an argument for its not existing, yet how else is one to prove its existence?

Earlier he had stripped off and swum in the loch, the freezing water closing over him, snatching his breath away at first and then, as he'd grown accustomed to the cold, raising an invigorating rush of blood to his veins. Drying himself off afterwards with his shirt, his skin flushed and mottled from the icy water, he'd found himself thinking back to the pamphlet he'd written on cold-bathing. Contagion, he'd firmly believed back then, had been in the air: it entered the body through the pores of the skin or by inhalation into the lungs. How certain he'd been on that point. How drastically his opinion on this matter has altered in the past ten days.

He can predict now, with absolute certainty, where the disease will strike. He needs only to learn the name of the birth attendant and he will know. It is so clear. Everything is suddenly so clear. From the moment Mary's pebble hit the ground, it was as if a great light had dispelled the darkness. The pebble went where his daughter's hand sent it. It was she who directed the pebble towards its destination. Watching her, he'd remembered: the Westminster Hospital, the rows of beds with their dark-grey blankets, twenty-five of them in all. The disease had not struck every patient. It had baffled the physicians, the way it seemed to prefer some sections of the ward to others. They could not understand what it was in the atmosphere that protected some women, but not others, ensured the disease landed on some beds, but not others. The fever had raged in three sections of the ward, but not a single woman had died in the fourth. It had soared over those beds, to find its target with deadly precision on others. No one could understand it. But he understands now. All the time they'd been looking at the problem the wrong way round. It was not the patients who drew the disease to themselves, any more than the squares draw the stone. Neither at the Westminster, nor in Aberdeen. All along, from the very first case, it was the birth attendant who selected, however unwittingly, where and on whom the disease would fall.

A specific contagion, indeed.

He was back at his desk in a moment, seeing the case notes and lists and tables as if with open eyes for the first time, seeing the pattern in the names and numbers, tracing the disease as easily as if it had all along been painted on the ground in thick black ink. Mistress Blake had delivered Harding's younger daughter in late December, then carried the infection from her to Elspet Garrow, the very next woman she attended. Case 1 in his table. Alec had inspected Mistress Garrow during her lying-in and then carried the infection from her to Jenny Duncan, Jean Anthony and Eliza Webster. Cases 2, 4 and 14. Mistress Elgin was in assistance at Jenny Duncan's labour and it was she who took the disease on to the third case, Iain Smith's wife. Case 3. And from her to Alison Mennie, whom she'd also delivered. Case 5. Mistress Blake had carried the infection to Alistair Brown's wife, Ann, then from her to Mistress Malcolm – and successively to every woman she delivered. Rabbie, who assisted at Jean Anthony's labour, must have taken the disease to Eliza Durward and in all likelihood also to Margaret Leitch in Carnegie's Brae. James Stuart's wife was delivered by Mistress Philp, who carried the infection on to the parish of Nigg, where she delivered George Duthie's wife, from where it spread through the whole parish. At Printfield a great number of lying-in women had been affected in recent weeks, and now he realized that it must be Widow Chalmers, another of the Dispensary midwives, who had carried the infection there from Agnes Meldrum's lying-in at Windmillbrae on the 10th of June.

Some midwives are carrying the infection, others are not. It is as simple as that. It explains why women in one neighbourhood have escaped the disease though they'd been delivered the same week or even the same day as others who fell ill. He himself has infected at least ten women, and Rabbie Donald too has been the means of carrying the contagion to two mothers, if not more. Who knows how many women Skene has attended since Mary McDonald, but Alec is willing to bet he's had other deaths from the same cause since. There must be other physicians too, no doubt, similarly and unknowingly condemning their patients to death. The disease is not in the air, but on their person. A contagious disease. A highly contagious disease.

Now, at last, everything made sense.

'It is not coming from the mother at all, don't you see?' he had told his apprentice, seeing but ignoring the incredulity on the other's face. 'It has nothing to do with her milk or bowels or her perinæum, whether it's torn to shreds or not. She can sniff as many flowers as she likes. Open or shut the windows as she pleases. Lie flat, sit up. She can turn cartwheels for all the difference it makes. It comes from us. It is we who are killing them.'

'Who will believe you?'

'They all will. They'll have to. It's the truth!'

Horrible, unspeakably horrible, truth.

He has chopped off the hydra's head, only to find another, uglier still, springing up in its place. A specific poison, invisible to the eye, more deadly than the plague, is attaching itself in some unknown fashion to the birth attendants and accompanying them about their work like an evil spirit, slipping through the door on their shawls and coat tails, peering over their shoulders at the labouring mothers, waiting only for the moment to strike. How is such an enemy to be routed? *Take away the cause and the effect will cease*, Dr Hulme had written in his treatise, but how in God's name is that to be achieved? And how is he to convince anyone of the truth of its existence in the first place? What he is proposing goes against not just vulgar prejudice but the opinions of the highest physicians in the land. Contagion cannot be carried as if it were a sack of oats, from one person to the next by a third party. There is nothing in the entire body of natural physic to support such an idea. But this is what he is saying, is it not? That the doctors and midwives are the agents of infection. That it is they who are carrying it from one woman to the next, while never falling prey to it themselves. Yes, this is *precisely* what he is proposing. But who will listen with sympathy and an open mind to so vile an explanation? He will be dismissed as a dangerous lunatic. Copernicus had needed Galileo's telescopes to prove to people what they did not want to know – but Galileo's telescopes did not yet exist. Alec's predicament is the same. He can tell them what is happening, he can show them the trail from birth attendant to patient, from patient to birth attendant; he can predict precisely who will fall ill and who escape. What he cannot do adequately is explain the 'it' in his account. What he cannot prove, or even begin to explain, is the stone in the equation.

Watching Mary at her game of beds and at last understanding, all the anxiety and uncertainty of the previous months had fallen away as if it had been nothing more than a slip of silk. There had been a moment of exultation, a brief pure moment of triumph. It had lasted an hour perhaps, no longer, gradually displaced by the appalling recognition of the implications of his discovery. He'd sat at his desk with his heart pounding. He could hear the hollow sound of it drumming against his breastbone, hard and fast, the reverberations extending up into the base of his throat. The whole of his chest felt tight and uncomfortable, as if his shirt were made not of linen but of lead. His throat, too, had become oddly constricted, and though the window was wide open and the air about him cool, the room had felt suddenly airless. He stood and paced round the room, trying to steady his breathing, but it hadn't helped. Instead, a sudden image had come to his mind of an experiment he'd seen conducted in Leiden: a cockatoo had been placed inside a sealed glass jar and the oxygen slowly extracted with the aid of an air pump; as the air in the jar had thinned, the bird's distress had increased and it had made desperate attempts to escape, battering the transparent walls of its prison with its wings until its strength was exhausted and the reserves of air in its lungs used up. It had taken less than two minutes for the creature to suffocate to death. Alec was younger then, had still not acquired that 'necessary inhumanity' which Mr John Hunter recommended to his students and which he, of necessity, had learnt since. What intellectual satisfaction he'd derived from the experiment had been tempered by the sickening sight of the creature's futile attempts to save itself.

His discovery. The beautiful truth he had worked so hard for, pursued with such relentless determination, risked so much for. Now he is trapped with it as surely as the cockatoo in its airless chamber. For ten days he has lived and breathed the fatal secret. He can see no way out that will not end in catastrophe.

52

Mary brings the letter to the top field. They've been at the farm for almost a week and she is thriving on the novelty of a freedom in which she can run from the farmhouse to the fields and be met with smiles at either end. The farm hands are happy to have her sit with them when they break from their work; they tell her stories of gypsies and whirriekows or sing their songs of long ago, of sieges lost and battles won. She likes best of all that her father is not busy all day with his patients, but close by in the fields with her uncle. When she comes with the letter, instead of taking it from her, he scoops her up in his arms and won't let her go until she has given him a kiss, holds her so tight to him that she wriggles to be set down again. The note read:

> I am obliged to leave Aberdeen in great haste. Please forgive me
> for not waiting for your return to explain. I hope my sudden
> departure will not much inconvenience you and that the enclosed
> information will be of some use. Robert Donald.

Alec re-folds the letter and slides it into his pocket.
'Bad news?' Jem asks, watching him.
'Nothing important. You go on. I'll catch you up.'
As the day passes Alec's bewilderment slowly congeals into anger. Leaving him? Leaving Aberdeen? Leaving him *now*? Taking flight just when he needs him most? When he has trusted him? If Rabbie has taken the news of his discovery this way, what hope is there of any of the rest? Skene is hardly likely to back a theory that will destroy him professionally. Bannerman is – has always been – averse to the slightest whiff of controversy. And Janet Anderson – what will she do with the knowledge?

The single sheet of paper enclosed with the letter has, at least, told him what he wanted to know. Jennifer Elgin had been treated for an erysipelas on her leg in late January and Meredith Philp two months later. Of the twenty-five dispensary midwives, eight had received treatment for the condition. But the Infirmary entries have revealed something else: a mild erysipelas in a relative or friend may also — somehow — render a lying-in patient vulnerable to childbed fever. John Webster had an infection in early March; his wife had died in April. Sir William Forbes's manservant had been treated in the same month for a sore on his left arm. He, in all likelihood, carried the infection from his wife in Aberdeen, who'd died after giving birth in April, to his sister in Fintray, six miles away. The midwife who delivered her had infected two others in the same parish, both of whom died soon after. This is as extraordinary as anything else he's yet discovered. Two diseases. Erysipelas and puerperal fever. But one and the same poison. Not a generalized contagion, but an entirely specific one, which by attaching itself to one person without fatal consequence could then be transmitted, catastrophically, to the next. Wherever the poison found a way into the body, it would seize its chance. If the point of entry was nothing more than a scratch or superficial surface wound, an erysipelas would ensue. But when an infected person was in attendance at a birth, the poison was capable of entering the body of the lying-in women and infiltrating her entire system. Dr Hamilton *had* been on the right track when he linked the two diseases, but he had thought the contagion was borne in the air. Dr White and Dr Clarke, from the hospital epidemics they'd witnessed, had also realized there was some connection. But no one before now has recognized the true nature of the poison.

It suddenly seems so obvious to Alec, as he recalls with mounting horror torn blood vessels after the birth and, long before that stage was reached, his own hands probing the wombs of his patients, his fingernails engrained with their blood and mucus, the touchings, the endless touchings, to determine the position of the unborn baby or the progress of the birth. No one before has understood what he now knows with dreadful certainty to be the case: that just as the erysipelas enters the body through a cut or wound, so the puerperal fever may enter the women's bodies through the exposed blood vessels during, or immediately after, the labour.

One and the same poison. Acting in one and the same way. It could be transferred from one person to another, from husband to wife, father to child, midwife to lying-in mother. It did not even die with its victims, but could be carried from the dead to the living. The women who laid out the corpses could transfer it. The physicians who opened the corpses could transfer it. But still the same question he can find no answer to: what is 'it'?

They're not back at the farm until late evening. The sun is slipping behind the line of the hills, the red stain of its going spreading like a cloth over the darkening sky, the night-chill creeping in off the sea. Megan has the fire lit and the broth ready. They eat sitting round the hearth, the bowls on their knees, and when the eating's done, Jem takes down his fiddle from the shelf and plays for them, the airs and ballads Alec has always loved, the aching beauty of the music enfolding them. Softly at first, Megan joins words to the melody.

> 'O waly waly up the bank,
> And waly waly doon the brae,
> And waly waly by yon burn side,
> Where I and my first love did gae.'

Mary, drowsy from the heat of the fire, rests in Alec's arms, eyes closed already, sucking on her thumb in sleepy spasmodic bursts. Her hair is warm and smooth beneath the slow sweep of Alec's hand. Love for her, pure as Megan's voice, tender as the bow on the strings, fills him, simplifies him. A single remote strain of wonder at this gift, his child. The miracle of life. The imperative of the forcing bud. His child. As she gradually subsides into sleep, he feels her growing heavy against him. When her thumb finally slips from her mouth, he carries her to the cot and gently lays her down, covering her with the blankets so she won't get cold away from the fire. Jem is playing still, Elizabeth and Megan seated on either side of him, their faces illuminated by the flames. From the shadows, Alec watches them. It's as if he is looking at a painting, they seem so utterly apart from him. As if in the short stretch from the fireside to the bed he has travelled an immeasurable distance, is separated not by a few short paces, but by vast tracts of space, seeing them as if from another world, impossibly far from theirs.

Instead of returning to the fire, Alec slips from the room and quietly lets himself out of the back door. The night is cold now and clear, the sky above his head filled with stars as far as he can see. The path from the back door leads through the vegetable plot to a small gate, beyond which lie the fields and woods, silvered in the moonlight. Alec stands in the lee of the building, breathing in the cool air, the stillness. Not really stillness: the longer he stands there, listening, the more his ears pick up the noises all around him: the sighing leaves; the intermittent rustling of voles and stoats and other nocturnal creatures; the bark of a fox; from the direction of the burn the creaking of frogs; from the woods, the high trembling cry of a nightjar. Jem's fiddle has stopped, he realizes. The women must be going to bed. Sure enough, a short while later, he hears the latch and his brother comes out to join him.

'I've something to show you,' Jem says.

He starts to walk towards the gate and Alec follows. They make their way through the fields, following the line of the flint dyke, Jem a little way in front, like they were children still, making their way across the fields that surrounded

Miltown, filing through the darkness on winter mornings on their way to the schoolhouse. Except that it's midsummer, not winter, and Chae is in Aberdeen and the others are in their graves, and Alec has no idea where his brother is taking him.

They're at the edge of the wood now, the moon so bright he can make out every blade of grass, every tree root, even the coarse weave of the wool on Jem's back.

'Where are we going?'

But Jem doesn't reply. He turns on to a small track that leads through the trees into the wood. It's much darker here, the moonlight obscured by branches, reduced to a hazy glimmer that flares in places where the foliage thins into shafts of startling whiteness. They walk on in silence for what seems a long time. Alec reckons they must be nearing the centre of the woods. Without warning, Jem turns off the path they've been following and begins to push his way between the trees to the left of the pathway. The ground slopes upwards through a dense sea of bracken as high as their chests, but Jem hardly slows his pace. And then at last he stops. They have come to a small clearing. At its centre, drenched in moonlight, is a circle of stones.

Was this what Jem had wanted to show him? Alec is surprised, a little disappointed. Standing stones such as these can be found in woods and fields throughout the shire. But as he continues to stand at his brother's side in the moonlit clearing, something about the stones begins to affect him. There are nine in all, some taller than others, none higher than his waist; together, they form a perfect circle. A profound stillness hangs over the place, as if it were not quite of this world. The stones are at once intensely immutable and intensely alive. It's not hard to see why folk might think them enchanted, weave tales of faerie trickery and devil's pacts to explain their presence: they have the look of once-living beings, arrested in time, caught for eternity in an attitude of private, sorrowing solemnity. A kind of wonderment falls over Alec as he looks at the stone circle, the same sense of awe that he'd experienced from time to time as a boy, in chapel or out in the fields at night: this awareness of the mystery of things, of sacred truths half-glimpsed but never fully revealed, of other realities hanging forever just beyond his reach. The feeling makes him uncomfortable and he looks away. Above the tree line, the night sky is thick with stars. Jewel-like Vega flashes blue and white directly overhead. The swooping eagle, ancient astronomers called it, seeing a bird of prey soaring upwards into the great expanse of the heavens. Alec picks out the constellation of which it is a part, tries to visualize the lyre it carries in its talons, the magical harp fashioned by Hermes as a gift for Apollo, and in turn gifted to Orpheus, the ill-fated bard, doomed to lose his wife to the underworld and wander the earth forever after, sorrowing at his loss. To Vega's left he can see Cygnus, the swan, flying south-west along the pale path of stars; to the right are the constellations of Hercules the giant and Serpens the snake, entwined in eternal battle.

The profusion of stars makes his head swim: those distant points of light, those infinitely far-off suns, and beyond them the enormity of space itself, reeling away, spooling out into eternity, without limits, boundless beyond imagination. Telescopes have revealed suns so distant the eye cannot detect them. Things now proven were once undreamt of. Nothing is fixed except in man's limited understanding of it. Even time is in a state of perpetual motion: stretching back into unknown pasts, extending forward into unknowable futures. All these months past it is simply this abyss of time that he has been peering into, trying to discern a future he cannot imagine and will never know. A future in which men might fly. In which wheels might move of their own accord. In which bairns might be born without pain and danger. In which diseases passed from parent to child might be isolated and extracted from the body in infancy or even before. In which all diseases might be curable.

'Do you remember the night our ma died?' he says suddenly. Jem nods.

'She was bleeding. I was holding her and it was all over me. In my eyes, in my mouth. The taste of her dying.' Alec shakes his head at the memory. 'The blood kept pouring from her mouth. She was choking on it. You'd gone for help and I was there with her on my own. I was terrified. I knew she was going to die.'

'You were just a child.' Jem's voice is gentle in the darkness.

'I ran away. I hid until I heard you coming back. She died alone, Jem. I left her to die alone.'

'Twas a long time ago.'

But Alec needs to say it all, now he's started.

'I made a vow. Never to let it happen again. Never to let a woman die if I could save her.' Alec stops, trying to find the right words. 'Now I find I cannot keep that promise.'

'What are you saying, man? What promise?'

Alec does not answer at once; when he speaks again, his voice is scarcely audible.

'What would you do if you discovered the identity of a murderer?'

'Jeezus, Alec!'

'And you had to choose between keeping silent, or making public the name of the killer, knowing the declaration would save hundreds, in time maybe thousands, of innocent lives, but that it would bring shame and ruin on yourself and on those you hold dearest in the world?'

'For God's sake! What trouble are you mixed up in this time?'

'I don't know what to do, Jem. That's the honest truth. I've gone too far to turn back, but can see no way forward that will not destroy everything I have worked for all these years. Other folk's opinions I have never cared for, you know that, not when there are lives and deaths in the balance. But this is different, and I can see no way through it.'

'This murderer,' Jem says. 'You're not mistaken? It is certain?'

'It is.'

For a long time neither man speaks.

This is how Cassandra must have felt – Alec is thinking – standing on the walls of Troy with the flames of the future searing her mind, shrieking her futile warnings, while her loved ones laughed in her face, or frowned and turned away, or told her she was mad. No wonder if she was! To tell the truth and never be believed. To be derided and defamed for it. Would it not drive anyone mad? And now he understands that science can give the same terrible gift, make prophets and seers of mere mortals, permit men to predict the future. Now he, too, can look into the future and see things no physician has ever seen before. Yet what a bitter gift. What a vile price to pay for knowledge. Now he is there, on the ramparts of the burning city, flailing his arms like an idiot, seeing everything so clearly, but shouting into an ignorance so dark and thick it is as if he were blind.

'Have you told Elizabeth?' Jem says at last.

'How can I?'

'Anyone?'

'Rabbie. Only Rabbie knows.'

There is one other, of course, besides Rabbie, but Alec cannot bring himself to speak of her.

'Hundreds of lives?'

'Maybe thousands. In time maybe hundreds of thousands.'

'Then there is no choice.'

53

It is said that folk have a sixth sense that tells them when
something is wrong, stirs in them an apprehension that some
ill is about to befall them or those dear to them, but no such
sense alerts Alec to what is awaiting him on his return to
Belmont Street. Even the sight of the front door hanging open
does not strike him immediately as strange. His mind is heavy
with his predicament, turning over and over the question of
how to proceed with his discovery and its implications. If
he has a sixth sense, he is too preoccupied with other more
pressing matters to pay it any heed. It's only when he's in the
hall with the house still and silent about him that he remembers that Annie had gone home to her mother while they
were at Logie and is not expected back until Elizabeth and
Mary themselves return at the end of the week. Even then,
Alec suspects nothing, immersed in his thoughts still as he
makes his way along the hall to his study. It's the sight of this
door, too, wide open when it is always kept shut, that makes
him stop, turn cold, hot, break into a run.

The devastation is total. Not a single piece of furniture has
been left standing, not a single picture left hanging. The side-
tables are upturned, all his instruments on the floor around
them in broken pieces. Morrison's wooden pelvis has been
trampled into shattered bits. The desk chair is sprawled on the
ground with its back split clean in two. The globes have been
wrenched from their stands, the surfaces slashed to ribbons.
Books lie everywhere, a hundred storm-smashed birds on the
Turkey carpet, their wrecked covers splayed like broken
wings. Through the gaping hole that was the storeroom door,
securely locked when he last saw it and now dangling loose
from the bottom hinge, Alec surveys the remains of his

ransacked collection: every jar and bottle swept from the shelves, the ground a stinking sodden mess of preserving fluid, mangled samples and smashed glass, the air a foul cocktail of vinegar, brandy, putrefaction and human shit: not content with destroying everything, the bitches have crapped their bowels out onto his floor. But the greatest violence has been reserved for the desk. The beautiful leather top is marked with deep scores far into the wood beneath, as if struck repeatedly with an axe. The drawers have been wrenched out and hurled to the floor, the papers crushed and thrown about the room. The lecture notes to the midwives have been torn to shreds. Alec sinks to his hands and knees amidst the debris, scrabbling frantically through the scraps of paper, picking up one crumpled fragment after another. His notebooks: his notebooks have gone.

54

August

If they will not heed his injunction and stop delivering bairns, how can he protect the mothers from the disease? If they will not let him bleed the mothers once infected, how can he hope to effect a cure? If folk will not trust him, how can he help them? The longer he considers the problem, the clearer it becomes that there is only one sure way to prevent further deaths. Yet what had seemed to him an unavoidable conclusion on the hillside talking to his brother, strikes him on further reflection as a measure so drastic, so decisive, that it must be avoided at all cost. The devastation wreaked on his study was a warning; from whom, he does not know, but the message is clear enough. There would be no way back from such a step, it would be tantamount to professional suicide for himself and certain ruin for many others. A disease that has a cause but no sure cure; that is transmitted by the very people to whom the mothers entrust their lives? Such a declaration would destroy the profession at a stroke. Any doctor encountering a case of childbed fever in his practice would be shunned forever. No midwife would be safe from condemnation once it was known that a single woman had died in her care. And besides, however sure he is of the veracity of his discovery, the explanation of it sounds feeble even to his own ears: something on their hands; something one can neither see, nor smell, nor hear, nor taste: who, *who*, will believe him? Rabbie had asked that very question the night before he left for Logie; now it rings day and night in his head like the tolling of his own death knell.

There has to be another way, Alec decides. He must wait.

He must forget the cause, forget the cure, and instead find some means of preventing the disease, some way of barricading the open door. Then and only then will it be safe to release his findings. The entire corpus of his discoveries – cause, cure, prevention, evidence – must be revealed at the same moment and not before.

While Alec frets, summer advances. Running contests are held on the Links, attended by young and old alike. Some days the races take place in mist so thick that the sea exists only as a low booming in the runners' ears, the race course and finishing line merely tests of faith. The cattle are fattened off for sale at the local fairs. Prices are haggled over and fortunes staked on returns the farmers won't see for months, their futures scrawled on scraps of paper that may be lost or thrown to the wind long before their merchandise reaches market. The drovers, sharp-featured, sharp-eyed, sharp-tongued ruffi-ans, who eat, sleep, breathe with their herds, wind their way steadily southwards, down through the glens to the great trysts at Crieff and Falkirk. The oats and biggs are harvested, the stooks dried and rigged, the stubbled land ploughed and harrowed. Fat red berries ripen on the rowans. The bairns' fingers are black with the juice of still-bitter brambles. Broom pods rattle in the wind.

Alec's efforts are directed now towards a new end: blocking the poison's path; preventing it from reaching its intended victims. He insists that the floors of the lying-in rooms be washed down with water and vinegar; instructs the mothers to inhale vapours of myrrh and camphire. Wherever possible, he orders the midwives to close up the chamber a few days before the birth and fumigate the air with brimstone heated over charcoal fires. He procures, with some difficulty, a store of gunpowder, and when brimstone and charcoal are not to be had, he goes himself to the house and sets off the powder in the room where the lying-in is to take place, urging the mothers to remain where they are and inhale as much of the smoke as they can stand. Before each lying-in, he tells the birth attendant, she must fumigate herself with wood fires of spruce and pine; after every lying-in, she must repeat the process and burn the clothes she'd worn at the birth. The midwives seldom obey. If he'd had the means to whitewash the internal walls of every house in the town, he would have done it himself.

Alec treats his own clothing and person according to the same prescription. He dare not fire off gunpowder or light brimstone fires in the house, so carries out the operation in the garden instead. Awareness of the contagion's presence has become an obsession: sometimes he imagines he can smell it on his fingers; sometimes imagines he can see it, the faintest shadow on his skin. He piles up spruce branches at the bottom of the garden and one afternoon, when he's gathered enough for a good-sized bonfire, he sets it alight, stoking the flames with the bellows until it's good and hot, then dousing the fire, then stoking it again, repeating the procedure several times over until the smoke is rising in thick, black clouds. The fumes half choke him, until he has the idea of tying a damp cloth round his mouth and nose. When the smoke is sufficiently dense, he strips to the waist and picks up a long stick that he's set aside for the purpose. He threads it through the sleeves of his shirt, then lifting shirt and stick together, carefully suspends them over the densest part of the smoke. He can feel the heat from the fire singeing his thighs, but there's no way of holding the stick in place and at the same time standing further back. To keep from burning himself, he is obliged to hop continually from one foot to the other, at the same time twisting his body from side to side, away from the heat. In the midst of this undignified dance, it occurs to Alec how much he misses his apprentice, misses Rabbie's quiet loyal presence at his side. They might even have laughed a bit, doing this together. It seems to Alec a long time since he's really laughed.

Once the shirt is fumigated to his satisfaction, Alec does

the same with his coat, and when he's done his coat, he takes off his breeches and, hopping about in nothing now but his underkegs, he does the same with them, wondering as he does so how on earth he is to persuade the midwives to follow his example, when they will follow him in nothing else.

55

Elizabeth is crouched down behind the bed in the process of retrieving the *Ladies Friend* from its hiding place between the mattresses. It is just out of her reach, each attempt to grasp it succeeding only in nudging it further away. With her head turned to one side and her cheek pressed up against the edge of the bed, she can feel the soft leather of the binding but she cannot get enough purchase on any bit of it to pull it back again. Her belly is huge now, preventing her from getting any closer. The smell of the bedding, engrained with sweat and camphor, makes her feel nauseous. She sits back on her heels, breathless and dizzy, struggling with a wave of sickness eddying up her spine. She puts her hands under her belly, wishing for some way to lessen the drag of its weight. She closes her eyes and waits for the room to stop spinning. Breathes in and slowly out to steady herself. It is as she breathes in again that she catches the smell: not the mattress this time, but something else, acrid and dreadful and familiar. She knows this smell. From long ago. Fibres of cotton and wool blackening in the flames, withering to ash. She can see it exactly as she did then. The arm rising in a silent wave above the bonfire, the hollow sleeve inflated with hot air for a moment, before being sucked down into the red-gold heat. But the silent wave remained seared on her mind's eye: a firebrand illuminating her guilt, revealing her treachery. Now it's here again, that same smell, and it can mean only one thing: that he's come back, as she always knew he would. He has tracked her down, come for his revenge. A life for a life. One last life still unclaimed.

She is on her feet and lumbering down the corridor, down the stairs. Only one thought in her head: to find Mary. She is flinging open doors, one after another, but Mary is nowhere to be seen. The smell is getting stronger all the time, filling her nostrils, her mouth. Her breath is coming in short jagged gasps, but she cannot stop to rest. She must not. She has to find Mary and get away. McKenzie is here. He won't let her escape a second time. She wants to shout Mary's name, but dare not. Ahead of her is the passageway that leads to the back door. The door is open and through it, she can see the garden, a rectangle of framed green. And there, at last, she sees Mary, standing just outside the door, her back to the house, and beyond her, a bonfire, dirt-grey plumes of smoke billowing up from the flames into the sky. Through the haze, Elizabeth can see the figure of a man, turned away from her. He is hurling what look like rags from a mound at his feet on to the fire. 'Mary!' Her voice is shrill. The man turns at the sound of it. His face is almost entirely concealed by a cloth tied over his nose and mouth. Only his eyes are visible. Seizing her daughter's arm, Elizabeth yanks her back into the safety of the house, oblivious to the child's cries of protest. No more deaths. It is the only thought in her head. There will be no more deaths. She is snatching food from the table, whatever's there, shoving it into her bag, grabbing an armful of shawls, tugging Mary with her, out of the house, out of the nightmare that has finally returned after all these years as she knew it would. Except this time it will be different.

She crosses the Denburn by the little footbridge below the house, pulling Mary along behind her. Soon they are out in open country, the town falling away behind them, the long grass at their feet bright with flowers. Ahead of them are the hills. Elizabeth takes the path across the barley fields, following the plough furrows, the ground lumpy and sharp with the broken stems of the harvested crop. They cross a stile into the next field, and on into a third. After so long trapped with the ceaseless din inside her head, she is aware now of an immense silence within and about her. The cage door has flown open and she has stepped through, stepped out into the air and the light. It is as if the world has come into sharp focus, the leaves on the trees, the birds singing, the wind sighing in the gorse. She cannot recall when she last heard and saw so clearly. Something has gone, some noise she's hardly been aware of until now that it has stopped. She is conscious of its absence, of the open space around and inside her; a sensation of tranquillity flowing through her, clean and clear as the air itself.

'I'm tired!'

Mary's plaintive voice comes as a surprise. Elizabeth had almost forgotten about her. They have come to the far end of the field. Great drifts of thistledown float on the breeze. In front of them is a coppice of birch and oaks, all that remains of once thick woodland. The earth between the trees is soft with bracken and fallen leaves. Early mushrooms gleam white in the dark soil. Above their heads the leaves are starting to turn, the first dusting of yellow on the upper branches of the birch trees; the oaks a dusty brown. Clusters of rowan berries glow in the wooded half-light.

'Here,' Elizabeth says. 'We are here.'

The trees have thinned and they are standing at the foot of a short grassy slope. Immediately ahead of them is a large boulder, its surface clagged with moss and lichen like an old tombstone. Dropping the bundle of shawls and food beside the boulder, Elizabeth kneels down and starts to run her hands over the ground.

'It's here somewhere, I know it is,' she says aloud.

Lifting her head, she sees Mary watching her. But at that moment her hands find the opening she's been searching for: a flap of grass and earth that folds back as easily as a Turkey rug to reveal an opening, just as she remembers, not an earth hole such as animals make, but a rough stone rectangle the

size of a small doorway: the entrance to the sonterrain. Elizabeth crouches down on her haunches and peers in. Beyond the
opening, a tunnel curves away into the slope of the hill. It is
half her height, the floor, walls and ceiling constructed of
the same stone blocks as the entrance. Behind her, out in the
clearing, Mary is still standing beside the boulder.

'Come see here!'

Moving aside, she makes room for Mary in front of the
opening.

'Go on!' she says, sensing the child hesitate. 'I'm coming
too.'

She puts her hand on Mary's back and gives her a little
nudge. Reluctantly, Mary creeps through the opening into the
tunnel. Elizabeth throws the bundle of food and shawls in
after her, then hitches up her skirts, drops on to all-fours and
follows. As her body fills the narrow passageway, it blocks out
the light from the entrance and they are enveloped in darkness.
Mary stops at once, blunders backwards into Elizabeth, cow-
ering against her, afraid to move forwards into the blackness.
Elizabeth tries to twist her head to catch a glimpse of the
opening behind them, but the tunnel is too narrow.

'Go on! We have to go on.'

Ignoring Mary's whimpers of protest, she pushes the child
ahead of her, shoving her forwards with her arms and knees,
edging them little by little along the passageway. At length it
opens out into a small circular chamber. Now her eyes have
grown accustomed to the dark, Elizabeth can see that the
tunnel is in fact quite short: there is just sufficient light from
the entrance to see the stone walls and curved ceiling of the
chamber. It is high enough for Elizabeth to stand in and a
little more than the width of her outstretched arms. The walls
and ceiling are dry to the touch. The air, too, is cool and dry.
It is all as she remembers. In the faint light, Mary's eyes are
huge dark discs in the pale smear of her face. Elizabeth smiles

and holds out her arms. With a little moan Mary falls into her embrace. Folding her arms around her, Elizabeth holds the trembling child as close as the mound of her belly will permit.

'There now, hush now,' she murmurs over and over into her daughter's hair. 'We are safe here. No one can find us here.'

56

He'd thought nothing of it: the hazy glimpse of Elizabeth through the plumes of smoke. Utterly intent on the task in hand, he'd hardly noticed her until she was gone. Hours later, when he comes back into the house, exhausted by his exertions but with a sense of grim triumph at having cut off at least one of his invisible enemy's paths, he notices only gradually how quiet the house is, remembering with a little pang of anxiety that other time he'd returned to find the place inhabited by this same unnatural silence. The stillness seeps into him as he passes from one room to the next, calling for them, receiving no response, the chill of doubt turning to a deluge of dread and then he's shouting their names, flinging back doors, hearing nothing but his own feet on the bare boards, his own voice echoing back at him, offering nothing but their absence.

He forces himself to walk, not run, the length of Schoolhill and Broad Street to Chae's house. Knows the moment his brother opens the door that Elizabeth and Mary are not there. Isabella comes out from the parlour at the sound of his voice.

'What is the matter?'

'Elizabeth's disappeared.'

With a little cry of fear, Isabella's hand flies to her mouth. The depth of concern on her face tells Alec what he should have known himself.

'And Mary?' Chae says.

'I think she's taken her with her.'

They go first to the chapel, on Chae's suggestion, then to the Plainstanes and down Marischal Street to the quayside, but there's no sign of them, there or anywhere. They search the town, along every wynd, in every doorway, retracing their steps once, twice, three times, in the dwindling hope they've somehow missed them. Twilight has settled over the town by the time Chae finally says, 'Most likely they've gone home.' They have looked everywhere they can think of a dozen times over without success. 'I'd best be getting home myself. Come for me at once if they're not there.'

But the house in Belmont Street is as empty as when Alec left it. Alone in the darkening hallway, he gives in to the feelings he has kept at bay all the time that he and his brother have been searching the town: the many instances of his recent neglectfulness crowd in on him and he is filled with shame and guilt. For weeks now, months, he has thought only of his patients, of the epidemic, of himself; has spared no time for his wife, except to think of her with impatience and annoyance. At Logie he had left her entirely to Megan's care. Since their return to Aberdeen, they have barely exchanged a word. How can he go back to Chae and Bella and tell them Elizabeth and Mary are not there? The prospect of Bella's distress, and still more of Chae's unspoken condemnation, is more than he can bear. He will search again. Will keep searching until he finds them.

Hardly knowing where he's going, Alec sets out once more, heading west towards the bleaching green. As he crosses the burn, he stops and peers down into the rushing water, half-expecting to see their bodies floating there. Where can they be? Where would Elizabeth have gone? He cannot think. What a mess he has made of everything! What an arrogant fool he has been! Sacrificed everything to the disease: the public's trust, the midwives' respect, his patients' confidence. And now his wife and daughter too? With every step, he is more acutely and painfully aware of his folly. The disease has possessed him, infected him, poisoned his mind, blinded him to everything but itself. He has been like a man infatuated with a teasing, elusive mistress, his every waking thought given over to the next encounter, the latest glimpse, the previous assignation, brooding on each mood, each lock and curl, reading meaning in every glance, obsessed with a desire to know, penetrate, conquer; reckless in his pursuit; forgetful of every other legitimate claim on his time and attention. He sees it so clearly now: his love affair with the disease. He had begun by hunting a prey, but gradually it had become a kind of courtship, a pursuit of something not vile but precious. He has been transformed from hunter to lover, has circled the disease like a predatory suitor, pursued it like a man bewitched. It has entered his bloodstream, pervaded his soul.

When Alec finds himself in front of George French's house, it is as if, in the matter of a moment, all the anguish of the previous hours and days and weeks and months has found a target, and in finding it been converted into an unfathomable howl of rage. Every humiliation he has suffered at French's hands over the years, every obstacle French has put in his way, every opportunity for advancement that French has stolen from him, every occasion for scorn and ridicule that French has seized upon, every sneering expression of contempt, every malicious remark: all of it rises in Alec's mind in that moment. French was behind the decision to cut off the Dispensary. French was behind Robertson's appointment to the Infirmary post. Who knows what else French is behind? The mob who'd come to his house that night? The ransack of his study?

'French!' he roars, pounding on the door with his fists, careless of who hears him. 'French! Open this damn door!'

And when Dr French does indeed open the door, Alec all but grabs the man by the throat.

'What have you done with them?' he bawls into French's face, half mad with fear and fury.

French steps back with a look of distaste. 'Get a hold of yourself, man. With whom, pray?'

'With my wife and chiel, you damn bitch!'

French makes to close the door. 'I see no call for that kind of language, Gordon. We will defer this conversation until you are ready to mind your manners.'

But Alec shoves his foot between the door and the jamb.

'Damn my manners! And damn you, French! Where are they?'

'Good God, man,' French shouts back. 'Control yourself!' And then, with genuine sympathy in his voice: 'I assure you, I know nothing of your wife or child. Are they not home?'

The unexpected gentleness in French's tone takes the heat off Alec's anger.

'They've gone,' he says, suddenly too weary to conceal it. 'I don't know where.'

French regards him through the gap in the door for a moment, then opens the door fully.

'I am sorry for your troubles, Gordon, but I cannot help you on that score. Will you come in a moment? Take a drink?'

A drink strikes Alec as a mighty fine idea, and without considering further, he follows French into the house. While French pours them both a whisky, Alec glances about him, his anger rekindling at the sight of the ordered elegance of the book-lined library they're standing in.

'Since you're here,' French says, handing Alec his drink, 'there is something I should like to discuss with you.'

'Oh, aye,' Alec replies, bridling anew. 'We're coming to it now, right enough! Your wee mob. Twas you set them on my house, was it not?'

French looks surprised. 'I haven't the least idea what you're talking about.'

'No? And who else would have any interest in stealing my papers from my own desk?'

French meets Alec's glare head on. 'If you wish to talk about stealing,' he replies in a level tone, 'let us first discuss what your apprentice was doing in the Infirmary office after midnight when he should have been upstairs minding the ward. We could also talk about certain items, found in your storeroom, that others might not, perhaps, consider your right-ful property.'

'I want my papers back.'

'So you do, but they are safer in my keeping for the time being.'

Despite himself, Alec is somewhat knocked off course by this frank admission of guilt on French's part. He is still floundering for a response when the other man takes the argument in a new direction.

'This epidemic,' French says, taking a sip of his whisky, 'what do you intend to do?'

'Do! Why, I intend to save lives, just as I always have and always will – if only the ignorant eejits in this town would let me get on with it!'

There is a brief silence, then French says: 'I am referring, Dr Gordon, to your study of the disease, not your treatment of it. You have made a discovery, I understand. Of some significance.'

'Oh aye, and who'd you hear that from?'

'You believe,' French continues, 'the birth attendants are responsible for spreading the disease. Am I correct?'

Alec stares at him. Damn the man a thousand times over! How the devil has he found out so much? Even with the papers in his possession, French could not have known this: the bare facts are there, but what they signify is written nowhere but in Alec's head. Unless someone – Rabbie Donald or Mistress Anderson – no, that is inconceivable.

French takes his silence as confirmation. 'Have you proof?'

'Aye,' Alec says at last. 'Proof enough. And experience,' he adds, 'the surest proof of all.'

French nods. 'So, I ask again. What are your intentions?'

But Alec realizes he has given too much away. 'And what the devil business is it of yours?'

French, who has taken a seat in the meantime, leans forward in his chair. 'I assure you, Dr Gordon, it is every bit as much my business as yours. I hold the public good of no small account and am much concerned when I hear of any adverse matter pertaining to the public.'

Alec gives a derisory snort. 'Pertaining to your reputation more like.'

'And your own reputation?' French counters. 'Does it mean so very little to you that you will knowingly and rashly demolish it at a stroke?'

'If it will save lives.'

French laughs, a short mocking sound. 'Very noble, sir! And do your wife and daughter share your sentiments? Pray, have you considered how you will support your family once this noble sacrifice has been made and you have ruined every hope you ever had of pursuing your profession?'

'In Aberdeen, perhaps.'

'In the whole of Scotland, Gordon. I will make sure of it.'

For a long moment the two men stare at one another without speaking.

'Do I understand you correctly, French?' Alec says at last. 'You wish me to bury my findings?'

'I wish you to consider how it will help individual patients to destroy our standing in the eyes of the public. Think, man! What will happen to the women whose lives you are so eager to safeguard if they are too afraid to seek medical assistance?'

Alec does not reply. He has not considered this.

'I tell you, Gordon, take great care! Publish these findings and you will bring much suffering on others. It is vanity that drives you, nothing more. You've dressed it very nicely in your mind, see nothing but noble sacrifice, but in reality it is the prospect of fame that draws you on and is blinding you to the consequences for everyone beside yourself.'

'I have a duty to tell the truth.'

'And you think by telling the truth you can make the whole world think as you do? You are wrong. All of us will die, some way or another, maybe by this disease, maybe another—'

'This is a highly contagious disease!' Alec interrupts. 'More dangerous than the plague.'

'Perhaps. But it will pass in time, just as the plague did. What people need, far more than your fine truth, is certainty: the incomparable comfort of certainty.'

'You do not think very highly of your fellow humans.'

'On the contrary. I think rather more highly of them than do you. Where you see only ignorance, I see – and respect – the value of self-deception.'

There is a degree of passion in French's speech, a degree of sense in it too, that has taken Alec by surprise. He would not have suspected the man of holding such views. Perhaps he has underestimated him. For a long moment he is silent, struggling to reconcile his own convictions with the arguments French has put to him. He does not trust the man, but there is an undeniable force in what he has said.

'What would have me do?' he says at last.

Very softly, but without hesitation, French replies: 'Leave out the physicians.'

'What!'

'Leave out the physicians,' French says again. 'In return, I will see that your family is provided for.'

57

With nightfall the faint light from the entrance fades and the temperature in the burrow drops. Elizabeth wraps Mary in one of the shawls and wraps the other around them both. It is completely dark now and utterly still apart from the small rustling sounds of their own bodies, the whisper of their breathing. They have eaten the last of the oatcakes. There is still a little cheese left for the morning. Elizabeth can feel Mary shivering against her through the layers of wool. Inside her, the baby stirs, too, performs a slow lazy roll, pushing at her with bony knees and elbows. Elizabeth puts a hand to her belly, cupping the strange hard mounds that rise and recede from her own flesh: mysterious, defiant. Mary feels them too, against her spine: the silent prodding creature hidden inside her mother's body. Then the baby kicks: a hard, sharp jab of its heel that catches Elizabeth in the ribs and makes her gasp, then laugh. From somewhere near her in the darkness comes a little answering laugh. Elizabeth smiles, then laughs again. And suddenly there is no stopping them: it is like a spell breaking, like water pouring through a breach, like a storm breaking: each laugh provokes another until they are helpless with it, falling against one another in the darkness, their laughter filling the little chamber, rebounding off the curved ceiling and returning to them, setting them off all over again, sweeping them away on a new flood of helpless, gasping, sobbing relief.

Gradually their laughter subsides and the silence settles around them once more. Mary wriggles around under the shawls, shuffling down into the warmth of her mother's body. A few moments later, she is asleep. Elizabeth stares into the darkness for a while, then closes her own eyes, listening to

Mary's quiet, steady breathing, and to the deeper silence beyond the chamber, the low pulse of it out in the woods and the fields, and to the dark answering throb of it in her bones, her blood.

58

Alec has no idea how long he's been walking. After leaving French's house, he'd searched the town once more, several times thinking he'd spotted Elizabeth and Mary ahead of him, only to find he'd been following complete strangers, the woman far too tall or small to be his wife, the child at close quarters nothing like his daughter. Eventually he'd turned his back on the town and headed out past the Lochlands into open country with some vague hope of finding them there; after a while that hope, too, had dwindled away. He walked on anyway, distancing himself from the town and all it now stood for in his mind, his feet covering the ground without any conscious effort on his part, striding out into the darkness, moving beneath him in a hard steady beat, each step a blow to the earth below, as if he would brand it with his despair and anger, scorch his bitterness into the epidermis of the land. He cuts right across the fields and drops down through the dunes on to the beach. The moon has risen as he's walked and hangs now, full and bright over the bay. The shoreline is dark from the departing tide, the sand compacted under his feet. The beach stretches ahead of him, mile upon mile of smooth emptiness. On and on he walks, berating himself, hating himself.

At first all his thoughts had centred on the interview with French. He'd given too much away. Should never have gone there in the first place. It was madness to have imagined French would know where Elizabeth and Mary had gone, worse than madness to have let French lure him into the house like that, yet he had flown straight into the net without a second's hesitation, and once there, drawn on by his own stupid pride he had made matters a thousand times worse by admitting to his discovery. French had surely been bluffing, for how could he really have known so much? He might have gleaned something from the midwives, or maybe from Bannerman, but he could not have known for sure. Not unless Alec himself had revealed more to one of them than he'd intended. However hard he tries, Alec cannot quite remember what he'd said to Janet Anderson the night he called on her: he'd told her to keep away from the infected midwives, that much he recalls, but had he also told her why? And Bannerman? Had he told Bannerman? He simply cannot remember. And then, that infernal bargain! The man five steps ahead of him yet again. Until that moment, Alec had almost been taken in by French's fine words, had found himself wanting to believe that the other man's intentions were honourable, that French truly wished to protect the public, when all along, from the first moment he opened the door and asked him in, French's sole concern had been to protect the physicians' reputations. How could he have been such a fool? A new thought strikes Alec for the first time, and despite his mood of self-condemnation, it permits him a flash of grim amusement: for all his wily astuteness, French had assumed and feared that Alec intended to do the one and only thing he had fully decided against: set down his findings and publish them. How near Alec had come to confessing that he had no such intention! Only his reluctance to give French satisfaction on that score had overcome the scruple, persuaded him to hold his tongue and let the man stew a little, let him imagine Alec to be as dangerous as he seemed to think. Any pleasure that French's one error gives him is short-lived, however, for as he turns French's words over and over in his mind it becomes painfully apparent to him that in another, more important, way French had seen the situation with limpid clarity, had understood what has only slowly become clear to Alec himself: whatever course of action he fixes upon matters very little. All the time that he's been trying to decide what to do with his discovery he has failed to see that another kind of contagion had seized the town, as surely as the epidemic of puerperal fever: a deep-seated prejudice directed at his own person, which no discovery, however brilliant, however just, can succeed now in dislodging. French was the one who'd seen the future, not he. Doubtless French had heard how the public meeting had gone, from Ross or Duncan or one of the others; doubtless he knew precisely how desperately the Dispensary finances stood, how far Alec had sunk in the public's confidence. The fact is, and Alec can no longer ignore it, his reputation in the town is in ruins. Whatever he does or does not do about the disease, his standing as a physician is damaged beyond all hope of repair.

He is way out along the bay now, the dunes rising up in dark hunched mounds on his left, the sea quietly shifting and sighing to his right. Seabirds bob on the swell, white heads gleaming in the moonlight. Even if he turned, he would not be able to see the town, which is tucked away behind the bending line of the coast. But Alec has no wish to look back at a town that has so unequivocally turned its back on him. He sets his face to the north.

Where has it all got him? All his striving after truth? All his unshakeable faith in facts and evidence and progress? To here. To nowhere. To this long, wide, empty stretch of sand. To this arbitrary present moment and no further. A thousand other pathways might have led him to some different place. French is right. People want certainty; they want small clear steps across the burn; they want to see the stones beneath their feet. They don't want to leap from one bank until they are sure they will reach the other. Tell them the stones are there, hidden beneath the surface of the water, but solid enough to bear their weight, and you are in the realm of faith and trust. People want to see truth, too, with their own eyes before they will believe it, just as children need to smell a rose before they'll believe it is perfumed, need to feel the flames burn their fingers before they'll believe that fire is hot. Why had he not seen this? What use is a truth that no one wants to know, a light that no one else wishes to see by? What is the value of truth when others deem it worthless? And in the end what difference will it make if he is right or wrong, if he does or does not reveal his findings? Someone else will blunder towards the same discovery, in ten years, or fifty years, or a hundred. With or without an Alexander Gordon. At some point, in the near or distant future, a remedy will be found, some plant or extract or distillation, as yet unknown, undreamt of, a substance with the power to destroy the disease once and for all, in every case. But it is an undiscovered country, far beyond the horizon of the known world. It is beyond Alec's grasp. Beyond his time. Perhaps French had been right about that, too: it is nothing but vanity that has made him believe that he, and he alone, should be the one to discover the cause of the disease, uncover its mysteries, proclaim the truth to the world at whatever cost, when the truth – another truth! – is that his life is of no real consequence. He is a tiny nothing, who for a while believed he could make a difference.

What a fool he has been! A vainglorious fool, duped by the illusion of influence, the seduction of reason. He has gathered evidence, pursued facts, sought proof, followed the precepts of his profession with all the unquestioning fidelity of a novitiate. But as he thinks back over the past year, he sees how false his faith in scientific truth has been. Now that he stops to dissect his discovery, to anatomize the discoverer, what does he find, but sudden hunches, impulsive whims, motivations of the most irrational kind? These equally had driven him on in his quest. Unpredictable happenings. Spontaneous moments of insight. Illogical linkages. These too had played their part, and in far greater measure than he's ever wanted to acknowledge to himself or anyone. Resentment, pride and guilt had informed his actions as much as a disinterested pursuit of progress. And ambition. And, yes, vanity. Who did he think he was? A Copernicus? A Galileo? A Newton? The true picture, if indeed there were such a thing, would always remain beyond the reach of any one individual, even the very greatest of them, for what could any man do but look through his own limited field of vision at the particular, circumscribed part of the whole that was visible from where he stood? How could any man hope to see further than that? How could any man imagine the unimaginable? The unimagined, perhaps; the unimaginable, never. One little lifetime. One little human mind. How could it hope to encompass such vastness? And yet, it must hope to: it did hope to! A doomed eternal quest for answers. That surely was the human condition: the continual asking why; the only ever partial grasping of the because; the unending reckoning with unreckonable-with truth.

Well, he wanted the truth and he has it! Ignorance comes at a price, and so too does knowledge. He has invested everything to purchase this truth: mortgaged his reputation, his professional prospects, his security, his family, his marriage. What else does he have left? He thinks miserably of his wife and daughter. What depths of unhappiness and fear could have driven Elizabeth to this? And how had he failed to notice? Had she gone mad, as her mother had done? If so, what desperate acts might she now have in mind? And where on earth could they have gone? How could a heavily pregnant woman and a five-year-old girl simply vanish into thin air?

Ahead of him, a thin trail of woodsmoke threads upwards into the milky night air. As he draws nearer, Alec sees that it is coming from the remains of a small fire, left by one of the fishermen and still smouldering slightly in a shallow of sand. He crouches down beside it and blows into the charred logs, remembering the long, carefree afternoon he and Mary had spent on the beach at the start of the summer. His breath makes the logs flare into life and the fire throws out a sudden belch of heat. With a violent lurch of longing, Alec thinks of his daughter's hand in his own as they'd jumped the breakers together, of the frown of concentration on her face as she'd brushed the wet sand from the sea-shells, then peered inside them in search of vanished signs of life. With savage intensity he longs to feel her hand in his again, to enfold her small body in his arms, to smell the salt and sweat in her wind-knotted hair.

Alec holds out his hands to the fire's warmth. He cannot tear his eyes from the glow even though it hurts his eyes. Crouching in front of the fading embers, he is aware of a new sensation, coming from somewhere deep within himself: a craving for release; a profound desire to be finished with it: all the struggling and battling of the previous months, the dying mothers, the grieving families, the stench of decaying flesh, the accusations and denunciations, the mounting opposition and endless criticism. He has had enough. He wants an end to it. He wants Elizabeth and Mary back safe and an end to it. That is all he wants now.

Alec shuts his eyes, fighting an overwhelming sense of desolation. He waits for the feeling to subside, then opens his eyes again. His gaze falls on the toes of his boots. The worn leather is encrusted with tiny grains of sand. He is conscious of his own body, swaying slightly above his feet, and of his weight, suspended in the great hammock of the beach, and of the beach itself, stretching into the distance on either side of him as far as he can see; of the cavernous dome of the sky, filled with innumerable, invisible points of light, wheeling slowly and silently above his head; of the sighing, shifting ocean, reaching away to the endlessly receding lip of the horizon; of his own insignificance in all this vastness. There is more than one truth. That is where he has been so wrong. Everyone has their own truth. Why had he never realized this before? Greed was a truth. And fear. And anger. And love. All this time he'd thought he was in pursuit of Truth, when it was merely facts he was pinning down. There was not one unassailable truth, but a dense labyrinth of competing, con- flicting truths. It all depended on where you were standing, how the sunlight shone through the leaves, what shape the clouds took as they slid past your head, how strong the dam looked, how fierce the current. His arrogance appals him. How can he have expected the midwives and physicians to congratulate him for revealing to the world that they were the angels of death not mercy? Had he seriously expected them to praise and reward him for calling them murderers? How blind he'd been, blinded by the glare of truth. His truth. Midwives needed to eat. Physicians had bills to pay. He'd given no thought to these things. Assumed his truth outweighed all others. Now he can see only how wrong he has been. Truth is a many-headed monster and it has devoured him.

A great choking sob rises up in him. He gives into it, lets his body fall sideways on to the sand, lies there, the grains in his mouth and eyes and nose, the harsh, racking sound of his own grief filling his ears, issuing from somewhere deep inside himself. He gives himself up to it, the waste of it, the pointlessness of all his battling, bitterness and despair and rage breaking out of him in unstoppable, heaving, jagged sobs.

How long he lies there, he cannot tell. Gradually the frenzy of grief subsides. Eventually he must have fallen asleep. He wakes to find himself curled on his side on the sand, chilled through. It is growing light. The sky over the sea is banded with long thin fingers of cloud: a rose-tinted grey high above the horizon, darkening to a slash of deep red at the point where the sun is about to rise. Alec sits up and brushes the sand from his eyelashes, cheeks, mouth; spits out the grains clinging to his lips and tongue. His bones ache from lying so long on the damp sand. The fire has gone out. Beside its remains he notices for the first time a pile of driftwood, intended for the fire but not used. Reaching over, he lets his hand close around the one nearest. The sea-smoothed wood is soft against his palm. It has a delicate solidity that he finds strangely comforting. He twists the stick between his fingers, then plants it upright in the sand between his knees, looking beyond it to the ocean and the rocking waves, stained a dark pink in the sunrise. Imagine parting the seas as Moses had; imagine walking between towering walls of water that might engulf you at any moment, you and the thousands of people following behind you, but you keep walking anyway because there is no way back, because the future lies ahead of you, because the promised land is on the far shore, whether you yourself will live to see it or not. It was not a matter of reason, but of faith. Would Moses have gone on without faith? Would reason alone have guided him and his people so far? How completely and entirely wrong he has been to think reason was everything. Facts and figures and proofs and evidence. He'd thought that was the way forward; that reason could override all else, conquer stupidity, ignorance, fear; that feelings were a distraction, an irrelevance, or worse, a dangerous diversion. He had prided himself on being a man of logic, a man of reason, a man guided by rational processes. He had sneered at the notion that men were ruled by their passions, had regarded emotions as a weakness to be overcome. He had never accepted the maxim that reason was slave to the passions, had rejected the notion as antithetical to everything he valued; only now does he see that he has been as enslaved as the next man, only blinder than most to his chains. And perhaps they were not even chains. Perhaps this has been his biggest error of all: the failure to recognize the value of passion, of faith, of feeling. After all, would he, Alexander Gordon of Miltown of Drum, have done all that he has without passion, without faith in something far beyond mere provable facts? What a fool he has been! The blindest fool in Christendom! To have cursed the passions of others and not seen how ruled he himself has been by his own. Reason is not everything. Reason is only a part of everything. Without passion, reason is as cold and dead as the fire at his feet. All his life, for as long as he can remember, he has thought of feeling as a hindrance at best, an inconvenient obstacle to progress. Now suddenly he sees it is the other way around. Passion maketh the man. What worth has a man's life without it? Reason leads to progress, but it is passion that gives warmth to man's endeavours, actions, thoughts.

Alec pulls the stick out of the sand, then plunges it back down again. Nothing. The stick remains a stick. No miracles for him, then. He pulls the stick out again and gets to his feet. The beach lies all around him like a blank sheet of paper. On a sudden impulse he starts to draw shapes in the sand, as he used to as a boy: circles; triangles; big untidy rectangles. The long-ago memorized laws of algebra singing in his mind. The rhythms and patterns of the equations: the certainties they offered. He stops and looks back at the tracks he has made, then, more slowly, in a smooth piece of sand, he traces his initial: A. Alpha, the beginning, an idea in God's mind, a beautiful, magnificent idea, an entire world, complete with night and day, the sun and moon and stars, mountains, seas, rivers, and life: creatures great and small, birds, insects, fish, and finally man himself. To the A, Alec adds three more letters. D – A – M. Adam. The first man, the most exquisite, extraordinary idea of all, 'adam', the Hebrew word for 'man', and in that one word, also the idea of woman. Adam's dam, his Eve, his chava. The companion, made from his rib to rescue him from deathly solitude. His salvation and his damnation. Drawing him to the poison of the apple, the catastrophe of knowledge. Enticing him towards his fall from grace, his expulsion from paradise. Alec looks at the letters in the sand. A D A M. He adds another A and another N to spell out M A N. Alpha, the beginning, Adam, the first man, Eve contained within him, drawn out of him, completing him. A DA MAN. And yes, a damning, too, a devilish soulmate, a fork-tongued gift, to lead him so swiftly from that place of bounty to a barren stony land where rewards are small and brief and life eternally hard, death always at hand, close coupled with life, manacled together from then on. A D A M A N. The story of life in those six letters. But there was a seventh day on which God rested. If this is the story of life then there must be a seventh letter. Yes, a seventh letter, but what? Alec's mind winds round and round on itself like a caged thing, searching for the answer, and suddenly finds it, like an arrow loosed from an archer's bow, like a dislocated bone sliding back into its socket, like truth itself falling into his open hand. T. The answer. The only answer. *Look to the rock from which you were hewn, and to the quarry from which you were dug.* It is not over. Not yet. It is not time to give up. The word is there in front of his eyes, set in the sand and set free in his mind, like a kestrel from the jesses. It will fly. He will let it fly. Not only for his own sake and the sake of his unborn child, not only for the mothers who have died and the mothers in generations to come who may perhaps be saved, but for every prophet there has ever been, for every bearer of unwelcome truths, for every individual past, present and future, who has known what no one else wishes to. In the last few moments one thing more has become clear to Alec: in attempting to silence him, French has helped him to a simple, unambiguous understanding – that the one and only thing left him now is his voice.

59

She wakes to the sound of rainfall. *Tp-tp-tp.* Big fat drops on the leaves over her head. There are flowers on the graves. Two small bunches of scarlet hibiscus. And a woman's back. A primrose-yellow shawl draped over white muslin. Someone is weeping. The flowers are wilting before her eyes, the petals curling and browning in the heat. The earth on the graves is soft. It shifts and slowly opens. Without a sound, the shrivelled bouquets slip down into the black yawn of the earth. Elizabeth is falling, too, unable to stop herself, sliding down into the soft dark mouth. She tries to shout out, but everything is mixed up, the woman in the yellow shawl has vanished, the flowers are nowhere to be seen. She is alone in the forest, the rain falling fast now, the drops running together, thundering on the leaves, streaming through the branches on to her head and arms. Her dress is wet through, the thin fabric clinging to her skin. She tries to run but the tree roots snare her ankles, wind around her bare legs like hands, cut into her flesh with their nails. Beyond the trees she can see Tommy's legs stretched out in front of him. He is lying on his back with his eyes closed. His face is tilted forwards on to his chest. The bucket is lying beside him, tipped on to its side, and the fish have spilled out on to the ground. Their scales shine like mirrors on the hard brown earth. Willie is sleeping next to his brother, curled up in a ball, head tucked down in the cradle of his arms. The rain doesn't wake them. Nothing wakes them. McKenzie lifts his rifle and fires, once, into the air. The sky rips. Birds screech upwards from the treetops. 'No!'

Elizabeth opens her eyes, her mouth stretched in a sound-less scream. For a moment she cannot think where she is. There is not a shred of light anywhere. The blackness is so dense it seems alive, a soft living thing pressing against her. She strains to hear something, anything, in the silence. Sliding her arm out from under Mary's body, gently so as not to wake her, she eases herself on to her hands and knees. Feeling her way with one hand along the walls of the burrow, she begins to edge her way in what she hopes is the direction of the passageway. From somewhere behind her, Mary stirs, turning into the warmth left by her mother's body, sighing in her sleep. The sudden noise sets Elizabeth's heart racing and she lurches forwards, her knees tangling in her skirts. Her face collides with the stone wall and she cries out in pain. But she has her bearings now: she is in the passageway. Ahead of her she can see the dim outline of the entrance. She can feel the lick of night air on her face.

The clearing is bathed in a queer milky light. Above the tree line, a vast chalky moon, round and full as Elizabeth herself. Ribbons of mist sidle over the ground, rising in a thin haze around the trunks of the surrounding trees. Underfoot the grass is wet with dew, silvery-grey in the moonlight. Elizabeth's face hurts where it struck the wall of the chamber. When she touches her fingers to her cheek, they feel damp. She is wearing nothing but the summer dress she left the house in three days before; her shawl is back in the chamber, forgotten in her haste. She is cold to the bone, her whole body shaking uncontrollably. In her mind, thirty years have fallen away. The dam has crumbled. The sandbank has subsided. The long-bolted door has flown open.

There were no flowers. There were no graves. Not then.

They'd been fishing. Willie was furious that she was going too. 'She'll only cry and want to go home. She'll tell Ma.' But Tommy said they had to take her or she'd tell anyway. He'd shoved his face up to hers: 'One word to anyone and I'll lock you in the cellar with the rats.' Charlie wasn't with them. He was in bed with a fever. Mo was sick too. The yaws had come out a few days before and Papa had sent him back to the huts.

They'd walked for a long time, through the forest behind the house, until eventually they came to a stretch of scrubland that led down along a rocky path to a small, secluded cove. McKenzie was waiting for them there. He frowned when he saw her, then he grinned. 'And why not?' he said, glancing up at the sky as he did so. 'The more the merrier.' While the others fished, she looked for shells and bits of coral. She'd found enough to spell out her name in the sand. Every now and then she looked back over her shoulder to check they were still there: three black silhouettes perched on the rocks, facing out to sea, the air trembling above their heads. From time to time one of them let out a shout and stood, a dark wavering line against the turquoise ocean. After a while they tired of fishing and followed McKenzie back up the hill and through the scrubland to a wooden shack on the edge of the forest. Tommy had five grey fish in his bucket. Water slopped over the sides as he walked, leaving a dark trail in his wake. McKenzie's horse was tethered to a stump to one side of the shack and in front of it stood a huge tree, speckled all over with tiny red flowers.

The afternoon was close and sticky Willie kept slapping at his legs where the insects were biting. Out of the breeze from the sea, the air barely moved at all. They sat on the ground in the tree's shade while McKenzie went into the shack. A moment later he came out again with a coil of rope looped over one shoulder and a yellow gourd slung over the other. In his hand he was carrying a knapsack, from which he pulled a loaf of bread and a large hunk of cheese. He held out the bread to Elizabeth, but she shook her head. She didn't want any of McKenzie's food. His breath smelt bad and his neck was lumpy with boils. *McKenzie like rotten mango.* That was what Marie said. *Nothin but black an stink under dat skin.* Elizabeth wished she hadn't come. She got up and walked away from the others towards the trees. No one paid her any notice. Willie and Tommy were taking turns to drink from the gourd.

McKenzie was grinning and laughing. Her brothers were laughing too, lolling on the ground, throwing back their heads at McKenzie's jokes. McKenzie kept looking up at the sky and grinning and passing the gourd around. Willie's face was very red. When McKenzie picked up his gun and fired it into the air, a furious cloud of parrots rose screeching into the sky. Willie and Tommy laughed louder than ever. Elizabeth thought of Mama and Charlie and the cool of the house. Mama would be angry when they got home. Papa was sure to whip them when he found out where they'd been. Thinking of the whipping they'd get, Elizabeth was afraid and angry. She couldn't see what Willie and Tommy were laughing at. There was nothing funny about being whipped. It was too hot to be outside. The back of her dress was wet and prickly with sweat. Angry and bored, Elizabeth wandered further into the forest. It was cooler here. She could hear her brothers and McKenzie still, but she couldn't see them. She wondered if she could find her own way home. Despite the trees, the heat was growing thicker and heavier by the moment. The light had a bruised, purplish tinge to it. Around her the birds had fallen silent.

When the first drops of rain fell, she was sitting in a nest of ferns some way into the forest, out of sight of the others. As the storm broke, she shrank back into the shelter of the ferns, but within moments the rain was pounding on the tree tops, streaming through the branches in shining torrents, bouncing off the leaves, turning the earth to liquid black. When she heard the gun fire a second time, she shut her eyes, buried her face in her lap.

How long did she sit there? It seemed like hours. Someone was calling her name, but she did not answer. When footsteps passed, so close that she could feel the ground shake, she did not lift her head, did not open her eyes.

It was a long time later, after the storm had stopped and the raindrops slowed to a lazy tapping, that she dared to move, creeping back in the direction she had come. Everything was quiet now outside the shack. McKenzie's horse was gone. The clouds had blown over and the sky was a clear watery blue. The sun had shifted round and the big tree in front of the shack no longer cast any shade. In the sunlit ground beneath the tree, her brothers lay sleeping. She could see Tommy stretched out on his back, his legs stuck straight out in front of him. Beside him, Willie was curled up on his side. Snaking over the ground, joining them one to the other, was the rope.

In the dew-soaked dawn, Elizabeth clutches her hands to her belly, hunches over as a sudden spasm of pain grips hold of her. *Not now! Please God! Not here!* But almost at once the next throe has begun, rolling up through her, squeezing the breath out of her, squeezing the life out of her. She staggers forwards a few steps, then stops. She cannot move. The baby is coming. Now. Here. There is nothing she can do. Already another wave is upon her, bearing down on her with such force it is as if the whole weight of the sky were pressing her downwards. The next throe forces her to her knees. The grass is wet and cold against her forehead. She is inside the pain and outside of it at the same time. She is tearing, splitting, breaking apart. Far away someone is screaming. The child will be born here. The ground is opening to admit her. There is no resisting it. It is drawing her down. With infinite, ruthless tenderness. Welcoming her in.

60

They bring her back to Belmont Street, alive but barely conscious. Her screams had roused Mary, sleeping in the souterrain. She'd fled into the nearby fields, her cries for help eventually heard by a farmer, who managed to extract from the terrified child what had happened. The baby was still in Elizabeth's arms when they found her, a greying scrap, the cord wrapped twice around its tiny neck. Mary has not spoken since. Alec puts Annie to watch over her, while he himself remains by his wife's bedside, watching her slip in and out of awareness of the room around her. For three days she wakes only to stare wildly about her, raving names that mean little to Alec, seeing people where there is no one but himself. Isabella pleads with him to get some rest, let her take his place for a while, but he stubbornly refuses, will not have Elizabeth wake to find him anywhere but at her side. He is so tired that he is hardly aware of the others quietly coming and going in the dimly lit bedroom. At one point he turns to find Rabbie standing beside him, but when he looks again he is gone and Alec thinks perhaps he has dreamt him.

It's five days before the delirium finally lifts. Alec has fallen asleep in the chair, but wakes instantly at the sound of Elizabeth's voice.

'Alec?'

'Yes.' He takes her hand between his own, more grateful than he's ever been for anything in his life. 'I'm here.'

'Is it over?'

'Yes, it is over. You are safe now.'

61

Rabbie and Alec are in the study, having left Elizabeth sleeping quietly. She is quite returned to her senses, though still very weak. When she'd woken earlier that evening, she'd been perfectly calm. She'd looked about her and asked after Mary. Alec assured her the child was well and safe. She did not ask about the baby, for which he was grateful. Chae had been over in the morning to say he'd found them a house in Queen Street, available for a third of the price. Though smaller than their present accommodation, it was light and well-appointed, with a study and a cellar and a south-facing parlour – but that was a conversation that would have to wait until Elizabeth was stronger.

It is the first time that Alec has left her since her return, the first time he has allowed himself to register the extent of his fatigue, the toll events have taken on him. His body is leaden with it, the blood vessels behind his eyes stretched to bursting from the effort of staying awake. Rabbie pours them each a whisky, hands a glass to Alec, then takes up a position beside the fireplace, one elbow resting on the over-mantel, one leg extended in front of the other. The posture of a confident man, Alec thinks, looking at him and struck suddenly by a change in his apprentice. He studies him more closely, but Rabbie's appearance is not obviously different: his dress is unremarkable; his face wears its usual mild and kindly expression. Nevertheless, something is altered. There is, unmistakably, a new assurance to his general demeanour. They have not been alone before and there has been no opportunity to discuss the reason for Rabbie's abrupt departure, but perhaps he'll get an explanation now. There are other questions he needs to put to Rabbie; other matters he needs to clarify.

Before he has found a way to frame any questions, however, the younger man speaks.

'I have changed my name,' he says suddenly, with a little awkward smile.

Alec, taken by surprise, looks at him uncomprehendingly.

'Perhaps, with everything else, you've not heard?' Rabbie says, a little embarrassed. 'That Uncle John died?'

Alec shakes his head. 'When?'

'The day after you left for Logie.' Rabbie looks down at his glass, then back at Alec, his face breaking into a wide smile. 'He left me everything: the Grenada estate, his house in Exeter, the farms – the whole lot!'

Alec sits back in his chair and stares at Rabbie. He cannot speak for the moment, relief and envy vying for ascendancy in his mind. So Rabbie hadn't abandoned him. He had left for reasons that were nothing to do with him. Only now that all suspicion of it is lifted, does Alec fully realize how heavily the thought of Rabbie's betrayal has weighed on him. But the entire inheritance gone to Rabbie at a stroke? That news gives rise to more complicated sensations. Rabbie is a rich man now. A very rich man indeed.

'There was one condition – that I change my name to Harvie.'

'You accepted his terms?'

Rabbie laughs. 'I did, Dr Gordon! Indeed, I did!'

Alec is not the man to grudge him so astonishing a turn in his fortunes. He lifts his glass.

'Well, then! To you, Mr Robert Harvie! I am heartily glad for you.'

The old devil! His entire fortune in exchange for a name.

Rabbie grins back, raising his own glass in return. 'And to you, Dr Gordon. To your discovery!'

These words bring Alec back to one of the questions he'd been on the point of asking. It's not the disease or the discovery he's thinking about now, but Elizabeth.

'Does the name McKenzie mean anything to you?'

Rabbie's smile fades. He nods.

'Aye, it does,' he says.

'Elizabeth kept calling out the name. All the time she was sick.'

Rabbie nods again. 'McKenzie was the overseer on my uncle's plantation.'

An odd expression has come over the younger man's face that Alec cannot interpret. There is something between pity and embarrassment in his look.

'You don't know?' he says.

Alec shakes his head.

Rabbie looks down at his lap.

'I thought – I thought everyone knew,' he says at last. 'It was never spoken of, of course, but I thought it was common knowledge in the family—'

'What was not spoken of? For pity's sake, man!'

Rabbie lifts his head and looks Alec in the eye.

'McKenzie murdered her brothers.'

'Murdered?' Alec is stunned. 'But I thought—'

And then Rabbie tells him: how the boys were brought back to Harvie's End on stretchers, not the youngest boy, Charles, he died of a fever, but the other two, Thomas and William; how no one dared touch them, not even to lift the bodies to the ground. The bearers wore thick leather aprons to protect themselves from the poison and the bodies were burnt right there in the courtyard, just as they were. McKenzie swung for it, of course. They'd caught up with him a few days later, hiding in the house of one of his mulatto women, and at the trial it all came out: how he'd got the boys drunk on rum, then bound them to a menachie tree and left them there, with a storm coming, knowing the rain that fell from its poisoned leaves would finish off the wickedness he'd started. He was not sorry in the least. Said it was his revenge, and the sweetest moment in his entire life. Said he was glad he'd lived long enough to savour it and that his sole regret was being deprived of the chance to settle his score with Mr Harvie to his complete satisfaction.

Alec stares at Rabbie, appalled. 'What score? What wrong had Harvie ever done him that he should wish to exact such a price?'

Again Rabbie's composure falters.

'She never told you? About her father? About the bairns?'

The look of bewilderment on Alec's face is answer enough. Rabbie puts his glass down on the floor between his feet. He has the look of a man squaring up to facts he'd rather have left forgotten.

'It was way back, in forty-five, forty-six, just after Culloden. You know how things were then. So many killed. The crops razed. Folk starving to death in their beds for want of food. Perhaps that was the reason, I don't know, but somehow or other my uncle got involved in the trading of bairns. My mother always said it was a young man's folly and in later life he was deeply ashamed of his part in it. McKenzie was around eight years of age at the time. They trapped him on his way to school one morning, stowed him in the grain store at the docks, then shipped him to Virginia with about fifty or sixty others, where they were sold as slaves. He was in Virginia many years, in the cotton fields, bound to a man by the name of Ferguson, a pretty savage master by all accounts. McKenzie eventually served his term and, having discovered that my uncle had meantime settled in Antigua, he made his way there and sought him out. My uncle, it seems, was persuaded to take him into his employ in return for a promise of silence. Any goodness there'd been in McKenzie's heart had long since withered away and he never missed an opportunity to make trouble on the plantation. But my uncle could see no way to be rid of him without having his own guilt revealed, which for his wife and children's sake he could not countenance. So he tolerated him, with no notion that McKenzie all the while was biding his time to seek revenge.'

There is silence in the room when Rabbie has finished speaking.

'I am so sorry,' he says softly, daring at last to glance at Alec's stricken face. 'You knew none of this?'

'She never said a word.'

Later, after Rabbie has gone, Alec goes back upstairs to Elizabeth. He slips quietly into the room and sits down on the bed beside her. She is sleeping, her face small and pale against the bolster, but her expression peaceful. As he takes her hand in his own, she stirs and opens her eyes, her dark gaze settling on him.

'You should have told me,' he says gently. 'You should have trusted me. We promised there would be no secrets.'

'I did trust you,' she says, her voice so faint he has to lean forward to catch the words. 'For so long.'

'But why did you never tell me?'

She does not answer and for a moment he thinks she must have fallen asleep once more, but then she opens her eyes again and looks at him once more and this time he hears her say, in barely more than a whisper: 'Too late now, Alec. Too late for us.'

62

September

The mist has thinned a little. For days it has hung over the town, muffling all sound, so dense that you feel you could reach out and run your fingers along its cool grey surface, grasp hold of its spongy weight and suck the moisture from it. There's a chill in the air, and the smell of autumn: mulched leaves and estuary mud. Along the quayside figures form and dissolve in the half-light. It's hard to tell how far or near they are in the blanking flatness. Alec stands with his back to the town, watching the wind riffle the surface of the water into tight little folds. The cold air catches in his lungs and sets him coughing. It gets into his bones these days, the damp, and is not so easily got out again; his health is not what it was. Alec pulls the muffler tighter about his throat and peers out into the mist for sight of the ferry. There is no one on the quayside to see him off, at his own request. Elizabeth and Mary were asleep still when he left the house. He'd thought about going to say goodbye, then thought better of it. He's had his fill of farewells, has no heart for any more. His apprentice, however, had heard him leaving and run down the street after him. They shook hands for a final time, and Alec saw there were tears in the younger man's eyes. 'Away wi ye, Rabbie,' he'd said brusquely. 'I've a boat to catch.'

There has been so much to do in the past fortnight: settling his accounts and professional affairs, clearing the house, ensuring all the paperwork is in order for Elizabeth and Mary's move to Queen Street. There's been no time to think forward to this moment and it has come upon him with strange suddenness. As if the clock hand had stuck some while ago at eleven, then jolted without warning to twelve. He has been preparing for this moment for days, yet somehow now it has come he finds himself unprepared, has the feeling there are important things he has forgotten to do, although it eludes him what they might be. He wants more time, but for what exactly he could not say. In any case, Alec rebukes himself now, time will not change anything, at least not any of the things that matter.

On the quay at his feet is the same small trunk he'd arrived with five years before; inside are the few items of clothing and even fewer belongings that he is taking with him: the leather case containing his lancet and fleam; a small travelling box of chirurgical tools, the lid monogrammed with his initials; a curl of Mary's hair, folded in a small piece of parchment, and, wrapped in a square of green silk, the miniature of Elizabeth that had been her wedding gift to him. He has kept only three books; the rest he has donated to the Medical Society, along with his lectures to the medical students and the midwives. He and Rabbie have spent much of the last fortnight copying them out from the torn and crumpled scraps he'd managed to salvage from the wreck of his study. Perhaps someone would publish them one day. Perhaps not.

The ferry is in sight now, edging alongside the harbour wall. The *Adamant* is anchored in deeper water further along the estuary. Alec had laughed out loud when he heard the name. As the ferryman flings the painter up on to the quayside and moors the boat, Alec looks back once more at the town. The granite walls of the tenements along Ship Row are lead-grey in the overcast light. The shuttered windows on the upper floors give the buildings the appearance of a long line of haughty faces. A fine send-off indeed! Alec shifts his weight from one foot to the other to relieve the discomfort in his right knee. This presentiment of frailty is something new to him: joints aching, bones stiffening, things not moving as smoothly as they were wont to; this coughing, too, is a damned nuisance he could do without. 'You'll take care of yourself, Alec?' Elizabeth had asked. He'd not understood at first what she meant by the question. It is not something he has ever given a moment's thought to, the care of himself. He picks up the end of his trunk and drags it towards the waiting boat.

How little he has to show for his years in Aberdeen. How insubstantial it had turned out to be, the life he thought he had. By tomorrow evening he will be a ship's surgeon once more, back where he began, as poor and as unknown as he had been then; poorer, for then at least he'd had a wife, a child, a home. Now he has nothing but the clothes he's standing in and the contents of his trunk. It is as if it had been merely a dream, from which he has awoken at last to find himself possessed of – nothing. All the effort and toil, the grand schemes, the streets and houses he knows like the sound of his own voice, the many people, loved and loathed. All gone now, like figments of his imagination, no more substantial than the mist. Maybe it had been a mistake, to take his leave alone like this. It feels somehow like death, this unremarked slipping away. But maybe in its way this is a kind of death.

It seems far longer ago than nine months that he'd quitted Jenny Duncan's lying-in. With what high hopes and ambitious plans he'd walked back through the town that night. And with how little idea of what lay ahead of him. When he thinks back to the first weeks of the epidemic, the disease settling over the town, taking it in its deadly embrace, enclosing all their lives in a net of fear and suspicion, it seems impossibly far away. Throughout those black nights last winter, called to one deathbed after another, crisscrossing the town in pursuit of the elusive trail laid by the disease, consumed with a determination to hunt his quarry down, to find the answers, to save lives, never once had he imagined that it would end like this. Would he have done as he had if he'd known all that he would forfeit in the process? If he'd known that it would take everything he'd ever had or ever wanted? His work, his reputation, his livelihood, his family? Alec thinks of all he has lost, he is filled with a terrible aching sorrow that makes the ground sway beneath him and the sky turn dark. The bitterness and anger of the past months have gone, as if all used up, like a well run dry, but what is left is this dark seam of grief, embedded within the fibres of his skin and muscle and bone. Elizabeth had come back from whatever place of madness she'd been to, and for that he was grateful, but he had lost her. They would not meet again. It was Elizabeth as he'd known her who let him take her hand in his and raise it to his lips, who had looked into his eyes with that lovely clear gaze of hers. *Too late for us*, she'd said and he'd accepted it. He'd failed her in so many ways.

It is Mary he cannot bear to think of.

The boatman lifts Alec's trunk on board and Alec steps in after it. The moment of departure is here. There is no turning back. He can feel the water nudging at the hull of the ferry. Overhead, concealed by the wall of mist, the gulls scream. The wind has dropped. Ahead of them, the river is smooth and glassy.

Alec feels for the consoling bulk of the manuscript stowed in the leather bag across his shoulder: he has worked into the early hours every night for the past month to get it done, writing so fast the ink was still wet on one page as he began the next. His case notes and tables had been returned anonymously one morning soon after his meeting with French, leaving little doubt in whose keeping they had been. Had French learnt since, Alec wonders, of John Harvie's bequest to his nephew? If so, he would have realized at once that it released Alec from all obligation to the bargain they had struck. It had not been immediately apparent to Alec, taken up as he was with other troubles. It was Rabbie who'd spelled it out to him. *You may write whatever you wish to now, Dr Gordon. I give you my word. Elizabeth and Mary shall not want for anything.*

It was finished two nights ago. A few phrases here and there betray, perhaps, too much of his true feelings, lapse somewhat from the impartial tone of scientific enquiry he'd striven for, but there will be time later to see to that. What matters is that it is done and in his bag and on its way to London, along with the letter from Mr Robinson of Paternoster Row, agreeing to print the work on presentation of a fair copy. Robert Chalmers had all but slammed the door in his face, but Alistair Brown has given his word he will sell it at the Homer's Head if Alec can procure the subscriptions and pay for the shipping.

The ferry pulls slowly out into the estuary, the boatman working the oars with firm steady strokes that barely disturb the oily surface of the water. The harbour wall has dissolved into the mist. Behind them, the boat's wake is a narrow dart, a swallow's tail. Around them, the liquid stillness.

What was it Janet Anderson had said in the physic garden all those months ago? *They will come to understand. In the end.* They had met one last time. There'd been no awkwardness between them. He had taken her in his arms and it was as if she was always meant to be there, with her face to his, his mouth on hers. 'Tis not an ending,' she'd said. He was sitting beside her on the bed, steeling himself to go, and turned to look at her when she spoke. Her hair like streams of flame over the white of her shoulders. She reached up her arms and drew him to her, taking his face between her two hands as if he were a child, her eyes level with his. 'Tis a beginning.'

And perhaps, after all, she was right. He is ready to leave: there is nothing left to stay for. The long fight is over. He will not think of failure. Something has ended and something has begun. He has achieved what he set out to, has he not? Distilled the pure from the impure. Turned ignorance into knowledge. It is there, incontestable, whether the world is ready to recognize it or not. The evidence laid out for all to see. The truth set down in the pages of his manuscript. *A Treatise on the Epidemic Puerperal Fever*. Tucked safely in his bag. The nugget of pure gold.

The mind's work is done and the heart's work too. Always as a boy Alec had thought of Jem as the alchemist, with his stones that flew forever across the surface of the burn. But, truly, was there not something of the alchemist in the midwife's art? All those years and he's never seen it until now: that birth is the greatest transformation of all, life itself the philosophers' stone. He has guided hundreds of women in his time through the transforming months of pregnancy and the final perilous passage of birth, and in these past nine months of battling with the disease he has wrought a transformation of another kind. He has death on his hands, yes, but he has life too. No one can take that from him. No one. It is enough. It is everything.

The waters part before the keel of the boat. The sea is ahead, a sheet of silver. Alec will not look back again. His reward lies elsewhere. There is nothing else now. It is an end. It is a beginning. It is done.

Author's Note

This novel is based on actual events that took place in Aberdeen between the years 1789 and 1795, but the account of those events is a fictionalized one and, while I hope it is faithful in spirit to what actually occurred, many names and details have been changed. The old infirmary physician, Thomas Livingston, for example, has been merged with his son, also a physician, to make one character. William Forsyth, the gardener, has been make a contemporary of Gordon's, whereas in reality he was several years older. Elizabeth's sister Isabella was in fact called Mary, like her niece, reflecting the widespread custom in Aberdeen at the time of giving close relatives the same name; to avoid confusion I have given her the name that she and Charles chose for their infant daughter. More crucially, the epidemic that struck Aberdeen lasted for three years, from December 1789 to the spring of 1792. I have taken the liberty of compressing the epidemic into one calendar year, basing the timescale on a very similar outbreak of puerperal fever that occurred in 1813 in the market town of Abingdon in Oxfordshire, and which in many important respects closely resembled the epidemic that struck Aberdeen with such devastating consequences.

Alexander Gordon did indeed leave Aberdeen to board a ship named the *Adamant*, a detail too poignant to change or omit. His *Treatise on the Epidemic Puerperal Fever* was published in London later the same year.

As far as is known, Gordon never again lived in Aberdeen and never again practised as a midwife. On leaving Aberdeen he rejoined the navy, retiring not long after as a result of ill health. He went to live on his twin brother's farm in Logie, where he died in October 1799, aged forty-six, of pulmonary pneumonia. Elizabeth Gordon remained in Aberdeen, surviving her husband by forty-four years to die at the impressive age of eighty-three. Their daughter Mary married her cousin, Robert Donald, in 1805. She died at the age of thirty-four, after the birth of their sixth child. Robert went on to become a distinguished Aberdeen doctor, with a special interest in midwifery. Alexander, the fifth of Robert and Mary's children, would certainly have made his grandfather proud: amongst his many achievements, Alexander Harvey served as Physician to the Aberdeen Royal Infirmary, Physician to the Aberdeen Dispensary, Professor of Materia Medica at Aberdeen University and President of the Medico-Chirurgical Society (the former Medical Society that Alexander Gordon had helped found). Today a fine portrait of Robert Harvey hangs in the current Medico-Chirurgical Society and a bust of Alexander Harvey stands in the entrance to the Medical School in Aberdeen.

Alexander Gordon dedicated his *Treatise on the Epidemic Puerpural Fever* to his old tutor and friend, Thomas Denman. Denman amended later editions of his own influential work on midwifery to take account of Gordon's findings, but he did so without ever acknowledging Gordon's momentous contribution to the understanding of the disease. Nowhere in Denman's later writings does he mention Gordon by name or cite his *Treatise*. The omission is puzzling. Perhaps Denman wanted to distance himself from the controversy surrounding Gordon's *Treatise*, wary of bringing a similar fate upon himself. Or perhaps the disagreement over the use of bleeding proved fatal to their friendship. The real reason will probably never be known, but the warmth of Gordon's dedication is all the more moving for the resounding silence it met with from Denman.

For the best part of the nineteenth century Gordon's *Treatise* fell into oblivion. The significance of his breakthrough was first recognized by the American physician Oliver Wendell Holmes, who referred to Gordon's *Treatise* in 1847 in a ground-breaking essay on the subject. But there was a still a long way to go. Even after the work of Joseph Lister, in the latter half of the nineteenth century, made clear that Gordon had been not just correct but extraordinarily prescient in his understanding of how the disease was transmitted and the way in which it entered the bloodstream, Gordon remained uncredited. His claim to fame was further overshadowed by the unwarranted heralding of Ignaz Semmelweis, a Hungarian obstetrician working in Vienna in the 1840s and 50s, as the first person to realize the role of midwives and doctors in transmitting the disease. Only relatively late in the twentieth century did Gordon finally begin to receive the credit he deserved. In the words of H. Thoms, one of his belated champions, writing in the *American Journal of Obstetrics and Gynaecology* in 1928:

> Alexander Gordon was not an uneducated country doctor who stumbled on a few facts and published a few scattered obser-vations. He was a finely educated physician who practised in one of the three great cities of Scotland ... and was in a position to observe accurately and in a scientific manner hundreds of cases of childbirth during his ten years of practice. Not only did he discover a great surgical principle but with great courage he proclaimed it in the face of opposition amounting to persecution.

Puerperal fever was responsible for more maternal deaths than any other disease except for tuberculosis well into the twentieth century. Throughout Europe, maternal death rates from puerperal infection were horrendous. The importance of antisepsis was not widely recognized or adopted until the end of the nineteenth cen-tury, and it was not until the invention and widespread availability of antibiotics in the 1930s that puerperal fever finally became a curable disease. Giving birth remains, however, one of the riskiest events in a woman's life. Every minute of every day a woman dies in pregnancy or labour. In developed countries today deaths from puerpural fever, or post-partum sepsis as it is now known, are mercifully rare. But, in many parts of the world where women still give birth without access to modern medicine or adequate hygiene, puerpural fever remains an extremely dangerous illness, killing as many as 250,000 women each year, a figure equal to five million women in every generation.

As well as telling the story of a brave and brilliant man, *Touching Distance* is about the women who suffered and died during the horrendous epidemic that struck Aberdeen in 1790. These events happened in the past, but they are still happening in an almost identical form in many parts of the world today. At very least, I hope that this book will help to draw attention to the many dangers that still accompany giving birth, and to the many people who are working as tirelessly as Alexander Gordon did in the eighteenth century to make childbirth a source of joy, not tragedy.

Acknowledgements

A great many people and institutions gave invaluable assistance during the researching and writing of this book. In particular, I would like to thank Dr Irvine Loudon, for his book, *The Tragedy of Childbed Fever*, an indispensable and compelling history of this terrible disease, and for his subsequent help with various fine points of obstetric history. I am also grateful to the Authors' Foundation for a timely grant to carry out research in Aberdeen. Michelle Gait and staff at the Special Libraries and Archives at King's College, University of Aberdeen, were most helpful in providing me with access to Alexander Gordon's published and unpublished manuscripts, and kindly granted permission for me to use Gordon's work directly and indirectly in my book. Fiona Watson at the Northern Health Services Archives, Aberdeen, spent many hours helping me to find my way through the fascinating records of the Aberdeen Royal Infirmary, and was tireless and painstaking in answering my numerous queries and questions about the workings of the Infirmary and Dispensary in Gordon's day. My especial thanks to Dr Geoff Gill and to Elma McMenemy for the time and care each took in showing me the beautiful and varied countryside around Aberdeen, and for sharing their contemporary and historical knowledge of the region with such unstinting generosity and enthusiasm.

Thanks, too, to Alex Adam and his team at the Medico-Chirurgical Society, Aberdeen, for access to the records of the Medical Society and other relevant papers; Jennifer Melville at Aberdeen Art Gallery; Mike Dey and John Edmunds at the Maritime Museum, Aberdeen; Neil Curtiss at Marischal College Museum, Aberdeen; Dr Colin Milton, Dr Joan Pittock Wesson and Dr Ian Olson at the University of Aberdeen; Sister Columba at St Margaret's Episcopalian Convent, Aberdeen; Catherine Taylor at Aberdeen Library; Eleanor Rowe at Aberdeen City Archives; Helen Shivas at the Aberdeenshire Museum of Farming; John Fisher at Drum Castle; Diarmid Mogg and Sandy Stronach for advice on Doric; David Potter, Kincardine and Mearns Ranger; David Frodin and Michael Holland at the Chelsea Physic Garden, London; Graham Hardy at the Royal Botanic Garden, Edinburgh; Jim Bennett at the History of Science Museum, Oxford; Simon Chaplin at the Hunterian Museum, London; Karen Howell and Kirsty Chilton at the Old Operating Theatre, London, and Annie Smith, midwife at the Hopitaux Universitaires de Genève.

Besides the works of Alexander Gordon, a number of other primary and secondary texts were important sources of historical detail, in particular James Beattie's *Day-book, 1773–1798*, John Luffman's *A Brief Account of the Island of Antigua* (1788), Thomas Denman's *Introduction to the Practise of Midwifery* (1794), John Hunter's *Cases in Surgery* (1825), *Alexander Gordon of Aberdeen* by Ian Porter (Oliver & Boyd, 1958), *Death, Dissection and the Destitute* by Ruth Richardson (Routledge and Kegan Paul, 1987), *Bury the Chains* by Adam Hochschild (Macmillan, 2005), and *The Knife Man* by Wendy Moore (Bantam Press, 2005).

On a personal note, for essential refuge at various key moments in the writing of this book, heartfelt thanks to Susan Gelpke Doran, Sos Eltis, Mark Haddon, Henry and Claire Dunne, Hannah and Shannon Stevenson, and to all at the Société de Lecture and La Sixième Heure in Geneva. For much-valued input, support and sustenance of other kinds, thank you to Flora Alexander, Rosamund Bartlett, David Bodanis, Peter Bradshaw, Amanda Craig, Natasha Edelman, Jo Frank, Susan Jane Gilman, David Goldie, Kathryn Heyman, Ellen Jackson, George Levvy, Alan Lightman, Michael Ondaatje, Sally Potter, Julia Saunders, Henry Shukman, Hannah Stevenson and Rebecca Swift.

I am extremely fortunate in my agent, Peter Straus, who has been a skilled and patient midwife to this book at every stage of its development, from imaginative embryo to publication. My editor, Imogen Taylor, has been a wonderfully encouraging and sensitive presence in that process too, and I am most grateful to her, and to Trisha Jackson and Liz Cowen at Macmillan for all their editorial support.

TOUCHING DISTANCE

Jessie, Solomon and Hugo Slim have lived with this book almost as intensely as I have, and with admirably good humour throughout. Their unflagging interest, tolerance and encouragement has meant more to me than I can say.

My final thanks go to Alexander Gordon himself, without whom it is entirely true to say that this book would never have been written. I first encountered Gordon in Irvine Loudon's *The Tragedy of Childbed Fever*, although in truth it was not so much an encounter as an outright assault: Gordon reached out from the pages of Loudon's book, seized me by the collar and – true to everything I subsequently learnt of his character – refused to let go until his tale was told. Alexander Gordon, thank you. It has been an extraordinary privilege to spend the last five years in your company.

Oxford, 2008